THE TALIESIN AFFAIR

STEVE TURNBULL

TAU PRESS LTD

The Taliesin Affair by Steve Turnbull.

ISBN 978-1-910342-92-3

Published by Tau Press Ltd.

Cover by Jane Dixon-Smith (jdsmith-design.com).

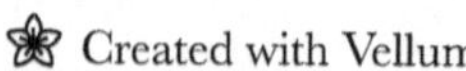 Created with Vellum

For Chris

Because without you, none of this would have happened.

AUTHOR'S NOTE

In the chronology of the Maliha Anderson stories, this one occurs first. However, it can be read at any point. As the first book in the series, the last, or somewhere in between. The only place I wouldn't recommend doing so is between *Thunder over the Grass* and *Under the Burning Clouds*.

1

It had been a long time since she had thrown up after a school lunch, so finding Ethel Jordan's bloody body in the library—where Maliha had retreated after forcing down the meal—did not make her stomach turn over at all. But that didn't mean she wasn't surprised. Of all the events she might have contemplated, finding the most notorious bully in the school bludgeoned to death would not have figured among them even as a slight possibility.

It did not require a genius to see the girl was dead, this was not the first dead person Maliha had seen. But she knelt beside the head to examine the corpse more closely, just to be sure her assessment had been accurate. The girl's skin, where it was not stained with blood or broken, was pale and there was no movement in her chest. Maliha sat down in a chair nearby, after checking it was not bloodied, and contemplated the body.

Another unlikely aspect was that Ethel Jordan was not known to frequent the library much, if at all. She was not studious and barely read anything she was supposed to, and certainly nothing for her own pleasure. Her only delight, as far as Maliha knew, was beating seven bells out of other girls.

Unable to prevent it, the teachers had redirected her violence to the hockey pitch which was, thankfully, an all-year sport. There could be a hundred pupils that might have wanted Ethel dead—Maliha herself had suffered more than once at the girl's hands—but somehow, she could not imagine any of them committing the act. Except herself, of course. The attack had been far from subtle. The poor girl's head had suffered numerous blows and there was blood on her hands.

Maliha looked around. Another curiosity was that Ethel—who had not been in the main hall for dinner—was lying with her head towards the door as if she had been going that way when attacked. And yet, despite the violence of the assault there was no evidence of a fight. One thing was certain, unless caught unawares, Ethel would have been able to put up a fight against even a grown man. She was very masculine in her build and her constant hockey playing had made her devastatingly tough.

No, it had not been one of the girls who had done this.

The assigned monitor, somewhere in the building, rang the hand bell vigorously for the next lesson and the sound echoed through the corridors. Maliha sighed, she was going to suffer for being late, even though her justification would be perfectly acceptable—if she had been white. She pulled out her journal and ripped a page from the back. She had a very nice Birmingham fountain pen with which she wrote "Do not enter. Infestation of rodents. By order."

It wasn't a very clever sign but it would keep other girls out for the short period of time needed to alert someone in authority.

As she left the library, she made a hole in the paper, looped it over the door handle and shut the door. She was aware she was leaving fingerprints but she did not think she would come under serious consideration as the murderer. More likely she would be disregarded completely.

"Where do you think you're going?"

Maliha ignored the voice. It was Rainie Lane, Lower Sixth bully and, of course, a prefect. Maliha was in the Upper Sixth now and would be leaving the school at the end of the final term after seven terrible years. The only Indian girl in a boarding school devoted to the education of the children of the titled classes. Plus, those whose parents had money and hopes of making good connections.

Rainie Lane was typical product of the school. Her name was Erin because her family were Irish but the nickname had been applied in her first year and stuck.

"Stop, Anderson!"

Maliha rounded the corner and judged the distance to the school office. Running was an offence but she pelted down the corridor as fast as she could for five seconds before returning to a fast walk and turning right. There was no further shout so she must have managed the second turn before Lane had reached the first.

Maliha ran again, grateful that classes had commenced. She no longer needed them and had not done so since the end of her fourth year. She devoured the books and recalled everything she read in utter perfection.

She reached the school office and knocked rapidly. She was a little out of breath but judged that would add credence to her story.

"Enter."

Like the rest of Roedean School, the office consisted of dark oak panelling, heavy curtains and heavier furniture, most of it inherited when the building had been purchased ten years earlier by Wimbledon College, moving from London to the South Coast of England. The school secretary was a slight woman with no fashion sense, but what she lacked in stature she compensated for with discipline. Though Maliha was aware of the woman's passion for pulp romance of *certain* type.

"Anderson? Why are you not in class, and have you been running?"

"Mrs Clemence, it's Ethel Jordan."

"What is Ethel Jordan?"

"I found her."

"I was not under the impression she was lost."

"Not lost, Mrs Clemence, she's dead."

Perhaps it was that Mrs Clemence did not expect to hear those particular words in that order coming from the mouth of one of the girls but she hesitated as if attempting to understand them. So Maliha pressed her advantage.

"In the library. I just found her. There's blood everywhere." The exaggeration should appeal to the woman's tastes.

"Ridiculous."

At that moment Rainie Lane stumbled in without knocking, clutching a piece of paper, and her face pale as milk. It seemed she had seen the note on the door handle and entered the library anyway. Maliha felt sorry for her, that was not something she needed to see.

Mrs Clemence fixed her eye expectantly on Lane but though the girl opened and closed her mouth several times no sound emerged.

"You saw the body," said Maliha, wanting to move things along.

Rainie's gaze locked on Maliha and nodded, the horror in her eyes said everything. Maliha turned back to Mrs Clemence. "I think you should call the police, Mrs Clemence, and perhaps ask Mr Gunnell to lock the library in case anyone else stumbles in on the body." Maliha pointed at one of the chairs. "You better sit down, Lane." Like an automaton, the girl did as she was told. "Let me take that." Maliha relieved her of the paper and she put it in her bag.

Mrs Clemence still hadn't moved. Maliha felt as if she could see the woman's thoughts as they marched across her face: Things like this simply did not happen in a girls' school.

This must be a prank. The Indian girl is probably behind it, just trying to cause trouble.

"Please, Mrs Clemence, this is not a joke. You must call the police. I will find Mr Gunnell."

Maliha did not wait for confirmation but stepped out into the corridor. After lunch on a Tuesday? The caretaker would be cleaning, down in the furnace room, located on the other side of the building.

She ran. It was too late to worry about rule-breaking now.

The heating system for the school was not efficient but it stopped the whole place from freezing solid during the cold months. Though there had been plenty of mornings over the seven winters Maliha had been here that the pipes no longer flowed and everyone went without washing for days at a time, except when buckets were brought in.

It was 1908 and King Edward had ruled for seven years since his mother, Victoria, had finally had the good grace to die. Technology was bounding forward by the day but still they could not stop the pipes from freezing.

She opened the door to the furnace room—out of bounds to all pupils at all times—and headed down the familiar stairs. Mr Gunnell had been a major in the British Army in India. He even spoke a little Hindi which pleased Maliha since it reminded her of home, though her native tongue was Tamil. The caretaker was the one person in the whole place she considered a real friend, and he seemed to welcome her visits. He had a sweet tooth and always offered her a little something from a tin. She stopped halfway down the steps and leaned on the railing.

"Ethel Jordan has been murdered and we need to lock the library to stop people stumbling on her body and possibly erasing any evidence."

Mr Gunnell also took her entirely seriously. He had been scraping dust from a corner—he kept the place spotless—but no sooner were the words out of her mouth than he dropped

the brush and headed for the stairs picking up his patched
tweed jacket on the way.

He did not run, but marched double time at a speed that
ate up the distance. Maliha had to run to keep up with his
long legs. As they approached the library he fished his keys
from his pocket. Two teachers were outside the room. Mrs
Lancaster (English and French literature) was comforting the
sobbing Mrs Fenoughty (Home Economics and Physical
Education). Mr Gunnell pushed past them, took in the scene
in a moment, disappeared inside then returned, slammed the
door and locked it.

"Is she…?" said Mrs Lancaster.

"Not a doubt," said Mr Gunnell.

Maliha liked Mrs Lancaster, she was enthusiastic about
language and was one of the reasons Maliha had taken to
reading—the other reasons being the acquisition of
knowledge, avoidance of boredom and hiding from potential
troublemakers. The colour of Maliha's skin, even though she
was only slightly off-white since, while her mother was
Brahmin, her father was a Scot, seemed to attract trouble. She
had learnt how to stay away from it.

It was only three months until she escaped this terrible
place and could return to India.

Then the school secretary arrived, with Lane in tow still
looking as if she was the one who had passed away.

"Can you help her?" Maliha asked Mr Gunnell quietly. "I
think she's in shock. A whiskey perhaps?"

Mr Gunnell looked at the girl and nodded. "Seen that
before. Raw recruits when they first see death. Not sure how
the school board would react to me giving a girl a slug,
though."

"Medicinal."

"Right you are, Miss Anderson."

He moved away and spoke to Mrs Clemence, who insisted
on tasting the drink first. Apparently, it required considerable
tasting before she agreed to let the girl have some.

Maliha did not watch. She suspected the sight of the dead girl was going to haunt Rainie Lane for the rest of her life. So, instead, she turned and stared at the door. How was it possible that Ethel had been so brutally murdered within the confines of the school?

"The police are on their way," said Mrs Clemence. "Perhaps we should all just carry on as if nothing has happened."

"Excuse me, Mrs Clemence," said Mr Gunnell. "What would be best is that everyone who has seen the body should go to the school office and wait for the police. They will want to take statements. The less this affects the rest of the school the better. Don't you think?"

"Oh dear, and with Mrs Ramsey away in London today."

The headmistress seemed to spend remarkably little time in the school, Maliha had observed. However, she was aware of the constant efforts to generate donations from benefactors and this required a considerable number of personal meetings.

That the murder might have a negative effect on the school itself, and on her, seemed to strike Mrs Clemence but then she relaxed. "Thank heaven, Jordan's parents are only in trade."

2

———

The police arrived less than an hour later in a steam-powered van. From the office window overlooking the main drive, Maliha watched them come to a halt at the main doors and the men pile out. Three uniforms, one of whom was a sergeant by his stripes, and a detective who seemed relatively young—perhaps in his thirties.

The atmosphere in the office had been difficult and no one spoke, except when Mrs Lancaster tried to comfort Lane. She wasn't crying and Maliha did not think that was a good sign. Though nobody questioned why she herself seemed unaffected.

Mr Gunnell had been left to guard the library.

There had been a series of frantic telephone calls by Mrs Clemence until she finally succeeded in tracking down the headmistress and was able communicate the terrible news. Although Mrs Clemence had made the call from the head's office, the volume of her voice was such that every word could be heard plainly. With only one side of the conversation to follow, Maliha gathered that Mrs Ramsey was suitably horrified, but that emotion was quickly followed by anger.

Mrs Clemence assured Mrs Ramsey that only the police had been called and that the press was not involved at all. Maliha suspected that would not last and, worse still, something of this nature was bound to attract national coverage. This did not bode well for the school.

By the time the police had found their way to the office the call was finished and Mrs Clemence was back.

All four men looked particularly tall. The helmets on the three uniformed ones made their height even more pronounced.

"I am Detective Inspector Ralph Williams, and this is Sergeant Hughes," said the plainclothes man, taking in the faces of the room with a sweep of his eyes that paused on Maliha. "Perhaps you would care to enlighten me as to why I and my men have been called out. Someone said a girl had been found dead?"

"Ethel Jordan," said Mrs Clemence in a breathless rush. "In the library. I think she was murdered."

"Perhaps we should leave that kind of judgement to the police. But this is true? This Ethel Jordan is dead?"

"The caretaker is standing guard over the body," said Mrs Lancaster. "These girls found her."

Maliha held her tongue. She had experience of how this was likely to go. If it had not been for the grey school uniform she wore, she doubted the policeman would have even noticed her.

"Both?"

Since Lane was unlikely to respond, Maliha spoke up. "I found her. After the midday meal."

"You?"

"I usually go to the library after lunch. She was on the floor and clearly dead."

"You are used to seeing dead people?" His tone was mocking.

"In India it is not uncommon to see the dead and dying on the streets, Detective Inspector Williams. I may have been away from home for a long time but I have not forgotten. And given the amount of blood on the outside, I do not think she could have been alive. I would have been happy to be incorrect."

"You hated her."

Maliha was surprised at the sudden outburst from Rainie Lane. What was she doing?

"She was not a popular girl, Detective Inspector," said Mrs Lancaster quickly.

He held up his hand. "I am only interested in facts. I will interview you one at a time. In the order in which you discovered the body or found out about the incident."

With that he sent the two uniformed men to find the crime scene and to send the caretaker back. Meanwhile he appropriated the headmistress's office for his interviews.

"But what about the rest of the school?" said Mrs Clemence. "There will be rumours and when the next class begins they will see your policemen. There may be panic."

"Your girls have dormitories I take it?"

"Of course."

"I want them all returned there and a full head count of both pupils and staff, both academic and all those who provide other services. I want to know if anyone is missing now. And everyone will need to be interviewed."

"But some of the pupils belong to the aristocracy. And even those who are not have extremely rich and influential parents. When they find out many will want their children sent home."

"Then you will keep the news to yourself and any that are requested must be told this is a police investigation and no one is above the law. They will be allowed to leave when I say so, not a moment before."

He stared thoughtfully at the window for a moment.

"I also want details of any trade deliveries for today."

"Yes."

"Good." He looked over at Maliha. "You first."

He sat in the headmistress's chair and pulled out his notebook. The sergeant remained outside and closed the door after her. Maliha sat opposite without being asked.

"And you are?"

"Maliha Anderson, from Pondicherry in French India."

"French India?"

"Yes."

"I had no idea."

Maliha bit back a caustic comment and kept her face still.

"Tell me in your own words the events leading up to your discovery of the body."

"I thought you would want to look at the body first."

"It's not going anywhere."

Maliha sighed. He was right, of course, but that was not how it worked in stories. "As I said before, I usually go to the library after luncheon."

"Why?"

"Because I find it more pleasant to sit by myself and read than put myself in a position where I might be insulted, struck, or otherwise denigrated by other pupils in the school." In her mind she dared him to disagree or argue the point.

"Carry on with your rendition of the events."

"I opened the door to the library——"

"It's not locked?"

"Only at night and on Sunday mornings."

"Why Sunday mornings?"

"We are to go to the chapel for weekly prayers and listen to the sermon, and then we are supposed to study and contemplate the Bible."

"Supposed to?"

"It is not generally done."

"Do you?"

"I have read it."

"All of it?"

"Yes, all of it. Even the parts young girls, such as I, are not supposed to read," she said.

"I was not aware there were such passages."

"Then you should study your Bible more, Detective Williams. You will find it quite revealing, I am sure."

He nodded and made some notes. "Continue with your story."

"I opened the door—"

"It was shut."

"Yes, otherwise I would not have had to open it."

He looked up and smiled at her humourlessly. "I find it important to clarify the details. If it is something you do every day it's entirely possible you might confuse the actions of one day with another."

"I don't get confused."

He did the smile again and waited.

"I opened the door and stepped inside. I was about to close it behind me when I saw her lying in the middle of the floor. I assumed she was dead immediately."

"Ah, your Indian experience."

"She had severe blows to her skull and I could see bone where her hair had been separated and stuck down with blood from the blows."

"How do you know there were multiple blows?"

"I looked."

"You did not find it unpleasant looking at a dead body?"

"I found it very unpleasant. I was trying to determine what my action should be. If she was alive and mobile I could help her to the infirmary, as it turned out there was nothing to be done."

"I thought you hated her?"

"You want the truth about Ethel Jordan, Detective Inspector Williams? Ethel was an utterly obnoxious girl. She took pleasure in causing other people pain—I believe the correct term is *sadist*."

This time he really was surprised and looked directly at her. "How do you come to know such a word?"

"I am extremely well-read."

Let him ask whether she had read the works of *de Sade*. She knew he wouldn't. If he had read them at all, it would be in the watered-down English not in the original French.

"I realise this is a progressive school, but I doubt they carry such books here."

"You are quite correct, I have read them outside of the school."

He decided that course of questioning was not relevant. "Tell me more of Miss Jordan."

"The school did their best with her and channelled her violent nature into hockey."

"The Beast of Roedean?"

Maliha smiled. "You have heard of her then."

"But you say you did not hate her?"

Maliha shrugged. "I disliked her intensely and abhorred her desire for violence. That is no different from any other girl in the school. I know with certainty that Rainie Lane suffered severe contusions when Ethel Jordan decided to kick her in her right leg until she could no longer stand."

"You're suggesting Lane was deflecting the possibility of guilt to you because she had more reason to kill the girl than you?"

"I am not suggesting anything. I am giving you some appropriate facts," said Maliha. "Linda Trafford was hospitalised from a blow to the head with a hockey stick."

"Could she be the murderer?"

"She never returned to the school, I believe her general health was so severely impaired she was moved to the south of France by her parents."

"Yet the violence of this girl was never reported to the police?"

Maliha smiled. "That incident was an accident. Hockey is notorious as I'm sure you're aware."

"But these other incidents?"

"The school relies on the parents' trust. I am sure they would rather not have any sort of scandal."

"They have one now."

"Yes."

Maliha waited while he scribbled several pages of notes.

"So, after you had established the girl was dead?"

"I wrote a note to put on the door in an attempt to prevent any other girls going in there and discovering the body. Then I went to the school office to report the incident. Unfortunately, Miss Lane saw me leaving the library and tried to stop me. I ignored her but assumed she would chase after me."

"But she did not."

"It seems she saw my note and decided to look in the room."

"And she was not as resilient as you."

"No."

"Where's the note now?"

Maliha reached into her school bag and handed it to the detective. He scanned it.

"Infestation of rodents?"

"The prospect of mice and rats should have been good enough to keep most girls out for the short amount of time needed to raise the alarm."

He nodded and wrote it down. He folded the note and put it in his pocket.

"Is that everything?" he asked.

"I spoke to Mrs Clemence who did not believe me until Miss Lane came in. I told the secretary she should ring the police and that I would fetch the caretaker to lock the door to the library."

"Very practical of you."

"Thank you."

"Is that something you learnt in French India as well?"

Maliha withheld the frown from her face. He would seem

to relax into being a decent human being and then he came out with that pointless reference to her heritage.

"No, Detective Inspector Williams, I learnt it from my mother and father."

He closed his little black notebook and leaned back in the chair.

"How much do you know of the suffragist movement, Miss Anderson?"

"I know a great deal. I read the newspapers and the pamphlets."

"And are you one?"

"A suffragist? I suppose I am, though not a member of any organisation. I do not think half the population of the country should be ignored."

"Deeds not Words?"

"You are attempting to lead me into a trap, detective, though I have no idea why."

"It's part of my job to determine whether there are any threats to public safety."

"You think this is a training ground for Suffragettes?"

"A girl's school run entirely by women. Yes, I think that is a distinct possibility. Those women are causing a great deal of trouble."

"Let me reassure you that while some of the girls might discuss the subject, the headmistress, Mrs Ramsey, is utterly opposed to the behaviour of the Pankhursts and their associates. And the sermons we receive every Sunday, particularly since the march in February, have all been about women staying in their place."

"I am reassured."

"Have you finished with me?"

"I will need you to write a statement as to the events and sign it."

"I can do that straight away if you wish."

"That would be acceptable."

Without being told, Maliha stood and went to the door. "You'll be wanting to talk to Miss Lane next?"

"Send her in."

Maliha hesitated. "Be gentle with her, detective, it was a terrible shock and she is not well."

"I will do what I need to do, Miss Anderson. A girl has been murdered."

Maliha swallowed an angry retort and left.

3

———

Maliha waited in the office. When Rainie Lane returned it was clear she had been crying again. Maliha somehow doubted the policeman had been gentle.

Given so much time for speculation she wondered what would happen to the school. There was no question in her mind the scandal would be all over the national press in the morning. A wide variety of vehicles—steam, diesel and electric as well as one donkey trap—had arrived in the road that ran along the cliff above the sea in front of the school. Men had left the vehicles and stood looking towards the buildings, some were taking photographs. Clearly word had got out.

The school lay in its own grounds with nothing between it and the sea except for the main road that ran between Brighton and Rottingdean. There had been efforts to extend the narrow gauge electric railway out this far, and perhaps further, but there was nowhere to put the tracks except the road or the fields, and the school would not give its permission. Mr Volks, who owned the railway, had attempted

to run it along the beach built up on scaffolding to keep it dry.
It had not been a success.

Once the interviews were complete—in the late afternoon
when the light was starting to fade from the sky—Inspector
Williams told them they could go about their business but not
to discuss the case with anyone. Which was not a problem
from Maliha's viewpoint, no one talked to her anyway, and she
suspected Rainie Lane would not be saying very much for a
while. The staff, however, were another matter completely.

Mrs Clemence told the girls to go back to their
dormitories. The teachers were responsible for one dormitory
each and had a room next door. Maliha returned to hers with
Mrs Lancaster.

"This is a terrible thing, Maliha."

"Yes, miss."

Mrs Lancaster was the only teacher who called her by the
name she preferred. It was not that they had a special
relationship, but since Maliha could speak French as fluently
as she could English, Mrs Lancaster seemed to think that
made them almost friends. She loved France, not that Maliha
had ever been there.

"It's very upsetting and I'm really not sure how I'm going
to cope, let alone look after the girls."

"No, miss."

They climbed the stone steps to the top floor of the
residential wing.

"You seem untouched."

"I suppose that's true, miss," said Maliha. The silence
from her teacher suggested she was expecting a more
complete answer. "I had no love for Ethel Jordan, she was not
a good person, but I am sad she was killed like that."

"You shouldn't speak ill of the dead."

"I do not think she will rise from her grave to haunt me.
And surely the truth is more likely to lead to the person who
killed her."

"You are more sensible than I, Maliha. I doubt I shall sleep tonight. I will never be able to forget what I saw."

They reached the dormitory to the sound of a great deal of shouting from behind the door. Mrs Lancaster went through first and the wave of noise dissipated in a moment as if it had never been. Maliha followed her in and went to her bed which was the first on the left. The accommodation was arranged alphabetically up the left and down the right. The water closet and bathroom were located at the far end but shared with the dormitory on the other side.

The headmistress had a passionate interest in birds, particularly exotic varieties, and each dorm was named after one. Maliha lived in Sea Eagles with seven other girls, her immediate neighbour being Margaret Creighton-Ward, daughter of a ridiculously rich aristocrat though she was not entirely unfriendly.

Mrs Lancaster went to the other end of the room, thereby fully gaining the attention of the Upper Sixth girls and then turned to face them. There was a long silence before she spoke.

"You—" and her voice broke there, and she had to take another moment to compose herself. "—you may have heard some rumours. And you are almost women now so I will be honest with you because truth is better than lies. *Honneur aulx dignes*. Though I have been asked not to communicate any details and I would ask you not to make things up."

She stopped again and cleared her throat. Maliha was impressed that the teacher had included the school motto which meant 'Honour the worthy' on the assumption that the girls would be worthy because she was honouring them with the truth.

"Ethel Jordan has been found dead in the library."

Of the seven girls, three squealed in horror. The drama queens who behaved the way they believed was expected of them. Margaret Creighton-Ward and Mary Laker began to cry, while the others seemed too shocked to react—or were not capable of understanding.

Mrs Lancaster extracted a handkerchief from her sleeve and dabbed at her eyes.

"The police are in the school and have interviewed those of us who were witnesses in one way or another."

"Are we in danger?" said Jennifer Wendlefield. Though they did not speak often, Maliha considered Jennifer to be one of the more sensible girls. An opinion confirmed by the question. She was also very beautiful and elegant, her every move seemed calculated to please. There were girls in all years who looked at Jennifer Wendlefield with longing, either to be her, or to be with her. But Jennifer had eyes and lips only for Antonia Dumont who, thankfully, was on another floor, in Kookaburra dorm.

Maliha considered how unbearable it would have been to have the two of them in the same room every night, but Antonia was a year younger. Maliha recalled that Ethel Jordan had also been in Kookaburra; she could not imagine how the girls there might be feeling now, probably utter relief in not having to face the girl's violence for a single day longer. And then they would feel guilty for being glad she was gone.

When it came to an answer to Jennifer's question however, Maliha knew that Mrs Lancaster did not have one to give. Was this an attack aimed only at Jordan? Or was it something that could happen to any of them?

"I'm quite sure we are not in any sort of danger but I think it's important that no one goes out alone," said Mrs Lancaster. "We will go down to dinner at the usual time but we will travel as a group, and we will return the same way."

"What if we have to use the facilities?" asked Annabel Leeming, who got up three or four times every night with that particular need.

"If you are here in the dormitory, Annabel, you only have to go in there as usual and you will be surrounded by fifteen other girls and two teachers. Anywhere else, just be sure someone goes with you."

"I'm scared," said Eliza.

"There's no need for that. I know it is very unsettling but we are British."

And that was that. Mrs Lancaster fetched a book and a chair then sat with them until seven o'clock. Maliha read her own book lying on her bed while the rest of the girls talked in subdued tones until the dinner bell rang.

The meal passed without incident save for a speech by Mrs Dixon, the deputy headmistress, who repeated most of what Mrs Lancaster had said. By now all the school knew what had happened, either having been told or through rumours. Maliha could feel the suppressed fear and panic that lurked just below the surface. There were nervous glances and hand-holding.

The teachers were in no better state, the science teacher Mrs Crumpsall, in particular, looked as if she would fall to pieces where she sat. However, the teachers had a responsibility to the girls and that helped them maintain a more relaxed exterior.

Eventually, the girls were dismissed back to their dorms as the catering staff came in to clear everything away.

Which was when something extraordinary occurred. Maliha was leading the way down the central aisle with Margaret Creighton-Ward—and from the looks she was getting she assumed the rumours included the fact that she was the one who found the body—when someone jostled her. It was not unknown, since anti-Indian feeling often boiled to the surface with name-calling and physical attacks, but in this instance something was pushed into her hand. She clasped it automatically and found it to be a piece of paper.

She glanced round but could not see who had done it, beyond the fact that most of the girls in the immediate area seemed to be in the third year. Maliha never had anything to do with girls so young, particularly not since she had entered the sixth form, where they had considerably more autonomy.

However, it seemed someone had passed her a note. Most likely it was some racial slur, or perhaps even an accusation that she had committed the crime, but she always read them. It helped to remind her of who she really was, and how she did not belong here among the white girls. She tucked the note up her sleeve and followed Mrs Lancaster.

She did not attempt to read the note immediately but waited until she needed to use the W.C. because it meant she could flush the note away after reading and no one would be the wiser. Once sitting down, she extracted the piece of paper and unfolded it. Contrary to her expectations it was neither a threat, slur, nor an accusation. It was a request for an assignation.

"Midnight, outside the refectory kitchen."

The time was pure melodrama, why not eleven-thirty or two o'clock? Either would be just as suitable, in fact earlier would be nice. The location indicated the sender had given the request some thought and, because of that, suggested this was a genuine request.

On more than one occasion notes received had specified a time and place so that she could be threatened or attacked. But the kitchen was a place the girls sometimes visited for midnight snacks. By setting that as the meeting place they could, if caught, simply claim they were raiding the larder. Clever. And it was almost certainly to do with the death of Ethel Jordan

Maliha disposed of the message and waited to ensure it had disappeared. She had read all of Conan Doyle's stories about his detective, as well as Poe, and she was now quite curious to know what this person had to say.

4

There was little she could do for the rest of the evening. For the Upper Sixth lights-out was ten o'clock. Mrs Lancaster anticipated nightmares for some of the girls and brought in the bedside lamp from her own room. She asked Maliha to fetch the table that went with it.

It was cold in the corridor, and the white electric bulbs shone without heat. She had been in Mrs Lancaster's room once or twice previously and liked the scent the teacher had in a little spray bottle on the table.

Not that the wearing of scent was allowed during the day. But Mrs Lancaster wore it when she went out on her free Saturday afternoon and evening. Although she was referred to as if she was a married woman, that was simply a tradition. None of the teachers were married, they would have to leave their employment if they were. But Maliha was quite certain Mrs Lancaster had a gentleman friend, there was always a smell of tobacco on her when she returned—not strong, but it was there. More importantly, it was always the same brand.

A small amount of personalisation was allowed. Mrs Lancaster favoured the French Art Nouveau movement and had a framed colour print of an Alfons Mucha painting on the wall. It was too intricate to appeal to Maliha's taste, and very romantic in style.

The bedside table was very basic, lacking even a drawer, and was easy to carry.

However having the light at her end of the room did not suit Maliha, since she planned to leave in the night.

"Shall we set up another light at the end next to the toilet?" she said to the teacher. "For Leeming?"

"No, let's put this light at the other end of the room. If anyone needs to come out to me in the night the light will be on in the hall."

Maliha smiled gently to herself and then felt a twinge of guilt for manipulating her teacher, but it would be ultimately for the best.

Once all that was done she went back to her bed and pulled out her copy of David Copperfield, she did not find the long-winded narrative to be particularly enthralling but Dickens' study of the life of the poor was interesting. It provided a more vivid representation of that time than cold—and frequently incorrect—history books.

Ten o'clock came. Mrs Lancaster uttered a few platitudes and turned off the main light. Maliha listened as the teacher closed the door of her own room and heard her going through the motions of going to bed. Mrs Lancaster would herself read for about twenty minutes by which time it would be half-past ten and then she would sleep.

"You saw the body, Anderson?"

Maliha should not have been surprised they were happy to talk to her after all these years, given the circumstances. But even now this was Margaret, one of the least reticent. The light from the bedside lamp cast everyone in dark shapes with highlights from Maliha's position at the other end of the room.

"Yes."

"What was it like?"

"Bloody."

Another voice spoke up, Annabel Leeming, the serial W.C. visitor. "Was she murdered?"

"The police said I was not to talk about it."

Tenby spoke up. "If it was an accident they wouldn't be so worried about the rest of us, would they? Even if she had done herself in, she's not going to come back and do it to us."

Maliha said nothing. Mary Laker, two beds down, started to cry again.

"Well done, Tenby." That was Jenny Wendlefield, her voice was as gentle and mellow as the rest of her was attractive. Perfection.

Maliha did not bother to look at her watch. It could not even be eleven yet. She would give herself fifteen minutes to get to the kitchen entrance.

"Did you do it, Anderson?" Tenby again. "You had enough reason. And you go to the library all the time."

"My liking for the library is why I found her. Jordan never went to the library normally."

"Just stop it, Tenby, why do you have to upset people?"

Nearly all the girls were sitting up now which really was not helpful from Maliha's viewpoint. It was not unknown for them to have very quiet parties and talk for hours. Partying might be unlikely this time but talking was.

"I'm going to sleep," she said and lay down. This was also inconvenient, she could not be certain she would be able to stay awake if she was lying down. She just hoped the rest would take the hint—or at least Jennifer because if she did the others would definitely follow.

"Why would someone kill, Jordan?" and that was Jane Porter-Smythe. Maliha shook her head, this was never going to work. She sat up again and realised everyone was looking at her as if she was going to answer—except Constance Oliphaunt who was fast asleep.

It was a perfectly reasonable question, of course, precisely the question the police would be asking, along with who and how. She realised there hadn't been a murder weapon in the room.

"Jordan was the least popular girl in the school apart from me," Maliha said. "Is there anybody here she hasn't hit?"

"Me," said Jennifer.

"She was probably in love with you," said Margaret.

The whole place became very quiet, it was almost as if no one was even breathing. Constance snorted and mumbled in her sleep. Nobody laughed.

Everyone knew about the relationships, the crushes, the little night noises, and the things that went on between certain girls. Nobody talked about it. Nobody ever mentioned it. Margaret had crashed straight through that rule and Maliha was not even sure she realised what she had said.

But it was fair comment, if ill-judged. In fact, almost certainly true.

"Yes," said Jennifer. "She probably was, everybody else is."

The awkward silence deepened. That Jennifer herself was now admitting what everyone knew just made it worse.

"I'm not," said Maliha in attempt to lighten the mood, and then realised she might hurt the girl's feelings. "But I do like you."

"Thank you."

"So what reasons could someone have for killing Jordan?" said Tenby. "Perhaps we can solve the crime."

"Money," said Porter-Smythe.

"Love," said Jennifer.

"Jealousy," said Margaret.

"That's part of love," said Tenby.

"It doesn't have to be. Lust then."

There was some embarrassed laughter.

"That's even more part of love than jealousy."

"Keep your voice down," said Jennifer. "We don't want Mrs Lancaster in here."

"She's got a man-friend."

"And don't gossip, it's unbecoming of a Roedeanian."

"Secrets," said Maliha. It was always secrets. She glanced at her watch. It was now eleven o'clock how could she get them to sleep in the next forty-five minutes?

The door opened and Mrs Lancaster stepped in silently in her slippers.

"Girls, I understand that this is a very upsetting time but I insist you go to sleep. And if, when I come back in ten minutes you are not asleep I will be forced to issue demerits against you all. And some of you—" she looked pointedly at Eliza Tenby, "—cannot afford that. Lie down and go to sleep."

Maliha thanked whatever deity might be responsible for making Jennifer's warning come too late. Now all she had to do was make sure she did not drop off herself.

She came awake suddenly not entirely sure why there was light in the dormitory. It all came back to her and she grabbed her watch. Ten to midnight. She cursed herself for being weak-willed but congratulated herself too on being so concerned about the meeting she had managed to wake up.

But she would be sensible. She did not get up immediately but listened to the breathing in the room. She did not think anyone else was awake. She sat up and slipped on her slippers then picked up her dressing gown and headed for the door. The squeaking of another bed caught her attention and, with her hand on the knob, she turned to see Margaret sitting up in bed and staring at her.

Unable to do anything else Maliha put her finger to her mouth and opened the door just enough to let her out but, as she pulled it closed, someone else's fingers wrapped themselves around the edge and pulled back.

Not wishing to start a fight of any sort Maliha left the door open and Margaret padded out after her. By mutual and silent consent, they did not speak until they had gone down the first half-flight of the stairs. It was cold and Maliha's dressing gown did not provide any protection. Margaret was only wearing her nightgown and no slippers.

"I knew it," she said. "I saw the note. What did it say? Where are you going?"

"Just go back to bed, you don't need to get into trouble."

"If you don't tell me what's going on I will wait five minutes in the dorm and then tell Mrs Lancaster you're missing. Can you imagine the uproar?"

Unfortunately, Maliha could imagine exactly the kind of uproar. She would be lucky if she wasn't expelled from the school—which she wouldn't mind except for the shame it would bring to her parents—there was even the possibility the police might consider it proof of guilt. Regardless of how impossible it would have been for her to have done it without getting blood on her uniform.

She sighed and checked her watch. There was no way she could get to the assignation in the five minutes remaining.

"Someone wants to talk to me I think it's someone from Jordan's dorm."

"But why you?"

"I do not know, Margaret. And if I don't go now I may never know because I'll miss them."

"Very well but if you don't tell me everything when you get back I will tell on you."

Maliha did not have time to explain that if Margaret did not report her immediately that would make her complicit in the crime and she would be in trouble herself. Instead she hurried as quickly as she could down the stairs.

She reached the longest straight corridor in Britain that ran on the first floor from the end of one wing right through the building to the end of the other. But she was not interested in that. She crossed from the stairs to a panel in the wall. The disguised door here was for the cleaning staff.

She went through and descended the steep stone steps as quickly as she dared. It spilled out into another corridor— again for the catering staff and not used much by other staff.

The pupils were forbidden to use them. And every one of them had done so at one time or another. What was the point of forbidden fruit if you did not taste it?

Besides this was the quickest and safest route to the kitchen. The policemen who were still on the premises would have no idea about it.

She turned a corner and crashed into someone else. Both of them cried out and their voices echoed noisily down the corridors. Maliha grabbed the other girl by the wrist and pulled her along behind her past the stairs to a store room. They both slipped inside, into the pitch black.

It was only at this point that Maliha realised she might have made a fatal mistake. What if this girl was the murderer?

"Who are you?" said Maliha.

Instead of answering the girl burst into tears. "I didn't think you were coming."

"I was delayed."

There were voices outside and the girl cut short her sobbing with sharp intake of breath. Male voices. And a powerful electric torch shining along the dark corridor. The two ducked instinctively as the light swept through the frosted glass of the door.

The light played across the girl's face revealing dark hair and large nose. Maliha recognised her—she knew and remembered everyone in the school. Those who excelled were the ones she knew best but this person had not been anyone of significance, at least until now.

Once the lights had passed, they stood up again. Just shadows in the dark storeroom.

"Why would you want to talk to me, Amelia?"

"You know who I am?" There was a northern twang to her voice which confirmed her identity.

"Amelia Johnson, Kookaburra. Daughter of Linton Johnson, sole proprietor of Johnson's Bicycles."

"Why do you know me?"

"I know everyone," said Maliha. "Though honestly that's

about the limit of it. Except that your father's business has been tremendously successful over the last fifteen years, especially since the introduction of the Faraday grid into the frame. So successful his bikes are the only ones used in the touring races now, despite the competition."

"Yes, well, I don't like bicycles."

Maliha said nothing. Almost every girl here expressed some sort of problem with their parents, ranging from dislike to outright hatred. Amelia's seemed to be somewhere in the middle. Maliha supposed it was because they had all been sent away to be here. The aristocrats seemed to have the least problem with the arrangement.

"You wanted to talk to me. Why?"

"Eth."

"Ethel Jordan?"

In the dark the girl nodded. It was a difficult motion to make out.

"What about her?" Maliha kept her surprise to herself. The fact that this girl had a nickname for Jordan seemed very odd indeed unless they had a relationship. Although it was hard to imagine a brute like Jordan having any decent emotion in her.

"I—I mean, we—"

"You had a pash for her?"

"No, I mean," the girl was very flustered, "it wasn't like that. I mean I'm in Kookaburra, I know about Dumont and Wendlefield. Eth and I weren't like that."

She stopped talking and started crying again.

Maliha sighed. "You asked me to come here and listen to you but right now you're not telling me anything and I don't even know why you wanted to talk to me. People usually don't."

"I know you're very clever."

"I'm not clever, I just remember things." *Everything.*

"I thought you might be able to help."

"Help who? Ethel Jordan is dead."

"I know!"

Maliha thought that anger was healthier than the self-pity.

"Very well, let's continue but I need you to answer my questions and not start crying again."

Amelia nodded.

"You said you weren't like the other two, so what *were* you like then?"

"We got on together. She talked to me."

"That seems very unlikely."

"It's true." Despite her emphasis, Maliha knew there was something else going on. The girl was trying too hard to be convincing.

"You mean she didn't hurt you like she did everyone else?"

"I mean she talked to me."

"What about?"

"There was a man."

"You're saying she had a boyfriend?" Maliha was now convinced that Amelia Johnson was making it all up. She knew there were people who would do that, particularly if they wanted to be the centre of attention.

"She had met him at a hockey game, and he fancied her."

That wasn't unheard of, plenty of times boys from the area would lurk outside the grounds and sometimes even come in to meet with the girls. And some girls were too stupid not to avoid it. Caroline Frankel had left the school because of just such a dubious relationship a couple of years ago.

"Did you see this man?"

"No."

"How do you know she wasn't making it up?"

"She didn't need to make things up. Besides, he brought her things and she showed me."

"What sort of things?"

"A penknife and some Brighton sugar sticks."

Maliha considered that for a few moments. She still thought Amelia was lying, but what if she wasn't? Was it really likely a man might take a fancy to Ethel Jordan? She shrugged, not *unlikely*, the doctor who visited the school was known for touching the girls unnecessarily. It was something they all just put up with—and they avoided seeing him as much as possible. Though he hadn't touched Maliha beyond the absolute minimum, clearly he was not a man who liked girls with darker skin. It was stupid but she felt insulted at the same time as being grateful.

"Have the police been to look at her things yet?"

"Not yet."

Maliha hesitated. If this went wrong she would be in a great deal of trouble. "Take me up to your dorm and I'll look through her cupboard. If I find anything that says you're telling me the truth we'll talk more."

"When?"

"Now."

5

K ookaburra was in the other wing. For speed, they could
have gone up to the first floor and used the long
corridor, but that would also make them easier to discover.
Maliha allowed Amelia to lead even though she could have
taken them there just as quickly, if not faster.

Maliha stopped her when they reached the top of the
stairs. "Describe which bed she's in."

"Second on the left."

That was something, at least it wasn't at the far end of the
room. The rooms were almost identical apart from overall
proportions and there were usually more girls in the
dormitories for the lower school. Many girls left after the fifth
year to be married off—despite sending them to the most
prestigious school in the country for the best possible
education, their parents still treated them like chattel.

"We'll go in together but you go straight to bed and then
if I'm discovered you can pretend you had nothing to do
with it."

"Why?"

"Why what?"

"Why would you do that? Protect me."

"Because I am not concerned what happens to me, if I am expelled I will go home to India and no one will care. If you are caught up in this it could affect your father's business."

The girl was silent for a moment and then approached swiftly. Maliha thought she was going to receive a hug. But Amelia pressed her lips against Maliha's—only for a moment—then she opened the door and Maliha managed to be sufficiently composed to follow her through.

Amelia went to the right with Jordan as the earliest and to the left.

The bed was still made up as if the girl might return at any moment and occupy it. But Maliha was not prone to morbid thoughts. Ethel Jordan was dead and would not be coming back. Unlike her own dormitory, the teacher for this one, Mrs Crumpsall, had chosen not to give her pupils a light for the night. However, this room gave on to the front courtyard which had electric lights fitted and they were blazing despite the time of night—possibly under instruction from the police. The result was sufficient illumination to allow Maliha to see well enough.

She sat down against the wall and opened the bedside cabinet. Maliha's cabinet was neatly stacked with her school exercise books, text books and some personal items arranged neatly. Jordan's was a mess. All the school-related materials were thrown into the lower part while her own things were scattered on the upper shelf.

Maliha went through them carefully, putting them on the floor once she had established what they were. There was a penknife. Maliha wanted to examine it in more detail but there simply was not enough light, she paused and then chose to pocket it. It was stealing evidence and interfering with a police investigation but she wanted to examine it in daylight. Amelia would never speak to the police about her suspicions.

There were several sheets of some waxed wrapping paper that smelled slightly sweet, large enough to hold a stick of rock, but this proved nothing. Ethel could easily have bought it herself on her trips out of the school. Amelia could simply have seen her eating it. Maliha pocketed one of them. Dried crumbs littered the surface, and an opened packet of biscuits lay near the back.

And then she found three slim tins piled one on top of the other. Maliha knew what they were instantly, supplied by the school for all the girls when they started their cycles: Southall's Menstrual Pads. It was tremendously embarrassing but at least, in this school, everyone was in the same situation, even the teachers. There was barely any education on that matter, and what there was came from Matron who supplied the materials, but the girls explained it one to another as the years went by.

Maliha's reading, on the other hand, had provided her with an extremely detailed understanding of the subject, and everything related to it.

She pulled the tins out and frowned. They were heavy, which meant they were unused.

And that was that. She returned everything to the cabinet and tried not to be tidy about it. The quiet dorm was filled only with the sound of sleeping girls. Maliha climbed to her feet and glanced at where Amelia lay. She was asleep, so Maliha stole from the room and headed back.

She was tired the next morning having had considerably less sleep than she preferred. She usually ended up being the last to wash simply because everyone else assumed that was her place. She was barely higher rank than a servant. This particular morning, she did not mind since she was having trouble pulling herself together. She almost felt stupid.

Breakfast was run the same way as the meal the previous evening and once again they were marched in twos down to the refectory.

"Well?" said Margaret.

"Hush."

"I want to know," she said. "Or else."

Maliha looked at her companion and spoke quietly. "Since you did not report me last night you are now part of the crime. If you tell on me now you will simply get yourself into trouble."

Margaret absorbed that information. "You'll get into more trouble than me."

"That would be true even if our crimes were identical. You just have to ask yourself whether you think it's worth your suffering, and how it will reflect on your parents."

"They won't care."

"Then I pity you."

Margaret was silent through breakfast and on the return trip.

"Is there anything I can say that will make you tell me?" she said finally.

Maliha frowned. "You think me so stupid that I would tell you how you might coerce me into doing something I choose not to do?"

"You could decide to tell me because you want to. Because it gives you someone to talk to because nobody ever talks to you."

"I will consider it."

Once back in the dormitory they were given an impromptu French lesson by Mrs Lancaster, Maliha was excused since she spoke French better than the teacher herself. Growing up in French India with a Scottish father and Tamil mother, Maliha spoke four languages although Hindi was her least practised one and there was barely any occasion to use it here. She had not uttered a word of it in all her years in Britain, except to the caretaker.

Mrs Lancaster had chosen to teach from the toilet end of the room which left Maliha in a position where she was not being watched by any of the others. She pulled out the waxed-paper wrapper. It was indeed for Brighton rock but these were not from the cheap varieties available at every tourist shop along the front. The paper was of good quality and printed in colour. The pattern was a tartan in red and green. The manufacturer's mark indicated Craven's Confectionery in York and, along with an illustration of the domes of Brighton Pavilion, there was a royal crest featuring the three feathers of the Prince of Wales with the date 1840.

The Brighton Pavilion had not been owned by the Royal family for a very long time. The capital had moved north from London to Manchester in the 1870s, and the Royal family removed with it to their new official residence. There had been no connection between Brighton and the Royals for even longer, over fifty years, but that didn't stop local companies playing on the old relationship, and requiring the producers to wrap their goods in "royal" trappings.

But who was this man who brought Ethel Jordan sweet rock and with whom she had indulged in the ultimate intimacy to her own ruination and death? Was she sure that Ethel had given herself to this man? Maliha thought it through. Yes, there was no doubt. The full tins were proof of it.

Had he killed her because of it? But if that were the case would he risk coming into the school to do it? And how?

There was no further she could go with the information she had to hand. She wanted to look at the penknife but that would have to wait until she had some privacy. Which in the current situation would be when she next went to use the privy, and not until Mrs Lancaster finished her lesson.

Maliha listened with half an ear to the girls attempting to form coherent sentences in a language they abhorred. Margaret Creighton-Ward was the best at it but she spoke the language with an English accent so sharp it could have sliced stone.

There was a knock at the dormitory door and Mrs Clemence entered. As was appropriate she waited at the back of the room until Mrs Lancaster acknowledged her.

"The policeman would like to talk to Miss Anderson again."

It wasn't as if she would be missing anything. Mrs Lancaster said that would be acceptable and Maliha followed the silent Mrs Clemence to the library corridor.

"You go," she said. "I'm never going down this way again."

"Thank you, Mrs Clemence." Maliha turned away.

"Wait."

Maliha turned back and waited. Mrs Clemence glanced at the clot of policemen around the entrance to the library, then back.

"The way things happened yesterday."

"Yes, Mrs Clemence. I came to the office and you sent me to the caretaker while you phoned the police."

"Yes."

Maliha found it hard to decipher the expression on the woman's face. It was a strange combination of anger and relief.

"Go on then, the detective is waiting for you."

"Yes, Mrs Clemence."

Only three months, Maliha thought. I only have to put up with this for another three months. Then home to the world I understand and food that doesn't make me want to throw up.

There were even more uniformed policemen than before but Detective Inspector Williams was at the heart of it. The body of Jordan had been taken away, but there were stains on the Chinese rug.

"Miss Anderson."

"Inspector."

The policeman made a space for her. There was another, much older, man not in uniform with a pair of magnifying spectacles and a small black bag. He was kneeling on the floor examining the rug—an activity that seemed awkward for a man of his considerable bulk.

"This is Dr Underwood—"

"Of Scotland Yard," finished Maliha. The man looked up but she must have just been a small grey blur among the blue blurs of the rest. "A scientific investigator of crime scenes."

"You've heard of me?" His voice was incongruously high in register.

"I read the newspapers, sir," she said. "I am delighted to make your acquaintance."

"Thank you, you too, Miss…er…"

"Anderson."

The inspector interrupted. "When you've quite finished?"

"Sorry," said Dr Underwood and went back to investigating the floor.

"Miss Anderson, I'd like you to go through the motions of what happened yesterday."

"You want to know if something jogs my memory?"

"That's correct."

"It won't, sir."

He smiled condescendingly. "This is a technique I have used very successfully with other witnesses, I'm sure you're no different. You'd be surprised at how much people forget."

"On the contrary, Inspector, and please understand that I mean no disrespect since I am sure you have had much success doing this, but I am different."

The smile did not leave his face, nor did it penetrate far beneath the surface. His eyes betrayed his impatience.

"You aren't."

"I have a perfect memory."

"People always think that."

"You don't understand, inspector. I remember everything with absolute perfection," she said. "Given time, I could recite the entirety of the Bible. Or quote back to you every word we spoke in the interview yesterday. I see you are wearing exactly the same shirt, there is an oily smudge just below the collar, although for some reason you have changed your shoes."

"You're one of those," said Dr Underwood from the floor. "That's astonishing, and also most useful I would imagine. At school, I mean."

"It is a both a blessing and curse, Doctor. It means I can learn things quickly but there is considerable jealousy."

"I can imagine." He laughed, although Maliha was not sure he appreciated quite what sort of reaction jealousy could invoke in a girls' school. Most of it did not involve humour, at least not for the target.

"I would still like you to go through it," said the inspector. "For my own understanding, if nothing else."

"Of course," said Maliha. "Where would you like me to start?"

The other police were ejected from the room and both Maliha and the detective went outside.

"The door was closed?"

"It was."

"Ajar or completely?"

"Tight shut as usual."

"But not locked."

"No, it's not locked during school hours nor into the evening when we might want to do additional study."

"You said you usually come here after the midday meal?"

"Yes."

"Very well," he said. "Just go through the motions."

Maliha backed up in the direction of the refectory and then walked to the door, turned the ornate handle and pushed it open. She felt the inspector's presence close behind her and his warm breath on her ear. He smelled of cigarettes and cologne. The former dominated.

"Don't mind me, I'm just trying to see it with your eyes."

She stepped into the room and he followed. The doctor had moved toward the window and was still examining the floor in great detail. She admired that level of dedication.

"So, you saw her the moment you entered the room."

"Yes."

"And you didn't faint?"

"What good would that do?"

"You didn't call for help?"

"She was dead, that much was obvious although, as I said, I did check just in case I was wrong. I did not wish to be right."

"You approached the body? Show me."

She knelt, contemplating the brown stains for a moment, before standing and sitting down on the chair she had used.

"You sat down? You didn't raise the alarm?"

"I was curious about her death, it was so unusual. Like a murder in a story, one of those locked-room mysteries."

"I do like a good mystery," said the doctor. "Have you read Conan Doyle, Miss … what was it?"

"Anderson, and yes, doctor, I do enjoy his stories."

"And what did you make of the death?" asked the inspector, he sounded tired, almost bored.

"The primary attack occurred elsewhere. She wasn't dragged, we could see that in the rug because it lay completely flat, but somehow she ended up here under her own steam. She was heading for the door probably trying to get help but died before she got any further. She might have been pursued and the final killing blow struck here. I'm sure the doctor will be able to confirm that one way or the other."

The inspector was silent for a few moments, his gaze shifted from Maliha to where the body had lain and then to the rest of the room.

"You worked that out?"

Maliha shrugged. "It seemed most likely."

The doctor gave a laugh. "Girls these days, eh? She'll be after your job next, Williams."

"It'll be a very long time before we see a woman doing a man's job in the police. It's hardly proper."

Maliha held her tongue since she had clearly

demonstrated that she was perfectly capable of doing his job. Nobody mentioned the fact that she was not white.

"So, you sat in the chair and contemplated the crime. For how long?"

"Two minutes."

"Did you consider who might have committed the crime?"

"Yes, I considered other girls but dismissed that idea because Ethel was physically strong."

"She might have been surprised."

"Even with the element of surprise she could have defeated a single opponent."

"A gang."

"Even I can account for the four girls absent from the meal. Jordan was supposed to be at hockey practice, two of the others were in the infirmary. The fourth is not in the school at present."

"Can you make a list?"

"Yes. Then I considered the teachers but they were all at lunch with us except Mrs Ramsey who was in London."

"You thought a teacher might have killed the girl?"

"She was an evil harridan who took pleasure in causing pain to others and indulged herself in that pleasure on anybody whenever she felt like it."

"Even teachers."

"I am not aware of any specific instances but they might have thought they were protecting the rest of us."

D.I. Williams made some notes. "Anyone else?"

"Will I get any credit for helping you solve the case?"

On the other side of the room the doctor spluttered with suppressed laughter.

"Your helpfulness will be noted."

"There's all the catering and cleaning staff but I can't comment on those. Then there's whoever she encountered during hockey practice and matches. There is no end of people she might have aggravated with her violent behaviour. And that would include every school team who has had the misfortune to come up against her in the last few years and suffered not only defeat but cracked ribs and miscellaneous broken bones."

"You're not serious."

Maliha chose to give him the look of disdain she had been practising. It was quite effective.

"It's not beyond the bounds of possibility," she said. "But we have to consider that whoever did this was either in the school grounds, or even in the school itself and managed to disappear completely. Presumably using the same method Jordan used to get into the library without being seen."

The inspector nodded. "Does the place have any secret passages?"

"Servants passages, yes, but secret? I don't know, they wouldn't be secret then, would they?"

"What about you?"

"You mean did I kill her?"

"Since we are being frank and not beating about the bush, yes, Miss Anderson, did you kill Ethel Jordan?"

Maliha had expected the question and did not react. "I would have been capable of it. I could have lured her to the library, taken her by surprise and beaten her over the head with a poker. She was not the brightest of girls, I could have used intelligence to counter her strength. But I did not. All I want, inspector, is to get out of here and go home. And that will happen in three months. I have waited seven years. I can manage to the end of the summer term."

"You are remarkably calm and collected, and that is in the nature of the coldest of cold-hearted criminals."

"If you wish to arrest me, please do so. As it is, I think I answered all your questions."

"Ha!" said the doctor. They both turned towards him standing beside a set of shelving. He was moving his head to and fro studying the books with his magnifying spectacles. Then he reached out and pulled a large red volume. Something clicked. He removed the spectacles and pushed at the shelf. It pivoted and revealed an opening. He laughed and turned to them. "You mentioned secret passages, this book has less dust on it than its neighbours. Bingo!"

Maliha stared. It was the section containing ancient copies of Hansards—she had never been sufficiently interested to read about what politicians, mostly long dead, had said in parliament. Though she berated herself for failing to ask herself *why* the school had these in the library.

But knowing would not have changed anything.

6

"Thank you, Miss Anderson."

Maliha looked up at the inspector standing beside her. "I'm sorry?"

"You may return to wherever you need to be now."

"Oh." She looked at the opened crack in the library wall. This was also an obvious conclusion and she had allowed her familiarity with the room to blind her to the possibility that she did not know all its secrets. "Yes, of course, inspector."

He seemed amused. "You have a good mind for a female," he said. "But you are not part of this investigation except as a witness and a possible suspect."

"You surely don't still think I might have done it."

"It certainly isn't a matter of what I might think, Miss Anderson," he said. "It is a matter of what the evidence and the circumstances may show. You admitted yourself that you, among all the girls in the school, would be able to kill Ethel Jordan."

"I also have insufficient cause. A year ago? Perhaps. But now?"

"I will weigh all the evidence as it becomes available. You are excused."

And that was that. The man stepped away from her and went out into the corridor where he called for his men to bring electric torches for their exploration of the tunnel.

Maliha looked at the doctor. He had been listening to the conversation and was staring at her.

"Do you know where this comes out?"

She shook her head. "I can honestly say that I do not."

He grinned. "A measured answer, Miss Anderson." He beckoned to her and went to stand by the window. Where the inspector smelled of cigarettes and the cologne he used to disguise it, the doctor was sweaty but Maliha was willing to forgive the man given that he, at least, appreciated her.

"What do you see when you look out the window?"

The library gave out on to the main area in front of the building and between the two square wings on either side. Roedean school was not a beautiful place. Brutish and functional would be a better description.

"Police cars, trees, the road, cars parked and probably members of the press—I imagine the news was in the broadsheets today, Mrs Ramsey will not be happy—and the tide is in. I think the inspector and his men should probably take their wellingtons."

The doctor laughed. "Good girl."

Maliha hesitated and then said: "Will you be doing the autopsy, Doctor?"

"Not me, no, not my area of expertise. Why?"

"I think Ethel Jordan was with child."

This time the doctor did not laugh. "Goodness me, how could you possibly know? Did she confide in you?"

"No, but I took the trouble to examine her bedside cabinet —" she did not mention it was the middle of the night and the doctor would have no idea whether it was permissible or not for Maliha to have done so, "—and I found certain evidence that suggested it."

"The inspector checked that early this morning. He said nothing of that nature to me."

"The inspector, no matter how skilled and worthy, is not a woman."

The doctor did not press the point. He could see quite clearly they were straying into areas that would be embarrassing to them both.

"The person doing the autopsy will use the Virchow procedure?"

"One wonders about the books you read, Miss Anderson."

"I read everything I can lay my hands on, sir."

"I see. Yes, Virchow is the accepted methodology. The pathologist will examine the girl's body and if, as you say, she is with child, he will discover it."

Maliha nodded. She most certainly did not want anyone asking her when she had the opportunity to discover that Ethel Jordan had not been using her sanitary products. She also did not wish to mention that there was one girl Jordan did confide in, she would protect Amelia Johnson if she could.

"You're still here," said the inspector returning with an electric torch.

"I wanted a chat with the girl, Williams. If you're to accuse anyone you can blame me."

The inspector grunted an acknowledgement, perhaps attempting to indicate that he still did not approve though he would not gainsay such an illustrious member of Scotland Yard.

"Will you be accompanying us, Doctor?"

Us comprised the inspector, Sergeant Hughes and one of the bobbies.

The doctor laughed again. "I think not, I'm not even sure I could squeeze through the entrance."

"So be it. Please make sure Miss Anderson returns to her teacher. I leave her in your hands."

"As you say, Inspector, enjoy your little expedition."

Maliha would not have been surprised if the inspector had

declared that he was not here to enjoy himself but he did not deign to give any reply at all. Instead he switched on his torch and slid through the gap into the tunnel beyond. The other two followed him into the dark.

From the light of their torches Maliha noted that this first part of the tunnel—wherever it led—was properly constructed. She surmised it would become rougher as they proceeded. She would have liked to have gone as well, but she was not dressed for it—even if she had been permitted.

"Well," said the doctor. "He's going to be gone for a while no doubt. I have completed my investigation of this room."

"What did you find?"

"A small piece of seaweed and a little sand as might fall from a shoe that had already travelled a distance from the shore."

"I didn't look at her shoes," said Maliha. "It didn't even occur to me."

"Don't berate yourself. Every good investigator must start somewhere. I can confirm that her shoes did have sand on them but even I did not consider the possibility of a secret passage. We are victims of assumption, Miss Anderson, some more than others. You must train yourself out of it if you are to see the world as it truly is."

"It is not a pleasant place, Doctor. That much I am aware of."

He sighed. "To be so cynical at such a young age."

"Isn't that what you're advising with your 'see the world as it is' speech?"

"Am I? I did not think so." He paused. "Will you give me a tour of the school? I would like to gain a better understanding of how it works that I might better comprehend what has happened here."

For the next hour she guided him around the buildings, through each wing pointing out the various specialist classrooms for science and the more general ones for language, literature and home management.

He was suitably impressed and asked questions in each place, usually to do with how frequently they were used and by whom. However, when he wanted to go into the areas denied to pupils she balked. It was one thing to sneak through them at night but she did not relish the dressing down she would receive from the senior staff if she were to do it openly.

"But those are the most important areas," the doctor said as they stood beside the very entrance to the back stairs that Maliha had used the night before. "I must see them."

They went to the school office and Dr Underwood butted heads with Mrs Clemence.

"Girls are not allowed below stairs."

"I must be given access."

"You are with the police, Dr Underwood, you may go where you please. The girls may not."

"I require a guide."

"I will fetch the caretaker."

"I wish to be shown around by Miss Anderson, she has been a more-than-adequate guide *above* stairs."

"She is unfamiliar with any other part of the school. She is a pupil, she is not permitted."

"I must insist."

"The school rules do not permit it."

"What if there was a fire?"

"What fire?"

"I was speaking hypothetically."

"I do not understand."

"If there was a fire and the only means of escape was for the girls to go below stairs would you prevent them because it was against the rules?"

Mrs Clemence hesitated. Maliha wondered whether it was because the thought of the girls disobeying the rules as too much, or that she perceived the trap being laid for her. Sadly, Maliha suspected it was the former.

"In such an extreme situation, naturally the girls take priority."

"You are aware there has been a murder on these premises?"

She looked shocked at him for suggesting that she might somehow have missed it. "Of course."

"A girl's life has not only been threatened but taken from her by force."

"Indeed, it is very distressing and I would ask you not to word it in such a disturbing manner."

"But, Mrs Clemence—dear lady—that is precisely what it is. Most disturbing and the other girls may well be at risk."

Her hand went to her throat. "It is of great concern to everyone."

"And the business of the police to ensure it doesn't happen."

"We all hope that."

"Indeed we do. So why are you preventing the police from doing their job?"

"Me?" Mrs Clemence squeaked.

"You, madam. I have determined that I require Miss Anderson for the most efficient functioning of my police work. And you are preventing that." He paused for effect and then. "As if you know better than I."

Mrs Clemence deflated like a pierced balloon. Maliha could not but admire the skill with which the doctor had turned it all around. It had been a long time since a teacher had inspired her the way she found this portly middle-aged man did.

"I suppose, since it is police business, then you must do as you will, sir," said Mrs Clemence, utterly defeated.

"I will, of course, take full responsibility for the girl. She will be under my protection and I will ensure she comes to no harm."

Maliha suspected Mrs Clemence would like to have that in

writing—in triplicate—but she would have to make do with his word.

"Dr Underwood?"

"Yes, Miss Anderson."

"The girls are all being kept in their dormitories. Now that the main investigation has been completed is that entirely necessary? After all, the catering staff are still using the below stairs area as if nothing has happened."

"You mean we should let the innocents out of their prison? I think that's a capital idea." He directed his attention back to Mrs Clemence. "The inspector is currently following a lead, so I shall take full responsibility but apart from the corridor with the library, the girls may once more go about their lessons as normal. Can't have them going doolally from being cooped up. Could you spread the word, dear lady?"

Mrs Clemence nodded dumbly.

"Spot on. Come, Miss Anderson, let us investigate this *terra incognita* below stairs."

It was two hours later Maliha was finally released from the doctor's service and allowed to return to the upper world in time for her Science lesson with Mrs Crumpsall. The woman was thin as a whip and in her late thirties. Her enthusiasm for science in all of its areas was infectious, at least among those girls with the mind for it.

The entire sixth form, both upper and lower, were present since their remaining numbers together barely made up enough for a full class.

Maliha was on the receiving end of stares from almost everyone as the lesson progressed—dealing with some of the more interesting innovations involving the Faraday device—it seemed she had achieved precisely the notoriety she had been avoiding for the last few years. She bore it stoically, even when a balled-up piece of paper bounced from the back of her head, when Mrs Crumpsall was adding the reduced-gravity ballet to the list.

It was true, humanity had been very inventive. From the ships that utilised the device to ply the Void between the explored planets; trains that ran in pneumatic tubes; beds that incorporated the device for the sick and injured; to the high-brow entertainments like the ballet; and the low-brow fairground rides supposed to mimic travelling through space.

Mrs Crumpsall turned to face them. "Now girls, I want you to consider your own lives and experience. Let's see if you can invent a new use for the Faraday device that has so transformed our world in the last sixty years."

Maliha looked around. The class were not in the right frame of mind for this experiment in ideas. Mrs Crumpsall was always looking for new ways to teach, naturally she would not go as far as the anti-authoritarian principles suggested by some, but she did adopt unusual techniques. Such as this one, getting the girls to think.

Under normal circumstances they could expect the usual selection of responses. Most of the girls simply ceased to function mentally when asked to produce an original thought, others worked at it as if this were an examination rather than a stimulant to their imagination. And then there were the few that loved the opportunity to allow their imaginations to soar.

Unfortunately, there was only one thought in everybody's mind and it related to the empty desk at the front. Jordan was always seated at the front so that she could not kick or otherwise torture the girl in front of her. This had been an early lesson learnt by the teachers.

But now it meant an empty space in front of everyone as a constant reminder.

Antonia Dumont, with Jennifer Wendlefield beside her, raised her hand.

"Yes, Dumont?"

"Is there any way a Faraday field could protect someone from violence?"

The silence that followed was awkward. Maliha had no doubt Dumont's question was honest, she was just the same as her lover, sweet and honest. Society would never allow them to be together but they were perfectly matched in every respect as far as Maliha was concerned. If Antonia had been anyone else than who she really was perhaps they could have gone somewhere. But unfortunately, she was a princess of the Prussian Royal House of Hohenzollern and, therefore, related to the present Kaiser Wilhelm II. Not that it was ever stated publicly and no other girl seemed to have worked it out. Maliha was entirely happy to keep her secret.

"No, my dear, all it can do is reduce the apparent weight of things by shielding the object from the effects of gravity. It does not create any sort of physical barrier."

Another hand went up. Maliha identified it as Katerina van Wyk. From overheard conversations she was aware that Miss van Wyk liked hunting, and she had an excellent seat. Her father was a diamond merchant.

"Miss van Wyk?"

While Antonia had a perfectly natural English accent having been brought up in Britain (though her German was excellent, unsurprisingly), Katerina was Dutch through and through.

"If someone shot a gun and they did not know of a Faraday device standing between them and the target they would miss their aim. The field generated would change the *traject van het projectiel*."

"English please, Miss van Wyk."

"I do not know the correct words, Mrs Crumpsall."

"Trajectory? Projectile?"

"*Ja*. The trajectory of the projectile."

"Yes. Very good. That is what would happen."

That it would have no effect on someone bludgeoning another to death with a heavy implement was not mentioned.

"This is something I have attempted to teach you girls. With limited success, I have to say. While the apparent weight changes, the mass of an object does not. These are different things. Even in a Faraday field the amount of energy to launch a bullet from a gun—" she nodded at van Wyk, "—is the same as needed normally."

At which point she lost most of the class. Maliha had seen it before. She understood it, most did not.

"Any other ideas that the field could be used for? Perhaps something more mundane?"

Maliha gave it some thought but she always found it hard to get beyond the inventions that already existed. Most vehicles whether land, sea, or air used it. Where it made sense to use it in recreation and the arts, it was being done. So, quite uncharacteristically, she put up her hand. There were mutterings.

Mrs Crumpsall looked delighted. "Miss Anderson?"

"Is it possible there are no further new uses that can be made of it? Merely adaptations of what has gone before?"

"I think that would be a rather depressing point of view, don't you?"

"I couldn't think of anything."

"And that's an end of it? What was your thought process on this matter?"

Maliha did not let her annoyance show. Mrs Crumpsall was implying that Maliha was saying that just because *she* couldn't think of anything, nobody could.

"I was considering that all areas of human endeavour that can use it already seem to be doing so. I have even seen advertisements for corsetry to provide additional support for women of generous proportions."

That caused a ripple of amusement, as well as admonishing sounds from the prudish.

"Not the sort of advertisement that attracts my attention," said Mrs Crumpsall with a smile.

"No, of course." Maliha now felt flustered. This was the most talking she had done in front of a group during the entirety of her stay at Roedean. "My point is that the device has a very specific effect. It is not some sort of cure-all. It can only apply in those instances where a decrease in weight is a benefit, and all of those have been discovered and the device applied."

"Have you considered the possibility of new medical benefits, Miss Anderson?"

She hesitated. "I have not."

"It's a thought."

Maliha went quiet with her mind whirling over what new medical benefits the Faraday device might produce. She glanced across at Antonia and Jenny. There was nothing the Faraday device could do for them. Nor for dead Ethel Jordan —even if some charlatans did claim that it gave them access to the Other Side.

The bell rang for the end of school. At this point there would normally be various activities including sports but while lessons had been reinstated, anything taking place outdoors had not.

She found it hard to believe that Jordan's death had only been twenty-four hours before.

She packed up her books but with the library off-limits she was prevented from accessing her usual hide-away. The girls were not permitted outside and that left her the furnace room as the only option, even if it was technically out-of-bounds.

7

———

"Did you know about the secret passage in the library?" she asked as soon as she had descended the steps and ascertained Mr Gunnell was present.

"Afternoon, Maliha. Nice to see you. Escaped from the clutches of the police then?"

Maliha went to the chair on the side away from the furnace and, having brushed away the dust and soot, sat on it.

"Do we need the social pleasantries?"

"They keep the world properly oiled and running, Miss Anderson. Just like your teachers tell you. Here, have a soft chew." He pulled a small tin from his pocket, decorated with the Union Flag, flipped it open and showed her the sugar-covered sweets within. She picked one but did not put it in her mouth.

"I am unconvinced. If everyone was honest and direct, I'm sure everyone would have a better time of it."

"You mean that Old Mrs Cuthbert should tell Cook to her face that she hasn't the slightest clue how to make Spotted Dick?"

"Should Cook be told her steamed puddings are tasteless

concoctions that would be better sealing the holes in brickwork? Yes, indeed, Mr Gunnell, it would be a favour to the world."

He put his head on one side and just stared at her.

She put the soft sweet into her mouth and chewed it. "Yes, very well," she said around the sweet. "If we do not wish for another murder on our hands it would be best if Mrs Cuthbert did not attempt to instruct Cook."

"Manners maketh the man, like it says in the good book."

"No, it doesn't."

"Eh?"

"I've read the good book from end to end. It doesn't say that. It says a lot of things, not that."

"Oh."

"And do manners only make man or do they make women as well?"

He changed the subject. "I had no idea the passage was there. If I had I would have told the governors and they would have had it blocked up pretty quick. No one the wiser."

Maliha nodded and hesitated then said. "She was with child."

"Who? The girl?"

"Ethel, yes."

"Blimey," he said. "Do the coppers know?"

"The doctor says they'll find out for certain during the autopsy. I think she was a couple of months along. Just enough for her to have realised."

"It's a bad do. She gets herself knocked up, the boyfriend finds out and does her in to avoid the scandal," he said. "Wouldn't be the first time. Won't be the last."

Maliha frowned. "That's probably what the police will say."

"You don't think that's what happened?"

"I don't know. Probably. But couldn't he have just abandoned her? Ethel's family aren't that important, just a successful businessman but not rich. Maybe that's why she hated everybody, she wasn't here because her family were rich or nobility."

"Unless the boyfriend is important."

"I know, and then there's the sweet papers."

"You lost me."

"She had wrappers for sticks of rock, they have a royal seal on them."

"Craven's?"

"Yes."

He nodded. "Shilling each, and they're no different from ones you can buy on the front for a penny. Daylight robbery."

Maliha sunk back into thought. She needed to talk to Amelia again. There were questions that needed answering but Maliha didn't really know what they were yet.

She sat back and took her book from her bag, found her page and read until the dinner bell rang.

Once again they were confined to the dormitory for the evening but at least getting out for lessons had relieved some of the tension. Maliha decided not to forewarn Amelia to expect a visit, the less she was seen talking to the girl or passing her notes the better it would be. Also she intended going out a little earlier. Midnight was something out of silly books.

She lay on her bed reading when Margaret Creighton-Ward sat down on the bed beside her but facing the wall with her back to the rest of the beds so her words were less likely to be overheard.

"You must tell me everything."

"I cannot, it would take too long."

The girl looked so crestfallen Maliha shook her head in despair. She wondered how much she could really tell the girl. Certainly nothing about the probable pregnancy. What did she want to hear? Something scandalous no doubt.

"Ethel Jordan had a boyfriend."

"Outside the school?"

"Of course."

"Oh, my word, that is so delicious. But who would have thought it of her? I always thought she was a man in disguise."

Maliha decided against suggesting that that would not be an impediment in some instances. It would be far too much for Margaret to take in. She would probably require some sort of explanation.

"And a doctor is going to cut her open to determine the cause of death."

"Oh, that just makes me feel sick." She had a pained look on her face just to show that she was telling the truth. Then she got an idea and a look of surprise, then horror took over. She leaned in to Maliha conspiratorially. "What if she's … you know … like Olivia Lettings-Brough."

That had been another event that had been thoroughly hushed up. When the third-year girl was clearly with child in the autumn term. Thankfully the timing was such that, however it had occurred, it had been during the summer holiday so the school was not culpable. Poor girl had only been fourteen.

Maliha had checked the papers but had never seen a reference to her since. It did not mean anything. She hoped it meant nothing but she was very aware of what could happen to girls who broke the rules—even if it was not their fault.

"Idle speculation and gossip do more harm than good," said Maliha. She preferred not to lie if possible. It could get you into deep water.

"But what if she was?"

"I'm sure we'll find out."

"What else? Why weren't you in lessons until Science? What did the police want with you?"

"Probably thinks she did it," said Annabel Leeming who must have been eavesdropping, although that would not be hard since Margaret was not very good at keeping her voice down.

"There was a Dr Underwood from Scotland Yard. I was showing him around."

"And did he touch you like Dr Jenkins?"

"Don't talk about him, Leeming," said Margaret and started to cry. Maliha wondered how this had got so out of hand. But at least she wasn't being questioned about the events of the day any more. She pulled out her book and started to read again, hoping that would be her defence against any other interruptions.

Her plan to stay awake until eleven and then head out shortly afterwards failed. Instead, she was woken by someone else sneaking out of the dorm. She lifted her head and scanned the room. Mrs Lancaster had left them with the light again. Whoever had left was already gone but Jenny's bed was the empty one—she had put the pillows between the sheets but that only worked when there was almost no light.

Maliha put on her dressing gown and slippers then headed out after her. There was no question who she was going to meet. Maliha was curious to know where, since it could not be the dormitory. She slipped from shadow to shadow thrown by the dim lights from the outside like a ghost. She moved quickly at first so that she could catch up with Jenny—at least enough to follow her.

When they reached the first floor she saw Jenny hurrying along the corridor—she had not headed into the servants' passages as Maliha had expected. She hung back until the other girl turned a corner and then ran along the passage, making as little noise as possible, until she reached the turn.

Where was she going?

That part of the school was mostly administrative and included the school office. It was a long way from the library, which was just as well because there were still police in the school. She stopped and listened. There was no sound of feet or breathing. Jenny had simply disappeared.

There was very little light here and Maliha gave her eyes time to adjust. Could there be another secret passage?

The cold was draining the warmth from her as she moved along the corridor. On the left was the school office. There was no light leaking around the door and when she pressed her ear to it she could hear nothing.

She moved on. There were two doors leading into the WCs. The only one for men in the main building was here, although she assumed there must be one for the male staff below stairs. The other was for teachers, administrators and female visitors. It said so on the door plaque. It was not for pupils.

Still, she paused at each trying to see if they were occupied. Again, there was nothing to suggest anyone was inside.

On the same side as the WCs was one of the main storerooms for school supplies. Also silent. And then on the other side the staff room. She froze as she heard a quiet giggle. Two voices murmured behind the solid wood door. Jennifer Wendlefield and Antonia Dumont no doubt. Maliha admired their boldness in selecting the teachers' common room for their assignations.

Though she wondered where they could have got the key, the place was locked up tight at night, and they must have a key each because they would not risk hanging around in the corridor waiting for the other.

They had not made any noise for a while and then there was a low moan. Maliha felt her face redden. Sounds like these were not uncommon in the dorms at night, sometimes a girl simply could not hold in her responses. But those were solo activities. This was two lovers. The sound came again and then a small cry.

Maliha crept away. She would not scare them by attempting to enter, they would have most likely locked the door anyway. Instead she headed up toward Kookaburra. It meant she would be able to confirm that Jenny was meeting with Antonia, which she assumed but did not know for certain, and still have the conversation with Amelia Johnson she desired.

She pressed open the door to the Kookaburra dormitory. The sound of sleeping girls reached her ears, they did not sound like the angels that men supposed them all to be. She had come to the conclusion that everyone snored at some point in the night. From which she could only conclude that she did as well, though it was not a pleasing thought.

Since there was only the light from outside in the room she crept to Antonia Dumont's bed and ascertained that the lumps were pillows, not a person. She was glad, it would have been a serious concern if Jennifer was an inconstant lover, a fact that Maliha would have felt compelled to reveal in order to protect the princess.

She returned to Amelia who was lying huddled on her side. How do you wake someone gently? Maliha crouched by the bed and stroked the girl's cheek. She had never touched any of the other girls before. Amelia's skin was soft and cool. It was strange. Maliha increased the pressure until she saw Amelia's eyes flick open.

"Say nothing, it's Anderson. I want to talk to you."

"What time is it?"

"About half-past three in the morning."

Amelia yawned. "Must we?"

"Yes, come on."

Maliha stood and stepped back as the girl sat up on the side of her bed. Maliha grabbed her dressing gown and held it out. Amelia shrugged it on and followed Maliha into the hall, then halfway down the stairs.

"What do you want?"

"I know that Jordan was pregnant and that she was meeting a man."

"I told you."

"You cannot blame me for not believing you. Jordan was no friend to anyone. How is it that she confided in you?" Maliha had a suspicion as to the answer and to find such a thing in real life that she had only read about was unnerving.

"We were just friends."

"She had no friends."

Maliha caught Amelia by the forearm.

"Let go of me," she hissed.

Maliha said nothing but tightened her grip.

"Stop."

Maliha dug her nails in.

"Don't."

Amelia's protestations were becoming less convincing. Maliha loosened her grip.

"No, don't stop."

Maliha released her arm completely. "Show me."

Amelia turned away. She hiked up her dressing gown and night dress to reveal her upper thighs covered in old bruises and scratches. The girl giggled. "I can go higher if you want to see more."

"No." Maliha hesitated and then said it. "You want pain."

Amelia just giggled again, like a child, almost as if she were a different person. What stray chance had put this girl in the same dormitory as someone who would happily give her what she desired? Was it chance at all? There were ways you could manoeuvre matters by saying the right things to the right people. After all, someone would have wanted to *not* be in the same dormitory as the Beast of Roedean.

"How did it start?"

"She hurt me, of course." Amelia giggled again. It did not sound sane and was unnerving. "My father used to beat me and I loved him so much. And he loved me because he said so every time. I made sure he always had a reason to beat me, nearly every day. I didn't want to come here but Grandma said I must and Daddy did as he was told. I miss Daddy so much and then Ethel hurt me and I knew I loved her too. We had to be careful because sometimes things would show."

"Did *you* kill Ethel?"

"Why would I do that? I loved her. You wouldn't understand. She was kind to me, she loved me too."

There was the sound of someone below. The two girls scooted back up the stairs as quietly as they could. Amelia dived into her bed and Maliha hid beneath Ethel's. She was barely settled when the door was pushed open and she saw the feet of the person she assumed to be Antonia. Moments later the feet disappeared into the bed beside Maliha which confirmed the girl was the Prussian princess.

There was little risk of her falling asleep lying on the cold floor, but Maliha kept her head up just in case. It took a little while but when it was all quiet she sneaked out and made her way back to her own bed. Jenny Wendlefield was already asleep. No doubt having very pleasant dreams.

Maliha found it hard to sleep with her mind in a whirl over the new revelations. There had been such a lack of rationality in this new Amelia she had discovered. She wondered about the girl's father, and the intervention to get the child away from him by the grandmother—who clearly had understood something bad existed between father and daughter.

Despite the insanity, she did believe Amelia had not killed her benefactor—what other word could there be for it? The girl desired pain and punishment, Ethel Jordan was the perfect person to deliver it. One would have hoped it would be enough for the both of them but it seemed Jordan's lust to inflict pain was more than Amelia could satisfy.

No, it seemed unlikely that Amelia would have stilled the hand that beat her. She needed it. Even though she had lost some of Ethel's attention with the advent of the boyfriend.

The boyfriend had killed Ethel because she had become pregnant, of that Maliha was certain.

8

———

Thursday began almost normally. The police only seemed concerned about the library now, so the rest of the school operated normally.

The first period for Maliha was private study. She was forced to use the drawing room since the library was no longer an option, and she did not think it was fair on Mr Gunnell to keep popping down. He might run out of sweets. Besides, if she were to do that too often someone would be bound to notice her constant absence. Being in the library was one thing but being missing from the only other choice of location was another altogether.

Amelia came in with her books and gave Maliha a wink. She pulled up the sleeve of her blouse where Maliha had held her to reveal bruises and a line of reddened indentations. The girl smiled.

Maliha returned to her book although she ceased reading it. This was not a good situation at all. What if Amelia had decided to replace Ethel with her? Inflicting pain was not something Maliha would choose to do to anyone. What she had done the previous night had simply been to test her hypothesis. It had succeeded beyond her imagining—too well apparently.

Annabel Leeming arrived, her green prefect badge sitting neatly on her cardigan. She glanced at Maliha first, there was an odd look about her, she seemed nervous and that was one emotion Maliha had never seen in her. She was a bully, though not the worst. It seemed that the bullies were always the ones who became prefects. Was it because they seemed to exude power?

In this case Leeming was exuding nothing of the sort but it seemed Maliha was not the object of her interest. She saw someone else, took a deep breath, placed a smile on her face—which looked completely out of place—and walked deeper into the drawing room.

"Mrs Clemence wants you to come to the office."

"Now? What's it about?" Amelia's voice. Maliha became very interested.

"She didn't say. Look, you know what she's like, don't be a pain."

Which was not like Leeming, she was being far too conciliatory. An outright threat would have been far more in her style.

"Yes, let me just pack up my things."

There was a long pause and then the two of them walked out together. Turning towards the office they disappeared. Maliha jumped up and left her book on the chair. She headed after them ignoring the stares.

Amelia and Leeming had already taken the next turn so Maliha moved swiftly along. At the end of the passage she went to the window and looked out. There was a Black Maria parked in the drive.

"Oh no," she muttered. There was a scream muffled by a heavy door. It didn't stop. The sound of men shouting failed to drown out the wordless protestations. Amelia must have gone wild. The sound turned Maliha's blood cold. The noise was filling the school and girls emerged from other rooms, they stood in the passages and listened with the same horror as Maliha was feeling.

The sequence of events clicked into place. Antonia must have heard them talking on the stairs, and concluded Amelia was the murderer. She had reported it to either Mrs Clemence or perhaps the police directly. Maliha felt some pity for Annabel Leeming, having to lure the girl into the office, she may be a bully but she was not a fool.

Amelia's screaming became muffled and then stopped.

Three uniformed bobbies emerged from the office carrying a writhing bundle. They had her in a straitjacket. D.I. Williams came out, he looked down the corridor.

"Don't you go anywhere, Anderson, I'll be wanting a word with you!" His voice echoed the length and breadth of the school.

Maliha turned back to the window knowing that every eye was now on her. All she ever wanted was to be left alone. Less than two minutes later the police emerged below and bundled Amelia into the back of the Black Maria. Two of them climbed in after her and the other went to drive the vehicle. It puffed away with D.I. Williams watching them go. His hands on his hips.

Turning back to the school, Maliha collected her things from the drawing room then returned to the school office. She entered without knocking and sat waiting for the policeman. Leeming was sobbing in another chair with nobody comforting her. Mrs Clemence was staring into space. Maliha imagined Mrs Ramsey in her office drinking whiskey wondering how she might fix this problem.

Maliha thought only of poor Amelia. Just another victim.

The detective arrived a few minutes later. "I want you down at the station," he said directly to Maliha, ignoring Mrs Clemence. But his words must have sparked an automatic response in her.

"Girls may not leave the school precincts during the school day."

"This is a murder investigation."

"It is not permitted."

"I'll charge you with interfering in a police investigation."

"Do your worst!"

The detective went silent. "It is not my intent to cause any disruption of the school's workings but I should like to point out that I represent the law of this country and have the weight of England on my side."

"And the parents of the girls in this school are your betters as well as foreign princes and such like."

Maliha felt her speech could have done with a better ending but it seemed to work.

"I will not be prevented, Mrs Clemence. However perhaps you can think of a way that the school rules may be bent but not broken in this instance. Bear in mind that I have just arrested one of your girls for murder."

Mrs Clemence gripped the edge of the counter and her knuckles were white. "It would be permitted if she were accompanied by one of the teaching staff."

"Good. Find one."

Saying nothing further. Mrs Clemence released the counter form her death grip, walked around the bench and stalked from the room.

From behind the door to the headmistress's office came the sound of a woman talking very earnestly. Mrs Ramsey must be on the telephone. Perhaps she was dealing with an upset parent. The advent of an arrest would mean the school would be able to return to the way it was. Most of the girls would remain—it would be far too inconvenient to find somewhere new for them if the trouble had passed. The news would linger in the press for a couple of days and then it too would be gone, leaving nothing except a sour taste in the mouth.

And one dead girl, and another falsely accused of her murder.

Maliha understood only too well how this would go. In a

school occupied by the offspring of the upper classes any result, no matter how wrong, was to be preferred over none. The inspector would be under pressure to resolve the case and have a perpetrator brought to justice.

And if that perpetrator could be bundled away to a sanatorium without a trial to titillate the press once more, so much the better. Amelia was the perfect person to blame.

The bell for the change in lessons rang. Mrs Clemence returned with Mrs Lancaster, carrying Maliha's heavy outdoor coat, and together they set off for the police station.

The ride in the car was uneventful. It did possess a Faraday, though not an efficient one. The vehicle looked as if it was a cast-off from a rich family. The driver's cab was separate and the passengers sat in the back on cracked leather seats which had probably been comfortable at one time.

"Hold this up to your face," said the inspector as the vehicle approached the exit on to the road. He held out a large sheet of cardboard that had once been a box. She frowned at him. "Quickly, before the press can photograph you."

Understanding, she snatched it from him and brought it up just as they pulled out on to the coast road. Flashes lit up the interior and Mrs Lancaster held up her hand to cover the other half of Maliha's face as some of the photographers were on the other side. Questions were thrown at them but it was such a cacophony there was not a single distinct word.

"I'd arrest the bloody lot of them."

"Language, Inspector," said Mrs Lancaster. "Miss Anderson is a child."

The car left the photographers and reporters behind.

Maliha and Mrs Lancaster were facing forwards while the inspector was opposite and could see behind. "It's a parade. Keep your head down."

"Perhaps you'd like me to wear a cloth sack over my face."

"That would work."

They glared at one another.

Despite her bravado Maliha would have been happy to have something. The idea of being in the newspapers did not appeal, even if they couldn't get a good photograph the reporters would describe what they could and make the rest up.

The car bounced along. The tide was on the way in and the pebble beach stretched away. However, the road veered away from the coast and headed inland. After a couple of minutes, they reached the gasworks on the edge of the town, turned south and then west again.

The police station was in the town hall, not far from the Royal Pavilion. Maliha had passed it and its mock Roman columns on several occasions. The vehicle chugged slowly through the crowded streets.

"The box, quick."

Maliha raised it just as someone ran up beside them and clicked through the window.

"This is quite intolerable, Inspector, putting Miss Anderson through this utter circus."

"I believe Miss Anderson has been withholding vital evidence in this case, missus," said the inspector. "I'm going to determine whether she needs to be charged. In fact, whether she was an accomplice in the murder or even the mastermind."

"Mastermind?" said Mrs Lancaster. "I believe you have been reading too many penny novels, sir."

The car drew in through a gate at the back of the building and came to a stop. A crash indicated the gates had been closed.

"Quick," said the inspector, "before they get into the building opposite and try to get your picture from the roof."

"Can they do that?" said Mrs Lancaster.

"I think they pay the owner monthly."

Maliha and the teacher were bustled through a side door into the echoing stone interior. It seemed strangely quiet compared to the hustle and bustle of the world outside.

Almost calming. But Amelia would be here somewhere in a cell underground… a cell that would at one time or another held drunks, thieves and even real murderers.

"Inspector?"

"Chief?"

The person approaching was a middle-aged man in a senior policeman's uniform, perhaps beginning to put on a little weight. Maliha's memory delivered his name though she had never seen him: William Gentle, Chief Constable for Brighton. The newspapers always referred to him in a positive light and mentioned his wide experience both in England and abroad.

"Are we arresting all the girls in the school now?"

"No, sir, Miss Anderson has particular knowledge of the crime and the girl we have arrested."

The Chief Constable's face fell and he shook his head. "Arresting young girls for murder. I wonder what the world is coming to."

"She didn't do it, sir," said Maliha but he held up his hand.

"Save your evidence for the inspector, young lady." And then he smiled at her and it was so genuine that she smiled back. She could not recall the last time she had met someone with such warmth. It seemed the newspapers were right, for a change.

"I was hoping to find Mrs Birkett, sir. Have you seen her?"

"Matron? She's with that other poor girl."

"I would prefer to interview Miss Anderson with her present."

Mrs Lancaster took a step forward. "I understood that was my reason for being here."

"With respect, missus—"

"My name is Lancaster. I would appreciate it if you would use it."

"With respect, Mrs *Birkett* is familiar with police procedures."

"Then I shall become familiar," said Mrs Lancaster. "I was sent here to chaperone the girl and that is precisely what I will do."

"It seems your problem is solved, Inspector."

There was a moment's silence. "Yes, chief."

The inspector led the way along passages that became progressively narrower until they came to a room containing only two chairs one on each side of a table.

"You don't expect me to stand, Inspector."

He left the room and returned with a third chair that he placed in a corner.

"Mrs Lancaster—"

"Miss."

"I'm sorry?"

"We're called Mrs in the school to give the impression of authority. However, I am not married. Miss Freda Lancaster."

"I see."

"I thought you'd like to know."

"Well, *Miss* Lancaster, I would appreciate it if you do not interrupt while I am interviewing *Miss* Anderson."

"I will interrupt if I consider you are being too aggressive in your questioning."

"Very well."

The inspector waved Maliha into the chair further from the door and sat facing her. He opened the folder and laid it out on the desk in front of him.

"Can I have your full name?"

"Alice Maliha Anderson" she said. "But we've already done this. Shall we just get down to the important part?"

"All right," he said. "Did you or did you not meet with Amelia Johnson last night between the hours of two and four o'clock?"

"It was about three thirty. Yes."

"You admit you did then?"

"Yes," she said. "Obviously. I just said so."

"For what purpose?"

"I wanted to ask her some questions."

"Why?"

"Because the relationship she described herself having with Ethel Jordan just didn't make any sense."

"In what way?"

"As has been described to you by many people and discussed at length with me," said Maliha. "She was a violent and unpleasant girl who took pleasure in hurting others and did not really care who they were. Why would she make an exception with Amelia Johnson?"

"Perhaps she had what you girls call a 'pash'."

"A possibility with any other girl but this is Ethel Jordan."

"What did you conclude?"

Maliha glanced across to where Mrs Lancaster was sitting. This was going to be difficult, the teachers were not aware of the extent of her reading.

"We discussed, as you recall, the fact that she could be described as a sadist."

Mrs Lancaster flinched at the word and her eyes grew wide but she kept to her word and said nothing.

"Well," said Maliha. "There is another type of personality, the inverse of the sadist, the masochist. The one who likes to have pain inflicted on them. It occurred to me that if Amelia had that nature then they would be a perfect match for one another."

"You confronted her with this idea?"

Maliha hesitated. "Yes. It was—it was unnerving. Her entire personality changed. As if she had a switch inside her. She admitted that she welcomed the pain and she showed me the back of her thighs which were bruised and cut. She offered to show me more—she *wanted* to show me more. She expressed her love for Ethel and mentioned her father as someone who beat her every day but professed to love her, and how her grandmother had intervened to send her away to school."

The inspector nodded. "We have had communication from the grandmother but not the father."

Maliha felt she was on the brink of tears but she forced them back. She refused to show weakness in front of this policeman. Instead she took a deep breath and continued. "So, I asked if she had killed Ethel, and she said she hadn't. Her logic, though twisted, made sense inasmuch as why would she harm the person who gave her what she wanted?"

There was a long pause while the inspector made notes. Maliha looked at Mrs Lancaster. She was dabbing her cheeks with a handkerchief.

"So, she's completely crazy and nothing she says can be considered truthful," said the inspector.

Maliha frowned. "I knew it. You're just going to make her the guilty one, but she'll never stand trial because she's off her rocker. Everything gets brushed under the carpet, you wrap it all up with a pretty little bow, and the real culprit goes free."

"There is no evidence of another party being involved."

"The boyfriend."

"What boyfriend?"

"Amelia said Ethel had a boyfriend."

"Amelia is crazy and would use any excuse to escape the blame."

Maliha fumed, she glanced at Mrs Lancaster. This was also going to be extremely awkward. "Please explain to me then, Inspector, how Ethel Jordan could be pregnant?" She got to her feet and leaned across the table. "Are you suggesting she was impregnated by Amelia Johnson? Or perhaps it was single cell division? Or perhaps a virgin birth? Generally speaking, there has to be a male involved in the process, in case you were not aware!"

He stared at her looming over him. "Sit down, Miss Anderson."

She sat down and glanced at Mrs Lancaster's horrified face.

"Why do you think she was pregnant?" said the inspector.

"Have you had the autopsy report?"

"Not yet."

Maliha sighed. "The first night Amelia was very upset and, for some reason, decided I should be the one she would ask for help."

"Why?"

"I have no idea."

Mrs Lancaster cleared her throat. "Because you're the cleverest person in the school, including all the teachers."

"I try not to be."

"That just makes it worse."

Maliha nodded. "She asked me to meet her and she said Ethel had a boyfriend. I didn't believe her because Ethel was so violent, what man would tolerate that? Nor, to be brutally honest, was she an attractive girl. I sometimes wondered whether she was some sort of throwback to an earlier time."

"Please stick to the point."

"Sorry. I examined Ethel's bedside cabinet and that gave me two clues."

"I examined that, what clues?"

"The tins of sanitary pads—" Williams pulled a face and Maliha pointed at him. "—and that's why you couldn't see the clue. You're a man." She turned to Mrs Lancaster. "She had three months of unused pads."

"Oh goodness. She's right, Inspector, Ethel Jordan was almost certainly pregnant."

He remained sceptical. "And the other clue."

"Wrapping papers from very expensive Brighton rock."

"And that says she had a boyfriend?"

"The pregnancy told me that, no other clues were required."

"And what do the sweet papers mean then?"

"I have no idea."

9
———

"Am I still on your list of suspects?" asked Maliha. "Nothing you have said has made me think otherwise."

Mrs Lancaster spoke up again. "Why not? It's perfectly obvious, Miss Anderson is being as open as possible about everything that happened."

"Because nothing she has told us suggests otherwise," said the inspector twisting round in his chair. "There are some parts of her testimony that are true. Those are verifiable. Everything else could be complete fabrication. There is certainly evidence of prolonged violence against the person of Amelia Johnson. It is reasonable to assume, given her nature, that it was inflicted by Ethel Jordan. But who found the body? Who is spending a great deal of time directing my attention away from the school? Away from her?"

"But Amelia?"

"Is not in her right mind. Nothing she says can be trusted."

"So," said Maliha. "You think I planned the whole thing. Arranged for Amelia, probably, to kill Ethel in the library and then 'discovered' the body? Then concocted the whole boyfriend idea to throw you off the scent?"

D.I. Williams turned back to face her. "You're clever enough, as your teacher has attested."

Mrs Lancaster was horrified and mouthed *sorry* at Maliha.

"Are you going to arrest me?"

"My investigation is continuing."

"I can go?"

"For the time being. Do not attempt to make a run for it."

Maliha stood up. "You're not serious."

"I am deadly serious, Miss Anderson."

"You think I would get far in this country with my face? Even assuming I was planning to run, which I am not because I am not guilty. Besides," she added, Her voice a mix of anger and hurt. "I am not about to give you the advantage of being able to claim I went on the run on the supposition I am guilty."

Mrs Lancaster came up beside Maliha and put her hand on her shoulder. "Do you really think Maliha is guilty, Inspector?"

He also stood now. "As I said, my investigation is ongoing. I will consider the school to be responsible for ensuring Miss Anderson does not go missing."

"I will take personal responsibility."

"Very well," he said. "I will hold you to that."

They had been given umbrellas with which to hide their faces from the photographers when they returned to the car, without the inspector.

Rather than sit by the window, Maliha perched in the middle of the rear bench seat. Mrs Lancaster held up her umbrella, still open, on one side while Maliha dealt with the other. The vehicle was besieged as they exited the gates and drove slowly through the town. The roads were filled with bicycles, motor vehicles large and small, plus corporation omnibuses as well as horse-drawn carts. They had to keep the umbrellas in position the whole time.

"I am so sorry," said Mrs Lancaster.

"It was to be expected," she said. "You know, even if they don't tie me into it, they'll just say it was Amelia."

"They already are."

"What do you mean? I beg your pardon, if you don't mind me asking, of course."

Mrs Lancaster patted Maliha's knee. "I don't mind. I think in this matter you have a right to know everything. You see, Mrs Ramsey has been speaking to her patrons and the more forward-thinking of the aristocratic parents. She announced only this morning to the staff that there is to be a dance at the school."

Maliha could not think of anything she would like less. "A dance requires men unless they are expecting the girls to dance one with another." Though she did not doubt Jenny and Antonia would be quite happy with that arrangement. "Nor can I see why that would be beneficial to the school if males of the local gentry were involved. Oh. She has arranged something rather more prestigious."

But despite everything she could not think what it might be.

"You are very clever," said Mrs Lancaster. "Where would your mind jump if I said: The Isle of Wight?"

"Osborne Naval School. And Prince Edward is attending." Maliha was impressed. "A dance between Roedean and Osborne would be unprecedented."

"There's more," said her teacher. "The Royal Pavilion has been booked. It will be as if the royal family were back in Brighton."

"It's not a dance," said Maliha. "It's a royal ball."

"Every girl of the nobility will be there, and any girl in the Fifth, Lower and Upper Sixth."

"I will not attend," said Maliha. Even though she had

been forced to learn to dance, the idea of being required to do so in public made her skin crawl.

"I do not think you will have a choice."

Mrs Lancaster peered out to see whether they were still being hounded, and having satisfied herself there were no reporters nearby—and with the roads clearing as they left the town—she let the umbrella drop.

"What do you think of the inspector?" said Mrs Lancaster in a rather different voice, almost in a dream.

Without a moment's hesitation, Maliha responded: "Boorish and lacking in imagination."

"Oh." There was a pause. "But a fine figure of a man, despite that?"

Maliha opened her mouth and then shut it again. Perhaps saying what she actually thought might not be what was required here. She was not familiar with social niceties and considered them to be a waste of time as well as leading to trouble. It was better to be forthright and honest, wasn't it?

"I am afraid that was not something I considered." There, that wasn't even a lie. However, she was under the impression her teacher already had a beau. Perhaps they had parted company.

"I wondered if he might be able to attend the dance. After all, they will require protection with the heir to the throne in attendance."

"I think both his grandfather and father have to pass away before he gets to be king."

"The king is very old, and George isn't young."

The car was heading downhill towards the coast now. They would soon need the umbrellas again.

"Mrs Lancaster?"

"Yes, dear."

"Do you think I'm guilty?"

"Of course not, even if the inspector—for all his good points—intends to ignore the father of poor Ethel's unborn as the most likely suspect, that does not make you guilty."

"But that's the problem, do you not see?" said Maliha. "He can arrange the evidence, circumstantial though it might be, to put me in the frame. His masters want the case resolved rapidly and quietly."

"I'm sure he wouldn't do that."

"The only way I can be certain to save myself is to find the perpetrator of the crime myself."

Mrs Lancaster went quiet.

"That would require a level of freedom that is not usually afforded to girls in the school. Even those of the Upper Sixth."

Maliha felt that this was not the time to speak. Let the teacher arrive at her own solution to the problem Maliha had presented. It didn't take long in coming.

"If you were, perhaps, to become ill, perhaps overtaxed by being at the centre of this terrible situation, it might be wise to place you in an isolated room on your own. And perhaps exempt you from lessons, honestly, I don't believe we have taught you anything you did not already know for years. That might leave you free to pursue your own investigations. Though I could not condone you leaving the school premises."

"Would this require a trip to Dr Jenkins?" That was not something Maliha relished, it did not matter what the ailment, he always found a reason to have a girl remove her outer garments, and his attitude towards her skin colour might have changed given that her figure was now more womanly. Maliha was not even sure if the teachers were aware of the man's proclivities.

"I don't think that will be necessary. I will simply say that I have observed you and the way you were treated by the police. I suppose it's possible you may have to see him but perhaps we can avoid it. Matron is more than adequate for the majority of concerns."

The school came into view and within a few seconds the

road was filled with reporters and photographers. They raised the umbrellas.

A cry of "Show us yer face, Anderson!" sent a shiver through Maliha. They already knew who she was. Too late to hope she would not get in the papers now. At least they had no picture.

The car drew up close to the main door and Maliha had never been so grateful to enter the school buildings than now. For once it was a haven from the crazy world outside.

Mrs Lancaster's plan went remarkably well. The teacher's explanation may have seemed logical and sensible, but Maliha suspected a desire to get her out of the dormitory was also in play.

There were announcements at lunchtime, which Maliha took as usual in the dining hall. It was as Mrs Lancaster had said, there was going to be a dance. Naturally, the lower portion of the school were severely disappointed they would not be allowed to take part—and Maliha expected the younger girls whose parents could regard themselves as noble had mixed emotions about being allowed in. The presence of the prince was not mentioned but there were a few who knew he was at Osborne. Word got around fast, it turned the proposed dance into a fairy-tale ball as far as the potential attendees were concerned, Maliha wondered how many of them realised the prince had not reached his fifteenth birthday.

They probably didn't care.

The other announcement was that the police would be quitting the school finally but that the library would remain locked for the foreseeable future. And that was news Maliha found gratifying.

Looking around the room, with the girls and teachers eating, and subdued discussion in the background, it was as if nothing had happened in the school after the last couple of days. Two girls had disappeared, and one of them to the relief of everyone except perhaps the sports mistress who had lost her most useful player.

If they considered it all, it was over and done to them. They could pretend nothing had happened, except perhaps when they passed the locked library. It might never be reopened. And tales would start of it being haunted by the dead girl. People would forget what she was really like, she would become some romantic ghost stalking the halls. No more than a story to scare the first years, which ultimately no one would believe had really happened.

But she knew. And if the spirit of Ethel Jordan was wandering the world because she had been so unjustly cut down—though the justice of it was debatable—Maliha would do her best to let her soul rest in peace. If not that, then karma would result in the girl being reincarnated as something unpleasant and there was justice in that.

The other girls went to their lessons and Maliha took three journeys to move her belongings from Sea Eagle out to a room in the infirmary building at the back. Matron fussed about her and insisted on taking both her temperature and her blood pressure with her new sphygmomanometer with which she could measure both levels. Matron was very keen on modern medical advancements, which was one reason why she disliked the very old-fashioned Dr Jenkins.

"If it were up to me, I would say you are completely normal, young lady. But if Mrs Lancaster wants you in a room by yourself, well, I can see the wisdom in it, if not agree with the reason. Do you play whist, Miss Anderson?"

"Don't we need four players?"

"Oh, I have other players if you're not above slumming it with the staff?"

"I'm sorry, Matron, but I have an unfair advantage."

"Cleverer than me, is it?"

"I have a perfect memory. I can remember all the cards."

"Can you now? I might have you in as my partner in that case. We could certainly clean up."

"That would be cheating."

"Using natural talent is what game playing is about, miss. Don't you ever think otherwise."

So Maliha had to agree she would be willing to play whist with Matron and other staff. Under other circumstances she might have welcomed it.

She spent the remainder of the afternoon examining her new surroundings. The room was almost as large as the dormitory and had a high ceiling. Unfortunately, it did not have the same quality of heating. The bed was bigger than she was used to, while the storage in wardrobes and boxes was far more than she needed.

The main window looked out to north, away from the coast and into the farmland behind the school. The track that ran along the northern boundary of the school was barely more than a hundred yards away. Beyond it was Cattle Hill and behind that, out of sight, was the village of Ovingdean. It was the vicar at St Wulfran's church who delivered their services. Along the track towards Brighton was the coastguard station, and then the track met the main road as it came up from the cliffs.

It would be possible to get into Brighton that way and it would avoid the reporters camped outside the gates. But she did have an alternative idea.

Mrs Lancaster had made it possible for her to prove Amelia's innocence, but Maliha had precious little beyond some sweet wrappers to guide her to the evidence she needed.

10

The evening meal came around. Maliha was not going to be served in her room, Matron made that very clear, so she headed off back into the school to join her dormitory at the table.

If she had not been the complete centre of attention before, she certainly was now. Every face looking in her direction desperate to know what had happened to her and the police, what had happened with Amelia. The emotion behind that desire ranged from morbid curiosity to fear. Or excitement in the case of Creighton-Ward, who sat herself next to Maliha as if it was her right.

"The girls in Kookaburra said Johnson started screaming as soon as she realised it was the police."

"Yes, I heard her."

"You were there? You get all the best stuff."

"I was just along the corridor."

"It must have been so exciting."

"It was horrible."

"Oh yes, I suppose so," Margaret said, trying to look sad.

"But still nothing like that ever happens here. Stops everything being so dull."

"Well, you've got a ball to go to now."

"That? I was always going to that. My dad's a lord."

Maliha was perfectly well aware of his status but Margaret never meant anything in a hurtful way, so there was no point taking offence. However, the revelation about the ball was another thing altogether.

"You mean it wasn't just organised?"

"Well, it wasn't going to involve the school before. That's new, I think. But yes. It was going to be at the time of the prince's fourteenth birthday but they've moved it." Margaret started to dig into her food. "It's rather inconvenient, my dress will have to be rushed."

"Terrible."

"Quite so."

Maliha stared at the plate of liver and bacon with mashed potatoes and peas. Seven years of being forced to eat western food had dulled her palate but she still hated it. She sighed. It wasn't true really, she kept telling herself she disliked it and would be glad to get back to a diet that did not involve overcooking red meat and mulching vegetables. In truth, while it still looked unappealing, she quite liked it. Some of it. There was no point starving herself as she had when she first arrived, until she had become so hungry she would eat almost anything.

"We thought they must have arrested you, too."

"They didn't."

"That's good but—" she said pausing with a fork of mashed potato halfway to her mouth, dripping with gravy. "—why did they think you were involved?"

Maliha wondered how much to say. If it had been any other girl Maliha would have known that asking for this information would have been about gaining status. The only person with more social standing than Margaret Creighton-

Ward was the secret princess, Antonia Dumont. And since it was a secret that didn't count.

"Because I was there. Because I'm clever. And because of the colour of my skin."

There. She'd said it out loud, finally. Their conversation wasn't private, of course, the people around pretended not to be listening but they weren't engaged in any other conversations.

"Some people are very stupid" was all Margaret said which rather deflated the anger Maliha had prepared.

They ate in silence for a few minutes. Other conversations grew up around them.

"What else can you tell me about the ball?" Maliha said.

Margaret shrugged. "What sort of thing?"

"Who else is invited?"

"The usual great and good. Some royals, aunts, cousins that sort of thing. And now we're getting hoi polloi as well."

"Thanks."

"Oh. Sorry, I didn't mean you, Anderson. It would be lovely to have you there."

"Don't bother, I won't be going anyway."

"Why not?"

"It's not something I'm interested in. Vacuous dancing to terrible music and mixing with people who don't even have the good taste to hide their prejudice? No, thank you."

"Oh."

Maliha hesitated. "I didn't mean you."

Margaret waved her hand dismissively but said nothing.

Dessert arrived and they ate. Maliha tried again. "Was the ball always going to be at the Royal Pavilion?"

"I thought you weren't interested."

"I can still be curious."

"Yes."

"It's surprising to think that Mrs Ramsey can pull enough strings to change the date and add the school to the invitation list. Don't you think?"

Margaret shrugged. "She just used the Old Girl network. There are enough ex-pupils married to men in positions of power. Royals, politicians, bureaucrats… she could probably make anything happen if she wanted." She moved closer to Maliha her previous annoyance already evaporated. "This is where the real power of the Empire is, Maliha, haven't you ever realised? I thought you were clever. My mother bends my father to her will, so cleverly he doesn't even notice it's happening. But the school is under threat, not only would it affect the reputations of every girl here, but there would be a backlash against the Old Girls, too, because they went to *that* school. A hundred influential parents here, and who knows how many more hundreds out there? And Mrs Ramsey can call on them all."

Maliha realised she had been thinking far too small for all the time she had been here. In her desperate desire to be back home, she had viewed this place as a gaol and the girls just prisoners. It wasn't that at all. It was a place where dreams could be driven into reality.

It was a revelation. She shook her head gently as she realised she had not been listening to what her teachers had been saying all these years. She had thought it was all platitudes, like a drug to obliterate the pain. On the other hand, they had been talking to the rich English with their pale skin. Not a half-breed who looked as if she had been out in the sun too long.

"You should go," said Margaret. "You don't have to dance and you don't have to tolerate boorish men talking in crude innuendo. We can go together."

For a moment Maliha thought Margaret might be propositioning her into a relationship like Jenny and Antonia. But no, she expressed none of the underlying *something* that was almost palpable between those two. It was innocent, and that was far more fitting for Margaret Creighton-Ward.

"I can't afford a dress."

"Daddy will pay."

"I couldn't."

"It will be a gift from me."

"I have two left feet."

"There will be lessons, I have no doubt, but it doesn't matter. I've done this before, even if you make a mistake it's always the man's fault. It means they haven't been leading well enough. They will apologise."

Maliha doubted they would apologise to her but she appreciated the thought. It seemed that Margaret was now her friend, which was something of a novelty. She wondered how far she could push it. Having an extremely well-to-do friend had the potential to open doors.

"Do you want Daddy to have a word with the Home Secretary about the police?"

Maliha found that her mind stopped functioning for a few moments as she processed the words, but finally managed to say. "What do you mean?"

"Well, if the police are being difficult, I can talk to Mummy, she'll talk to Daddy, he'll talk to the Home Secretary and he'll have a word with the Chief Constable and then you'll have no more trouble."

"No, I—I mean thank you for the offer, but I would rather do this my way."

Even though I have no idea what that is.

The end of the meal arrived but Maliha was loath to lose the opportunity Margaret's friendship had now offered her. "Would you mind coming back to the infirmary, to talk more?"

Margaret's face lit up. "I'd love to." And she bounded over to Mrs Lancaster who was gathering up her girls. There was a brief conversation and other girls once more glanced at Maliha.

As Margaret came back with a huge grin on her face, Maliha got the impression of a puppy. "I have to fetch my books, Mrs Lancaster said that you have to coach me on French and I must not stay past eight."

Maliha went back to the infirmary, found Matron, and explained about the visit. She looked a little put out. Maliha mentioned she would be available for cards after eight and that seemed to cheer the woman up.

Margaret duly arrived and was impressed by the size of the room, then suitably jealous that Maliha now had a room of her own. "No more having to watch Jenny sneaking off to her lover! Or listening to Oliphaunt talking in her sleep. Or the snoring, or the little night noises."

Little night noises. The girls' euphemism for when a girl did the thing they were warned not to in their beds. In her time in the Brighton bookshop Maliha had read every book she could lay her hands on and that included learned treatises on female biology and behaviour. All written by men and, she hoped, all wrong—certainly everything that she could compare to her own experience was incorrect.

Maliha made Margaret go through the French poem she was supposed to learn by rote. Not that Maliha could see any point in that at all, but that was the work and Margaret had promised she would.

Then they sat at opposite ends of the bed while Maliha wondered how she could bring up the subject of what she needed.

"You do have lovely hair," said Margaret. Hers was black and curly, there wasn't a lot that could be done with it. Maliha's was long, thick and straight.

"Thank you."

The conversation faltered again. This was not something Maliha was used to.

"You must live in a big house?" She said it and then cursed herself for saying something so inane.

"I suppose so. It's about the same size as the school but it's got more grounds," said Margaret. "What about you? What's it like in India?"

Maliha gave a half smile. "I don't even know how to answer that. It's so different, I couldn't say where to start."

"I suppose its hotter than here."

"Yes, much hotter but wetter a lot of the time where I live. But it's on the coast like here." Her smile widened. "I was pleased about that when I got here. I thought: At least I have the sea and that means my home is just over the horizon because the sea joins us together."

"But it's not, is it?"

"No," she said. "No, it's so far around the world that it's tomorrow morning there now."

"But that's a lovely idea, you could just get in a boat and sail there."

"A Faraday flyer would be quicker. Even a balloon."

"I suppose so. I flew to Paris once."

"That must have been nice."

"I was sick and they all spoke French."

"They would."

"I know, I expect you'd be fine in Paris you'd understand what they were all saying."

Maliha couldn't stand the small talk any longer and just blurted the one thing that was foremost in her mind. "I need a disguise and I can't think of one."

"What?"

"I need to get out of the school and do some investigating in Brighton. I don't know how. Mrs Lancaster helped by getting me in here so I have more freedom. Can you help?"

"Why do you need a disguise? Just go in mufti."

Maliha stared at Margaret in quiet astonishment. And was now regretting that she had been so stand-offish all these years when the person she could have talked to had been there all the time.

"Sometimes it needs adversity to bring people together," said Margaret as if she was reading Maliha's mind. "I've always admired you."

"Oh, thanks," said Maliha. "But I can't just go out in my ordinary clothes."

"Why not?"

Maliha pointed at her cheek. Margaret looked confused for a moment.

"You go out on Saturday afternoons—where do you go, by the way?"

"Usually the bookshop."

"All these years? You must have read every book there."

"Not all of them," said Maliha. "But I have to go out in my school uniform. I can't do that. And I don't have very much else." *And most of it is too small for me now.*

"I've got more clothes than I need."

"Why?"

"Because we're friends now."

"I had friends in India but don't think I know how it works anymore."

Margaret got off the bed and stretched. "Who knows how it works, but would you have said that to me a week ago?"

"I wouldn't have said it to you this morning."

They laughed and Maliha relaxed. Something changed as if she had been holding herself taut as a bow string every moment for so long and now she let it go.

"Do friends cry in each other's presence?" Maliha asked, feeling her cheeks warm with embarrassment.

"Always, but—" Margaret grabbed her things, "—crying will have to wait. I need to get back before Mrs Lancaster notices the time. I'll sort out some clothes and bring them before breakfast tomorrow."

"Thank you."

And she was gone. The room seemed quiet and empty. Maliha had been used to sleeping in a room filled with people for so long she felt lonely. Even though she hadn't even liked them.

"But that might have been my own fault," she said to the mirror.

She went out and found Matron sitting with some of the staff from below stairs. They were introduced but Maliha excused herself saying that she was tired from having a troubling day. Matron asked if she wanted a tonic and Maliha said no—she had a good idea of what was in Matron's tonics.

At least the infirmary had electricity and she was able to read before turning out the light and trying to sleep. She still was not sure what she was looking for but at least she might have a chance now.

11

Margaret was as good as her word and arrived ten minutes before breakfast on Friday with an armful of clothes.

Her opening line was "I didn't bring underwear." And that almost before the door closed. "I didn't think you'd want to wear mine, and you have your own."

"School regulation," said Maliha and they grinned.

"I have seen some interesting items in the fashion magazines," said Margaret as she dropped the clothes on the bed. "I'm going to get some for the ball. Do you want some?"

"No, please you don't need to. I'm not planning on letting anyone see under my clothes."

"Honestly—" and then she stopped and frowned. "Can I call you Alice?"

"No."

"Friends usually call each other by their first names, or nicknames, you know."

"I know, but Alice is my father's mother's name and she's a Scottish woman who lives in Glasgow. If you're not going to call me 'Anderson', then I'd prefer Maliha."

"Oh, that's so pretty."

"It's Indian. I was christened Alice Maliha Anderson."

"You are Christian then?"

"Not really, that was for my dad. I had the *Namakarana* ceremony as well for my Indian side."

"Maliha. That's good. Does it mean anything?"

"Beauty and strength. And Alice means nobility."

Margaret smiled. "That's lovely. Margaret just means 'pearl'."

"Pearls are beautiful, they fish for them in my home, Pondicherry."

The bell echoed through the passages, though they could barely hear it.

Breakfast came and went. Margaret went to lessons and Maliha returned to sift through the clothes and decide what she should do. There were three white blouses, two skirts, one dark blue and the other dark green. Very demur. And a green cardigan to round them off. The size looked about right but then the blouses were puffy and the skirts only tight around the waist. There was nothing that wouldn't fit. Thankfully corsets were a thing of the past—at least for young ladies with an appropriate figure. Maliha had two pairs of suitable boots and socks to accompany them.

Now there was the matter of escape.

She left her room and fully acquainted herself with the two floors of the infirmary building. The upper floor, where she was, was divided between a small ward with four beds, and the private rooms. One of which she was occupying.

The lower floor consisted of three store rooms, and an examination room. Maliha looked in disgust at the room Dr Jenkins used. She shook her head. His behaviour was completely unacceptable but who would believe any of the girls over the doctor himself. He would just claim they were hysterical.

The main corridor led into the school directly through a modern addition that meant no one who was ill had to go outside. There was another door, kept locked, that led out to the grassy area at the rear of the school. She tried the doors of the storage areas. They were locked but she was sure from the arrangement of rooms their windows would also lead outside.

She had no desire to go out at night so she needed a secure way of escaping and returning without anyone seeing. All she needed to do was get out onto the footpath or track in ordinary day clothes and no one in the school would give her a second glance looking out from a window.

Acquiring a key was a little problematic and there were two choices. The first, stealing one from Matron, did not seem like a good plan. She would notice eventually and Maliha had no way of creating a duplicate. The second option was probably in the furnace room and that's where she headed.

"Shouldn't you be in class, Miss Anderson?"

"I'm excused."

Mr Gunnell held up his newspaper and shook it. "On account of being in here?"

Maliha's heart sank. She walked over and took it from him. The murder in the school was all over the front page, she followed it to page six where there was an engraved image of the school. No photograph, just a general description of two girls being taken into questioning and one of them being released while the other had been incarcerated as dangerously insane.

She sighed. At least she was safe. Photographs were not common in newspapers, but it did happen and it would be quite possible for them to take a picture of her and create an engraving to make reproduction easier.

But not this time.

"Do the police think you done it?"

"I don't really know. On the one hand they want it hushed up as quick as may be, on the other I think that inspector just has it in for me. To be honest I don't think he likes women at all."

"Perhaps he doesn't." Mr Gunnell grinned slyly and winked.

"I don't think he's a homosexual."

"A what?"

"It's the word used in a book I read, well, the translation from the German text. Means what you meant." She handed the paper back. "It won't matter anyway if I can prove who really killed Ethel Jordan."

He pulled his little sweetie tin from his pocket and offered her one. "How are you planning to do that?"

"I have to get out of the school."

"And you're looking for some help?"

"Please." She placed the little sweet on her tongue. It tasted of nothing except sugar.

He stood up and checked the gauges on the furnace and water heater. "I like you, Miss Anderson, but it would be my job if anyone found out I helped you get out. I can't, not this time." He picked up a rag and rubbed at an invisible spot on a copper pipe that almost gleamed in the half light.

"I just need a key to the storeroom in the infirmary, the one nearest the back door."

Mr Gunnell kept on cleaning.

"If a spare key was accidentally left where someone might pick it up then no blame could be applied."

"Sound like you might be getting into very murky waters, Miss Anderson."

"Amelia's family will have to live with the shame of a daughter driven mad by her unnatural desires. Why should they also have to live with the lie that their daughter killed another girl? At least if I prove her innocent—and myself into the bargain—I have done something good for them and they might at least be able to bring Amelia to live at home with them instead of being locked up in Bedlam with the truly insane criminals?" She paused for breath. "I can't do it if you don't help me."

This was a lie, she had considered the possibility of leaving by the window in her bedroom. The climb down would be tricky but not impossible. Getting back up might be problematic. There was the passage from the library to the beach, but the library was also locked.

Mr Gunnell had stopped cleaning and was standing facing the pipework.

"I'm sorry—" she stopped as he held up his hand.

"You really think you can find the real culprit?"

She looked up at him but he kept his back turned. "I don't know but at least I'm trying, which is more than the police are doing."

He was still standing and facing the pipework.

"Is there something wrong, Mr Gunnell?"

"Maybe, maybe not."

"What is it?"

He turned around slowly, pulled the sweet tin from his pocket and looked at it. "I may have done something I shouldn't've."

Maliha wondered whether this was really something she wanted to know about. "What?"

"You know how you sent me up to lock the library after you found the poor girl?"

"Yes?"

Mr Gunnell looked in every direction except at Maliha. "You see, I had a good look round before I shut up the room, just to make sure there wasn't no one else there."

He stopped again.

"What did you do?"

"I took something."

"What?"

He didn't answer but instead went to the other side of the
room where he had a table with a lamp and his chair. There
was a small bin on the floor which he picked up and pulled
out something white. Maliha followed him and took it. It was
a small white bag, the sort used to give out quarters of sweets.
It was waxed on the inside but otherwise unmarked.

"You've been eating the evidence, Miss Anderson. Sorry
but you know what I like. I didn't think it could have anything
to do with anything. Leastways that's what I told myself."

"The ones in your tin, they're from here?"

"I didn't have no others."

"Can I have them?"

"You want to tell the police?"

"I need to be able to get out of the school without being
seen," she said. "If you have a spare key to the library I'll have
that as well if you don't mind."

"Are you blackmailing me, Miss Anderson?"

"I don't want to."

Mr Gunnell sighed and Maliha knew that this was the end
of their friendly relationship. There would be no more chats
about India and the state of the British Empire.

He pulled out his tin of sweets and handed them over.
Maliha emptied the contents into the sweet bag and slipped it
into her skirt pocket as Mr Gunnell found his keys and went
through them carefully sliding the ones he wanted off
the ring.

He handed two of them over. One was fairly modern and
made of steel, the other was larger and of iron, the latter one
would be for the library.

"I'm sorry, Mr Gunnell."

She wanted to say more, about how she would be doing
the right thing by using the keys to get out of the school but
somehow the words wouldn't come out. They would be simply
justifications for the crime she had just committed. The only
positive side to their exchange was that she had forced him to

give up the keys, he had not handed them over willingly, and that might serve as some sort of defence should he need one.

With her words stuck in her mouth she turned away and headed back up the stairs determined all the more to succeed in her goal—if only because that would provide the justification she needed for what she had just done. She could not even say goodbye.

She checked her watch. It was still early-morning and the change in lessons was still a few minutes away. She wanted to try the tunnel in the library but she had no light. It was worth a look though and, strangely, she was keen to return to the peace the library gave her.

The corridor was empty as she hurried down it. The door unlocked easily and she slipped inside as the bell was rung. She shut the door against the increasing noise and locked it again.

There would be those girls who avoided passing the door because of what it now meant. And those who would stop outside for exactly the same reason. She stood with her back pressed against the wood and listened to the subdued voices, unable to make out any of the words.

But soon it went quiet again as the girls went on to their next lesson.

Maliha stopped staring at the patch of brown that stained the carpet. The police were completely finished here so replacing the carpet would be a priority.

It occurred to her that the police had not mentioned a murder weapon. Even if the post-mortem examination of the body had revealed what sort of implement had been used to kill Ethel Jordan, they had not found one. And they would also know how tall the person who used the weapon would have been. Unless she had been sitting down.

That was why they had not arrested her. She might have a

motive, and even an opportunity, but the method still escaped them. She looked around. They would have checked everywhere in here, the police were, at the very least, methodical. But there had been so little blood splattered about the place it was a certainty that most, if not all, of the damage had been done somewhere else and Ethel had run back here —perhaps to get help—before dying of her wounds.

She realised this was very important. And that she needed to get down the tunnel and examine it to see if Ethel had been bludgeoned anywhere there.

Ha. The inspector had been bluffing all along. He knew she had not done it because he did *not* find evidence of the attack in the tunnel either and that meant it must have happened a good distance away. Perhaps even in Brighton. He knew neither she nor Amelia had committed the crime. A wave of anger went through her because that meant he did not even care that Amelia had not done it. He was happy to pin the murder on her just so he could brush the whole case under the carpet.

She walked across the room, avoiding the bloodstains, to the window. She did not approach it too closely, some of the photographers had telescopic lenses on their cameras. Maliha wondered for a moment whether the rules about using curtains at night in the dormitories were being fully applied. She shrugged, that didn't matter to her now.

The day outside was grey with a light mist. The sea was foreshortened and the rolling grey waves seemed to come from some nether world instead of the horizon. The reporters' vehicles were still there, although she counted three less than yesterday except one was completely new.

She intended to see how far she could get along the secret passage without light and went to the bookcase of government proceedings. She wondered whether perhaps she should have read them after all. It might be interesting to see what was being said by the men who ran the world. Except there were so many of these books and—*one of them was upside down.*

For an absolute certainty, she knew it had not been like that the last time she was in here. It was on one of the higher shelves and she needed to get one of the chairs from the table. She climbed up on it and extracted the inverted book. It was in the right chronological sequence so it had not been misplaced and it was completely clean, brushed free of all dust.

She held it in her hands and stared at it. This was not an accident. It was a message. And, if it was a message, there was only one person who could have sent it: Dr Underwood. The inverted book might have attracted someone else's attention but they would most likely have ignored it. Maliha knew it had been changed since she had last been here. Dr Underwood knew that she would remember explicitly—assuming she had been telling the truth, and she had no reason to lie.

That meant he had left it for her. A clue to something. But what?

Still standing on the chair she flipped through the pages looking for a message but no loose paper was revealed. She stared at it once more. If the book itself was the clue… she checked the spine: this was the fourth series, volume 146, covering the 11th to the 20th May 1905. She checked the contents and on the 11th were three entries dealing with India. She smiled grimly. The last of those was related to 'Home Accounts'. She opened the book at the appropriate page and under the very brief entry was a handwritten message.

Miss Anderson, well done. Of course I cannot be sure you will ever read this but I shall assume you are doing so right now. It came to my mind you would wish to investigate the tunnel to determine whether Miss Jordan received her wounds there. I could tell you the answer but I choose not to, since that would make it less enjoyable for you. On the off-chance you do not find yourself equipped to traverse a dark passage I have placed an electric torch on the bookcase above you. If you find yourself in need of someone to speak to, I can be contacted through my club, the Savile, on Piccadilly. Yours, Justinian Underwood, Doctor.

He had even arranged the need for her to be standing on a chair. She reached up and after moments fumbling in the dust she located the torch and brought it down. She replaced the book the right way up and climbed down from the chair, she put it back by the table.

She located the book that activated the door and pulled it. A mechanism clicked. She pushed on one side of the shelving and it turned in place allowing her access behind. She entered and ensured she could operate the unlocking mechanism then pulled it closed until the lock clicked once more. She opened it again, just to be sure, and satisfied herself she would not be trapped.

She flicked on the torch and its bright beam illuminated the narrow passage leading along the outer wall for a short distance and then down into darkness. Maliha cast the light around. The walls were plastered and the floorboards extended under the bookshelf into the tunnel indicating this had once been part of the room itself and partitioned at a later date. The dust on the floor had been disturbed by many feet, so even if there had been any clues they were all obliterated.

She frowned. That stupid policeman could have checked the footprints to see how many different types there were. Or perhaps he had, there was no way for her to know without seeing his reports. She rejected that idea completely, she was not going to sneak into the police station just to read them.

Moving along the short passage she reached roughly made stairs going down, the first few were made from wood but they changed to chalk and descended precipitously for at least twenty feet. Using the wall to aid her balance, she made her way down. Until she hit the damp and dirty chalk floor.

The tunnel did not run straight, nor were the walls even, but it was relatively easy to traverse. She kept her eyes open for anything that might indicate Ethel had been struck here, but there was nothing on the walls that looked like it might be blood splattered from a violent attack. The floor was dirty and wet. As the tunnel progressed the small stream in the floor increased in size.

Eventually, she saw the walls ahead lit up with daylight. And she switched off the torch to conserve its power. The sound of sea echoed along the tunnels growing in volume until there was a final dog-leg at the end. The tunnel doubled back on itself once, descended another series of rough-cut steps and opened on to the world. The exit was a narrow slit that, she imagined, would be barely noticeable from outside, and from inside she would be invisible in the dark against the white of the chalk cliff.

She stood there and looked out at the sea rolling in, its small waves tumbling infinitely on to the rocky shore. She was still wearing her school uniform so dared not exit into the daylight, but she would need to investigate this route to see how easy it was to get down on to the beach and what route Ethel must have taken, escaping from her attacker.

It was hard to imagine Ethel Jordan fleeing for her life. She had been the one who made others run or cower in fear. But she had met someone who had been able to dominate her and bring her to heel. Had she been violated by this person against her will? Or had she engaged in the act willingly?

Maliha stood and tried to imagine what it might be like to be Ethel Jordan. The sea moved endlessly while fishing boats crossed its undulating surface. Further out there were still some sea-going vessels that had not been replaced by the Faraday airships, though even the water-borne vessels were now vast since they, too, could use the Faraday effect to carry far more cargo than was possible without the invention.

Perhaps the poor girl had arrived by boat. If true there would be no way of knowing since the tide would have removed all evidence of it.

She sighed. There was nothing more she could do here and now. But this afternoon she would go in search of sweets in Brighton. It was not a prospect she found attractive, the number of shops selling rock and sweets must be in the dozens. This was a tourist town, after all. Still, there were ways to narrow the process down.

With that thought she turned her back on the sea and the light to make her way back through the tunnel to the school.

12

———

S he had to change her school uniform when she got back
to her room as it had been stained by her unplanned trip
through damp chalky tunnels. There would have to be some
discussion with Matron about what the arrangements would
be for cleaning her clothes here in the infirmary.

In preparation for a quick change when she returned from
lunch, Maliha laid out her 'disguise' she had been a little
concerned about her skin colour but as long as she didn't
make a fuss it should not be a concern. She headed back to
the main building when the lunch bell rang and was waylaid
by Margaret coming in the opposite direction who fell in
beside her as they made their way to the refectory.

"What have you been doing?"

"Finding out if Jordan was killed on the school grounds."

"Really? I mean, I thought she was."

"No." Maliha knew the secret tunnel was still not generally
known about so she chose not to mention it. But she realised
she had talked herself into a corner. "Well, yes."

"That doesn't make any sense. Either she was or she
wasn't. I'm not stupid, you know."

Maliha sighed. "She died in the library but she had been beaten elsewhere."

"Oh, that's terrible. So, whoever did it forced her into the library to finish her off."

"Yes."

"I suppose that makes sense, the library is a place mostly no one goes. Except you."

"I don't think the murderer knew that."

Which seemed to satisfy Margaret, for which Maliha was thankful, since the sequence of events she had just painted did not stand up to any real scrutiny. Her friend chose not to examine it.

Lunch passed swiftly. The interest in Maliha had subsided now the mystery was solved—and a day old. Once back in her room Maliha picked up the outdoor clothes, locked her own door, and headed downstairs as quick as she could to avoid meeting anyone. The storeroom opened easily and moments later Maliha was inside with the locked door behind her.

She set about getting changed. Some of the fastenings were awkward since they had been designed for someone who would have help being dressed. Such was the life for an aristocrat like Margaret, and in school there were always those who would help. Not that Maliha had ever asked for any, she was not sure it would have applied to her.

The storeroom consisted of shelving on which bedding and clothes were airing before being put on the beds. Even if someone had come in, Maliha could have hidden easily. Once changed, she secreted her uniform beneath a pile of sheets and addressed her attention to the window. It had frosted glass, which was a benefit. The mechanism was a simple latch and cord arrangement to unlock it and lift it open.

She looked out into the cold and damp, the grass stretched for a short distance to the wall and trees beyond. To the right and left she could see the various school buildings and the wall that linked them together to provide a suitable barrier. Whether it was to keep interlopers out, or the girls in, was a moot question. Running along the buildings was a gravel path edged with stones from the beach.

She sat on the window ledge and lifted her legs over and then slipped out on to the path. The gravel crunched beneath her feet She was reluctant to let the window close all the way so found a pebble just the right size to provide a gap she could get her fingers under. The final stage was to walk west along the outside of the buildings until she reached a line of trees that led away to the track.

It was more nerve-wracking than she could have imagined, though she knew she was unlikely to run into any trouble. There was a gate used by some of the serving staff and for deliveries, only unlocked at certain times of the day and in full view of the kitchen. She passed the chapel, which stood in the corner of the school, and noted that it too had a door. And then she was at the corner with an open space between her and the trees. Just a few yards but for those moments she would be visible to anyone in a room on this side of the school who happened to be looking out.

But then, what would they think? Would they assume one of the girls was making an unscheduled trip out of the school? They might wonder who the woman was, but then the female of the species was never a threat. Taking a deep breath, she stepped out and walked as casually as she could across the intervening space.

The trees and bushes swallowed her up as the path went on. Less than ten paces further in was a gate in the fence that marked the boundary of the school. Maliha clicked the latch and went through onto the main track. This led down a gentle slope and then up again. To her left was the coast and the sea. To her right, Cattle Hill. And ahead was Blackrock Coastguard Station. With the sea so quiet, and the weather inclement, none of the coastguard personnel were outside to speak to her. It was possible they might wonder whether she

was from the school. If she were in lower class garments she
might have claimed she worked there. As it was, there was
no need.

She came out onto the road that led into Brighton and
pressed on. She was without gloves, the ones she had were two
years' too small, so put her hands in her pockets.

It took only five minutes to reach the gasworks, though she
could smell it before she saw it with its great gasometers rising
above the town beyond. This end of the town comprised of
poorly built housing for the workers, but Maliha turned south
towards the coast before she reached the main residential
area. Even so, the cobbled streets, despite the cold wind, was
occupied by children playing and shouting at one another.
They were young, and no real threat but she preferred to
avoid any sort of confrontation.

"You lost, missus?" shouted one urchin. This was followed
by some raucous laughter. Children in India would not be so
disrespectful. At least that was how she preferred to remember
it.

She chose not to reply; her goal was in sight. The
Blackrock terminus of Volks Electric Railway lay at the end of
the street, right on the beach. There was no other person in
the small two-carriage vehicle when she got on board but a
man in a kind of railway guard's uniform left the small
building and hurried over.

"Aquarium, please."

"Sixpence, miss," he said. He looked very cold even
though he had a scarf.

"Don't they let you wear a coat?" she said as she fished the
small silver coin from her purse and handed it over.

"That would cover up the uniform, miss." He cranked the
handle on his machine and tore off the ticket. As he handed it
to her, his cold fingers brushed hers. "Anyone else joining
you?"

"I'm on my own."

"Not a day for sightseeing."

"No, but it's good to get out. I'm staying nearby." That white lie was necessary if she chose to return the same way, otherwise he might consider it strange.

"As you say, miss." He gave her a sort of salute with one finger touched to his cap, exited the carriage and climbed into the driver's cab.

He pulled a cord and the bell dinged twice. Maliha went up to the front and sat so she could see him operate the controls. He threw a switch and she found herself lighter. She had not been aware the light railway utilised a Faraday device but then why should it not? Still she did not think it was a very efficient one. She might feel lighter but not by very much.

"We used to have the most efficient Faraday money could buy," he called back to her as he pushed a lever forwards and the carriage pulled away. It was silent except for the clack of the wheels on the tracks. "Two problems with that. The carriages tended to derail and when they did they lost contact with the power rail."

Maliha tried to imagine a carriage full of people suddenly gaining full weight as they bounced off the rails. "And the other one?" she called back through the glass.

"Not everyone likes it. Tourists and their offspring who have eaten too much, suddenly get light. And they discharge the contents of their stomachs. It's just not good for business."

"And you're stuck running between Blackrock and the Aquarium."

"Two problems there," he said. "Corporation won't let us extend any further west and won't explain why." He paused for a moment as the train clacked through a set of points. "We tried extending towards Rottingdean was tried with the track on stilts. The cliffs keep collapsing and the sea will take anything away in a bad storm. Nobody would let us build alongside the road."

"That seems unfair."

"It is. We are a major attraction of the town but they treat us badly. I think it's because Mr Volks is of German descent."

The carriages rattled through a set of points where the track split for short distance—about the length of the two carriages, and then merged back into one. The buildings along the coast road were Georgian houses with the occasional area of green between them. Most were hotels now. A hundred years ago, Brighton had been the playground of the aristocracy, so entrepreneurial developers built holiday homes for them—every single building was in the same style. But Queen Victoria didn't like Brighton—it was too crass and common for her—plus the capital was moved from London to Manchester, so the buildings were sold off. Then, as is often the way, the ordinary people, crass and common though they might be, came here and they needed somewhere to stay, and the houses became hotels.

Brighton had survived and it thrived still.

The railway ran along the edge of the beach, which here was sand. Bathing machines stood in rank upon rank blocking the view of the sea. In India, playing in the sea was something children did. Adults generally did not, unless it was part of some religious rite. The sea was a dangerous place for the unwary.

The train paused at a station. No one boarded. They set off once more. Ahead, Maliha could see the Aquarium building looming inland and, in the water, Brighton pier was taking shape, thrusting out into the sea. All along the front there were two roads running parallel. The one closest to the beach was for all through traffic. The other ran along the front of the hotels—once upon a time that would have been only for the carriages of the rich. However, the arrangement kept the traffic moving.

Beyond the Aquarium it was another story. The traffic in the city was notorious and never any better than what she had experienced in the police vehicle. Even at night.

The driver brought the carriages to a stop at the end of the line and Maliha disembarked.

"Thank you," she said to the man as he stepped out and stretched. "I will be returning in an hour or so."

"If I'm not here, I won't be long," he said.

"I was wondering if you could help me."

"The Royal Pavilion is straight up that road past the Aquarium," he said. "You can't miss it."

"It's not that," she said and rummaged in her bag, pulling out the sweet bag. "I wanted to get more of these but I don't know the best place."

"Lots of sweet shops, miss."

"I think these are special—they are very nice—I wondered if you might know what they are?"

She held out the bag. He hesitated then poked two fingers inside and managed to get a sweet between them. He studied the yellow sugar-sprinkled confectionery.

"They have different flavours, that's lemon but there is an orange one too. They're like Rowntree's Fruit Pastilles to taste but are hard-boiled. And they have that sort of marbling inside."

He smiled. "Barnett's Oranges and Lemons, miss. A real treat, as you say, not the cheapest though. If you're wanting more of them you'll find the only shop in Brighton that sells them, opposite the Royal Pavilion," he indicated the direction he had before.

She thanked him and took the stairs up to the road.

Despite it being a dreary and damp early spring afternoon, she had to fight her way through hordes of tourists. She made sure she kept her own belongings safe. Despite the strong police presence, the pickpockets were bold hereabouts. Tourists were careless with their money.

It was less than ten minutes past the gardens to the Royal Pavilion. She stopped and stared like any tourist. It was a ridiculous example of royal excess with its Russian-style domes. But she was not here to see it—and it was not the first time anyway—this time she was more interested in the shops.

Keeping close to the shop fronts and far from the animal deposits in the street she examined each window as she passed. There was more than one sweet shop mixed in with the small restaurants, and public houses. But she passed them by until she reached the one with the words "Langthorpe's Sweet Emporium. Exclusive purveyor of Barnett's Confectionery. The Sweets of Angels."

She went to the door and pushed it open. The bell above rang out.

13

———

The woman behind the counter was large with a round countenance. The sort of person one might expect to have the word 'jolly' applied to them. However, Maliha could see immediately that the word that really applied here was likely to be 'angry'.

"Good afternoon," said Maliha in her best accent, honed through all the years she had been in England.

The woman sniffed.

"Can I have a quarter of Barnett's Oranges and Lemons please?"

Without a word the woman turned to the racks of sweet jars behind her and pulled down the appropriate one. She unscrewed the lid and with what was clearly a practised move she turned it on its side and a shower of sweets came tumbling out and rattled into a hopper on the scales. The quarter-pound weight was already on the other side and the pointer moved straight into the vertical position as the last sweet joined its fellows in the brass pan.

She pulled a sweet bag from beneath the counter, flipped it open with one hand, lifted the pan and let the sweet slide in.

With a flourish she held the corners of the open end of the bag and flipped it over twice to seal it. Finally she plonked the bag on the counter in front of Maliha.

"Thruppence."

Maliha handed over the coin. "Do you have a stick of Craven's rock?"

The woman glared at her for a moment then pointed at a box near the window. "That'll be a tanner."

The wrapping was exactly the same as the ones she had found in Jordan's locker. "I heard you're the only shop in Brighton that carries Barnett's confections."

"That's right, you want the rock or not?"

"Sorry, I just wanted to know if you had it."

"I don't need no time-wasters."

"I'm sorry," said Maliha. "But I'm trying to find someone who I know loves Barnett's Oranges and Lemons, and Craven's rock. I thought, because you're the only stockist you might be able to help."

"Why would I help the likes of you? I sold you what you wanted."

Maliha knew her time here was limited; the woman would throw her out. She had to move quickly. "It's the girl who got murdered at the school."

The look on the shopkeeper's face told Maliha everything she needed to know. "That's got nothing to do with me."

"She came in, didn't she? Who was she with?"

"I don't have to tell you nothing."

"I could just nip over to the Town Hall and have the coppers here in a heartbeat. I know Inspector Williams." Not that she intended to do any such thing. He was the last person she wanted to see, at least not for a while. Besides, it would be difficult explaining how she came to be here without mentioning the sweets which would mean revealing her source.

The woman's face became redder as if she was fighting some internal battle and was going to explode.

"Look," said Maliha trying to soften her tone, "I don't want to get anybody into trouble. All I care about is the poor girl who's being accused of the murder. I know she didn't do it but I need to prove it. If you can tell me where to look next, your name doesn't even have to be mentioned. But when you read the real murderers hanged for the crime, you'll know you helped."

"Didn't like her much, nasty piece of work if you ask me."

"You're right, she was an unpleasant girl. Very violent."

"Why d'you care then?"

"Because the murderer is getting away scot free. And an innocent girl is being blamed."

"Newspaper says she's mad as a hatter."

Maliha sighed. "Yes, she is not in her right mind, but she still didn't do it. You saw the girl, Ethel Jordan, do you think a girl smaller than me could bludgeon her to death?"

"I seen her play hockey. Beast of Roedean was right."

"You don't have to do anything except tell me where to find her friend."

The woman grinned. "You really want to know? I can give you the address. He works at one of the hotels on the front. The Pier Majestic. I seen him in the kitchen when I was delivering Barnett's for some do they was having."

"Do you know his name?"

The face took on a cunning look. "For a half-crown I might remember."

Somehow this had gone from blackmail to bribery. Half a crown would buy the woman a few drinks. It was probably worth it. Maliha fished around in her purse again, she didn't have a half-crown coin but she had the two shillings and sixpence. She dropped the coins into the woman's hand.

"Patrick Hogan. She called him Pat."

"Thank you." Maliha went to the door and turned. "You did the right thing."

"We'll see."

<h1 style="text-align:center">14</h1>

Maliha debated whether to tackle the hotel immediately, but she felt pressed for time. The longer she stayed outside the school the more chance there was that she would be caught. So, instead, she went back to the sea-front and waited for the train to arrive.

The wind had got up and the breakers crashed onto the beach in a continuous roar. She stared at the almost hypnotic waves, not thinking at all until her reverie was broken by another thunder that grew by stages.

She looked up and around as a flyer went over heading along the coast. It was one of the small, and new, four-rotor models designed only to carry a few passengers, though smoke still belched from the stack. It was not travelling fast and the rotors were angled halfway between vertical and horizontal—still providing lift as they drove the machine forwards.

There were bigger ones like this. Her parents had already booked passage for her return home aboard the *RMS Macedonia*. It was a huge vessel belonging to the P&O Line that took hundreds of passengers across the sky, driven by six rotors. Her journey home would take only a few days, even with the stop-overs which included Paris. She would have the opportunity to see some of it, she would have to tell Mrs Lancaster.

But this was not a commercial vessel. As it roared over she could see the Royal Ensign painted on its underside. A Navy ship. Fear gripped her—not the fear of something bad happening to her personally, but the fact that the ship might be heading for the school and she would not be there to witness the visitors and get some idea of what was going on. She doubted, if that really was its destination, that she personally would be missed. The place would be in uproar.

Maliha made certain that she read the flyer's registration number so that she might be able to look it up later. In the distance, the carriages of the electric railway had come into view, but they simply could not arrive quickly enough. If she had enough money she would have taken a cab and to hell with the consequences.

The vessel did not disappear into the misty distance, it reached a point something over a mile away where it turned inland and vanished behind a low hill. That settled it in her own mind, it was an emissary from Osborne College and she was absent.

It was another few minutes before the carriages rattled to a halt in front of her and she was on a knife edge as it pulled in. The sixpence for the fare was warm as she had been clutching it in anticipation of the train's arrival.

"When can we set off?"

The driver consulted his watch. "Five minutes."

"Can we not leave immediately?"

"I'm sorry, miss, I have a schedule."

"There's nobody here!" said Maliha pointing at the empty platform.

"I am sorry if you are in a hurry, perhaps you should have arrived for an earlier train."

Maliha clamped her mouth shut on a vicious response, she turned and faced the front with her arms crossed. She did not check her watch. She simply sat and fumed until the fellow climbed casually into the driver's seat, went through all the motions to ensure the vehicle was prepared to move. Rang the bell twice and set off.

The journey back felt tortuously slow. Maliha tried to engage herself by looking at the hotels and seeing if she could spot The Pier Majestic hotel.

It was a curious name, but there was probably a shortage of good options.

They were approaching the end of the line when she finally saw it: Close to the park at Kemp Town. It seemed to occupy a small part of a block, just one corner since another hotel was named directly beside it. All the better. She fully intended to gain access as soon as she could.

Today was Friday, so she would be able to leave the school with impunity tomorrow—if the girls were being let out at all. Although she would still need to change.

The train came to a stop. Maliha forced herself to thank the driver, she was still annoyed that he had not left earlier—but she also knew her anger was entirely unfair. Knowing did not help very much.

She strode at brisk pace up the road beside the gasworks, oblivious to the children. Her legs were aching as she climbed the gentle hill towards the coastguard station. The school did insist on the girls performing calisthenics to enhance their fitness—and their beauty, as Mrs Fenoughty insisted it did. But once in the sixth form it was not compulsory and Maliha had ceased to practice it. She preferred to read and she was certainly not concerned with how her appearance might affect men. She had no desire to catch a husband.

The path split away from the road and she followed it. One of the coastguards was now on duty and scanning the horizon with a pair of binoculars. He touched his finger to his cap as she passed. "Afternoon, miss."

She didn't want to say anything but that would be unconscionably rude. "Good afternoon." And she walked on.

Getting into conversation was out of the question, he would remember her too clearly.

Her watch told her it was getting on for four o'clock and the flyer had gone over about half an hour ago. It would have taken about five minutes for it to land and power down the rotors so that its passengers could disembark safely. Five minutes to get inside and then at least ten to fifteen minutes of pleasantries, tea and cake. Perhaps even twenty.

At her best estimate she would arrive when the visitors were in conversation with whomever they wanted to speak to. Probably just Mrs Ramsey. Assuming their discussions went on for about an hour she would have time to get changed and locate herself in the environs of the school office to see who had come all this way by flyer just to talk.

She had reached that conclusion, and was entirely satisfied with it, when she realised there was a military-looking person standing at the gate. A young fellow, but his uniform was Royal Navy and he carried a gun. There was no question that he had seen her and there was no way she would be able to change her trajectory without it looking very odd indeed.

"Sorry, miss, you can't come through."

"But I have to go to work."

"You work here?"

"In the infirmary, I assist the matron."

"I'm sorry but I have my orders."

Maliha glanced at her watch, grateful her coat covered the quality of the clothes she wore.

"Matron's not going to like it."

"I'm sure she'll understand when you explain."

At least he had swallowed her story. Maliha looked around for somewhere to sit, the ground was too wet. She was not completely ignorant when it came to men, she listened to what the other girls talked about, and she had read every available book on relationships. And not just non-fiction, she liked reading stories, too, because they gave her a more human viewpoint on the dry words she devoured.

There was a log which was also damp, but at least it wasn't muddy. She sat carefully making sure the ankle of her right leg, and a portion of the calf encased in a stocking, was on display. But casually. His eyes dipped in that direction.

His Navy blues were pressed but creased from the travel. She judged his age to be similar to her own, seventeen. His badges showed him to be a cadet, but he held the gun as if he knew how to use it. And he very probably did.

"I saw the flyer coming in," she said. "I didn't know it was royalty."

He smiled but said nothing.

She chose to pout at his lack of response. "It will get very boring if all we do is wait in silence."

"Sorry, miss."

"You're a cadet?"

"That's right, miss."

"And they let you have a gun?"

"A cadet isn't just someone who's new. It means I'm training to be an officer."

"What sort of officer?" she paused as if surprised at herself. "Are there different sorts of officer?"

"There are different branches of the Navy, miss, there is different training."

"What do you want to be when you…pass out?"

"Graduate, miss. I want to go into the Void Fleet."

"That's where the adventure is!" Maliha said brightly, it was the slogan the advertisements for the Royal Navy were using at the moment. It appeared regularly. There simply weren't enough men to go around, the Navy was expanding fast now that they were having to patrol the Void and planets as well as Earth. The newspapers had even reported on discussions in parliament about employing women in support, an idea which found favour among the suffragists.

"Yes, miss, I hope that is where the adventure is."

"Have you been up?" She glanced into the sky. The light was

beginning to fade but there were still hours to the evening meal even if she couldn't get in to see who the visitors were. All she had to do was persuade this sailor to reveal enough. He hadn't denied it was royalty. For a moment she had the idea that perhaps it might even be Prince George, it would certainly make sense for him to discuss the approaching ball with the headmistress.

"I have," he said. And he couldn't keep the grin off his face.

"Were you sick? I heard everyone gets sick, first time anyway."

He hesitated then decided it did not detract from his maleness to admit. "I was. Yes, everyone is. But I recovered quickly and I have to say that it was the most astonishing experience I have yet had."

"Did you see the stars?"

"Like crystals planted by the hand of God. So many of them, and so bright, and it's true what they say. They don't sparkle. And so many different colours."

She smiled, too, with genuine pleasure because he was so enthusiastic about it.

"That sounds marvellous, I would love to go up myself one day. But it's so expensive, I expect I'll just have to stay down here and listen to the stories."

"You could emigrate to Venus or Mars. They're always looking for the right people. Young people, like you, miss. And —" he had been talking in such a relaxed way he suddenly realised he was going to say something possibly awkward, "— not so many women want to go as men. They prefer married couples, of course."

She looked away and placed her hand delicately by her cheek.

"Sorry, if I said something out of turn, miss. I hope you'll forgive me."

She gave him a little time to suffer and then. "Let's not talk about that."

He went quiet. She turned back to him. "Did you fly the machine?"

"I'm not qualified to."

"Will you learn?"

"There will be training."

She nodded and then craned her head to look through the bushes at the buildings of the school. "Do you know how long it's going to be?"

"I'm sorry, I don't. The admiral will be as long as the admiral chooses." He grinned as if this was some sort of saying. Perhaps it was in the Navy. Perhaps it had a different implied meaning, some innuendo. She shook her head, she couldn't see it if there was. She took it at face value.

"Must be an important admiral for all this." She waved her hand at him and then in the vague direction of the school. "I suppose it's about the dance they're having."

"Will you be going, miss?"

"Ha, me? This isn't a fairy story for the likes of me. Maybe they'll want me in the kitchen or standing by in case one of those posh girls keels over from her corset being too tight, or not eating enough, or too hot, or taking too much of the hard stuff on the sly. No, sailor boy, I won't be there." *Not if I can help it.*

"Cadet Harris."

"You?"

"Me."

"Alice. Alice Anderson." She could see his mind working. Such a normal name—apart from the alliteration—how did that belong to a girl of her colour? "My dad was white, my mum's Indian."

"Oh."

At least he had the decency to look slightly embarrassed at having even thought it.

"What's your first name?"

"Bert."

"Hello, Bert."

"Hello, Alice."

Somehow, she didn't feel quite so bad about her Christian name when he said it. He had no distinct accent, just a type of generalised upper middle class. Which is probably what he was.

"Older brother?" she said.

"How did you know?"

"That's the way it goes, isn't it? Oldest brother takes over the family business. Next one joins the military, the one after goes into the clergy?"

"I think that's a bit old fashioned," he said. "But I don't have a younger brother, just a sister."

"How old is she?"

"Twelve."

Maliha said nothing about the age difference. The chances were that there had been pregnancies in between and lost babies. It happened everywhere.

"What are you planning to do in your military career?"

He smiled self-consciously. "The usual."

"What's the usual? I don't know I'm just a female."

"Try to climb as high up the ladder as you can get, more responsibility. Get married to someone suitable."

Yes, thought Maliha, *because if you don't get married you won't be able to climb the ladder. Someone like me would not count as suitable.* Not that she had any interest in him whatsoever. He wouldn't be going back to India with her.

"So, you have to start here guarding a fence."

"It's not so bad," he said and gave her a genuine smile.

Moments later there was a hail from inside the grounds. He looked round.

"Looks like you're off," said Maliha.

"I'm sorry I had to stop you going in."

"Just following orders, I don't mind. You better get moving, can't keep the Prince waiting."

There was a momentary double-take and he looked like he was going to say something then changed his mind. He went through the gate and headed along the side of the building.

Maliha smiled to herself as she walked through. As she crossed the grass she turned to watch him go. He looked back for a moment then went on when he saw her heading for the corner of the building.

He had almost said something that would have confirmed what she thought. But that change in his mind was confirmation too. He had realised what he was about to say would have revealed the truth, but by then it was too late. Speaking or silent, she now knew today's visit must have been from young Prince Edward's father, the heir to the throne, George. And, considering the health of Edward VIII, likely to be King very soon.

But to have a visit from him? It seemed so unlikely, could the ball be so important? But then was it unusual for a father to be concerned for the safety of his son when the British Royal family was a potential target for any anarchist?

It was getting quite dark as she pushed up the window and clambered back inside. She changed quickly and then headed back upstairs to her room without being seen by a soul. She heard the flyer taking off with the vibration of its rotors pounding the air and thrumming through the stone of the school walls.

There was a knock on her door at half-past six.

"Come in, Margaret."

The handle turned—Maliha had already unlocked it to give the impression she had nothing to hide—and Margaret poked her head round. "How did you know it was me?"

"Because nobody else is likely to visit me."

Margaret closed and locked the door. "Did you get out this afternoon?"

"I'm not sure I should tell you."

"You did! I would never be that brave. Did you find out anything?"

"Yes, but nothing conclusive yet."

"Well, while you were out something truly astonishing happened."

"The future King arrived for a chat with Mrs Ramsey."

Margaret's face fell. "Who told you?"

"A handsome sailor."

Margaret absorbed that but then her face lit up again. "You don't know, do you? Ha!"

"What don't I know?"

"Who also came to the school—" Maliha opened her mouth. "—No! I forbid you to talk, you mustn't guess because you'll be right and then I won't have been able to tell you *anything*."

"I can't imagine who else visited."

"Prince Edward!"

"I never would have guessed."

"I shall pretend that is true." She came and sat on the end of Maliha's bed. There was a perfectly good chair, but it seemed the habits of so many years in a dormitory meant she could only sit on the bed.

"But," said Maliha, "I was stuck outside of the school talking to the guard so if you have any other information about the visit from these royal princes I would be very interested to know."

Unfortunately, Margaret's ideas regarding what was important did not match with Maliha's.

All she did was confirm what Maliha had deduced: that princes had arrived, gone up to a meeting with Mrs Ramsey, and then left after about an hour. They had been in their naval uniforms which were, naturally clean and sharp, but not dress uniforms which indicated this was a very practical discussion.

There had been no pomp or ceremony, the visit had not been arranged in advance. In fact, there had been the curious image of Mr Gunnell wielding a shotgun before it was established exactly who had arrived. After all, the flyer could have been stolen.

"What did you think of the young prince then?" asked Maliha quietly as they headed out to the evening meal.

Margaret paused before answering. "He seems very young."

15

———————

To satisfy Matron, Maliha spent the evening playing
whist, they sat in the otherwise empty infirmary,
permanent inmates were not common. Their opponents were
Cook, who was physically large and quite intimidating—she
also drank a great deal of gin—and the school baker, Mr
Pimm, a very precise gentleman. They did not win too much
and, besides, the nature of the game meant that her skill was
not as useful as it might otherwise be. A great deal was
dependent on probability and likelihood, it was not something
she wanted to bend her mind to.

Maliha kept silent and let the adults talk. As time went on
they relaxed and their discussions ranged from the
management of the school (which they knew they could do
better) to the nature of the girls (most were abominable but
you couldn't help feel sorry for them), and the visit from
royalty. They liked the old King even though he was a
scoundrel, he was a decent monarch who cared about his
people—which was more than the old Queen had done—
meanwhile George was an unknown quantity so they hoped
he was like his father.

"My aunt on my mother's side has a nephew who works at Osborne," said Mr Pimm. "It is not a pleasant place for the young fellow. He is bullied, they say."

"Why would his father put up with that?" said Matron.

"It's not done to talk about it," said Mr Pimm. "It is not manly."

"The girls do it," said Cook. "And they're worse than any boy."

Maliha could vouch for that. Not that she had been bullied by boys for comparison. But she said nothing.

"How they expect me to plan and organise all the food and drink they're going to need for this ball in just three weeks I do not know," said Cook.

"Perhaps they'll bring in outside help," said Matron.

"Over my dead body," said Cook then crossed herself.

It hadn't occurred to Maliha that Cook was a Catholic, and her Irish accent was not very pronounced, but then she had nothing to do with the woman apart from eating her meals. The Royals might not like that, after all she might be a Fenian and take the opportunity to poison the prince, along with the flower of British nobility.

Then again if she hadn't done it yet, she wasn't likely to do it now. It wasn't as if she could have been lying in wait for a random opportunity like this.

Except, Maliha thought as she played out her cards, that wasn't the way the police thought about things. Inspector Williams had made it very clear that he thought this was a hotbed of suffragist activity. It would be a simple enough leap to suggest the Cook was a Fenian loyalist looking for an opportunity for murder.

But she did not say anything and took the next three tricks smoothly.

"She's a devil with the cards," said Cook. "Certainly, keeps them close to her chest."

Maliha was not offended that Cook did not speak to her

directly. After all it must be odd playing cards with one of the pupils.

Then she realised something. "I thought the ball was going to be at the Royal Pavilion." Because that would have its own caterers, Cook would not even expect to be involved.

Cook and Mr Pimm almost jumped at her words, partly perhaps because Maliha had said almost nothing up to now, or because she had been quite forthright in her phrasing but, Maliha suspected, mostly they had just told a pupil something that perhaps was supposed to be a secret.

"It's all right, I won't tell anyone."

Cook did not seem convinced although Mr Pimm relaxed.

"You can trust her," said Matron.

Maliha could not think of any reason why Matron would think she could be trusted, particularly, perhaps the woman just did not want to lose a cards partner who could help her win.

"It'll be known to the whole school by tomorrow morning," said Mr Pimm. "You know what these girls are like."

"Never mind the girls," said Matron. "I've never met a teacher yet who could keep herself from gossiping."

"That's so right," said Cook. "They are terrible gossips."

Maliha did not state the obvious but for a moment she locked eyes with Mr Pimm and she detected the hint of humour there. She had never even seen the man before, despite being here all these years, but she knew from the quality of his breads, buns and cakes that he was very skilled at his profession. Why would he be here rather than somewhere better?

Perhaps she would get the chance to ask him some time.

In the next three months.

The card playing wound up at about nine-thirty when both

Mr Pimm and Cook had to get back to the kitchens to direct preparations for the next day.

"You did well, Miss Anderson."

"Thank you, Matron."

They had remained sitting in the infirmary and their voices echoed. It was warm enough though and kept that way in case there were girls in need of medical attention. Matron brewed a cup of tea in her little kitchen located in an alcove at the end.

"Though I have to say that sneaking out of the school in the middle of the day does not seem the best of plans if you want to remain in school and do your exams."

Maliha was silent in astonishment. She had been so careful.

"You think I am unable to notice what happens in my own domain? How you managed to get the key from Mr Gunnell I have no idea—" Maliha opened her mouth to speak but Matron held up her hand. "—I am sure you did nothing untoward but more than that I do not need."

"I can assure you I did nothing inappropriate." There was nothing *appropriate* about blackmail, but that was not what either of them had been referring to.

"I do not want your assurances. Nor will I demand a promise from you that you cannot keep."

"I am doing this for Ethel Jordan, and for Amelia Johnson."

Matron shook her head and sat down heavily in the chair opposite. "Oh, those two."

"You knew?"

"Suspected. Amelia's excuses for her injuries were ridiculous but she did not seem concerned so I let it pass. That she was in the same dormitory as Jordan was what made me suspicious." She sighed. "I thought perhaps if one girl willingly accepted the violence of the other then perhaps others might be spared." She sighed. "We all try to maintain the image of the school as a bastion of female perfection. And we all lie about it."

Maliha nodded. *Even I am doing it.*

"Have you been told Ethel was pregnant?"

"Why would I be told? How do you know?"

"She had three months of unused pads."

"She was bright enough to keep fetching them. Foolish enough to not need them," said Matron. "She wasn't the first and won't be the last. Some just can't help themselves. I sometimes wish—" She stopped with the look of someone who has started on a course and then is unsure whether they should complete it. She decided. "I sometimes wonder whether it would be better to let the girls play together." She went red in embarrassment at her own words. "I mean, not forbid it. Let it happen, they will grow up and go their separate ways in the end."

Maliha smiled. "I can't see Mrs Ramsey making an announcement about that."

Matron paused and then burst out laughing. "I can! To be at that meal and listen to it. The teachers' faces, the girls."

"Jenny and Antonia would be happy."

The laughing stopped. "Jennifer Wendlefield? Antonia Dumont?"

Maliha realised she had exposed a secret and felt her skin crawl with guilt. It was not that she had ever promised to keep it a secret but it was an unspoken agreement among the girls. You did not reveal secrets to adults, and especially not teachers.

Matron was suddenly very serious. "They can't do that."

"Because Antonia is a German princess?"

"How do you know that? Never mind. No, that would be very bad if it got out."

"Jenny will be leaving school this year. Antonia has another year to go. They'll forget about it, just like you said." Maliha said the words but she had seen the two of them together—and heard them—she somehow doubted they would accept being parted. She hoped Matron would accept it, Maliha did not want to cause any difficulty for the girls.

"There were specific instructions in regard to Antonia," said Matron. "She was to be protected at all times, she is the great grand-daughter of Wilhelm I. They plan to marry her off to a Russian to try to keep the peace."

Given the state of Russian politics, Maliha was not sure that was a very good plan. But nobody was going to listen to what she thought.

"Matron, you won't tell anyone about my trips?"

"I won't, dear," she said. "But I won't help you either. It's more than my job's worth. If you're found out I'll just deny knowledge."

Maliha nodded. It was perhaps the best outcome she might have hoped for.

Saturday morning she slept late and missed breakfast. The other girls had lessons until lunchtime although it was usually personal study for the sixth form. She found the lack of regimentation in her life a little difficult to deal with. She preferred knowing where she was supposed to be. This level of freedom was unnerving.

Then Margaret knocked on the door. Maliha was not sure why she always knew who it was but there was something in the rhythm and strength of the strike. The door was still locked and she was still in her nightdress but she padded across the cold floor and let the girl in.

"Are you feeling all right?" said Margaret.

"Yes, I am fine."

"Good because I'm taking you home."

"What? No."

"Yes! You must come because this is the only chance to have you measured for a dress."

"I'm not going to the dance."

"You have no excuse, with it being here."

"I'm trying to find out who killed Ethel Jordan, had you forgotten?"

"It will wait until Monday."

"But—"

"Are you telling me you would rather spend another weekend moping around this place? Or wandering off to the bookshop to read one of the volumes you haven't yet touched?"

The idea of spending the afternoon in the bookshop, reading in the corner Mr Kennington had arranged for her, was very appealing indeed. Although she did find the man somewhat unnerving. He liked to stare at her for long periods of time, especially if she was reading something improper for a girl of her age. She did not think he would ever touch her, unlike Dr Jenkins, so she was willing to tolerate his odd behaviour in order to read the books.

"My father's cook is excellent," said Margaret. "And we have a *couturier* coming all the way from London."

"But—"

"I insist that you get dressed and prepare for a weekend away."

"How long will it take to get there?"

"Daddy is sending a car, it's only a couple of hours by road. Foxley Heath." Maliha must have looked blank because she added. "Near Royal Tunbridge Wells. I thought you knew everything."

Which did give Maliha some clue as to the destination, about twenty-five miles north-east.

"When?"

"Ten o'clock and we'll be just in time for luncheon."

"Will your parents be there?"

"Mumsie will be but Daddykins is staying at his club."

Somehow the nicknames fitted with Margaret's behaviour perfectly.

"Does your mother know I'm—" she searched for the best way to say it. "—not white."

"Oh, she won't care."

Maliha wondered how sure Margaret really was about that or, even if she had absolute certainty, whether that would be true. Perhaps *Mumsie* would think twice about spending a ridiculous amount of money on a girl she did not know and turned out to be a half-breed.

The more she thought about the potential consequences— being stuck in the wilds of Kent being the cause of a battle between Margaret and her mother.

"I really can't."

"You must."

And Maliha saw this argument descending into the sort of foolish yelling and name-calling she had seen so often in the dorms. Though here there would be no one to stop them. Matron wouldn't interfere.

"Would I be able to have a bath?"

Margaret laughed. "Of course! If Mumsie doesn't have too many people over then you'll be able to get a lovely suite all for yourself. Otherwise we might just have to share and I have my own bathroom. I think sharing would be super, don't you?"

Maliha allowed herself to smile. She felt as if Margaret was the irresistible force, while Maliha was certainly not an immovable object.

"What sort of people does your mother have over?"

The car arrived promptly at ten. Margaret had helped Maliha pack and they had both gone to the school office to sign out. Mrs Clemence was not happy and had sent for Mrs Lancaster.

Margaret's leave of absence had been arranged by her mother. Maliha had no one to do that for her so Mrs Lancaster was the obvious choice. If Mrs Clemence had secretly hoped Mrs Lancaster would deny permission she was disappointed, although the teacher did take Maliha to one side.

"Is this what you want to do? I know Margaret can be forceful once she gets an idea in her head."

"I was reluctant at first but I warmed to the idea."

Unfortunately, her answer made Mrs Lancaster more concerned. "Under other circumstances I would encourage this activity, it is good for you to make contact with people who may be able to assist you in later life. It's how the world works. But you don't have to go if you don't want to. It will be my fault and not yours."

"It was pointed out to me that there will be excellent food, superb sleeping arrangements, and an interesting variety of people to talk to."

"If you are sure."

"I am."

"Then I will approve your leave."

So, with Maliha carrying her overnight bag—Margaret didn't need one since she was going home—they headed out through the school. Faces watched from the windows as the driver quickly relieved Maliha of her bag and stowed it in rear of the vehicle.

Maliha was impressed. It was a Daimler—as used by the Royal Family—and a recent steam model. Except the steam engine did not drive the wheels, it generated power for both the electric motors and the Faraday grid. The design, through the use of battery storage, meant it was always ready to start. A second crewman, for want of a better term, attended to the furnace but that, of course, was out of sight.

The entire passenger and driver cabins were entirely enclosed with considerable headroom, and inside the smell of leather was intense, while the brass fittings gleamed. There were table-like cabinets set in the centre of the bench seats dividing them in half.

"This is new," said Margaret. "I thought we'd be getting the old one. It was very noisy."

This machine was not. Once the two of them were safely seated on the well-upholstered bench seats the car set off. There was far too much space inside, it could have taken eight people with ease, and twelve if they were friendly. The machine made so little noise Maliha could hear the gravel crunching under the wheels.

The Faraday effect was most welcome as they accelerated down the long drive. But the suspension seemed to absorb every bump and hole, giving them a gentle and smooth ride. Within minutes they pulled out on to the main road and turned east, away from Brighton. There was a strong wind and the water had been whipped up into big waves and breakers. Spray threw itself into the side nearest the sea.

Maliha wished she could see how fast they were travelling. It looked to be in excess of thirty miles per hour, possibly even forty which, on such an uneven road, ought to have been very uncomfortable. But the ride remained smooth. She knew from her reading, the limousine had a maximum speed of ninety miles per hour, but that was on a race track.

They turned off the coastal road when they reached Rottingdean and headed north into the South Downs.

Maliha's stomach rumbled. The quiet of the car meant that it was clearly audible. Margaret giggled and opened the cabinet. "Mrs Thurley is a dear." She pulled out a small wicker basket and undid the straps. "Elevenses."

She handed Maliha a small package wrapped in wax paper and tied up with string. The smell of smoked ham hit her. Maliha groaned. Why did it have to be ham?

On the one hand, from an intellectual viewpoint, she understood that religious dietary restrictions had a great deal to do with how life was lived in the past. That didn't stop her from wishing the people in Britain would stop giving her pig meat. However, her stomach had already decided for her. And she ate her way through the sandwich as fast as she could. The bread was thick and soft, the butter flavoursome and there was mustard too. The ham was, well, it was ham which she told herself she did not enjoy because she was not supposed to.

She was just getting hiccoughs from eating something quite dry too fast when Margaret offered her a bottle of lemonade.

"No glass?"

"It's easier just to drink it out of the bottle, less chance of spillage."

The journey took two-and-a-half hours. Once they were off the trunk roads the driver had to reduce speed. The country lanes were barely wide enough for the vehicle at all, and more than once they ended up trapped behind a slow-moving horse-drawn cart.

Rain came down in deluge as they pulled through the main gates of the estate. There were smaller buildings at the gate "The gamekeeper and head gardener live there." The tree-lined gravel driveway wound through the lawns and disappeared over a low hill. The main house wasn't even visible.

They passed a farm on the left just as the road curved to the right and the edifice—there was no better word for it—came into view. With its Roman columns in the Palladian style, it looked bigger than Roedean It seemed astonishing to think this was someone's home.

It was still raining, but there were three people standing outside waiting for the car, all carrying large umbrellas. A man who Maliha assumed must be the head butler and two maids standing back from him.

"Lassiter!" squealed Margaret as the vehicle came to a stop and she threw the door open.

He came forward and held the umbrella above the car so she could get down. "Lady Margaret."

"I brought a guest, Miss Anderson, she's in my dorm at school and she's very clever."

And with that she bounced out, stumbling slightly as she shifted from the low gravity inside the vehicle to the full amount outside. She did not wait for the umbrella—or Maliha—but ran for the steps to the front door.

Maliha took that as her cue to get up and move to the door. That was the moment the driver chose to disengage the Faraday and already off-balance because she had to stoop inside the vehicle Maliha fell to her knees. She felt her cheeks flush with embarrassment and felt the driver must have done it deliberately.

"Miss Anderson, may I assist?" Lassiter had put out his hand. After a moment's hesitation she took it and used it to help lever herself back on to her feet. Not an easy task in a long skirt. He maintained his grip as she stepped out and down to the ground. So close to the building and, looking up, it was very imposing. She did not suppose that was an accident: people visiting needed to know who the important person was here.

"This way, Miss Anderson."

She admired the sensibilities of the butler as he indicated the direction with a sweep of his hand to guide her and yet allowed her to lead the way, still holding the umbrella above her head. That was a sign of real quality. But then, she thought as she mounted the steps to where her friend was waiting, it was like Margaret herself, she seemed completely oblivious to Maliha's heritage—Margaret didn't ignore it, it just did not matter to her.

Once she was undercover, Lassiter removed the umbrella.

"Her Ladyship has a number of guests for the weekend, miss," he said. "What sort of accommodation would you like for Miss Anderson?"

"Can you have another bed made up in my room?"

"It will not be of the best quality, miss."

"I really don't mind," said Maliha. "I'm used to a Roedean bed."

"If I may make a suggestion?" said the butler. "The guests

have claimed all the outward-facing rooms, but the Green
Suite is available."

"But that's miles from my room," said Margaret.

"For both of you, miss."

The light dawned for Margaret, if not Maliha. "Excellent
idea, Lassiter. Remind me to tell Daddy to give you a raise."

The butler smiled as if this was a joke they shared.
Strangely, Maliha did understand this relationship. It was like
her and Mr Gunnell—then she remembered. It was the way
they used to be.

"But there's no one actually in my room?"

"Naturally not, miss, you room is sacrosanct."

"You think so? Well, I think some of my playthings went
missing between summer and Christmas."

"If you say so, miss."

The two maids returned from the rear of the car, one of
them carrying both umbrellas while the other held Maliha's
case. They did not stop but went through into the house. She
wondered if she would ever see it again.

"Where's Mumsie?"

"Her Ladyship and her guests are in the drawing room at
present. Luncheon is at one o'clock."

"We better get our skates on then."

"You have ten minutes, miss."

Margaret shucked off her coat and almost threw it at
Lassiter who managed to acquire it mid-flight without the
slightest flicker of surprise. Maliha took hers off more slowly
and handed it to the butler who took it gently from her.

"Right-o. C'mon, Maliha, let's run."

Maliha seldom ran but with Margaret disappearing into
the house, she set off at a hurried walk. There was almost no
time to take in the great hall with its red and white
chequerboard floor; the doors and arches; huge paintings.
Margaret was already halfway up the curving staircase taking
the steps two at a time with the experience of it being her
own home.

Giving up on decorum, Maliha chased after her, although she found the steps to have a very awkward spread, which changed as she climbed. She reached the first floor and her friend was out of sight. Then the words "down here" floated from the left. Maliha hurried along the corridor set at intervals with doors. The floor was covered with a deep carpet that absorbed any sound her shoes might have made.

She felt embarrassed about her shoes and then wondered at herself. She had always thought she did not care what other people thought of her. That their judgements on her meant nothing unless she herself considered them to have value. Yet here she was, worried what a member of the aristocracy might think, even though that person had not gained their wealth for any other reason than an accident of birth.

Since she had not encountered Margaret she took the corner to the left again and carried on. Finally, near the end of that passage, reaching a door standing ajar.

"Margaret?"

"In here."

Maliha pushed her way inside. She got the immediate impression that this was a room that had been tidy right up until a couple of minutes ago when a whirlwind had struck it. Said whirlwind was, at that very moment, in a side room Maliha took for a dressing room and throwing clothes everywhere.

"Grab the hair brush if you need it."

The sound of a dinner gong echoed up through the house.

"We shall be late," said Margaret stopping her fevered activity for a moment and turning to Maliha. "Fashionably late."

Maliha wondered about this, after all they had absolutely no idea who the other guests were, perhaps they would not appreciate an interruption from two schoolgirls. One of whom was particularly silly.

There was little point worrying since Margaret insisted on having her way. So, with some help, Maliha spruced herself up—even allowing Margaret to pin up her hair. Though it was a little ragged since they were hurrying.

Which is how, some forty minutes later, led by the giggling Margaret, she entered a large dining room occupied by eleven mature women in very feminine dress. All of whom looked at them with interested eyes.

16

I t took Maliha a full forty seconds to fully comprehend the
situation. The first distraction was a woman with skin
darker than hers, and similar features, though dressed in fully
western clothes. Then there was the predominance of purple,
white and green colours. In the dresses, skirts, blouses and
ribbons. And then the faces.

"Oh my," she said. Quite unlike herself and yet she had
never been in the presence of so many luminaries.

"Hello, Mumsie," said Margaret as she walked forward,
while Maliha was rooted to the spot. She reached the woman
who gave her a peck on the cheek which was accepted without
comment. "I hope we're not too late for food." She didn't wait
for an answer and went across to the table where lunch had
been laid out as a buffet. The room was arranged with several
separate tables but the women were all grouped together as if
whatever meeting they had been having continued through
lunch.

"Margaret, will you not introduce your friend?"

"Oh, this is Maliha Anderson. We're in the same dorm at

school and she is terribly clever—much cleverer than that policeman who came about the murder."

Maliha felt as if she wanted to fade into the wall and disappear but she couldn't keep her eyes from the Indian woman in the group. She then realised that this would not do at all. So, she walked forwards and curtsied.

"Your Highness, I am honoured." Then she turned to the others. "I am afraid I do not know all of you but Mrs Pankhurst, Miss Sylvia and Miss Christabel. I believe I am in the presence of the executive committee of the Women's Social and Political Union."

"Clever indeed," said Emmeline Pankhurst.

"I only read the papers, madam."

"Scurrilous rags."

"They are, but sadly my only source of news. I believe I am able to sort the truth from the lies for the most part."

Lady Henrietta Creighton-Ward stood up. "If we have all finished let's adjourn to the dining room." The others stood as well, except the Indian woman. "Sophia?"

"I'll catch you up."

The hostess did not argue and led the rest of the group away. Maliha realised she was staring after them in a most undignified way. Meanwhile, Margaret was piling food on to a plate.

"Maliha Anderson, is that right?"

Maliha's attention was whipped back to the woman in front of her. "Yes, your Highness."

"Oh, just call me Sophia. It's not as if I have any land or rights back home. I've lived here all my life."

"But the old Queen gave you your own apartments."

"Victoria had a soft spot for my father. It was just her way of showing appreciation. I don't think Edward ever liked me," she shifted and stood up. "So, you're at Roedean? Is your family well connected?"

"My father is quite well off."

"Anderson? He's English?"

"Scottish." Maliha didn't mean the word to come out quite as defiantly as it did.

The Princess Sophia Duleep Singh smiled. "Ah yes, Scottish. He is the inventor of the Anderson Valve?"

Maliha nodded.

"You see, we both know each other by reputation. We are quite equal. And where is your family from?"

"Pondicherry, your—sorry, Sophia."

"The part of India the British would rather forget. And your mother?"

"Brahmin."

"I'm sure you take after her in wisdom and kindness."

"Thank you. I hope to see them again very soon."

"There was a death at the school?"

"A murder. I found the body." And this time she felt that she was saying it with pride as if she were trying to impress the woman. "I have been trying to find the murderer."

The princess raised an eyebrow. "Is that wise?"

"The police have decided to blame another girl who is not of sound mind, so that they can close the case. But she could not possibly have done it. The man who killed her must be brought to justice."

"And you think yourself capable of that task?"

Maliha bristled at the implication that she might not be. "I do."

A kind smile crossed the princess's face. "I am not a popular person to the British establishment. It is not just my association with the Suffragettes, but I recently returned to India despite being forbidden to do so, and I have to say that I was dismayed at the way our people are treated by the British. It is an injustice that I seek to right. Again, we are the same." She took a deep breath and looked out of the nearest window, even though there was little to see with the rain beating down on it. "Out there, no doubt getting very wet, are two members of the British secret service keeping an eye on me. And, Miss Anderson, you will now be noted as a person who associates with subversives and anarchists. I am afraid that may make your life a little harder."

Maliha knelt down and touched the woman's feet to honour her. Then felt the other's hand on her own head. "*Namaste*, Maliha Anderson."

Without another word she left the room.

"What was that?" said Margaret with a mouthful of food.

"A blessing."

And that appeared to be the limit of Margaret's curiosity, which Maliha was happy about since she did not really want to go into explaining their cultural differences. She went to the buffet and helped herself to a selection of food that was the least offensive to her upbringing. And definitely no ham.

Maliha would have liked to have gone out and explored the grounds but the rain was persistent and heavy. Instead she was forced to stand at an upstairs window while Margaret pointed out buildings that she could not see. As far as she could gather there was a large decorative lake around which were several other buildings, including a couple of follies.

If the princess's secret service men had any wit they would be hiding in those, although what they expected to see or learn from there she could not imagine. Perhaps their seniors just wanted to be sure their presence was known, and that would be sufficient to dissuade any problematic behaviour.

Clearly, if that was the intention, it did not work.

The dress designer arrived at three o'clock in the same limousine that had carried the girls from Roedean. They watched from the window as a woman dressed in striking black and white stepped down from the vehicle, half hidden by the umbrella held over her by Lassiter.

"That's not just 'a' *coutourier*, Margaret," said Maliha. "That's Jeanne Paquin."

"Of course it is. She designs all of Mumsie's dresses, anyway I thought that sort of thing didn't interest you?"

"How would you know what interests me?" Maliha said it without even thinking and the as the words spilled out she realised how bitter she sounded. Her regret was immediate. "Sorry, I didn't mean—" Except there were no more words to say, because she did mean it.

"Because you're interested in news, and politics, and machines," said Margaret sounding a little sullen, like a child who's been chastised for something they did not do and is trying to explain themselves. "And why would anyone as clever as you be interested in fashion?"

"I'm interested in everything," said Maliha, but somehow that did not seem to make anything better. "I'm sorry, really. I just react sometimes."

How could she explain to a girl who had never had a hardship in her entire life what it was like to be Maliha Anderson?

"It's all right. Come on, let's go down. She doesn't like people who are late, and she has no respect for the upper classes."

Then I think we should get on famously, thought Maliha.

The fitting for the dresses went well enough, though there were aspects of it Maliha found quite embarrassing, since she was required to disrobe almost completely and suffer the intrusions of the tape measure.

Jeanne Paquin was efficient but not chatty. She approved of Maliha's trim figure as being one that would show off the dress; and indicated that designing something for her particular skin tones was an interesting challenge.

Maliha did not take offence since the woman was simply stating her professional view. However, Maliha was not to get any say in the dress design, the colour, or the shoes to be worn with it. Everything was down to Madame Paquin. Though Maliha expected that both hers and Margaret's dresses would be silk and contain a great deal of black: the mark of a Paquin creation.

Less time was spent measuring Margaret since for her it was a matter of updating her measurements. Then the *couturier* disappeared to speak to Lady Henrietta, leaving the girls once more to their own devices.

Maliha was bored already and itching to return to the school so that she could continue to investigate the murder. This was an unnecessary distraction, although if she was truthful the idea of being able to attend the ball wearing a Paquin dress did appeal to her. It would be a slap in the face to the bullies. Then she chastised herself for being so petty. They were not worth even that much attention.

"Do you support women's suffrage, Miss Anderson?"

She was sitting at the evening meal and facing Christabel Pankhurst, which was terrifying. The tables were once again separate as if they were at a restaurant, but Maliha could see the point in it. If they were at a large dining table, the conversations tended to be stilted. To speak to the person on one side of you meant you ignored the other, and the person opposite tended to be a good distance away. This arrangement meant that you could see each of the other people at the table and include everyone in the conversation.

It was a much more feminine arrangement in her opinion.

On her table, apart from Margaret and Christabel, was Princess Sophia with two members of the movement Maliha had not heard of: Melanie Whittaker and Tamara James. The last two were quite young and perhaps new to the group as they did not say very much. Perhaps they, too, were in awe of the others present.

"I do, of course," said Maliha. "There is no logic to women being treated as a mere addendum to the male sex."

Christabel and Sophia both laughed out loud.

"I will suggest that particular phrase to my mother," said Christabel. "She will enjoy it and possibly even use it—if you don't mind."

"No, of course not, I would be honoured."

"And no charge for its use?" said Sophia.

"For one shilling I will transfer all copyright."

Sophia leaned over to Christabel at her side. "Our Miss Anderson is quite the detective as well as driving a hard bargain."

Christabel shook her head. "That was a terrible business, but they have the girl?"

"Amelia Johnson did not kill Ethel Jordan," said Maliha firmly. "She had not the will, the opportunity nor, if truth be told, the physical strength. Ethel Jordan would have been a formidable foe."

Leaning forward with a frown across her forehead, Christabel lowered her voice. "What exactly are you saying, my girl?" Her soft Manchester accent came to the fore.

"I am saying the girl is going to be committed to an asylum dedicated to dangerous criminals for the rest of her life, without trial but accused of something she could not possibly have done."

"I am no lover of the police—"

"Unless he's very handsome," said Sophia as if there was some story there.

"Hush. While I do not love them, this seems beyond even them if the evidence is as you say."

"There is no evidence, that is why it is convenient for them to blame her and consign her to a living hell," said Maliha.

"But why?"

"The reasons are twofold: The event is seriously damaging to the school's reputation and those in power need a quick resolution. And we have a dance which has been organised with the Royal Navy College at Osborne on the Isle of Wight. Prince Edward will be in attendance, once

more the crime needed a rapid solution so it would not
interfere."

She did not explain how the dance itself was being used as
a way of resolving any doubts the parents might have in the
school. After all, if a future king is allowed to be present in the
school, it must be a proper place.

"She is being used as a scapegoat?"

"She is barely sixteen."

"I heard," said Melanie Whittaker, "the girl is quite mad."

Maliha sighed. "She is unstable but not dangerous. She
should be in the care of her grandmother not in a place where
she may well become utterly lost."

"You are a little young be an alienist," said Christabel.

"I have spoken to her, I have spoken to her both in her
right mind and out of it. Even then she was no danger to
anyone but herself."

They had all stopped eating as the conversation became so
intense and passionate. All except Margaret who seemed to
have been listening with only half an ear at best.

Christabel sat back. "This is very sad but I do not think
there is anything we can do."

"I am not asking for help, Miss Pankhurst," said Maliha.
"You have your own concerns to deal with. I will save Amelia
Johnson."

"And how will you do that?"

"By finding and revealing the true culprit."

Maliha glanced at Princess Sophia, who was smiling and
nodding at her.

"Well," said Christabel. "I believe you would make an
excellent Suffragette but I will not try to recruit you to our
ranks. We stand beyond the edge of the law." Which remark
drew approving smiles from her compatriots. "I see that you
are more inclined to its support and I would not want us to be
less than friends by being in opposition."

"We are not in opposition, Miss Pankhurst. You work for
all the women of this country, and I work for just one."

"So be it, Miss Anderson."

Christabel held out her hand and Maliha shook it. The action did not go unnoticed on the other tables in the room.

"I wish you would hurry up and finish your main course," said Margaret. "Cook's desserts are simply to die for.

After dinner the women returned to the drawing room to play cards. It seemed that none of them chose to smoke. The weather continued unpleasant into the night. There was no further discussion of either the plans of the Suffragettes—a name coined as an insult, but which they took to themselves to confound the press—nor of the events at the school. Maliha did notice that neither Margaret nor her mother took particular pains to talk to one another.

She found this hard to understand. Perhaps having all that money drove them apart.

As it was, Margaret decided they would leave the grown-ups to their own devices and the two of them said their good-nights and headed up to the Green Suite.

It had no windows but there were skylights in the roof that would let in natural light during the day. The mansion was, naturally enough, fully equipped with electricity—and, from certain rooms, it was possible to hear the steam engine that ran the generator.

The suite had three main rooms: a central lounge with the door to the corridor, and two bedrooms, one on each side, which seemed more or less equal in size. The decor was, unsurprisingly, green. Maliha's clothes had been put into one room, they had also been unpacked and a steam iron run over them to remove any creases.

After the excitements of the day Maliha was tired and perfectly willing to go straight to bed. Margaret had other plans and insisted on talking about inconsequentialities for another hour. She seemed particularly interested in the dance and whether or not there would be any eligible men present.

"Of course, what I think is eligible and what Mumsie thinks are two entirely different things," she said. "Who would you like to marry?"

The question woke Maliha from her increasing stupor. "I hadn't given it a thought."

"You might find someone at the dance. A handsome prince."

"I don't have any interest in princes, handsome or otherwise. I'm going back to India when I leave school. That's it. I won't be coming back." Though she had a foreboding about what awaited her back in Pondicherry. One of those was her grandmother who would be trying to marry her off. Even her parents would probably be interested in that. She wasn't.

"Well, you can be sure of a lot of attention, you're very beautiful."

"Don't be ridiculous." *Am I?*

"Of course, you're a sultry eastern beauty. The type for whom dreams are made."

"If that's what they think then what they'll get will be nothing more than a nightmare."

Margaret sighed. "I'm only trying to help."

"I know, and I understand but that kind of life just isn't for me," said Maliha. "I'm not some trophy to be won and stuck on the wall next to their other kills."

"You're saying I'm a trophy?"

"No." *Yes.* "Look, you are what you choose to be. If that's the life you want then that's perfectly fine. It's just not what I want. Don't you want to be like your mum?"

"She's been trying to get herself arrested and so has that princess you like. I don't want to be arrested."

"Don't you think having the vote is important?"

Margaret got up from the chair she was sitting in, went through into her room and shut the door. Maliha stared at it. Was she coming back? Each of the rooms had its own W.C. so was she utilising the facilities.

But she knew Margaret wasn't coming back. She had been pushed too far and simply escaped.

Maliha felt guilty now but it was the sort of thing she expected when dealing with the other girls. Margaret was nice enough but she wasn't interested in a world beyond what was directly around her.

She might change as she got older but she might not.

Maliha went to her room. Not only did this house have electric lights but there were electric heaters in every room. They were needed. The sky lights let in the cold as well. Maliha got undressed and slid under the thick eiderdown. She was asleep almost before she noticed.

Since it was still March the dawn did not occur too early but when the light finally woke Maliha she could see blue sky and the sun cutting across the opening above her. The room was warm and she threw back the covers but continued to lie there. There was something comforting about having no windows and being alone. A quiet privacy that she truly appreciated.

She checked her watch. It was only seven o'clock but she had no idea when breakfast would be served. Or even whether they would have to go down for it. Or if it would be served in the room. She wrapped herself in her dressing gown, pulled out her book and put on her slippers. The door opened soundlessly and she stepped out into the middle room with a certain amount of caution. She did not know if Margaret was up and whether she would be holding a grudge after the insults of last night.

Maliha was still cursing herself whenever she thought about it. She had been tired and had said the wrong things. It wasn't that she didn't believe what she'd said but she had not intended to upset her friend.

She had got along for years without one but now that one had turned up she was keen to keep her.

It was another hour before noises in the other bedroom informed Maliha of the imminent arrival of Margaret. She decided to pretend she didn't hear her coming, it would seem more normal.

The door opened and Margaret shuffled out. Her hair was a complete rats' nest.

"Morning," said Margaret.

"Good morning, look I'm really sorry—" she stopped as Margaret held up her hand.

"It's fine."

"Really?"

"Really." And as if to prove the point Margaret came over and kissed Maliha on the cheek. Then wandered back to her room and shut the door.

Maliha was aware, from several years of observation, that Margaret did not do well in the mornings. It took her a good half an hour to wake up properly, and that was on a good day. It had never occurred to her before but she knew the people in the dorm better than her own parents.

The door opened again and Margaret stuck her head out. "Breakfast in the lounge from eight. Buffet because the staff go to church. Mostly."

"Are we going to church?"

"Do you want to?"

"No, I'm not a Christian."

"But you always go to church."

"I'm not given a choice, am I?"

The door closed again. It was already gone eight o'clock. She headed back into her room to get dressed then returned to the chair to read. She did not think it was polite to go down without her host.

They finally arrived for breakfast at half past nine. Only the lesser members of the WSPA were present so, apart from typical British nods and smiles, they did not speak. The girls ate kedgeree followed by buttered toast with plenty of marmalade. Maliha washed hers down with tea. Margaret had coffee.

Meanwhile, the sun rose slowly and bathed the house in light. The warmth coming through the windows was pleasant, and Maliha felt that growing up here might not have been so bad. From the window she could now clearly see the woods and buildings poking up through the base branches. The sun glistened on the still water of the lake.

"We should go for a walk," said Margaret. "I'll show you all the secret spots before lunch." She gave a little sigh. "We'll have to head back to school straight away after that so we're back before evening."

"Won't some of the other women need the car?"

"They're packing up this morning. They just need to be taken to the station in Tunbridge Wells."

But they did not get a chance for the walk. Their attention was attracted by the noise on the patio just outside. The Suffragettes were gathering for a photograph. So, the girls grabbed their coats and went out. The sun was warm but the air still quite cold. Her years in Britain had acclimatised Maliha to the lower temperatures, except when it became particularly cold, while the summers, which the natives called hot, made no impression on her whatsoever.

Maliha watched them. It seemed strange to see such an impressive group of women laughing and joking. She had imagined they would be serious all the time. Their chosen task, to change the minds of men ingrained with centuries of dominance, was herculean—how could they possibly detach their minds and find humour in anything?

But they did. And in the simplest of things too, like an accidental bump that was countered with a mock accusation. The pretence of Christabel trying to upstage her sister, or block her face with her hat.

It was Margaret's mother who was taking the photograph but after a moment someone suggested that Maliha or Margaret could do it. The daughter demurred so Maliha found herself forced forwards to stand by the machine on its tripod. It had been set up next to the stone balustrade that ran around the edge of the patio. It meant she could stand up on it to allow herself to see through the viewfinder and hold the actuating lever easily.

There had been plenty of photographs in her time at Roedean, individual, year and whole school that traced her life. The pictures had been sent to her parents by the school. Maliha had not been allowed to see them, but the letters from home were appreciative.

And now she was about to take a photograph of the most powerful women in the country.

"Smile, please."

They smiled and she pressed the actuator. The shutter mechanism clicked.

"We'll take a few," said Emmeline Pankhurst. "You never know how they'll turn out, someone might have blinked just at the wrong moment."

Maliha had never operated a camera before but she had read enough magazines devoted to photography. The handle to move the film on was positioned where she expected and she wound on until it clicked into position. She noted that the device was remarkably easy to operate.

"Ready?" she called out as she peered down into the viewfinder once more. She waited a moment for them all to settle. "Smile." Click. Wind on. "Smile."

She depressed the actuator once more but this time
something tugged at the upper arm of her coat. A metallic
snap ricocheted from the camera. Then the sound of a
gunshot echoed across the grass.

"Get down!" screamed Emmeline. Maliha threw herself
off the wall to hide behind it. She peered between the stones
as another bullet ricocheted off the wall above her head. But
this time she had seen the tiny flash from a small domed folly
directly across the valley from them.

"Mummy!" wailed Margaret. There was something in her
voice that made Maliha turn. Margaret was still standing,
though everyone else was on the floor and a patch of dark
damp red was forming at her shoulder. "It hurts."

For a second, Maliha froze. On the one hand she wanted
to dash for her friend, but even as she looked she saw Tamara
James tugging at her and pulling her to the ground.
Scrambling awkwardly in her skirt and coat Maliha crawled
past the camera towards the end of the wall. It terminated
with a plinth carrying a large urn. She stood up behind it and
wriggled out of her coat.

She felt energised and ready to run, but she swallowed
hard though her mouth was entirely dry. She caught up her
skirt to give her legs room to move and set off at a run. There
were two steps down from the patio to the path which she took
in a single leap barely breaking stride.

"Miss Anderson! Stop!"

Another gunshot echoed across the valley but she had no
idea where it fell. She knew no one else would understand her
action. She hoped that applied to the marksman as well. And
she was relying on fact that he would now consider his
position to be compromised. He would be packing up and
leaving because the entire household would be alerted within
minutes and men would be pouring across the grounds in
search of him.

And that was why she was doing this.

Those men would obliterate any evidence at the scene well

before any policeman could arrive and cordon off the area. If the shooter had left any evidence, she needed to see it before it was destroyed.

These thoughts ran through her mind as she pelted along the path as it curved around the grounds. She could have gone in a direct line across the grass but the ground was wet from yesterday's rain and would be very troublesome. More importantly, a straight route would lay her open to a bullet through her heart.

She already knew how the events following the attack would play out. She had known from the moment the second bullet had pinged off the wall above her head.

The people behind her would be convinced this was an attempt to assassinate Emmeline Pankhurst. And they were completely wrong.

The distance across the valley was not too great but clearly his weapon was insufficiently accurate to make a precise kill. Even so, he had barely missed her on that first shot when it would have been easy to fire into the group of Suffragettes and, even if missing his target, hurt or killed another of the women. And he could have fired several shots in rapid succession before they ducked out of sight.

She found herself slowing down and she was panting terribly. She could hear shouting from the house, including continuing demands for her to stop. She should have paced herself better, and perhaps the calisthenics classes would not have been a complete waste of time.

She was around the bend and now heading along the straight that led towards the folly. She let herself drop to a walk, after all she did not wish to come upon the man before he had time to flee. She was no match for an adult male with a gun. At least not physically.

She glanced to her left at the house. The women had disappeared into the house. She could see Lassiter with a pair of binoculars looking directly at her while three gardeners were ploughing through the muddy grass with difficulty. Her assessment of the ground had been correct.

Having regained her breath, she picked up speed once more to a slow trot. She still needed time before the gardeners started to trample the ground. A series of worn stone steps led up to the right. She took them and within moments the folly stood there. A simple dome supported by Roman columns with stone benches beneath it. At least she was able to see that there was no one there now.

The scent of cordite hung in the air. She turned to look at the house. From this point it would not have been possible to carry out the attack. She climbed slowly until she reached the folly. A glance told her that this was the spot. It still looked an impossible shot but if the man had a telescopic sight he would be able to see far more clearly.

And if he leaned against one of these pillars he would be able to achieve better stability.

There. A smudge on the pillar closest to the house. She wished she had a tape measure she would be able to judge his height to within an inch. But she was not ready to step on to the floor of the folly just yet. Instead she studied it. There were several footprints but two were more clearly delineated, once behind the other. This is where he had held his stance with his shoulder against the column.

And fired two shots to kill her. Almost successful. And then the third a game shot as she ran along the path. She turned again and looked out. Yes, he had the opportunity to get that shot off but after that she would have been out of sight unless he changed position. It seems he had chosen not to.

Spent bullet cartridges lay in the damp mud and leaf mould at her feet. Two where she stood because he had fired twice from the same position and the other? She looked to her right. There. She reached down and picked it up carefully by its edges. Not that she had any means to take a fingerprint or, indeed, compare it with others. But she placed it in a pocket anyway. If the police were

thorough they might wonder where the third cartridge had gone
—but since they would not be able to find where the third bullet
had struck they might decide it was hysteria among the women
that said three shots. She knew where the third bullet had fallen.

Now she climbed on to the folly taking care not to
obliterate the boot marks. She knew little of boots but these
were very large and quite suitable for the terrain and weather
conditions. He knew what he was doing. She stood close to the
pillar with the scuff mark which, as far as she could tell, was
about a good six inches above the top of her own head. He
was a tall man, she did not need to know that his deep
footprints would lead the pursuers through the woods to a
track where he had another means of transport.

Quite possibly a horse, though it would need to be a big
one. Yes, almost certainly a horse given the weather
conditions. The only other alternative might be a flyer of
some sort. In which case they would have no chance of
following him. Not that she expected they would catch him
anyway. If she had planned this attack—even in the limited
time available—the horse would lead to something faster on
the main road.

Not expecting to find anything else, Maliha walked round
to the other side of the folly where something white caught
her eye. She squatted down to study it. A small piece of white
paper perhaps two inches square, wrinkles on two of the sides,
with something gooey red attached to it. She found a twig and
turned it over. There were no distinguishing marks. She picked
it up and stuffed it into her purse.

She heard the puffing of the gardeners before she saw
them. They appeared through the brown branches.

"He is gone," she said. "But his footsteps go that way." She
pointed in the obvious direction. One of them touched a
forelock and said nothing before heading off with the others
in tow.

18

Lady Henrietta berated her for being so foolish as to run off, then was consoling and pleased she was alive. Then allowed her to see Margaret who had been put to bed. The first bullet, that had just missed Maliha had caromed off the camera and hit the other girl in the shoulder. Much of its power had been spent but it had penetrated her coat and pierced her skin, lodging in the flesh.

Not even close to being a fatal wound, but painful.

One of the staff had served in the Boer War and had been trained in field medicine. He had checked her over, declared she was in no danger, and said they should wait on a fully trained medical doctor.

Both medic and police had been sent for.

Maliha heard arguments among the Suffragettes as she climbed the stairs, some of them thought they should leave but the senior members said no. They would report this attack on them because it would engender public sympathy. The exception was to be Sophia, since she was already problematic to the British government, she would leave immediately.

So Maliha sat with her friend and held the hand that was not in a sling.

"Mumsie gave me brandy."

"Did it help?"

"I feel quite light-headed but it hurts a lot still."

"I'm glad it's not any worse." She hesitated. She needed to apologise but was concerned where that conversation might lead. "I'm sorry."

"What for?"

"It doesn't matter."

"That's what Mumsie says when she doesn't want to talk about something."

"And I don't want to talk about this," said Maliha. "Except I have to."

Margaret yawned. "Better hurry up because I'm really tired."

"He was trying to shoot me, not the other women."

"Don't be silly."

"And I don't know if I should go back to school."

"Lassiter will take you. I'll be fine."

"That wasn't what I meant. Not go back ever."

"Why?" She really was sounding very tired now, her words were coming slower and less distinct.

"Because I'll put all the other girls in danger. Like you. Like the Suffragettes."

"Always in danger." Margaret's voice was barely above a mutter now.

Maliha rested her elbows on the bed and pressed her hands into her face.

"I can't afford to have friends."

There was no response from Margaret. Even if she had heard, she was too far gone to respond. So Maliha remained in that position, with her head in her hands trying to decide what she should do.

"The police want to talk to you, Miss Anderson."

She looked up with a jump, almost as if she had been

asleep herself. It was Lady Henrietta, her face impassive as if she dealt with attempted murder every day. Perhaps she did with the Suffragettes, simply not quite so close to home.

"Thank you."

"They are in the library. Do you need me to show you the way?"

Maliha looked at Margaret. Her face was pale but she seemed to be sleeping peacefully.

"I know the way."

Of course she did, one tour of the building had been quite sufficient to commit the layout to memory.

She paused at the door where Margaret's mother still stood. "I'm sorry."

"There is nothing you could have done."

I could have followed my instinct and never allowed her to befriend me. But she just nodded and went downstairs.

This inspector was older than Williams, which Maliha was glad for, and in possession of a very fine moustache. He would have more experience and would rely on it with complete self-confidence. But this was outside of his knowledge and whatever box he fitted it into would be the wrong one.

And here she was. A mere girl, and a foreigner. This interview would be for form alone. He glanced up as she entered and waved her into the chair facing him across a table. Both table and chairs were over a hundred years old if she judged them correctly.

"Alice Maliha Anderson?"

"Yes."

"I have been speaking to Detective Inspector Williams in Brighton."

She said nothing. He did not require a response, he was simply demonstrating his superior position in the interview.

"A murder and an attempted murder, and you're in the middle of them."

"I can assure you I would rather not be."

"And how do you feel about the women's suffrage movement, Miss Anderson?"

"I am in favour of it."

"I see."

"And what means do you consider acceptable in achieving those ends?"

"Am I under arrest?"

"You are an eyewitness in a shooting resulting in the injury of an aristocrat."

"I am not completely in favour of all the methods used by the Suffragettes, however I do appreciate that making the Government take notice of an unacceptable situation can be difficult."

"Would you allow yourself to be injured, or do yourself an injury for that cause?"

"I'm sure it would depend on the circumstances."

He glanced down at his notes then back at her. "You fled the scene. Why?"

"I did not."

"I have statements from witnesses present that after the second shot you ran away from the scene."

She had expected this question and had toyed with the idea of answering truthfully, but amateur detectives were not looked on with any favour. Pulp magazines notwithstanding.

"Yes, I did run but I was trying to draw the fire of the attacker."

"I beg your pardon?"

"I believe my words were quite clear."

"You were drawing fire?"

"I'm sorry, did you not understand my words."

She returned his stare. This was not a lie. But he would not understand the truth of it now, nor perhaps ever.

"I find it hard to credit."

"You asked how far I would be willing to go for the cause? I had no idea the house would be occupied by suffragists when

I arrived. I came because my friend invited me, and we were being measured for new dresses so that we can attend a Royal soiree in a couple of weeks.

"As I said, I am in favour of the movement. I am nobody, they are making changes in the world. I am young, they are less so. I chose to run so that the man attacking us might be confused as to the target. I hoped to distract him."

"There was a third shot I understand."

"I was quite scared, there may have been. I did not notice."

"So you have nothing to add?"

"I ducked behind the wall after the first shot, heard Margaret cry out, and after the second I decide to run in the hopes I might save others."

"The first shot hit the camera you were operating?"

"Yes, I was standing on the wall and there is a hole in the arm of my coat where the bullet went through."

"And the second bullet struck the wall behind which you hid."

"Did it?"

"It did."

"Goodness." Maliha did not like the way this was going, the man was not a fool.

"He was either a very bad shot being unable to hit a line of women standing still. Or he was a good shot but not quite good enough to hit you."

Maliha frowned. "Why would someone want to shoot me? I am nobody."

"That, Miss Anderson, is a question I would like to have an answer for. When I spoke to Brighton constabulary, Williams noted that you had withheld information from his investigation. I find that I am forming the same conclusion."

"But, Inspector, the decision to even come here was not made until yesterday morning. There was no plan to it and nobody knew until we left. I am quite sure the Suffragette meeting has been in planning for considerably longer. After all, Margaret's father had intentionally absented himself to spend the weekend in his club." Then she added as an afterthought. "Perhaps he arranged it to scare his wife into leaving the movement."

"And injure his own daughter into the bargain?"

"That was an accident, I think we all know that. A simple ricochet. Besides *he* might not have known his daughter was going to be here either. Perhaps shooting the camera was intentional to scare the attendees."

The inspector stared at her. Of the three options he had, the one that suggested that she was the target was the least likely. She was not sure he had even considered the idea that Lord Creighton-Ward might have done it.

"Then there's the question of whether the household has recently fired any of the staff."

"That line of inquiry is being pursued."

Maliha decided this was a good time to be quiet, before he decided her alternate solutions were simply diversions.

"So you have nothing to add?"

"I don't think so."

"You must remain available until we have finished our investigations here."

"I have to go back to school," she said. "But they don't let us out so you'll know where I am."

"Very well."

She stood up.

"But, Miss Anderson," he said looking up at her. "If I find the slightest evidence that you are somehow involved in all of this I can assure you we will speak again."

"In that case, Inspector, this will be our last goodbye."

She turned around and cringed inside at the bravado of her comment. She really must learn not to intentionally irritate people.

She went back to the Green Suite and found her things had

already been packed. She was not quite sure how she felt about that. It seemed that living this way gave you no privacy whatsoever. The servants knew everything.

The limousine pulled away from the house as the sun was dropping towards the horizon, somewhat later than the time she had been originally meant to leave. The cabin was hot and she explored the little cupboards and drawers until she located a bottle of lemonade.

She was not sure at which point she had decided to go back to the school. Or even whether it had been her own decision but the trip gave her time to think.

And now she could think about the attempted shooting, she trembled a little. Someone had tried to kill her. If the man had been a slightly better shot he would have put the bullet straight through her body and she would have died right there on the patio.

She looked at her hands. They were not shaking but she could feel the fear lurking inside her.

Someone had tried to kill her. But they had failed. Obviously.

The *why* was not in question: she was continuing to investigate the murder of Ethel Jordan. Someone did not want her to do that. But this attack had been very revealing. She may not have learnt much by way of detail but the scope of what she was investigating had opened up.

Ignoring for a moment how they had discovered where she was, it must be an entire organisation behind Jordan's murder, which means the murder was incidental to a bigger plan. Somehow, the girl had become mixed up in something larger, she had a relationship someone did not approve of and because of that they had felt threatened and needed to dispose of her.

They had attempted to kill her somewhere but she had proved to be tougher than they expected and made it all the way back to the school before she finally died.

Had they caught up with her and finished her off in the

school? No, probably not because if someone had added any
blows to her head in the library, there would have been
spatters of blood. And there were none.

They had left her for dead, or she had fought back and
escaped.

She nodded to herself and took a drink of the lemonade
from the bottle. Margaret was right, it was far safer than using
a glass. And it felt daring, the teachers would be appalled.

Who had known she was at Foxley Heath?

All the teachers, the headmistress and Mrs Clemence. The
staff would be able to find out quite easily. Certainly all the
girls in the Upper Sixth, and rumour would inform the rest.
And anyone who was watching the school, such as any of the
journalists still camped outside, or someone pretending to be a
journalist.

So, anybody.

But who knew she was continuing the investigation? Mrs
Lancaster, Matron, Mr Gunnell in the school … and the
woman in the sweet shop. Maliha cursed herself for being a
fool, the woman had been very forthcoming and given her a
considerable amount of information. What was more likely
than she was part of the cabal?

It was dark by the time Maliha arrived back at the school. She
should have reported to the school office but instead went
straight to her room in the infirmary as quickly and as quietly
as she could. The last thing she wanted was to have to talk to
people. Matron was waiting for her.

"Are you alright, Miss Anderson?"

"Yes, but I am exhausted."

"What about poor Miss Creighton-Ward?"

"Just a flesh wound. The bullet had ricocheted before it
struck her and most of its energy was spent. She'll be right as
rain in a few days."

Matron shook her head. "This is a bad business, someone taking pot-shots at Suffragettes is what I heard."

"The police don't want me to talk about it." *But go on believing that.*

"They come in threes, don't they?"

That piqued Maliha's interest tired though she was "Do they?"

"Well, you wouldn't know but little Ena has had bad news as well."

Maliha shook her head. "Ena?"

"She's a scullery maid, sweet little thing. Went off this morning to see her brother, as she always does on a Sunday, only to find he had taken his own life. Poor girl. Mrs Ramsey has let her have a day before she comes back to work."

"That is sad," said Maliha, whatever tiredness she had been feeling fled. "But I don't know any Ena." But she only knew a few of the non-teaching staff by name and face.

"You wouldn't have seen her. Only joined the staff a couple of months ago, such a sweet accent, too. Ena Hogan."

Maliha suddenly was at full attention. The name the woman in the shop had given her: Patrick Hogan.

Ethel Jordan's boyfriend was now dead, too.

19

———————

Maliha managed to persuade Matron that she couldn't go to dinner, and it was agreed that it would be brought to her. She made sure her door was firmly locked the rest of the time, and she stayed away from the window, which looked out to the north.

They were trying to kill her. They had killed Ethel. They had killed one of their own—Hogan must have been ready to inform on them to the police for their actions. Or, at the very least, they were unsure of him.

She sat on the bed and stared at the wall.

Was there any way she could escape this? If she ran away from the school, perhaps. But where could she go?

Tell the police? They had no reason to believe her. The woman in the shop would simply deny the conversation.

But she knew she would do none of those things because of what was inside her. She owed a debt to Margaret, for an injury that was Maliha's doing. And there was still Amelia Johnson, forced to live in a hell she did not deserve.

There was no option. Maliha must go on, but since there was a chance that she herself might be killed in the endeavour, she decided to start a journal. The rest of the evening was spent hunched over a school book detailing the events that led her to this point, along with her own conclusions so far. She returned the book to the rest, where it hid in plain sight.

And finally, feeling calmer and more resigned to a difficult future, she climbed into the bed and went to sleep.

Monday morning and Maliha was awake early as usual. She made some plans for the day, well aware that they might well be upset by what others wanted from her. She allowed time for the interview with Mrs Ramsey that was certain to occur.

Breakfast was strained. Without Margaret to provide a form of conduit between Maliha and the rest of the school, she sat completely alone in the middle of the crowded refectory. There were muttered words around her: Jonah, cursed, witch, murderer. But they were only words, she had heard things as bad and worse.

She was stopped by Mrs Lancaster before she could go back to her room.

"Mrs Ramsey wants to see you."

She simply nodded and headed upstairs to the school office. Someone jostled her on the stairs and she fell forward, catching her hands on the edge of the step. She was kicked in the ankle a couple of times before she regained her footing and hurried on. She told herself it didn't matter, as she avoided all the other girls in the corridor. She decided not to use any of the toilet facilities in the main school from now on, and to be sure to lock her room whenever she left it—though she had done that as a matter of course anyway.

As she entered the school office she emphasised the limp. It would help later in the day if people thought she were incapable of walking.

Mrs Clemence glanced at her once and then ignored her. Maliha sat down in one of the chairs provided and waited. For an hour. She could hear Mrs Ramsey on the telephone in the other room. Eventually however, on a signal that Maliha did not see, Mrs Clemence looked up.

"Go in."

Maliha limped across the room, entered Mrs Ramsey's inner sanctum, where she had been interviewed by the inspector less than a week before. The headmistress sat behind her desk with a look on her face Maliha could not quite decipher. Somewhere between worry and happiness. Almost as if the woman enjoyed the troubles she was dealing with.

"Sit."

Maliha did so in the same hard-backed chair as before.

Mrs Ramsey was not a tall woman and even behind her desk she was not imposing. Her hair was short and white. The wire-rimmed glasses held lenses that had almost no strength. Maliha had wondered more than once whether she really needed them and considered they might be an affectation. The faint smell of alcohol hung in the air.

"Death seems to be following you, Miss Anderson."

"Thankfully not, miss. Margaret suffered only a minor injury."

"She was shot!"

Maliha jumped, she had not been expecting such an outburst.

"One girl is beaten and another is shot and you are present on both occasions."

Maliha had the feeling nothing she could say would help, so she stayed silent. Those in power always preferred silence in their subordinates.

"Answer."

Oh well, it had been worth a try. "I don't know what you want me to say, miss."

"I want an explanation. Tell me now why I shouldn't simply expel you."

"I had the misfortune to be in the wrong place at the wrong time. I went to the library after luncheon and found Ethel. I could not have killed her—"

"Don't say that."

"But I didn't."

"Do not use that word."

If there was anything Maliha loathed it was people who wanted euphemisms because of a real, or pretended, inability to face the real thing. What on earth could she say to imply she had not killed the girl if that word could not be used?

"I didn't do it. The police agreed. And they have a suspect." *The wrong person.* "And I was operating the camera when the attacker fired his gun." She was almost expecting to have that word forbidden as well, but nothing came from the headmistress. "That Margaret was hurt was an accident. It could have been any of the women." *Two inches to the left and it would have been me.*

"Suffragists." The amount of contempt the headmistress got into the word was astonishing.

Maliha bit her tongue to avoid correcting Mrs Ramsey to *Suffragettes.* The suffragists were the peaceful ones, the suffragettes used violence. They would no doubt be considered a thousand times worse.

"So you're saying it had nothing to do with you."

"How could it, Mrs Ramsey?"

Maliha was certain that the woman was desperately trying to think of a way that it could be, and Maliha could even have enlightened her but that would be counter-productive. At the present time being in the school was safer than being out of it. Even though she was going to have to venture forth at some point.

"What am I going to do with you?"

There Maliha *could* help but she made sure to sound sad and concerned instead of pleased. "I am forced to live in the infirmary. I am not attending lessons. There is less than three months to the end of term and I will go home to India."

Mrs Ramsey regarded her then nodded. "You will stay in the infirmary for the rest of your time here. You will not take part in any school activities. You will keep to your room and avoid speaking to anyone. Your meals will be delivered."

Maliha did not let any of her elation show. This was utterly perfect. "Yes, Mrs Ramsey. I will do as you say."

"If Lady Henrietta makes a complaint, I will have you expelled."

"Yes, Mrs Ramsey."

"Go."

"Yes, Mrs Ramsey."

Maliha still limped, just to avoid the idea that she might have been faking before, but the limp would no longer be necessary. She had not felt quite so happy for a very long time. It was as if a burden had been lifted from her.

She would be free to carry out her investigation virtually unhindered.

The first thing she needed to do was talk to Ena Hogan. She wondered how that could be arranged. Since she was supposed to keep to her room she could hardly go wandering about the school. On the other hand, this was below stairs. Other problems presented themselves however, if the girl was nothing more than a scullery maid all she would be doing is washing and cleaning all day.

"Matron?" Maliha poked her head into the main ward.

"In here."

Maliha went through into Matron's office, where she found her with a pile of brown folders which looked to contain medical notes.

Matron waved her into a chair and went on studying the folder, working her way through what appeared to be a series of dated notes. There were two piles of folders on the table: one tall, the other short.

"Your news about Ethel's condition got me worried," she said. "I'm looking for anything in these notes that might indicate any change in the other girls."

"Is that likely?"

"Girls, Maliha," said the woman looking up and removing a pair of glasses from her nose. "Most of them manage not to get themselves in the family way, of course. Most of them manage not to cross swords with a man until she's at least left the school. But there are always those who cannot resist their animal urges, or simply engaging in what's been forbidden."

"I haven't," said Maliha.

"Of course, you haven't, dear. You have more sense in your little finger than most of them possess in their entire bodies."

"Can you tell from those notes?"

Matron shook her head. "Not really, unless there is something obvious."

"I could help."

"No, dear, these are private records. I can't let you see them."

She closed the folder in front of her and added it to the smaller pile. "Did you want something?"

"Mrs Ramsey has decided I have to stay in the infirmary for the rest of the year, not attend any lessons, have my meals delivered, and generally stay out of everybody's way."

"She's covering her back. If anyone asks she can say that she's done what was appropriate but," she paused for dramatic effect. "Cook is not going to appreciate giving you a separate meal nor having someone deliver it."

"Perhaps Ena Hogan could do it."

Matron laughed. "And what interest do you have in that little chit?"

"I'd like to ask her about her brother."

Matron gave her a penetrating look. "This is something to do with Ethel's murder."

Maliha said nothing but held the woman's gaze.

"I see. So you'd like me to have a word with my friend and make sure it's Ena who delivers the food."

"Just today, I don't care who does it any other time."

The was a knock on her door about five minutes after the lunchtime bell had rung. She had spent the morning working her way through more of David Copperfield. It was tough going but she was not going to be defeated by the long-winded descriptions.

She unlocked the door and saw a lanky girl with dark hair holding a tray. She stepped back and let the girl in. Maliha caught herself, she was calling the servant a girl in her mind and yet she must be ten years older than Maliha. Either that or her life had been hard. Or both.

"Put it on the table please."

She did and then turned to go. "You're Ena?"

"I am, miss." Irish. Maliha's mind went into a whirl, could this be a Fenian plot after all? She caught herself. No point trying to run ahead to the conclusion without any information.

"Sit down," she pointed to the bed. "Don't worry, Cook knows you'll be delayed. You're to wait until I've finished the meal." So Maliha sat at the table and looked at the stew with mashed potatoes and peas.

"Ena Hogan?"

"Yes, miss."

Maliha had considered how she could approach this but had decided that now they were trying to kill her she might as well be direct in her own approach. There was no benefit in trying to remain hidden.

"How did you discover the secret passage to the library?"

The girl made a noise of surprise but kept her hands at her sides. They were raw with cleaning and the skin drawn tight over the joints as the girl gripped the blanket. She did not answer the question.

"I just have to talk to Inspector Williams at Brighton constabulary and you'll be in gaol before you can blink. I have no desire to cause you problems but you *will* answer my questions. And if I can keep you out of the trouble that will come, I will."

"I've not done anything."

"Neither did Amelia Johnson but they've got her in Bedlam. Is that what you want?"

"You've got nothing on me."

Maliha dug her fork into the stew and took a mouthful. She chewed it slowly. She thought carefully. There was a small silver cross on a chain around the girl's neck.

"Your brother was murdered and they made it look like suicide. He won't be able to go to Heaven unless he gets the last rites and no priest will do that for a suicide. If you tell me what I need to know, and I can prove he was murdered, they will give him what he needs most now that he's dead."

Ena Hogan relaxed a little. "You would do that? Why should you care about my brother?"

"I don't. I only care about the truth."

She was silent again and looked at the door as if she was wondering if she could escape, and if she did whether it would do any good. Maliha noticed the stew was much better than usual. It was lighter and less oily, and the herbs were more delicate.

"Who made this stew? It wasn't Cook."

"New chef from London. Cook's in a right state over it."

Maliha nodded. "So, how did you find the secret passage?"

"I was cleaning. I like to read adventure stories."

"That was the tax section."

"Why would a school have shelves of tax books? In my stories there are always secret doors behind the shelves in libraries." Maliha laughed, and Ena looked affronted. "And I was right!"

"That's not why I was laughing," said Maliha. *You asked the one question I should have asked but didn't.* "Why did you and your brother come to Brighton?"

"Friend of Pat, his man, said he knew where we could get jobs. Things aren't good at home. So we thought, why not?"

"And Cook hired you."

"They were down a scullery maid and I ain't afraid of hard work. Cook's from County Cork and we're from Dublin but she didn't hold it against me."

"What happened to the girl you replaced?"

Ena shrugged. "Someone said she left one Sunday to see her mam but never came back."

"Convenient," said Maliha quietly and ate some more of the stew. It might be red meat but whoever had created this really did know how to do it. And the mash was a good consistency and free of any lumps, which must be a first for the school. She turned her attention back to her guest. There were two, perhaps three deaths, and one attempted murder, and those were the only ones she was aware of. It all pointed to this being something very big.

"So your brother and Ethel Jordan."

Ena shook her head. "I said he was crazy. That girl was a demon to everyone, I think she enjoyed causing pain, but for him she softened. You don't believe me. I didn't believe it and I saw it with these eyes. When she was with him she had a smile. So sad it was, as if she was broken inside and Pat was the only thing that made her whole. They would get together whenever they could. I knew what they were doing…you know, but what could I say? He was happy and he made her —" she struggled for a moment, "—complete."

Maliha listened, trying to squeeze the Ethel Jordan she knew into a mould that did not seem to fit.

"You told her about the passage?"

Ena shook her head. "I did not. She wasn't soft for me, I had more than one bruise from that harridan. I told Pat because it was the sort of thing his man wanted to know. Pat must have told her."

"Did Pat ever come into the school?"

"Not that I know. Though if he and that girl had planned anything there's no reason I should know."

Maliha thought about it as she continued to eat. No, probably not, otherwise Amelia would have found out. Chances are she stuck like glue to Ethel, at least as much as she could.

She finished the last of the food then placed her knife and fork together on the plate. Ena stood up.

"Thank you, Ena. That has been very helpful but there are a couple more things. Would I be right in thinking they had a special place where they would meet?"

"There was. A shed on the seashore, near where the railway starts. Pat used to call it his love nest, it was easy for both of them to get to."

Maliha knew the area from her walks along the coast.

"So, is Pat's man over here too?"

"He is not, but there's another Pat spoke to."

"And has this one ever spoken to you?"

"He has not."

"He will. And, when he does, I would like you to let me know."

Ena hesitated for a moment. "You think they killed Pat?"

"I'm very sure. I can only think they have a secret and suspected Pat told Ethel. Then perhaps Pat told his boss he'd made the girl pregnant. And they decided they needed to kill her, and then your brother." Even as she was saying it Maliha was less sure of herself. It was very vague.

"If they killed Pat, I'll do what I can to help."

"Is there anything you can tell me about Pat's 'man'?"

"Taliesin."

"What?"

"Taliesin. Pat said it once when he had been out with his friends."

"In what context?"

"He used it like it was an event. Something about Taliesin showing the way to the future."

Maliha filed it away. It had to be a codename. "These people are planning something serious, Ena, and they will not hesitate to kill again."

"If you can save my brother's soul, Miss Anderson. I will do what has to be done."

Then she put down the tray again and reached her hands to her neck. She withdrew a thin dark cord with a key hanging from it. "The police let me have my brother's things. I think you'll be needing this."

And she left.

20

Maliha paced the room. She wasn't happy for several reasons. The talk with Ena had been revealing and at least she now felt she understood Ethel Jordan better. But the intentions of the gang, of the Taliesin men perhaps, were unclear.

They might be Fenians and planning an attack but would they attack a girl's school? They had gone to great lengths to get someone on the inside, even made sure their girl was Irish so there was more chance Cook would choose her.

It was no good, there just wasn't enough information. All she could be sure about was that a murderous gang—including a sharp shooter—was interested in the school, and very interested in dissuading Maliha from investigating.

Perhaps they had not intended to kill her, only scare her. She shook her head. No, if that had been the case there would have been a warning message and then the shot. And it would only have been a single shot, not two more.

She listened for the lesson bell. It went off finally and she allowed another five minutes for people to settle, latecomers to arrive and the teachers to get into their lessons.

With her door firmly locked behind her, wearing her non-uniform clothes with a coat over the top she strode through the school corridors. She reached the library swiftly, unlocked it and was inside without being seen. She had about two hours but did not think she would be that long.

Maliha went to the window and looked out. The day was another sunny one although high clouds were scudding in from the south. The union flag was standing straight out from the flag pole and quivering. There were still two cars parked out on the road. A man lounged against one of them smoking a cigarette. He was looking towards the school but did not react to her standing there. The light on the glass would make her invisible to the outside.

Dr Underwood's electric torch was where she had left it the previous week. And it did not take her long to negotiate the tunnel down to the beach.

She realised she had forgotten to check the tides. The sea was in but was not up to the cliff. But the waves were big and crashed heavily throwing up spray that was blown in on the wind. She deposited the torch a few steps up to ensure it didn't get wet, pulled her coat around her with the hood up then stepped out on to the rocks and into the water-filled wind.

Turning right towards Brighton she followed the worn path. The day being bright, there were more people out on the beaches—despite the brisk breeze. A couple of kite-flyers were braving the blast over on the main beach. But no one else was chancing the path she was on.

It took her considerably less time to walk directly to the Volks railway terminus than it had before since she was following the direct route. She passed ranks of bathing machines with their canvas walls flapping noisily in a constant rattle. Slightly further up the beach were the sheds, seven of them.

They were all constructed of wood, a couple had rooves of corrugated iron, the others were just boards. The paintwork was peeling, weathered by damp and salt. In all cases, the main door faced the sea, though their construction seemed somewhat haphazard. They were not built in a line but looked as if God had held them in his hand and scattered them.

Maliha had no idea who owned them. She should have asked which one Patrick and Ethel used, but as she drew closer she could see one of them had a black ribbon tied to the handle. Something Patrick Hogan would have done before they killed him, Maliha suspected. She shook her head again, it still did not fit with her image of Ethel Jordan.

The door had a padlock. It was not very big but sufficient to deter the casual thief. Maliha brought out the key and it fitted. Sand in the lock made it grind as she turned and unhooked it. A sudden gust whipped her hair around her face and blew the door open with a bang. She stepped in quickly and pushed it shut against the wind. An oiled bolt slid smoothly into place when she pushed it and the door stayed closed, though it rattled.

Maliha turned her back on the door and faced the room. The window on the right had a net curtain in place and a heavier one pulled back. There was a single bed, neatly made and she recognised the school's required hospital corners in the smooth blanket. At the foot of the bed was a small round table and two mismatched chairs. The mirror on the wall was blotched in a couple of places but serviceable. In the corner was what had probably been a discarded wardrobe with its doors taken off. Some clothes hung in it, at least one dress, skirt and blouse. And a man's shirt and trousers. Nearest to her, on the left, another table, with a bowl for washing. Finally, there were pegs on the wall from which hung a couple of cups, and there was some crockery and cutlery all placed neatly.

They had been playing at happy families.

She noticed something flat lying on the table and approached. A picture frame with more black ribbon around it. She lifted it and saw a face she recognised and one she didn't. Ethel Jordan smiling and the young man beside her, their cheeks pressed together. It was Ethel's smile that caused Maliha to catch her breath. She was happy. Truly happy.

Maliha slammed the picture face down.

She stared around again. How could she be happy? How *dare* she be happy? How could a girl who delighted in the agony of others stir compassion? Maliha felt her sense of reason had been violated. Waves of hate and sympathy competed for dominance.

She pushed them both away.

Looking down, she noticed a rug that had become rucked up when she opened the door.

Why was a rug there when it would be moved every time the door was opened? Maliha kicked it away. The brown wood was stained and darker. Something clung in the cracks.

Maliha crouched down and touched the dark mark. It was dry, of course, but just slightly tacky the longer she pressed her finger. Ethel's blood stained the floor of her love-nest. This is where she had been beaten to death. She looked around; every other surface was clean even of dust. Someone had tidied up.

Ethel would have told him she was with child. She would have been proud that their happy family would be blessed with a child. Would he have been pleased? Yes. The photograph told the story. He was as happy with her as she was with him. Someone else had committed the murder.

Maliha stood up again. Was the weapon still here? The crime would have been committed in a rage. The number of blows told of the anger—as did the fact the murderer had failed to confirm she was dead.

Twice now she had seen the death of Ethel Jordan.

She looked at the bed once more and knelt down, avoiding the stain on the boards. The brass fittings of a case glinted. She reached in and dragged it out. The case felt light enough to be empty but something shifted inside when she lifted it. The bed creaked noisily when she sat and dropped the case beside her. The case wasn't new but hadn't seen a lot of wear.

Perhaps it was one the Hogans had used when they came over from Dublin.

The locks clicked open and she lifted the lid. Maliha jumped at the grotesque monkey face staring out at her. It was an ugly thing, but just a stuffed toy in what might be a circus outfit. Again, it was not new and some of the stitching was loose. What really attracted her attention was the Roedean exercise book, one of the thicker ones in which you might be expected to write lots of essays. And it was blue, which meant Religious Education.

Ethel had written her name on the outside and nothing else. Uncertain as to whether she really wanted to do it, Maliha gripped the card cover and opened it.

I Love Him. It hurts.

There was nothing else on the first page. It was certainly in a female hand and resembled the style the school tried to instil in all the girls. It had been written with a fountain pen but Maliha had not seen one here. Nothing of value had been left here. Either Pat Hogan or the person who had murdered Ethel had cleared the place. They did not want any evidence.

Something crashed against the door. Maliha thought for a moment that perhaps the wind had blown a chair, or piece of driftwood. Then it came again and she realised it sounded like someone slamming their bare palm against the wood.

"Alice Anderson! Open the door."

The voice was completely unknown to her: Male, middle-aged, London. And he did not know her, since he used the name that she did not. Not a policeman. Probably not one of the criminals since they were more likely to shoot than knock —regardless of how noisily he had done it. He slapped the door again.

"Open the bloody door, it's pouring down out here!"

She closed her eyes. There was no other way out of here and she had limited time. He might go away if she kept quiet but she doubted it.

"Step away from the door and I'll open it."

"Hurry up, Jeezus, I'm getting soaked."

The rain was now thundering on the roof and the wind was even driving it through the cracks. Maliha leaned her weight against the door and slid the bolt back. She stepped away but had her foot set to block it from fully opening. The wind and rain ripped through the room the moment there was a gap and a man's hand grabbed the door edge. He pushed it back against her shoe as he squeezed through and slammed it shut with the full force of his body.

She determined immediately that he was not properly dressed for the squall that had piled in from the English Channel. Just a tweed jacket that was too small to fasten across his beer gut, matching trousers and shoes unlikely to keep water out.

He had needed a shave a couple of days ago and if he had owned a cap it had probably gone in the wind. His hair was thin, straggly, and standing out from his almost-bald head covered in droplets of water. His front had looked damp in the moments she had seen it. His back was dripping with water.

He got the door secured but continued to lean against it as if he didn't trust the bolt.

"Christ. Give me a smog-filled alley any day over this fresh air and weather."

He turned slowly, and she could see him taking in the scene perhaps as thoroughly as she had. Perhaps he was a policeman after all.

"Who are you?" she said finally, since he did not seem keen on introducing himself after barging in on her.

"Anything good in that?" He was looking at the exercise book on the bed where she had dropped it.

"I am not going to enter into any discussion with you until you tell me who in the world you are."

"James Munroe," he said with a finality that suggested it would answer any question. "I don't answer to Jim, mind."

"A name is hardly sufficient, Mr Munroe."

When he faced her she was reminded of the occasion she

had seen a train being rotated on a turntable. Slow and ponderous but unstoppably powerful. His attention landed on her like a weight.

He thrust out his hand. "Agent of His Majesty's Special Investigation Service."

"I have never heard of such a thing."

He reached into an inside pocket of his jacket and pulled out a leather pouch. It was held shut by a thin purple ribbon wound around a tiny capstan. He undid it methodically and held it up so that the two folds opened and the paper inside was revealed. She glanced over it to make sure she had every word. The bottom of the warrant was most interesting: A small royal seal and what could be the signature of Edward VIII.

It could still be a fake, of course, but the fact that someone had gone to the trouble of faking a warrant using the name of service she had never heard of, seemed to confirm his story. It would be simpler to fake credentials for an organisation that did exist.

"Very well, what do you want?"

"Miss Anderson, I am here to offer you a job."

"You are offering me *employment*?"

"That is correct."

"Here?" She looked around at the sad little room. "In a shack on a beach in the middle of a storm?"

"There's a decent pub up on the front not far, but I don't think that would help, we'd both be sodden by the time we got there."

"I do not go into pubs, I am a pupil at Roedean School. You are aware of this?"

He dragged a chair from under the small table and sat. It creaked under his weight.

"I know who you are, Miss Anderson."

She remembered the man leaning against the car outside the school just before she took to the tunnel. "You have been watching me."

He shrugged. "It's not as if I could walk into the school and demand to talk to you."

"Not even with that warrant?"

He smiled. "Make no mistake, Miss Anderson, it gives me the authority to do that. But there are too many eyes on the school just now."

"A convenient excuse."

"You're very sceptical."

"Yes."

"What can I do to convince you?"

She paused for a moment, mostly for effect. "I cannot think of anything."

"How do you know I'm not here to silence you?"

"I don't."

"And that doesn't worry you?"

"Worry is a waste of time, Mr Munroe. Either you can do nothing about a situation, or you can do something. In either instance worrying has no value."

"Philosophical too."

"I consider it mere practicality."

"And if I attacked you?"

"You might find that I am not as defenceless as you think."

His eyes narrowed and he looked at her hands clasped in her lap. "You have no weapon."

"Don't I?"

He moved awkwardly as if discomforted. It was pure bluff, of course, but he could not know what cards she was playing.

Then he smiled. "Very good. You see that's precisely the kind of attitude that works in our organisation."

"And what sort of work do you actually do?"

"We investigate."

She gave him what she considered to be her best withering look.

"If you were to read my warrant in detail," he said. "You would see that I have the complete and full authority of the

Crown, and the freedom to move and investigate whatever I wish."

"*Outside of the British Isles,*" she said.

He was taken aback. "You … read that?"

"I did," she said. "So, Mr Munroe, what are you doing here?"

"As I said, I am offering you employment."

"I am not interested."

"Unlimited resources, excitement and adventure."

"I am uncertain as to why you might think any of that is of interest to me."

"Miss Anderson, ever since the unfortunate death of the girl in your school you have been applying yourself to the solution of that puzzle. That is why you left the school last week to go into Brighton. That is why you went to the home of the Creighton-Wards. That is why you are here. You cannot leave it alone."

Maliha allowed herself a gentle smile. He would not be able to interpret it for what it was. Clearly, she had not been as subtle as she thought she had, but he was completely wrong about the trip to the Creighton-Wards. That it had revealed something of the case to her was irrelevant, it was not why she had gone. He was right about one thing though, she could not leave it alone. It was like an itch that must be scratched but cannot be reached, but she was not going to tell him that.

"You have the better of me, sir. Which surely means I am not the right person for the job."

"Dr Underwood assured me that you are."

"Dr Underwood is part of this organisation?"

"I cannot say precisely, but he is important."

"I see." She looked at the window opposite. The noise of the wind had dropped. Perhaps the squall had blown itself out. She checked her watch and stood up. He jumped to his feet out of politeness. There was so little room he was uncomfortably close. "Well, I am sorry that your recruitment mission has been so unproductive but I can assure you I want nothing more than to return to my home in India once the school year is complete. Becoming an agent of the Crown is not something that appeals."

"That is a shame. We find that the fairer sex has at least as good a record of success as the men, and often in far more delicate situations."

"As a suffragist, I am pleased that you employ women, Mr Munroe, but I am afraid you will have to do without me." She did not fail to notice the way he almost flinched when he said *suffragist*. "But if I may ask a question?"

"Please go ahead, though I can't guarantee I'll answer."

"Was it you who shot at me at the Creighton-Ward house?"

"Shot at *you*?"

She smiled. "Well, that's good to know."

"But I didn't answer."

"Yes, you did," she said. "Do you think this is a Fenian plot to murder the princes and disrupt the Royal line?"

"Fenian plot?"

Now she frowned. "Honestly, Mr Munroe, you call yourself an investigator but you know nothing of this business whatsoever."

"Just one moment, miss. I have not been investigating this matter. Nor am I permitted to, according to the charter. I was only here to speak to you."

"Then why not do it when I ventured into Brighton last week? Since you were clearly following me."

"I had not decided whether you were the right material."

"Even though Dr Underwood—who is important in your organisation—said I was?" She drew herself up to her full height, sadly rather less than his. "You, sir, are a liar. You are extremely interested in this case even though you are forbidden to investigate it. Whether or not you were telling the truth about wishing to recruit me, I do not believe for one moment that was your motivation in seeking me out." She took a breath. "On the contrary, you are forbidden to investigate, but I am not and you sought to use me as your proxy until you had sufficient evidence to bring it to whoever you need to impress."

Even if her height was less than his, he seemed to shrink beneath the onslaught of her words.

"You know nothing of this case. And you will get nothing further from me."

She slipped her hand into her pocket and pulled out Ethel Jordan's pen knife. It was well-oiled and the blade snapped out just as Munroe took a step in her direction. She pressed the point into his gut. He stopped. She reached back and released the door bolt. The wind may have dropped but it was still strong and the door slammed open behind her.

"I warned you, Mr Munroe," she said. "I may not be able to do a great deal of damage with this knife but it will hurt and you will bleed. Consider what I am about to say carefully. You and I are not, and never will be, partners. I will not solve this case so that you can get a leg-up in your business. However, I *am* in a position to communicate with Dr Underwood any time I choose. Rest assured that I will write a letter to him and have it lodged in a safe place. If you bother me again I will have the letter sent. Do you understand?"

There was hate in his eyes. "Yes."

"But there's more. You see that shooting at the Creighton-Ward house, that you—along with everyone else—assumed was an attack on the Suffragettes, was an attempt on my life. That's why the first bullet hit the camera and made a hole in my coat. The second hit the wall just above my head where I had hidden. The third shot at me as I ran along the path, and not at the other women at all. They were such an easy target, the assassin could not have missed had he been aiming for them." She paused for breath. "I do not wish to die, but if I do that letter will be sent."

"What are you saying?"

"That you will remain here in Brighton and prevent any harm coming to me."

His silence told her everything she needed to know. He understood. Not that she cared whether he stayed or not.

"I am going to leave now," she said. "Please do not make a scene. The electric railway vehicle has just arrived and there will be a number of passengers. I can raise the alarm with a scream quite easily. I suggest you remain here for an hour or so. Don't worry, I am returning directly to the school."

She stepped backwards still holding the knife out. The wind whipped her hair as she pulled the door shut. She heard the bolt close on the other side and heaved a sigh of relief.

Gripping the little knife tightly, she hurried back along the coast. The tide was on the turn. She wanted to run but forced herself to keep an even pace. It would not do to injure an ankle on the uneven terrain.

It was only when she slipped into the tunnel and picked up the firm heavy weight of the torch that Maliha allowed herself to breath more easily. At the library end, she put down the torch, folded the pen-knife and put it away.

Her hands were still trembling.

21

———

Two weeks. That was all the time she had before the dance. It was obvious to her there was to be some attempt on the lives of the father and son, the Princes George and Edward. Perhaps just one but if they could get both that would cause tremendous disruption.

It must be a Fenian plot. There were plenty of countries that could benefit from such an upheaval, but it was the Irish who were the most active in that area. It couldn't be the Germans since their royal family was so closely linked. Likewise, the Russians would be unlikely to do it, besides they were wrapped up with their internal problems.

France did not seem a likely choice either because of the *Entente Cordiale*. While there were people who would be happy to see that agreement destroyed there did not, in her mind, seem to be a lot to gain. The British still did not really like the French, and the feeling was mutual. The Germans objected because they felt threatened by the Anglo-French accord— they had even tried to disrupt it three years earlier by confronting the French over Morocco, hoping the British would break their side of the agreement.

The move had failed, making relations with Germany more difficult. Perhaps it was the Germans, after all? But Maliha could not see how killing the princes would cause a breakdown of the agreement with France. Unless they could pin it on the French.

She shook her head. The Fenians were the only significant group to whom that action would make any sense. And there were already Irish people involved.

"But I'm just trying to solve the murder," she said out loud to the wall. "I mustn't get side-tracked."

Dinner came and went. It wasn't Ena who served it this time.

Then came another knock on her door. Maliha frowned, it couldn't be Margaret because she was at home nursing her wounded shoulder. She went to the door.

"Who is it?"

"Jenny," said the voice. "Jennifer Wendlefield."

Maliha had long since ceased to be surprised by the guests she was entertaining since the murder. She opened the door but it wasn't just Jenny, it was Antonia as well. They entered and stood awkwardly in the middle of the room. Antonia took Jenny's hand so naturally it was almost as if they did not realise they were doing it. Once the door was shut, Maliha gestured towards the bed.

"I don't have many places to sit," she said. "You two take the bed." *The way you prefer.*

The two sat so close their legs touched. Maliha took the chair by the table where the letter to Dr Underwood lay, half-written. Maliha was still not completely convinced that this Special Investigation Service was real, it made writing the letter more difficult. She glanced at the window that gave out on to the fields and hills. The curtain was heavy and fully pulled. No one could see in. She was acutely aware that James Munroe might be out there even now.

"How can I help you?"

The two lovers glanced at one another. Jenny was the taller and it seemed that she took the lead in their relationship.

"We're not sure," said Jenny.

"Well, there's not much to say then."

Antonia had dark eyes, almost as dark as Maliha's. "We need help."

And I have a sign outside my door saying 'help given'? "I don't understand."

"We want to run away," said Antonia. "We *need* to get away."

"Go somewhere," said Jenny. "Safe."

Maliha sighed, she was thinking about the words from Matron stating how the girls' relationship must not continue. "I don't know how I am supposed to help."

They looked at each other again. Jenny spoke: "Somewhere we can go where we don't need to hide."

"I doubt there is such a place, and besides," she said. "It's not that simple."

"What do you mean?"

Maliha looked at Antonia, she seemed very sad. "You're a Prussian princess, they have plans for you."

Jenny's hand went straight to Antonia's knee as if to protect her from Maliha's words.

"How do *you* know?" said Antonia. She did not deny it.

"Which part? That you're a princess or that they have plans for you? Your accent in German gave me the first clue. The vehicle that picks you up every holiday was another, the royals never could choose anything other than a Daimler. Once my interest was piqued, I read the papers and your parent's schedule coincided with your own travel. It wasn't that complex a deduction. And since you are the great granddaughter of Wilhelm I, yes, it's not hard to realise they have plans for you."

"I don't want any part of their plans," said Antonia. "They'll just marry me off to some old English noble to help the politics."

"The world has changed," said Jenny, leaning forward. "They just haven't realised it. The adults are still trying to run our lives but we don't want that."

Maliha shook her head. "It's not that I don't understand. But there's nowhere you can go where other people won't judge you."

"Do you?" said Jenny.

"No." Not that she had ever thought about it before but now that she did she realised she had spoken the truth. She did not judge. "As long as you're happy, why should it matter to me?"

"I knew you were the right person to come to," said Antonia.

"You were right." And the two of them faced one another, inches apart. Antonia glanced back at Maliha for a moment then she leaned forward and planted a kiss on Jenny's lips. They closed their eyes and savoured one another.

Maliha frowned. "That's not getting us anywhere."

They broke apart as if they had been naughty but with little smiles on their faces. Jenny in particular went red with embarrassment.

"We…" Antonia squeezed her lover's hand. "I'm sorry but we've never done that when anyone else was about."

"I should think not," said Maliha. "Even if one of you had been a man, the shock of such licentious behaviour would have split the foundations of the school."

"You really don't care?"

"Why should I?"

"Everyone else does."

"Except for the ones like you," said Maliha. "You haven't read Sappho, of course."

"Sappho?" said Antonia.

"Ancient Greek woman," said Maliha, "wrote poems about how she loved women, and men come to that. Quite detailed, some of it."

Jenny seemed the most surprised. "Both?"

"Why not?"

"I told you—" said Jenny to Antonia. "—we're not the only ones." She turned to Maliha. "Tonia was worried."

"Does that mean we could find somewhere in Greece, Miss Anderson?"

"No, I—" *or perhaps?* "—it depends on how much money you have and how far you're willing to go."

"I don't have a lot," said Jenny. "My parents spend most of theirs keeping me here."

"I can get plenty," said Antonia. "I just have to go home."

Jenny turned. "You can't steal, not even for us."

"I don't have to steal, I have my own. There's a lot of jewellery. Gifts from rich relatives, that sort of thing. We can get money for that, can't we?"

They turned back, this time with some hope.

What am I doing? "There are a lot of Greek islands, some are very small. If you went to one of those I don't suppose anyone will care who you are or what you do with each other. But you would have to cover your tracks very well. You would have to just disappear from here."

"That sounds wonderful," said Antonia.

"Does it?" said Maliha. Her voice became harsh. "Even if you could get away without being followed, you two have very little idea of what it's like to have to work for a living, even if you were able to find somewhere. You can't just live on the money. Yes, it would probably last a long time in a place like that but it would run out eventually. You'll need to work to live."

Antonia looked hurt and defiant in the way she lifted her chin. "I am not soft."

"Beautifully soft," said Jenny.

Give me strength. "Stop it, that's just the sort of thing that will get you into trouble. You're not dealing with the truth of this. Do you think this will be some fun adventure? The world is not a safe place. You could die or be killed. From disease, from animal bites, food poisoning, from thieves and murderers. Two defenceless young women, ripe for the *picking*."

"When you say picking…" said Antonia.

"You know what I mean. And that would be men."

Jenny squeezed Antonia's knee again. "You're trying to dissuade us but a minute ago you were giving us hope."

"Because you need to be shocked. You're living in a dream, here in this school. You have no idea what it's like to be ripped from your home and planted somewhere where everything is different and even the food makes you sick."

Jenny nodded. "I remember, Miss Anderson. Can I call you Alice?"

"No."

"Sorry. But I do remember when you came here," said Jenny. "You were not happy."

"This is not about me," said Maliha. "But I understand being an outcast and shunned by society in a way that you do not. I understand being dropped into a culture where nothing makes any sense. You do not understand these things. Why don't you simply be close friends and indulge in your passions when you can? The British are very good at looking the other way."

This time it was Jenny who got angry. "Because it's not about passion, Anderson. This is about love. If I were never permitted to touch Tonia again I would still love her until the end of the world. She is everything to me. We cannot be parted."

Antonia looked at her partner and then rested her head on her shoulder. "That's how it is, Miss Anderson. If you cannot help us find somewhere to settle then we will just run. Anywhere."

Maliha stopped arguing. Jenny opened her mouth to say something but Maliha held up her hand and the girl said nothing. Maliha got to her feet and paced, almost forgetting she had guests.

Why not do it? She had nothing vested in British society. It had done nothing for her and had even attempted to destroy her own world. She was a suffragist in her heart even if she did not wear the colours on her sleeve. Why not spoil the plans of a western patriarchal society? She understood the injustice of a girl incarcerated against her will for a crime that was not hers. Wasn't what they planned for Antonia just the same? A gilded cage is still a cage. Forced to give herself to the pleasures of some man whose very touch would make her want to kill herself?

Am I over-romanticising their relationship?

No. She had seen the pashes and affections girls had in regard to each other. But this was not the same. These two did care for one another. True, it was a young love and, because of that, over-sentimental, but she felt that it was something that would last. Romeo and Juliet cast as two women. Back when it was first produced Juliet would have been a boy. So, what difference?

I have become an old woman, and a matchmaker. Grandmother would be proud.

Except her mother's mother was not proud that her daughter had married a westerner and had this half-caste child.

The logical progression from a willingness to try was the question as to whether it could be done at all. But perhaps the decision came first. Decide to do it and a way would be found.

"Very well," she said turning very suddenly to face them. Antonia jumped. "I will assist you in this mad scheme of yours, but there are conditions."

"Name them," said Jenny.

"You will make enquiries on my behalf about the death of Ethel Jordan."

"Why?" said Antonia.

"Because only a fool would think that she was murdered by Amelia Johnson."

"I never liked Johnson," said Antonia. "She was odd. And

the way she hung around Jordan seemed like she wanted to
be hurt."

"She did."

That shut them both up. It was a concept they were not
equipped to deal with.

"But," continued Maliha. "She did not commit the crime,
it was impossible for her to do so. No reason, no opportunity,
and no means."

"But the police—"

"Are hushing it up because the ruling classes want to keep
this school running. They need somewhere to throw the girls
they don't know what to do with." *Even if the police think it's a
hotbed of suffragist idealism.*

Antonia was nodding at that.

"But my parents put me here so I would have a better
chance in the world," said Jenny.

"And mine," said Maliha. "How little they understand
how the world works. But that's not the point, I need to know
everything you can discover about Jordan."

Jenny hesitated and then nodded. "What else?"

"You will have to trust me with your money, so that I can
buy passage for you."

"We could hire a flyer," said Antonia.

"And you would need someone to fly it, and then that
person would remember you and tell the police about the two
girls he flew somewhere."

"Couldn't we bribe him?" said Jenny.

"Certainly, until the moment he decided he could make
more money by selling his story to the newspapers."

Antonia shook her head. "Not everybody is dishonest."

"That's true, do let me know when you have perfected the
means of telling one from the other," said Maliha. "Is there
anything of value you can get before next weekend?"

Antonia hesitated and then pulled off the small ring from
her little finger. She held it out.

"You don't even know if you can trust me."

Antonia gave a said smile. "We have kissed in front of you, I think it is too late to be worrying about that, don't you?"

Maliha walked over and held out her hand so Antonia could drop the ring into her palm it was heavier than she expected.

"It's gold," said Antonia.

Maliha handed it back. "Keep it. But I will need cash and plenty of it."

"Is there anything else you want from us?" asked Jenny.

"Not at present. However, come and visit every other evening after dinner. Although—" she glanced at her watch. "—not too late since I may be required to play card games with Matron."

The girls got up slowly, reluctantly, their hands entwined.

"Look," said Maliha. "I'm going to be off with Matron until about nine o'clock. If you two would like to stay here, perhaps talk about your plans. What you think you might like to do? That would be acceptable."

They stared at her. The unspoken part of her offer, that they could spend time alone together, to do as they wished without the likelihood of being discovered, hung in the air.

"Thank you," whispered Antonia.

"Don't make a mess of my bed."

Jenny went bright red.

"And you need to keep the noise down. I am aware of how loud your pleasure can be."

It was Antonia's turn to look horrified, her lips formed the word *how* soundlessly.

"I happened to pass the teacher's common room in the middle of the night."

Once more they were speechless with embarrassment.

"I will lock you in and slide the key under the door. If you would do me the service of leaving the key here and not locking it when you leave."

She went to the door and stopped. "One final thing, your relationship is known to some of the staff here, including

Matron. I may need you to pretend to have a break-up at some point before we spirit you away. Can you do that?"

They nodded, still unable to express a coherent thought after the discovery that their passion had been overheard.

Maliha shut the door behind her, locked it and slid the key underneath. She was quite certain she was not the only person to have overheard them at some point. They were very bad at hiding their actions, perhaps they would be better at being enemies.

22

—————

The card games with Matron and her friends had gone off smoothly. Nobody asked any awkward questions and Maliha had gathered that Cook's nose was very thoroughly out of joint since the organisers of the dance event had installed their own chef. This *man* was now getting the kitchen running on his own schedule and to his personal standards.

Which were a great deal higher than Cook's apparently. While, in private, Cook had nothing good to say about him or his techniques, the fact remained that those who were consuming the food created under his instructions were enjoying it far more than they ever had Cook's own. And that only made it worse.

"Surely Cook should take this opportunity to learn?" said Maliha to Matron.

"Her pride has been pricked. She'll never let that go."

Mr Pimm asked about Margaret's injury and was happy enough when Maliha explained it was not serious.

"But a girl from this school getting shot?" he said.

"It could have been much worse." *I could have been killed.*

But the time passed swiftly enough, and soon she was back

in her room. Jenny and Antonia had followed her instructions to the letter, and the bed had been made—it was less wrinkled than when she had left it. She pulled back the cover and sniffed. There was little in the way of lingering scent, for which she was grateful.

It had been a difficult day. The encounter with James Munroe had been upsetting, she suspected that perhaps he was not doing very well in his position and was concerned they might fire him. Well, if that was the way he treated women, or girls, then perhaps that was just as well.

She sat down and pulled the letter she had been writing from the desk. There was no lock on it so the lovers could have looked through her things. It did not matter, she had very little to hide and they were probably more interested in each other.

Although she tried, she could not concentrate on what she needed to say to Dr Underwood. She was lacking focus tonight. She sneezed and realised her eyes felt heavy. She had got quite wet this afternoon, not as drenched as Munroe but still wet and cold because the wind had gone straight through her coat.

Maliha could not afford to be ill. There was far too much to do. How would she help Jenny and Antonia if she was stuck in bed? Let alone solve the problem of Jordan's murder.

Her frustration with her weak and annoying body broke out in a wordless cry which cracked in the middle.

She sat back and sniffed. There was no point fighting it: She was sick. On the positive side, she was in the right place.

It had just come over her so fast, she shook her head then wished she hadn't because a headache had started as well. She growled and pushed herself to her feet. What was it the Buddhists said about the body? "To keep the body in good health is a duty."

The trouble was that Maliha saw her body as something that just got in the way, and she had not time for its foibles, or aches and pains. Getting ill was just an insult.

Unfortunately, getting annoyed about it was not going to help.

She found Matron in her office and promptly sneezed again.

Matron looked up. "I thought you were looking a bit peaky. Back to your room and into bed. I'll bring something for you."

Maliha said nothing but turned back to the door.

"And that'll teach you to go gallivanting about in a storm."

Why do people say things like that? thought Maliha. *It doesn't mean anything. And it won't even teach me to not go gallivanting about in a storm. If I need to.*

Getting undressed seemed harder than usual and by the time she'd pulled her nightdress on she was exhausted. Then she burst into tears and immediately became furious with herself for being so emotional when there was no reason. She didn't cry. She never cried.

She suppressed the emotion and forced it back down inside. She was sniffling when Matron came in with a tray on which was a bowl covered with a towel.

After putting the tray on the table, she brought the chair to the bed in front of where Maliha sat, dabbing at her eyes and nose. She then placed the bowl on the chair. Maliha could feel the heat coming off it and the acrid smell of something no doubt intended to be medicinal.

"Put the towel over your head and breathe the steam for a while," said Matron. "It will clear your sinuses."

Maliha did not argue. At least the state of her nose and eyes hid the fact she'd been crying. She had no desire to show that weakness to anyone—even less so when she had no idea why she had even done it.

Matron left again as Maliha leaned forward with the clothe draped over her head to keep the steam enclosed around her face.

She breathed deep. And coughed. She could not, however, deny that it was doing some good. The pressure in her sinuses reduced and her ears popped. Unfortunately, she would not be able to breathe it all night.

She tried to pass the time by thinking about the case but all she could think of was James Munroe. He really was a horrible person. To think he had planned to use her to forward his own career.

Her mind drifted and she found herself by the camera at the Creighton-Ward house. She jumped as the bullet ricocheted from the casing again. An inch or two to the left and she would be dead. Dead.

Why hadn't her mother and father paid for her to go back to India during the summer holidays?

Don't they love me? Don't they want me?

She wept again. It wasn't cheap to travel but they hadn't done it even once. They hadn't come to visit her. All she had were the letters and they did not say a great deal. No, that wasn't true, the letters were very long and spoke much about what was happening at home and what her relatives were doing. But they didn't *say* anything. Maliha replied in kind, of course, what could she say in her letters but describe what was happening in the school. Not that there was very much.

She never told them how much she disliked it here but she always told them she loved them and missed them. *Every time.*

Perhaps they thought she was happy because she never said that she wasn't. Perhaps they thought she wanted to stay here.

Perhaps they were protecting her from her grandmother.

She knew her mind was unfocused but she did not feel she wanted to concentrate on any one thing at this time. It was easier just to wander.

She brought the image of her grandmother to mind. She was not a bad woman—*I don't think she is*—but she was what an Indian grandmother should be. She nagged. Of course, with her mother marrying a British man, all the plans for her mother, and whatever children she had, had simply gone wrong.

Her mother should have gone to live with her father's family and been under the control of her mother-in-law. But instead Maliha's parents had their own home. It was not very grand but her father earned a reasonable amount, and he had his royalties from the Anderson valve he had patented.

But without a mother-in-law to tell her what to do, grandmother had decided it was her responsibility.

Maliha took a deep breath and coughed again. The amount of steam coming off the bowl was decreasing and the air was becoming clammy. Her face and hair were damp but she stayed there, leaning over the bowl with her eyes shut. Dreaming.

There had been a fight. Why had she not remembered that? Because when she was young she did not understand how valuable her memory was, nor how it differed from everyone else. She thought everyone recalled everything.

There had been that fight. Her mother and grandmother, who was staying, as she often did. They were shouting at one another in Tamil. Maliha's father was not home, he had gone to Bombay and would be there for a few weeks. Grandmother was staying to keep her daughter company.

Except.

Maliha could remember every word, but she had been young and had not understood. But now, seven years of living later, Maliha suddenly knew why they had been arguing.

Grandmother wanted Maliha betrothed and married before her father came back. But her mother was having none of it, she would not agree unless her husband agreed. Which, of course, he wouldn't. Grandmother was trying every argument she could think of, including the idea that their marriage was not even valid.

Maliha had never heard her mother lose her temper like this. Of course, she had been angry more than once, and certainly at Maliha herself. But never like this. Her fury was terrifying.

And Grandmother finally went silent.

Maliha, then, did not realise how significant that was. Maliha now remembered that Grandmother *always* got the last word.

The door opened and Maliha jumped. Her head was still over the bowl but it wasn't giving off any steam and was only lukewarm.

"You should be in bed," said Matron. She took the towel as Maliha tried awkwardly to drag it across her hair. "You silly girl, you should have stopped." She picked up a second towel and wiped Maliha's damp face and rubbed her hair.

"Fell asleep," Maliha tried to say but it came out as barely more than a croak.

Matron pulled back the covers and helped her into bed. She went away and came back with a second eiderdown which she laid over the top. It made the bedclothes oppressively heavy but Maliha said nothing. She felt detached from everything as if nothing meant anything to her.

Except for the pain in her head. She could not recall when that had started, and then panicked because she felt she must be losing her memory.

Matron put the light out. "I'll check on you later."

Then the woman was gone. The lack of light seemed to reduce the pressure in Maliha's head but the dark brought its own problems. She felt as if she was drifting again. Like the first time she had experienced the Faraday effect on board the small Dutch flyer that had taken her from Pondicherry.

It wasn't the day after the argument between mother and grandmother. Nor the next day, but it had been less than a week. Her memory informed her it was four days.

There had been a tense atmosphere in the house. Grandmother had not left and it seemed to Maliha that her mother now never left her side. As if she was protecting her.

There had been trips into the town, to see people, a journey to the airfield where money had changed hands.

Maliha now cursed her younger self for not paying attention. If there was no memory then there was nothing to remember. She told herself that spouting tautologies was pointless.

She drifted then woke up having a coughing fit. At least thinking about the past helped her to clarify the present. If she was recalling things accurately.

"Of course, I am," she croaked out loud. Then coughed again. She buried her head beneath the covers so that she could breathe the warm damp air there which was less irritating to her throat.

Mother had not dared let Maliha out of her sight because grandmother was going to grab her and take her away to be married. Maliha realised this with a sudden clarity that seemed to clear her head for a moment. Her mother had protected her.

A wayward fragment of imagination swirled in her head showing her the image of a twelve-year-old girl being forced to have carnal relations with a fully-grown man. She shivered. It happened. Where she came from it happened all the time. But it was no different here in England, it still happened; that it was frowned on did not prevent it.

The Dutch flyer had carried them across India in just two days. It was not a fast ship, having just one propeller and getting its lift from gas bags. Young Maliha had loved the feeling of lightness—and she loved seeing the world from so high up. Flying was a wonderful thing. Old and ill Maliha realised the bags had been filled with hydrogen and could have been set on fire so easily, which would have brought them down and dead.

But ships flew all the time with hydrogen because helium was so expensive and hard to get hold of—unless you were in Germany or America.

They had reached Bombay in the evening. Maliha had never seen so many people. Her home, Pondicherry, was a quiet town by the seaside, with French architecture and a relaxed attitude to life. But Bombay was terrifying and frenetic.

Even her mother was scared. Their saris marked them as southerners but they managed to steer clear of trouble.

They reached her father's hotel and managed to gain admittance. It was the first time Maliha had ever seen such open hostility from a white person. She did not like it.

Maliha had fallen asleep in the foyer. When she woke in the morning they were in a set of rooms with her father. But her parents were very serious and discussed things where they could not be overheard. Young Maliha did not care, she was happy watching the world go by from the balcony. The noise and the activity in the city was enough to overwhelm when you were in it. But from the balcony she could see the people like a flowing river and it all made sense.

Maliha woke up in a sweat in the bed. The sheets were soaking wet but she could not bring herself to do anything about it. There was no light showing from underneath the door, and no light creeping round the curtains. Whatever time it was, everyone was in bed and no one was getting up yet.

The air outside the bed was cold. She lifted the blankets weighing her down and let a flow of cold inside. It helped a little. Her mouth was intensely dry but getting up to fetch some water seemed far too much effort for something so unimportant.

Maliha screamed at her parents. She begged them not to make her go. She refused to eat. But nothing she did would change their minds. What could a young girl do in the face of such implacable parents?

If only they had explained to her why they were treating her so badly. But they did not. They simply told her they had arranged for her to go to a boarding school in England, and that she would stay there for the next seven years.

She did not understand why they were punishing her. Maliha now knew that they were saving her because they would not be able to protect her all the time. Father needed to go away and her mother had her own duties, she was not merely a wife but a scholar and there were studies and teaching.

All they would say was that it was for her own good. But she could not see what possible good there was in being sent away. *Out of the reach of an old woman who had her own plans for the family.* And if they had said that? Would it truly have made any difference?

Maliha now knew that it would have. Even then they underestimated her. Everyone did that.

And three days later she was put aboard a vessel bound for England. She did not cry and she did not scream. But she hated them. She kissed them dutifully but she could see in their eyes they felt her resentment.

When she got home she would touch her mother's feet and ask forgiveness for being a naive child. And she would hug her father and tell him she forgave him. And she would thank them both for saving her from an appalling fate.

She would not thank her grandmother. She would never speak to that woman again.

She dreamed she was running along a dark tunnel that seemed to go on forever, twisting and turning through chalky rock. In her hand she had the torch Dr Underwood had given her and she was trying to reach the end and to get out on to the beach so she could save Amelia.

But the tunnel never ended and she stumbled on. Always, ahead, there was a turn that glowed with daylight but, whenever she reached it, it was never the end and there was always another turn a little further on with the promise of escape.

She tripped and fell. And kept falling into blackness while her head throbbed.

"Wake up, Miss Anderson."

She lashed out.

"Careful!"

Maliha opened her eyes which didn't want to focus.

"Nightmares?" said Matron.

Maliha just stared. She had no energy.

"Come on, you need to get up for a little while."

"Why?" she croaked.

"So you can eat the orange on the table, drink the tea—I've put in lots of sugar—and see if you can eat that bread." With that she threw back the covers and cold air streamed across Maliha's body making her shiver. Matron caught her by the hand and gently drew her up. Maliha's head swam and she felt faint. "Just sit for a moment. Oh, goodness, you're drenched with sweat. We need to get you changed and change those sheets as well. Do you need to relieve yourself?"

"Not…no."

Matron fussed. She came and went. Maliha was stripped of her nightdress and bundled up in a thick dressing gown. She staggered to the table and tried to do as she was told. The sweet tea was welcome, and the orange refreshing. She chewed the bread but did not seem to have enough saliva to make it soft. She used the tea to wash it down.

Behind her the sheets were changed and a new nightgown—one of the infirmary ones—laid out.

"Why would Jennifer Wendlefield want to talk to you?"

"Don't know," Maliha muttered. That might not be true but at the current moment she really didn't care.

"I don't believe that for a moment, Miss Anderson," said Matron. "But let's be clear, young lady, you're not having visitors until you're on the mend."

"Yes, Matron."

"Good. All right now, back to bed with you."

23

———

I t took two more days. If she had started with a cold it
changed into influenza. Matron visited regularly, taking
her temperature and noting it down in her little book. Then
she would force Maliha to drink water or squeezed citrus fruits
mixed with honey.

The days passed in a drowsy haze but the nights were
interminable with nightmares that seemed to last forever. She
dreaded sleeping. More than once, in the middle of the night,
she pulled herself out of bed and paced. She tried to think but
the fuzziness of her mind defeated her. The cold floor and
cool air on her skin seemed to help but, in the end, she would
have to return to sleep again. And dream.

She had never been this bad before. There had been colds
from time to time, but she always ignored them as best she
could. This would not be ignored. In the occasional lucid
moment, she understood Matron's concern: influenza could
kill someone unprepared for it. But the girls in the school were
looked after well enough and had plenty of good food, they
seldom succumbed to disease. Though it was not entirely
unheard of.

But Maliha would never give in to such an ignominious end.

When she woke up on the third day she found herself once more in control of her faculties. She thought it must be Thursday though she was not entirely certain. She remembered Matron had said that Jenny had wanted to talk to her—her news was probably not critical but Maliha had been unable to move forward with any plan to rescue the lovers.

Matron came in at eight o'clock. Maliha was wrapped up against the cool air but sitting at her desk finishing the letter about Munroe to Dr Underwood.

"You should be in bed."

"I'm feeling better," said Maliha, though her voice was still a little hoarse.

"You will do as I say."

"I appreciate your concern, and I do thank you for your ministrations." Those words were spoken with honesty. "But if I am forced to remain in bed I shall go out of my mind, I have already wasted too much time."

"I do not wish to force you."

"Matron, I understand. But short of tying me to the bed I cannot be forced to stay there against my will." Matron opened her mouth to speak but Maliha continued. "However, one thing I desperately want to do is read the newspapers for the last couple of days. I would be able to do that in bed."

"I see."

"And I find I am extraordinarily hungry." Almost weak with hunger in fact, though she would not admit that since it would give Matron an additional argument.

Matron pursed her lips in clear irritation. "Very well, Miss Anderson. If you will return to your bed I will arrange for a suitable breakfast to be brought, along with the newspapers."

"Perhaps I could see Jenny Wendlefield, too."

"She has lessons I expect."

"Not first period."

"What day is it?"

Maliha hesitated. "Friday?"

"Thursday."

"Oh. Second period then."

"I'll see what I can do," said Matron. "So, if you will be so kind as to return to your bed."

"I'll just finish this letter."

The door slammed. Maliha sighed heavily and rested her head on the table. The headache was still there but she would not let it rule her. She closed her eyes. It wasn't that she was tired—she was utterly exhausted. The last few days had drained her, but the delays meant she must now work even harder if she was to solve the murder of Ethel Jordan.

Finally, she managed to summon enough will-power to lift her head and screw the lid from her Birmingham fountain pen. She could see that she was not forming her words very well and there was a distinct difference in style.

Never mind. It was important to finish at least this.

She managed to get her thoughts down on paper, detailing her meeting with Munroe, and his attempts to coerce her to do his bidding. She included the fact she had used a small knife to defend herself. She signed off with a paragraph explaining that while she was flattered he considered her valuable enough to join this service, it was not something she had any interest in.

She blotted the words, folded the sheets, slipped them into the envelope and sealed it. Then wrote carefully on the outside. *To be delivered to Dr Underwood of Scotland Yard, London, in the event of my death.* She paused, wondering if that perhaps that was overly dramatic, but concluded it was a simple statement of fact and signed it.

Once the ink was dry she slipped it into the desk.

She closed her eyes again. Her head throbbed whenever she moved it. She was thirsty but there was no water in her glass.

Then she forced herself back to bed and lay down. She closed her eyes.

She knew considerable time had passed when she opened her eyes again. She could see the newspapers resting on the chair beside the bed, on top of the tray with the smell of bacon, toast and the scent of tea. Her mouth salivated. On this occasion she was not concerned about eating meat.

"Sorry if I woke you."

Ena. Maliha blinked twice and pulled down the covers. The woman was standing a short distance away.

"I brought the breakfast."

Maliha floundered for a moment fighting with the blankets and eiderdown to sit up. Ena hurried over to help. "Matron said I should wait and take the tray away when you've finished. And report to her how weak you are."

Ena moved the pillows and then almost lifted Maliha into a sitting position.

"Me Nan needed lots of help before she died."

"Sorry."

Ena shrugged. "People die when they're old."

"Sometimes when they're young."

"I'll tell Matron you're doing well."

"Thank you."

Ena picked up the tray, deftly extended its feet was she held it with one hand, and then set it down in front of Maliha.

"Shall I feed you?"

"I think I can do that."

"Influenza was it?"

Maliha nodded as she brought the cup of tea to her lips and drank. Never had tea tasted so good, even if they did drown it in milk. It had been sugared, too. The plate was not overfilled but had a couple of slices of bacon, a sausage, mushrooms with fried bread on the side.

She started in on it slowly. Ena moved the newspapers to the table and sat without asking.

"The man contacted me."

"How?"

"In St John's on Sunday."

"That's the Catholic church in Kemptown?"

Ena nodded. "I was near the back and he put a letter in my bag."

"How do you know it happened there?"

"Because I noticed him doing it, but I didn't say or do anything."

"You didn't look at him?"

"I did not," said Ena. "I did not think that was wise. When we stood at the end he was gone."

Maliha bit into a mushroom, it had been fried quickly and retained its delicate structure and flavour.

"What's the new chef like?"

"Hard but fair. I like him. Cook is going off in a huff every day."

"I suppose she'll get her kingdom back after the dance."

Ena slipped her hand in her pocket and pulled out a folded sheet of paper. "It doesn't say much. But he's still wanting the information I would have given to Pat."

Maliha took the letter. The paper was cheap enough to be unidentifiable. The hand was very neat and the pen used looked to be a good one, similar to her own, but the sentences were curiously constructed.

"Do what we want, or you will be like your brother. You will come to church Wednesday, Friday and Sunday. Be a row before the back. Taliesin"

"Can you get to church that often?"

"I can, the school is good about religious observance and there are Catholic girls here I can escort for confession and the like. I spoke to the chef. He's amenable and he's the one who says."

Maliha smiled. "That's good. I expect they'll tell you what they need to know on Wednesday—"

"It's Thursday, Miss."

Maliha double-took and shook her head, then wished she hadn't. She took a sip of tea to wash down the food and hide her mistake. "Did you go?"

"It was too soon. I did not get permission until the end of yesterday."

"Tomorrow then," she said almost to herself. "This might be a good thing. They are up against a much tighter deadline than before, it may cause them to make a mistake."

"I just want the man who murdered my brother dead."

And I want the killer of Ethel Jordan brought to trial, then hanged. They are probably the same person, so we can both have our wish.

A wave of exhaustion went through Maliha and she put down her knife and fork. The food was only half-finished but she couldn't face any more. She leaned back into the pillows and closed her eyes.

Taliesin—the great bard of Wales. A strange choice of name for anyone except perhaps a Welshman, or someone from the southwest of England. It suggested a level of education, but Maliha had not for one second assumed the criminal was unintelligent.

Yet the attack on Ethel had been so brutal. She sighed. There was no rule that said an intelligent person could not also be brutal. If only she had managed to speak to Ena's brother before he was killed. All because she had been taken off to the Creighton-Wards.

The door shut and she opened her eyes. Ena was gone and the tray as well. She had not even noticed the weight of it being lifted from the bed.

If she was Taliesin she would want to know how to get into the building without being seen when the place was going to be thoroughly guarded. The secret passage would have been ideal but it was no longer secret. That must have galled them, Ethel had ruined their plan.

Maliha sat up straight. *That didn't make any sense.*

Ethel had been killed before the dance was moved. Assuming Taliesin knew about the event he would have been planning on it being at the Royal Pavilion several weeks hence. It was moved *because* Ethel had been murdered.

Could that have been intentional?

No, it could just as well have been cancelled. Taliesin had killed Ethel to keep her mouth shut because, when it became known she was pregnant, questions would be asked, she might say who the father was and that could have led to Taliesin himself. Better to kill both of them. He thought Ethel was dead in the beach hut and, if she had been, it would have been a long time before her body was discovered. But she had managed to get back into the school and that upset his plans completely.

But the secret passage had nothing to do with Taliesin's plan.

He was trying to kill the two heirs to the throne. The Royal Pavilion probably had a dozen entrances and exits. The school, however, had very few.

Maliha turned her attention to the newspapers. She felt the need to catch up after losing two days.

She read every article, and every advertisement. Just as she always did. A new trade agreement between Britain and France. Tensions with Germany. Concerns at the political situation in Russia. And that was Monday. Tuesday was much the same. Births, deaths and marriages among the nobility. Parliament discussing foreign policy. Reports from foreign correspondents. An attack by Indian separatists on a British military outpost, not far from Delhi. The new schedule of launches up to the Victoria Void Station over Ceylon. Discussions about decommissioning the old military orbital signalling stations. Schedules of flights to other parts of the world.

Wednesday was more of the same but this time with advertisements for people wishing to become colonists on

Mars and Venus. Or take up mining in the Asteroid Belt. The reach of the empires, not just Britain but Germany, the Americans and the Dutch, had extended far beyond the confines of the Earth.

There was a feeling that ran through almost everything in the newspapers. It whispered there would be war. So many people felt they would welcome it but Maliha had read the reports from the second Boer campaign. It had been fought with the new weapons and the flying machines. It was a very different conflict than had been seen before.

Some spoke of a global war. But the nations were capable of fighting across the vastness of the Void as well. And how could you defend against a vessel coming straight down from the Void to wreak havoc on, say, Manchester?

There was another knock on the door.

Maliha sighed tiredly. "Come."

Jenny Wendlefield entered. Maliha was grateful Antonia was not with her, she was not sure she could have tolerated their intensity. She waved the visitor to the chair.

"How are you?" said Jenny

"Better than I was, but this is the first morning I have been aware of anything since Monday."

"I wondered if you had been able to come up with a plan?"

Maliha felt a wave of annoyance and was unable to keep it from her face.

Jenny got up. "I'm sorry. You've not been well, of course you haven't."

"I have."

Jenny's face lit up. "You have?"

"It's only a skeleton of a plan but yes." It wasn't that she was lying but, with the pressure on her, the idea had simply sprung up. "I'll have to work out the details but leaving on the night of the dance is the obvious choice. The place will be in turmoil with everything that's going on and they won't be able on keep an eye on everybody."

She paused and Jenny sat down. Maliha recalled the schedules in the newspaper. "There's a flyer heading out from Brighton airfield about midnight heading for Central America via Portugal, the Azores, New York, and so on."

"South America?"

"But you get off in Portugal and head across into Morocco."

"But—" She looked awkward and slightly embarrassed.

"What?"

"White slavery."

Maliha looked to the heavens. "That was a complete fabrication by a very stupid man who went to jail."

Jenny looked almost disappointed.

"That's not to say you shouldn't be careful. Two white women unaccompanied is not the best choice but you want to escape, you will have to do your best. Just as you have been taught here." Jenny was still looking unsure. "In fact, I probably do not want to know where you go. I'm suggesting Morocco but if you disembark in Lisbon you could go anywhere from there. If I don't know then so much the better because I can be completely honest."

Jenny looked happier at that.

Maliha's headache was not receding and she was feeling annoyed. "Have you been able to find out anything?"

"Jeanne Paquin is coming to the school this weekend."

"Yes, I met her, she's fitting my dress."

Jenny simply stared at Maliha as if words had utterly abandoned her. Maliha realised it had sounded like a boast, which had not been her intention, but if it meant she had one up on the white girls, well, she would accept that triumph.

"I have some money for you," said Jenny after a long silence. She reached into a pocket and pulled out three white twenties. "Will this be enough?"

Maliha nodded and took the money, she noted they had been issued by Coutts which was unfortunate since that would make them more noticeable. "I will provide receipts and change."

Jenny gave a half smile. "I can't really believe we're doing this."

"You need to be ready. I'll sort out the times but you'll both need to leave the dance and get changed into travelling clothes." She thought about what Matron had said. "It's very important you stay separate that evening. Even if you have to pretend you've had a falling out."

A wave of fatigue went through her and she involuntarily shut her eyes.

"I'm sorry," said Jenny. "Matron said I could see you."

Maliha kept her eyes shut and her head was swimming. "I told her I was up to it." *I just wasn't expecting to have a long conversation with Ena beforehand.* Without thinking about it she rolled over in the bed so she was more-or-less horizontal, with the twenties still scrunched up in her hand. She did not notice when Jenny left.

24

It was past midday when Maliha woke again. The headache was gone and she felt refreshed and hungry. Although her legs were weak, she managed to get up and wrapped the dressing gown around herself.

It seemed that, while she slept, she had come to a conclusion. Perhaps it was the letter to Dr Underwood that had convinced her. She needed to inform the authorities of what she suspected—more than simply suspected, what she knew.

The local police force was not an option, they would not treat her with any credibility. The only person she believed would listen was Dr Underwood himself. She sat at the table and set about drafting the letter with every relevant detail. She knew there were holes in her knowledge and was aware that her assumptions were not all well-founded, but she was confident in the overall picture. She wondered if she should include the cartridge she had picked up at the Creighton-Ward folly. She dug into her bag and pulled it out. The square piece of paper had stuck to it.

She decided against putting it in. The police report would have the details if they wanted to enquire further.

Once she had finished, the letter spanned five neatly written pages. She signed it *Alice M. Anderson* on the basis that he might be more inclined to treat her seriously if she used her western name. Once the ink was blotted and dried she folded it, placed it in the envelope and addressed it.

She peeled the square of paper from the cartridge. She sniffed at it. The sticky red substance seemed to have no smell and it was crusted where it was in contact with the air. She touched her finger to her tongue to make it damp and gathered the slightest amount of the material on her finger and tasted it. It was sweet, almost pure sugar. The remains of a cheap boiled sweet most likely.

Just as she was dropping it into the bin, Ena entered with lunch: soup and bread. She did not stay this time and Maliha ate in silence and quiet. There would be nothing to do for the rest of the day and she should spend it recuperating because tomorrow she needed to go into Brighton.

She was progressing rapidly through *David Copperfield* when Matron arrived, in the mid-afternoon, pushing a trolley of equipment. She went through the rigmarole of taking Maliha's temperature, examining her throat and using the machine to record Maliha's blood pressure.

"You seem to be back to normal."

"I feel much better."

"Would you tell me if anything was amiss?"

"It would depend on what it was."

Matron made a derisory noise.

"Could you take this letter and have it posted?" Maliha indicated the one on the desk.

Matron picked it up. "Who's Dr Underwood?"

"He examines places where crimes have been carried out

to find evidence and help determine who committed the crime.”

“This is about Amelia Johnson?”

Maliha hesitated and then nodded.

“And it’s important?”

“Yes. I think so.”

Matron placed the letter on her trolley. “Is there anything you need?”

“I’m hungry again.”

“I’ll see if the kitchen can rustle something up for you.”

It took an hour, and Maliha could almost hear the complaints of the kitchen staff pointing out that it was only a couple of hours to dinner and they were busy. However, Matron prevailed on behalf of her patient. Even if it was only more soup and bread plus some fruit.

When someone else knocked on the door at about six o’clock Maliha wondered whether the constant visitations were her punishment.

She was very surprised when Margaret Creighton-Ward entered, not wearing her school uniform and with her arm in a sling. Maliha smiled though she was still concerned, the deeper she got into trouble the more people seemed to congregate around her. Margaret closed the door.

“I heard you were ill.”

“I have been. Matron says it was influenza.”

Margaret’s face became more concerned as she came over and sat in the same chair as the previous visitors had done. “Are you sure you’re alright?”

“Just tired and my joints ache, but I have been declared to have a normal temperature now and I’ve been hungry.” Her empty plate was still on the tray on the table.

“I’m glad you’re on the mend.”

“What about you? How is the shoulder?”

“Still hurts and I have to have the dressing changed

regularly but Mumsie declared me fit to return to school." She looked around the room. "Can't say I'm upset about that."

"It can't be comfortable?"

"I can only sleep on my back, otherwise it hurts. Then it wakes me up."

Maliha had noted the tired look around her eyes.

"Perhaps Matron can provide something to numb the pain."

"I'm all right."

They lapsed into silence.

Until Margaret said. "How did the man with the gun miss?"

"He hit you."

"I was not entirely in my right mind when I saw you immediately afterwards, but I remember you saying the man was shooting at you."

"Yes."

"And you said we couldn't be friends because of that."

"Yes, and I still think that."

"It's not the way we do things, Maliha, after all these years do you think a British woman would abandon her friend simply because of the danger?"

"But that's my point, Margaret," said Maliha. "We don't have to be friends so you do not have to worry about me."

"And that's not how that works either, you can't just stop being friends."

"I'm sure you can. All I have to do is insult you and send you away."

Margaret shook her head. "That might work on lesser individuals, ones who were not true friends in the beginning. For a true friend that would only make the bond stronger."

"Then I shall ensure that I do not make any more friends."

"You're not serious."

Maliha looked her in the eye. "I can assure you I am entirely serious. I managed with nothing better than mere acquaintances all these years. It's only the last couple of weeks that have changed that. Once I am away from here, I shall simply not speak to anyone."

"One cannot go through life without friends."

"Ask me in twenty years."

Margaret shifted awkwardly and winced in pain. Maliha almost felt it herself. If this was what being friends meant—feeling the hurt of others—then she could do without it. There was enough in her own life without the need for anyone else's.

"I hear Jenny and Antonia have been visiting you."

"How long have you been back?"

"I got back a couple of hours ago."

"Eliza Tenby?"

"With Constance as the choir. They were quite put out that the queens of the school were being entertained by the Indian girl."

"That is the obverse of making friends," said Maliha. "You gather enemies as well."

"It's just jealousy, not only are you being visited by the royalty of the dorms but you also have your own room and are no longer required to attend class."

Maliha shook her head and threw back the covers, she sat on the edge of the bed with her feet flat on the ground. "It's of no concern to me what others think. They have nothing to do with me." She stood up. She felt stronger already and that was pleasing. "And in less than three months I will be gone, and there will be nothing to bring me back."

Margaret stood out of politeness. Seeing the flash of pain across her face gave Maliha a twinge of guilt.

"Do you really hate it here that much?"

"There are some things I hate, like the food, though after so many years I think my sense of taste is completely corrupted. The weather is so cold and damp most of the time, I don't know why you people don't move somewhere better."

"We love our country, Maliha."

"I'm not British, Margaret."

"India is a part of Britain."

"Not all of it."

"Isn't it?"

"No. I come from the French part."

Margaret grinned. "Now I know you're joking, the French have no empire." Maliha did not smile and Margaret lost hers. "You're not joking."

"French India is on the east coast. Dutch India is along the west coast. The British may own most of my country, they do not own all of it. And my people were there first."

Now Margaret looked uncomfortable, she sat down again and stared at the bed.

"I'm sorry," said Maliha. "Yes, I am British, I am also French, but I am Indian." *Your people won't let me forget that.*

"It must be difficult not knowing who you really are."

Maliha sat back down on the edge of the bed. She had misjudged Margaret. People could be difficult to understand. And perhaps Maliha owed her something, after all Margaret had been hit by the bullet which had not been intended for her.

"I have to go into Brighton tomorrow."

"Why?"

"I want to go to a sweet shop."

"I don't think Matron will let you if you've only just recovered. You're not strong enough yet."

"She would if you went with me."

Margaret shook her head. "Is this to do with your case?"

"Yes."

"I don't think it's a good idea. I don't want to get shot at again." She said it lightly as if it was intended to be a joke but neither of them smiled.

"And I need to buy some things, the sooner I can organise it the better."

"And is that to do with the case?"

"No, it's something completely different."

"Is it a secret?"

"Yes," said Maliha and looked Margaret in the eye.

Margaret nodded. "You are willing to trust me?"

"I am."

"Very well." She stood up. "There's no time like the present. I will propose the trip to Matron and say it is for me, but that you would like to come. And that I think the sea air will do you good."

"I think we get plenty of sea air simply by living here."

"It's not the same as being out in it."

"Being out in it is what laid me up in bed, in the first place."

Margaret got to her feet and headed for the door. "Well, hair of the dog and all that."

"I don't think that refers to being ill, Margaret."

"Really," said Margaret in false innocence. "My father claims it's perfect for curing his blue devils after a riotous night."

Maliha considered that a reassessment of Margaret's intelligence might be in order since this appeared to make no sense whatsoever.

"Say whatever you need to convince her."

"I will, and if necessary I will offer a bribe." Margaret finished with some finality but still loitered by the door without exiting.

"Is there something else?"

"Can you call me Peg?"

"Why?"

"Or Peggy, or Meg, or Margie, Mags?"

"What are you talking about?"

"I've never had a nickname. Mumsie always calls me Margaret, and I can't even remember the last time my father used even my full name." She looked down in embarrassment. "I just always thought it would be nice to have a nickname that a friend used."

"Do you have a middle name?"

"Three. Margaret Leanore Penelope Sadie Creighton-Ward."

"I'll call you Sadie."

"But that's not a nickname."

"I think you'll find that it is a nickname for Sarah?"

"They called me a nickname all this time and I didn't even know?"

Maliha shrugged. "It would seem so. Perhaps they didn't know."

"My grandmother on my father's side was Sarah."

"That will be why then."

"Do you have a nickname?"

"No."

"Can I give you one?"

"No."

Margaret left quietly.

Maliha looked up to where she had disappeared and spoke to the empty air. "Yes, it is hard not knowing who you are, but I have a name that's part of my heritage and I will not let that be corrupted."

25

E na brought breakfast.

"When will you be going into church today?" asked Maliha as she hungrily consumed the rounds of toast, eggs and drank plenty of tea.

"For eleven o'clock, when the priest is available for confession."

"What are you going to tell Taliesin?"

"Should I tell him the truth?"

"Yes, unquestionably, there must be no hint of duplicity. If he thinks you're lying he may try to harm you, and we have no idea what he really knows."

"There's not a lot I can say. I don't know how else they can get in if they cannot use the tunnel."

"I've thought about it," said Maliha. "There are going to be a lot of deliveries between now and next week. They could smuggle themselves aboard a cart. Do you know where the orders are coming from?"

"I can find out. Chef has the details written in a journal he has in his office."

"Can you get a look at it without getting caught and questioned?"

"I surely can."

"There's a door in the chapel that leads in from the outside. I don't know where it leads to in the Church but you could mention it. Of course, there will be police and military patrolling the grounds but it's almost the new moon that night so it will be dark, even if it's not cloudy. And there's the brazen approach of attempting to enter as one of the guests. But if they can do that they don't need your help."

"Sound as if the school is more like a sieve."

Maliha shrugged. "It gives you something to say to him. We will find out what he's planning when he asks you to do something, like unlock the church door."

"Perhaps I should check it before I go?"

"If you can."

"I'll do that."

Ena left promptly and Matron appeared with a sour look on her face.

"Miss Creighton-Ward wants to take you into Brighton."

"Yes."

"Do you want to?"

"The Creighton-Wards are not a family you say no to."

Matron looked even worse. "I'm not an anarchist, Miss Anderson, but I sometimes wonder if the aristocracy has outlived its usefulness."

"That just makes you a republican, Matron."

"Do you *want* to go?"

"I am feeling stronger and I think it would do me some good to get out and exercise."

"Well, I may not be as enthusiastic on the subject as Mrs Fenoughty but I'm not one to decry the benefits of fresh air and exercise," said Matron. "But do not let her exhaust you."

"I think the same applies the other way with her injury."

"It does, so I'm charging you with her good health as well."

"Yes, Matron."

Finally, she was left in peace. She gave the impression that she was feeling better than she was but today there was no headache, her constant hunger had passed and, thankfully, the sun was shining. That would be something of a restorative.

"I'll have Mrs Clemence phone for a taxi," said Margaret.

"We could walk."

Margaret considered it. "There are still reporters on the road."

"We'll go the back way. No one will see us leave. A taxi with two girls in the back will simply draw attention, and taxi drivers have been known to sell information to reporters," said Maliha. "But we could get a taxi back."

Since they had permission to leave the school on this occasion there was no requirement to use the window in the storeroom but instead they simply walked out of the rear gate. Maliha led the way along the back of the church. She paused at the door in the chapel. It did not have a handle on the outside but the hinges looked as if they would work.

"What?" said Margaret.

"Oh, nothing."

"Don't tell me then," she said and walked off towards the trees on the school perimeter.

Maliha took one last look and hurried after her. "I'm sorry, Sadie, but if you don't know then you won't have to keep a secret."

"If you think you can get me into a better temper by calling me Sadie," she said with a sigh and a smile. "You're probably right." They passed under the bare branches of the still winter-bound trees with the sun shining through them. "The sun's warm."

But the wind wasn't, coming in off the sea as usual, but they were wrapped up against it. Margaret's arm, still in its sling, was under her coat.

They walked down into the dell and up the other side to the coastguard station. There were two men sitting on the flat roof. One of them with binoculars scanning the sea, the other one waved and Margaret waved back.

"I like the look of him," she said. "You can have the other one." She giggled—a sound Maliha had not heard from her before—and then sobered up. "If only."

"Something wrong?"

"Life. My life to be precise." She sighed. "You get to run away from here, back to India, and I'm going to finishing school then I'll be married off to some eligible bachelor decided by my parents. Never mind whether I like the fellow or not."

Maliha felt strange for a moment, and then she realised what was trying to escape from inside her and she burst out laughing. She strangled it into silence as fast as she could. She was not a person who laughed.

Margaret, however, had stopped walking. Maliha turned and saw her crying. Margaret raised her eyes and hissed. "How dare you laugh at me?"

"No, I wasn't."

"Yes, you were. I thought you were my friend. It was a hateful thing to do."

Maliha glanced up at the coastguard who were both looking down at the girls. "Come on, they're staring at us."

"I'm going back."

"Please, I wasn't, honestly," said Maliha. "It was just that you're complaining about the very reason I'm here. And what I'm going back to. My parents sent me here, and haven't allowed me back, because my grandmother wanted to marry me off when I was ten."

"Ten?" Margaret said with obvious horror. "But that's criminal."

"Twenty years ago the age of consent was thirteen here in Britain, Sadie."

"I'm sorry."

"No, I am. It was just…funny." She glanced back up at the coastguards, they were both grinning. Margaret's one was a good-looking fellow but Maliha's was quite a bit older. "Why do you get the young one, Sadie?"

Margaret turned and glanced up. "Because I got dibs on him. Come on." She put her free arm through Maliha's and they headed on. "It's good to be out without any adults telling us what to do or think."

It was half-past ten when they arrived at the Volks train terminus. Maliha checked her watch and did some calculations. They should be in time.

"I think we should go to church."

"You're not serious?"

"This is one of my little side trips. I think we may see the man who killed Ethel."

"How ghoulish."

Maliha bought tickets from the driver, the train set off and they trundled along the coast. The good weather seemed to have brought out the tourists though Maliha was not sure what rock they must have been hiding under. It was always the same, even on a Saturday in mid-winter, if the sun shone there were tourists walking the streets of Brighton.

They only travelled half the length of the track and disembarked at Kemptown. With the map clear in her mind, Maliha led the way off the beach. Beyond the road running alongside the beach was a continuation of the cliff that separated the school from the sea. A covered promenade ran the base of it. Maliha and Margaret crossed the road but, rather than take the promenade, they climbed the stairs that led up to the second road, Marine Parade, with its Georgian buildings forming a great phalanx running east and west.

They walked along the front, dodging sightseers. Maliha got a few odd glances from passers-by, they probably thought she had been out in the sun too long. A terrible crime for any woman who prized the paleness of her skin. The waves rolled in on the sandy beach and a daring few paddled bravely in the shallows. The water would be freezing cold.

They passed Royal Crescent with its extremely expensive apartments set back from the road and, at the next junction, they crossed the road and headed into the town. Maliha checked her watch once more. They were on time.

Moments later they reached the junction, with Bedford Street to the right and Upper St James Street to the left.

"Perfect," said Maliha and walked over to the small tea shop on the corner. The bell on the door tinkled as they went in. The place was crammed with tables which, in the height of summer, would no doubt be packed with tourists. As it was, at this hour on a Friday morning, the place was empty save for the serving girl standing next to the counter.

Maliha squeezed between the chairs and sat in the window, so she could observe people going in and out of the church. Margaret took the chair opposite. The place was not heated and they kept their coats on.

"Why are we here?"

"Just a moment," said Maliha. "Two teas, please, and do you have Battenburg?"

"We have got some, ma'am."

Maliha looked Margaret in the eye. "Do you like Battenburg?"

"Yes—"

"And two slices of Battenburg."

Then she relaxed and the ache of the walking they had done came to the fore. She closed her eyes for a moment. "This church is inconveniently located almost exactly between the halfway and aquarium stops."

"But why are we here?"

"Do you know Ena Hogan?"

"What year is she in?"

"She works in the kitchen."

Margaret hesitated for a moment. "No, I don't know her. Is she important?"

"She is an Irish Catholic and that church is the one she attends."

"I admit I fail to see the significance of this girl and the church."

"She and her brother were recruited, innocently I may say, to provide information about the school, for the person or persons attempting to assassinate the princes."

To Maliha's eye it seemed that Margaret was trying very hard to assimilate a great deal of information. It was clear she did not have enough information yet.

"Ena's brother was the one who fathered Ethel Jordan's child. And he too was murdered, but since it was all a secret no one connected the deaths."

"Except you."

"Quite so. Now the leader of the group, who calls himself Taliesin, is forced to deal directly with Ena and the only opportunity they have to pass information is here."

Margaret seemed to have caught up. "And you are expecting to see him."

"Yes."

Margaret nodded and was about to speak again when the waitress appeared from the back carrying a tray. The two of them went silent and allowed the girl to place the plates with cake, two cups and saucers, a small milk jug, tea-strainer and teapot—all decorated in a blue and gold pattern—on the table. She withdrew.

"You said assassinate?"

"Yes, I believe that is their intention."

"Then why are we here? We should alert the police, and have the man arrested."

"I agree, and I have sent a letter to Dr Underwood at Scotland Yard."

"You don't think anyone will believe you."

"I *know* they won't believe me, Sadie. Detective Williams

thinks I might be the perpetrator—he knows it wasn't Amelia.
Dr Underwood is the only one I believe I can trust." She
paused. "There they go."

"Who?"

"Ena and the Catholic pupils. They're going to
confession."

Margaret shook her head. "There's something about
Catholics I don't like."

Maliha put the strainer on Margaret's cup and poured the
tea. "Of course not, you're British aristocracy, distrust of them
is bred into you."

"You're saying I'm prejudiced."

"Don't take it personally. You can't help it."

"You can be extremely rude on occasion." She looked out
of the window. "I think there's a man looking at us. Could it
be this Taliesin you talked about?"

"Is he tall, thinning hair, large stomach and a tweed jacket
that's too small for him?"

"How on earth do you know what he looks like?"

"Pay him no heed. He's not Taliesin. Try not to stare
at him."

Margaret stared at her instead. "Who is he?"

"His name is James Munroe and he works for the
government in an investigative capacity. Though at present he
is working for me."

"For you?"

"Yes, he is ensuring that I do not die."

"Why?"

But Maliha did not answer, her eyes were fixed on a man who
had stepped down into the street from the church portico. What
was he doing coming out when confession had only just started.

He could have been first in the queue but would he have
had enough time? She wasn't familiar with the practical
aspects of the process but she did not think so since it could
only have been about five minutes.

As she watched he pulled out his timepiece and checked it. She judged him to be in his thirties. His hair was black and straight and there was something about his clothing that looked odd, though she could not put her finger on it. He turned in her direction and walked to the junction. He was barely twenty feet away from her, and between the various vehicles that drove past, and he looked tall. Tall enough to have been the man who left the scuff mark on the pillar of the folly at Creighton Manor.

Did he have a military bearing? She was not sure but he did walk with a steady and measured step, perhaps of shorter length than a man of his stature ought to have. She was certain he was not seeing her inside the shop but she chose not to turn her head in his direction, just in case. Instead she watched him cross the road from the corner of her eye and saw the flutter of something white fall from his person as he walked.

"Wait here!" she said suddenly, making Margaret jump, and leapt to her feet. She pushed her way carelessly and noisily through the chairs and tables, then yanked the door open. She hesitated as the bell rang out loudly. She stepped out slowly and turned away from the junction and took three steps. If he had heard the bell and looked that should be sufficient time for him to realise there was nothing of interest and continue his journey.

She turned back and was relieved to observe him heading away along Upper St James St, in the direction of the centre of town. She was far more interested in what he had dropped. While she took the trouble to avoid the unpleasantness's left by the livestock that pulled the carts, the small piece of paper had no such scruples. It had landed in the gutter. She was loath to pick it up and chose to crouch down at the side of the road to study it.

It was a small square of waxed paper, creased and folded. There was nothing on this side but she was certain that if it were turned over she would find a trace of a sticky sugar material.

She stood and stepped back into a doorway from where she looked up the street but he was gone. The only person she recognised was a very irritated James Munroe. She did not acknowledge him.

Back in her seat in the tea shop, she ate the Battenburg cake and drank her tea.

"What was that about?"

"Taliesin is the man who tried to kill me and shot you. Now I know what he looks like, I believe I know where his compatriots are and, once I have spoken to Ena, I will know his nationality."

"This Ena is Irish?"

"Yes."

"Then it is a Fenian plot. My father says the Fenians are a murderous bunch of anarchists."

"Perhaps."

They paid and left.

Maliha led the way back towards the beach. "We need to get a cab."

"I thought we were going to a sweet shop."

"We don't need to now."

"I wish I knew what you were thinking."

"I'm thinking we need to go to the Town Hall, and that both of us are tired from walking."

"The police station is at the Town Hall."

"Then we shall have to be careful not to bump into any policemen."

26

____

They obtained a cab from the front of one of the hotels and let it carry them through the busy streets to the impressive building, into which Maliha had been forced. Having paid the cab, they stood beneath the columns of the entrance with people coming and going around them. Maliha glanced up the road, she couldn't see it from here because of the bend but the sweet shop was little more than one hundred yards away.

"This is something I need you to do, Sadie."

"Me? You mean I get to be more than just an attachment?"

"You're white and your accent labels your class. We need to see the records of the transfer of businesses in the town for the last, well, two years at most."

"Why don't you ask?"

"Because I am not white, and my accent would betray my origin even if my skin did not."

"I'm sure that's not true," said Margaret but it was clear from her uncertainty that she was only saying it to please Maliha.

"You are not that naive."

Margaret sighed. "Very well."

"I'll be your companion."

Margaret did not respond but headed inside. They negotiated the receptionist easily enough since he was easily awed by Margaret's obvious rank, and she could title herself Lady Margaret without it being a lie. She was a true member of the aristocracy.

They were directed to an office on the second floor, which was something of a relief to Maliha since the police station was in the lower levels and this meant they were far less likely to run into anyone who would recognise her.

The clerk in the main office was a young fellow, probably in his late twenties but somehow conveying the impression of someone much younger, and he seemed very surprised when two women appeared at his door. He had a cup of something poised before his lips. It went back to the desk in such a hurry that it spilt. He did not notice and jumped to his feet.

"Hello?" he said in a voice that quavered a little. "Can I help you? Who are you looking for?"

Margaret pointed at the door where the engraved glass declared the *Clerk of Business and Land Rights and Ownership*. "Are you the clerk?"

"The assistant to the clerk," he said. "He's out but will return in the afternoon."

"I am Lady Margaret, daughter of Lord Creighton-Ward. I have an enquiry but it is a simple thing and I am sure you will be able to assist."

He looked flustered at her introduction but rallied. "Would you like to sit down?"

He indicated the hardback chair. Margaret sat awkwardly. Maliha simply stood behind and off to one side. The clerk glanced over and then ignored her. He went back to his own side of the desk and sat. He now noticed the spreading stain of the spilt tea, grabbed his handkerchief and lifted the tin mug. Whatever document had been under it was now stuck and he was forced to peel it off before mopping the liquid with the cloth and setting the mug down on it.

"Would you like some tea?"

Maliha could not see Margaret's face but could imagine the look of disdain she likely cast on the tin mug.

"We have proper crockery" was his response to her silent criticism.

"Let's not bother with that," said Margaret. "Are you familiar with Langthorpe's Sweet Emporium?"

"On Pavilion Parade. Yes, I know it."

"We're off to a good start then," Margaret smiled and for some reason that brought colour to the fellow's cheeks.

He must be starved of female companionship, thought Maliha. She studied his face, he did not seem to have an unpleasant disposition and while not what one might call handsome he was—she looked for the right word—*satisfactory*.

"We are curious to know whether it has changed ownership in the last couple of years."

Maliha was certain that it if had been sold, it would have been in only the last eight months since the young prince had not arrived at Osborne College prior to August of the previous year.

The man reached for a dark green file on his desk, he slid it closer and opened it. She saw it had the words *Business Transfers* and the date *October 1907*, on the cover. There were not a great number of items in the folder but he flicked through them and extracted one.

"Yes, here," he said. "The deeds were signed on the 23rd October."

"Well, that was very easy." Margaret stood up awkwardly, and the assistant clerk popped to his feet. Maliha took the difficulty her friend was having, lacking an arm for balance, to move across and assist her, and also whisper in her ear. "*Who bought it?*"

Maliha had to acknowledge that Margaret took her new

instruction smoothly. "What were the names of the signing
parties?"

He frowned for a moment then Margaret smiled at him
and if he had an objection, it disappeared. He looked back at
the sheet he was still holding. "Well it was sold by old Mr
Langthorpe, obviously—" he stopped and frowned at the
sheet. "I'm afraid I can't read this."

Margaret stuck out her hand imperiously and he handed it
over as if mesmerised.

"Diederich Hößler," was what Maliha saw on the sheet.
Margaret pronounced the surname *Hossler*. But now Maliha
was confused, the shop had been bought by a German? The
man's clothes had looked a little off, did that mean he was
German?

Why would a German want to kill close relatives of the
Kaiser?

But Margaret was taking her leave of the funny fellow.
They had probably made his day—unless he preferred
working with dull documents. She was not in a position
to judge.

Once outside, Maliha took charge once more and they hailed
another cab, it was steam-powered with a Faraday grid but
quite modern, this time she ordered it to head for Brighton
Airfield.

"Why are we going there?"

"I need to buy some tickets."

"Are you not staying to the end of the year? I insist you
stay for the ball, after all you do have a dress designed by
Jeanne Paquin."

Maliha hesitated then replied with a safe: "I am not going
away yet."

The taxi negotiated the bustling streets of Brighton and
then headed west through the adjoining town of Hove. The
entire area consisted of more Georgian-built residences in a

regular pattern of streets. These had been cheaper since they were not in Brighton-proper and for that reason they had remained private, though many had now been subdivided.

The taxi passed a gasworks that looked the same as the one at the other end of the town and the houses ended giving on to fields—and the one of particular interest to Maliha. Even though it was still March, there were plenty of flyers on the ground, having just arrived or ready to go out.

A couple of balloon vessels lay at rest by some warehouses. Maliha leaned forward so that she could get a better view as vessels were revealed and hidden by the buildings. At least two fixed-wing craft, a number of dynamically adjustable aero-thrust models in various sizes—always at least four rotors but sometimes six for the bigger ones.

This was one thing that gave her pleasure. She loved flying machines.

Finally, they were all blocked by the great warehouses and hangars. She sat back and then saw Margaret smiling at her. Maliha frowned.

"Where do you need to go, miss?" called the cabby from the front.

"Jordan Airways."

In saying the name of the company out loud, it hit her like a piece of lead piping.

"Who was Ethel Jordan's father? What does he do?" she said abruptly.

Margaret looked as surprised as Maliha. "I don't know. Nobody talked to her—at least not like a normal human being. You think her father runs Jordan Airways?"

"I believe so."

The cab pulled up at a very unprepossessing brick-built slab of a building attached to one of the smaller hangars. Jordan did not use gas-filled flyers then. She could not see into the hangar from here but she guessed he would use one of the bigger passenger fixed-wing flyers. They were reliable and fast.

A large sign directed them to the reception area. The walls were covered in photographs showing the flyers of the Jordan fleet and their pilots. There was no one at the desk so Maliha took some time to look. She smiled when she saw an ornithopter, the same manufacturer as the Iron Pegasus, flown by the Edgbaston sisters years ago. Only ten years, but it seemed like a lifetime away. Maliha loved to read the books about them. Some of the few books she would read more than once, even though she could remember every word.

There were books but the sisters were real, as were their adventures. The writer of the books was Winifred Churchill, who had attended Roedean. It was a strange world where there were so many connections. But the stories had stopped a few years ago, and the Edgbaston sisters were not heard from any more.

"Can I help you?"

The gruff man's voice interrupted her reverie.

Maliha turned. The man was too young to be Ethel's father. He sported a neatly trimmed black moustache that matched his jet-black hair. Then she noticed he was addressing Margaret, who looked to Maliha helplessly.

"I wish to buy passage for two to Panama."

"Do you now?"

"Yes. I believe you have a flight next Saturday?"

"Not tomorrow."

"No, as I said, next Saturday."

"That's forty-five pounds return," he said in a way that suggested he did not think she was able to pay. "Each."

"One way."

Maliha could almost feel Margaret ready to explode with curiosity beside her.

"Thirty each."

"I can pay you in cash now. Can you do a discount?"

He paused. Maliha was unsure whether it's because she

claimed she was carrying so much cash with her, or because she had the audacity to ask for a discount.

"How good is your money?"

Maliha reached into her coat and slid out one of the twenty-pound notes. She unfolded it and laid it out. She pointed to the name of the issuing bank. "Is Coutts good enough for you? It's good enough for most of the aristocracy."

"I can do it for fifty."

"Thirty."

"Forty-five."

"Thirty-five."

"Forty-five."

Maliha took the twenty-pound note from the counter and placed it back in her coat pocket. She turned toward the door. "Let's try Lemans, Lady Margaret."

"Lemans? They have terrible machines, they're all ancient. Their grids will go in mid-air. You'll never get to your destination."

Margaret followed Maliha.

"Forty," he said.

Maliha smiled to herself. "Done."

"Five pounds for food and drink."

She returned to the counter. "Very well." She handed over the three notes and received a fiver and a tenner in change. Not issued by Coutts.

The man pulled out a ledger and prepared his pen.

"Is Lady Margaret travelling?"

"No, I'm not," said Margaret abruptly.

"The names of the passengers," said Maliha calmly, "are Mr Trevor Wicks and his wife Adelphi Wicks."

He wrote the names down. "Very well. If the *Wicks*—" Clearly he was not taken in by the subterfuge, but it was no skin off his nose if a couple of young lovers wanted to elope to the Americas, they wouldn't be the first. "—can arrive at eleven on the evening in question they can board with the other passengers."

Maliha nodded. "They'll be here." How he might feel if he knew the two lovers were of the same gender she could not imagine. Perhaps he would not care even then. The British were strange that way, there was so much stated in public about what was allowed and what was not between people and yet, when it came down to the individual, most of them just did not care. As long as no one was being harmed. The male and female impersonators on the stage were a case in point.

The British could be very contrary.

The man pulled out two printed tickets and wrote in the booking details and the names on each and handed them over.

"Thank you, Mr—"

"Kenilworth, Jeffrey Kenilworth, pilot."

"Will you be taking this trip?"

"I do the European flights mostly."

"I see," said Maliha. She looked down at the counter as she tucked the tickets into her coat pocket. "It was sad about Mr Jordan's daughter."

"Well, he was upset, of course."

When Maliha looked at him again he was looking in every direction other than her. "You don't seem so upset."

"Mustn't speak ill of the dead."

"I suppose not."

"Does Mr Jordan fly?"

"Sometimes, special clients, if you know what I mean."

"Oh?" said Maliha. "How special?"

"Let's just say this isn't the first time I've seen a note issued by Coutts, and the ones I've seen have been higher denomination than yours."

Maliha smiled. "Well, then, I definitely came to the right place. The Wicks are certainly looking for discretion and I can see you have that."

Inside she was entirely unimpressed. He'd as good as told her he was talking about royalty. Though which particular royal family was another thing altogether. The Saxe-Coburgs usually flew with the Royal Navy, but perhaps they would use a private company if they wanted to be inconspicuous.

Perhaps.

Maliha said her goodbyes and left with Margaret. They had had the taxi wait and soon they were on their way back into Brighton.

"Is that it?" said Margaret.

"That's it. Are you hungry?"

"Starving."

Maliha thought for a moment. "We could get some fish and chips."

"That would be brilliant."

The driver knew a very good chip shop out of the usual tourist areas which was, therefore, cheaper. He even fetched it for them, and they paid for him to have some as well. They had finished eating by the time they were in sight of the coastguard station, where they had him drop them off.

Maliha paid him. "Can I ask your name, sir?"

"Bob Roberts, miss."

"Mr Roberts, can I book you in advance?"

"What do you need?"

"Would you be able to come to the back entrance to Roedean school, next Saturday?"

"Not tomorrow."

"No, *next* Saturday, at ten-thirty to convey two passengers and minimal luggage to Jordan's at the airfield?"

"There's a big do on then, ain't there?"

"There is and there is also a couple who wish to leave unnoticed to continue their life which their parents would deny them."

"Are they of age?"

"They are old enough, Mr Roberts, and they are fully cognisant of the repercussions and consequences of their actions."

He grinned. "You been reading a dictionary, miss?"

"You know what I said, sir. Will you do it?"

"Sounds a bit romantic."

"It's very romantic. They are deeply in love though they are forbidden because she is promised to another." *Though we don't know who the other is, but that's not important.*

"Then I'll do it."

"You are a gentleman, Mr Roberts."

He touched his cap and got back into the cab.

Exhaustion gripped her suddenly and she wavered. Then she stood up straight again and headed back towards the school with Margaret beside her.

27

Maliha slept late. It had not been her intention, she had wanted to rise early in order to prepare herself for the day, unfortunately the exertions of Friday had taken their toll. She had declined Matron's offer of a card game and retired early. She had not been able to concentrate on her book and woke at some point to find the corner of it jammed into her cheek.

That had been two in the morning. With the lights out she had pulled back the curtain and looked at the sky—clear and filled with stars. Then she had returned to bed and was aware of nothing until she was woken by the gonging of full milk churns being unloaded. Followed a short time later by the clatter of the empty ones for the return to the creamery.

Saturday had always been a strange day in the school. In the lower years there were still lessons in the mornings—after all, too much idleness was a bad thing—and the afternoon was given over to voluntary physical activities. But on the whole, it seemed neither one thing nor the other. For someone who enjoyed simply reading, it was a good day.

But not today, because Jeanne Paquin was coming to fit

her ball-gown. Maliha had seen photographs of the designs Madame Paquin produced for more celebrated individuals, and her designs were the talk of Society. But Maliha was not part of that, nor did she ever want to be. However, her original decision not to attend had been overtaken by events, let alone the persuasion of Margaret.

More than that, though, she had no idea what to expect.

She realised she was prevaricating. She needed to act. Breakfast had been left outside her door—which she discovered when she went in search of Matron. There had been no discussion of what to do about having a bath, and Maliha felt she should be as clean as possible for the fitting. It would undoubtedly involve getting changed with Madame Paquin, and possibly an assistant, being very close and touching. Cleanliness was a matter of good manners.

Matron indicated that Maliha could use the bath and showers. The only occupant of the infirmary at present was a third year who had inhaled something noxious in the science class. It was not entirely clear whether this had been accidental. Matron was quietly fuming since she was certain the girl had been pushed as a practical joke. "Some of these girls have no ability to see the potential consequences of their actions."

Maliha bathed and dressed in a fresh set of clothes, courtesy of Margaret. Then she sat down to eat the cold toast and egg, which she washed down with tea that had managed to stay lukewarm—which was worse than stone-cold.

Afterwards Maliha set out in search of her friend and met her coming down the stairs from Sea Eagles.

"Are you ready?" said Margaret with a smile on her face. "This is going to be so exciting."

"I am ready. I cannot say I am excited."

Margaret came up beside her and slipped her arm into Maliha's, who realised she had dispensed with the sling.

"How is your shoulder?"

"Twinges a bit but it'll be fine."

"You must tell Madame, if she asks you to move your arms too much."

"I will."

The school possessed a guest suite that combined a small lounge, two bedrooms and private toilet. This was the location for the fitting, and as it turned out Madame Paquin was dressing more than just Maliha and Margaret. Waiting in the lounge area was Emily Solsbury, a resident of Blue Cranes—the dormitory that shared facilities with Sea Eagles—and also Antonia Dumont.

Emily was new money. Her father had been lower middle-class but now was a successful investor with a large and profitable portfolio. Maliha had come across the name of Solsbury in the paper on more than one occasion, not always mentioned in a good light. He might have been the perfect demonstration of how a man might better himself through hard work and wise dealings. That did not mean that he was accepted into society—he was merely tolerated.

Unfortunately, that attitude had coloured the temperament of his daughter. Emily disliked the aristocrats and nobility, but she was clever and had gathered a coterie of like-minded girls.

Antonia's face lit up when she saw the other two entering.

"Well, look who it is," said Emily. "The rich one and her murderous maid."

Margaret smiled. "Hello, Solsbury. Antonia."

Chairs had been placed in the room on either side. The three sat down on the opposite side to Emily.

Antonia looked up and stared at the other girl. "It doesn't matter how much money your father throws at you, Solsbury, you'll never be a lady."

"Oh, but I will, we've already sorted out a broke aristocrat. He'll do anything to save his precious estate. I'll be married next year while you're still sniffing after your bit of skirt."

"You can wear the most expensive dress in the world," said Margaret, "but you'll still be a guttersnipe."

"World's changing. There isn't room for the likes of you and your darkie friend." She looked at Maliha for the first time. "You don't belong here and you'll come to a bad end. And it's people like me that'll make sure you do. We know it was you that did for Ethel Jordan."

The door slammed open and four women, impeccably dressed, even though it was in everyday wear, entered carrying long cases and what were clearly clothes but hidden beneath layers of paper. And then Madame Paquin stalked in followed by Mrs Ramsey. The four girls stood up.

The next three hours went by in a rush yet seemed to take forever. Madame Paquin and her staff set up in the bedroom. The headmistress fluttered about ineffectually, but her presence ensured that Emily Solsbury kept her vicious tongue to herself.

The girls went through in alphabetical order which mean that Maliha was first, followed by Margaret, then Antonia and Emily last. Maliha was undecided what was worse for Emily Solsbury, the fact that Maliha went first, or that she herself was last.

The first round of fittings did indeed involve the removal of outer garments—behind a screen, and there was a silk dressing gown for modesty—and the trial placement of the dress. Maliha was astonished when she saw it. Deep blue silk cut almost as if it were Empire line but loose around the bosom. The décolletage was daringly low and Maliha was extremely uncomfortable showing so much skin. There was a mirror in the room and she could see a grown-up woman looking back at her.

"It has been very short notice," said Madame. "This was the only material suitable."

"It's beautiful," said Maliha and, to her own surprise, she really meant it.

"I believe it complements your skin tone, but a midnight blue would be better. I will also provide a wrap in the same

shade but gossamer, it is not yet ready. It will be like one of
your Indian sari, I think."

"Thank you."

"Also the shoes. And undergarments. This disgusting
material you wear cannot be permitted beneath my dress."

"Thank you."

"And your hair. I will send a stylist. You will have your hair
up to expose your neck. And appropriate jewellery. Paste, of
course. This will make you a princess. Yes?"

"Yes." Maliha did not want to say thank-you again. She
was already wearing it out. "But the cost?"

Madame Paquin waved her hand dismissively. "Your
friend's mother is an excellent customer."

Before Maliha could utter another thank-you, she was helped
out of the dress and returned to the screen to get changed.

"We will finish these other girls and perform the necessary
work until this evening when we will perform the final fitting.
The dresses will be delivered next Friday."

Maliha nodded but she was behind the screen at the time
so that would have been invisible.

"Do you have a man to stand up with?"

"No."

"There will be no shortage of suitors when you are in one
of my dresses."

Maliha was not entirely sure how she felt about that. She
brought back the image of herself in the dress. She did not
know who that woman was, or whether she enjoyed the
company of men. There had been very few men in her life up
to this point and most of them were either old or dangerous.

"Was it good?" said Margaret.

Maliha glanced at Emily and decided a simple nod was
sufficient.

Since she did not have to wait, Maliha left so that she
would not have to endure any more of Solsbury's vicious
commentary. She felt slightly guilty, leaving Antonia alone but

Maliha did not trust her to keep her mouth shut about their plans. Besides, Mrs Ramsey was there, her mere presence would prevent the worst of it.

She returned to her room. Margaret arrived about half an hour later, beaming with delight.

"My dress is lovely, it's all pink and flowery, not too daring because my father doesn't like that, but it will look lovely in a photograph. My arms are all exposed and I have nicely shaped arms, don't you think? I'm so looking forward to this. We can't invite any boys but they will supply them and they'll be Navy cadets. I mean I know we can't really do anything but we might be able to catch a kiss. What's yours like?"

"Which?"

That confused Margaret for a moment and then she realised and grinned even more. "Your dress, of course."

"It's blue."

Margaret waited for further description but Maliha disappointed her. "Is that all you're going to say about it?"

"I think it's very elegant and very modern. It seems that Madame has decided that since I am not her usual clientele she is going to experiment."

"How wonderful," said Margaret. "But did you like it?"

Maliha looked down and her face softened into a smile. "I thought it was beautiful. And when I looked in the mirror it was like seeing a stranger."

"I know! Isn't it tremendous?"

Then she calmed down and sat on the bed beside Maliha. "I've been trying really hard not to pry."

Maliha turned away and stood up. "Don't ask."

"I have to know. Those tickets are for the evening of the dance, who are they for, Maliha?"

"I can't betray that confidence."

Margaret was silent for a few moments. "I know anyway. You think I have nothing between my ears."

"That's not true, I know you are intelligent."

"But perhaps I don't apply the intelligence God gave me to the right things?"

"Perhaps."

"That's what the teachers always say." She sighed. "The tickets are for Jenny and Antonia, aren't they?"

"I cannot say."

"You're helping them run away."

"Don't ask."

"But perhaps I can help? I mean," she said, "if you didn't want me to know why did you take me with you yesterday? You could have just gone on your own and I would have been none the wiser. I think you wanted me to know so you'd have someone to talk to about it."

Maliha leaned on the desk and closed her eyes. Was it possible she had done it deliberately? In retrospect her actions did not make a great deal of sense. "I needed you for the church and the Town Hall."

"You didn't even know you were going to the Town Hall. You were going to the church and then to the sweet shop."

And if I had I might be already dead.

Margaret stood up and cleared her throat. "I don't think you're safe to be let out on your own."

"What?"

"You heard me," said Margaret and pointed at Maliha. "You, Miss Anderson, are a fraud. You're just deluding yourself half the time."

"Yes."

"Which?"

"Yes, I'm deluding myself and yes, it's Jenny and Antonia."

"Oh God. You mean I was right?"

"You were right. About everything."

"Don't tell anyone, it'll ruin my image."

"Your *image*?"

"Of course, it's very important not to appear too intelligent, you'll drive the suitors away."

"I'll bear that in mind."

"So, if I'm going to be your trusty assistant, your Dr Watson, how can I help?"

Maliha shook her head. "I don't know." She sighed and leaned her head against the wall by the window. "Half the time I don't know what I'm going to do next myself."

"Well if that's the case you're very good at pretending as if you know what you're doing."

Maliha said nothing.

"What's the plan with the elopement?"

"It's hardly that, they can't get married, can they?" Maliha frowned. "You don't seem very surprised or concerned they want to run away together."

"I said it before, Maliha," she said. "You really don't understand the way the aristocracy thinks. I mean the real thing, not those recent additions of the past hundred years. My Uncle Jeremy is a complete flower. He's very sweet but terribly effeminate. And enjoys the company of men like himself. Everybody knows and nobody minds. He's not hurting anyone, after all."

Maliha stared.

"You're like everybody who isn't us, Maliha, you think we're stuck-up and intolerant. But it's the other classes that fail to encompass life." And then she went from being very serious to smiling again. "I know half the plan. You get them into the taxi with that nice Mr Roberts, who takes them to the airfield where they catch a Jordan flyer to South America. That's the easy bit. So why don't you sit down and tell me how you're planning to get our two love birds out of the school?"

They had afternoon tea and shortly before the evening meal they were called back to the guest suite for the final fitting.

The change in Maliha's dress in that short time was

astonishing. She had been overwhelmed in the morning but now it was almost transformed. From the high waist down to her hips the material hugged her body and from there it fell generously to the floor. It trailed behind but was high enough at the front that she could walk.

"I will send the shoes before Wednesday. They will have heels that will raise you up and improve your posture, but you will need to practice, otherwise you will stumble about like a new-born lamb."

"Is that entirely necessary?" said Maliha.

The glare from Madame pierced her like a dagger. "You wish to look *élégant*, no? Of course. But you must also be *gracieux*. Like a swan. You have a body that can wear the best of my fashions and so you must move to their best advantage."

So I only exist to display your skill, thought Maliha but knew better than to express it.

Madame stepped back. She walked round Maliha and then looked at her in the mirror. "It is good. There are ornaments to be added but they will be minimal. They will highlight, not overwhelm. Less is more, *n'est pas?*"

So Maliha changed back into Margaret's clothes and seeing herself in the mirror she had the impression she was looking at an old woman.

And that was that.

28

Maliha was not able to avoid church on Sunday morning.

The younger girls were ranged in the front pews with the older ones further back. This was based on the theory that the younger ones were less responsible. It did not make a great deal of difference since teachers and other staff sat at the ends of the pews to ensure there was no disorder.

They sang the hymns, to the accompaniment of the small organ, played by Mr Gunnell on this occasion. He and the music teacher, Mrs Lampton, took it in turns, though she was the more competent musician. They prayed and they listened to the sermon.

Seeing Mr Gunnell playing gave Maliha a little pang of guilt and sadness. Perhaps he would not hate her for doing what she did, especially if her actions saved the princes and, more importantly, brought Ethel's murderer to the gallows.

But what progress had she really made in that direction? She had no real proof, all she had succeeded in doing was revealing the conspiracy. Hopefully, on Monday, she might get a message from Dr Underwood,

or some other sign that her message was being
acted upon.

Most of the catering and cleaning staff were at the back
but Ena would not be there, she would have gone into town
again. The events of the previous day had driven all thoughts
of Ena from her mind. She resolved to speak to her at some
point today, hopefully she would bring the evening meal.

The service ended with a processional and the girls slowly
came out of the pews from the front towards the back. When
it was the turn of the Sea Eagles, Maliha stepped out and
began to follow. Without warning someone pushed hard on
her back, she tried to stumble forwards but something
obstructed her ankles. She flailed for the edge of the pew as
she fell forwards. Misjudging the distance, her fingers hit the
wood hard and then the cold tiled floor came up to meet her.
She managed to get her other arm under her head to prevent
smashing her nose but it hurt nonetheless.

The organ went silent mid-bar and as the notes echoed
into silence, she heard giggling.

"Careful, Anderson," hissed Emily Solsbury. "Don't want
to hurt yourself."

Maliha picked herself up as the rest of the girls filed past.
Mrs Lancaster helped steady her. They both stood there as the
others retreated along the nave and out through the vestibule.

"Are you all right?"

"I think so."

"Did you trip?"

"Yes." The single curt word was all that was needed. "I'll
just sit here for a few minutes."

"Shall I wait with you?"

"Thank you but it's not necessary."

Maliha sat in the pew and leaned on the shelf in front of
her. She listened to Mrs Lancaster's shoes clicking into the
distance. Then the door of the chapel squeaked shut.

It could not have worked out much better if she had
planned it, although bruised fingers had not been a price she

wanted to pay. She got to her feet. The door to the outside
was not on this level but must be in the crypt.

Maliha hurried along the nave to the exit and opened the
door on the left. There was a robing room with cupboards and
a table. A second door opened on to a set of stone stairs
descending into the dark.

She looked around but was unsurprised to see that electric
power had not been brought this far. There was a candlestick,
candle and safety matches. She lit it and made her way down
the steps. The stone was dry and floor with it. An arch on the
right led into darkness, a quick look revealed the crypt proper
but the corridor continued parallel to it.

The flagstones that comprised the floor were worn but not
uneven. It took less than a minute, even taking care, to
traverse the corridor's length and arrive at the door at the
other end. There was a large padlock through the loop of a
generously proportioned bolt, with other bolts at the top and
bottom. It was locked, of course, and the door very firmly
shut. Just as she had experienced on the other side.

She went back to the crypt and went through just so she
could get a good picture in her mind's-eye. A set of six stone
coffers were placed evenly around the room. There was no
other exit. The church pre-dated the school by at least two
hundred years and these were the final resting places of the
original owners of the land, the Crevesey family.

Maliha nodded to herself. This was all looking quite
promising for the escape of Jenny and Antonia. All she had to
do was determine how to get the keys to open the church and
the back door. Then deal with the guards that would
undoubtedly be stationed all around. Particularly since she
had given the warning about Taliesin.

If Dr Underwood really was part of this secret
organisation it meant he would have access to the royals
themselves. It was not in their nature to avoid danger—after
all, even the young prince was attending the Royal Navy
college and being trained in warfare—and they could not call

off the dance, otherwise they would not catch the conspirators.

She climbed back up the stairs, snuffed out the candle and replaced it exactly as it had been. If someone tested its warmth they would realise it had been used, however it seemed unlikely. Maliha shut the door to the stairs and studied this room in more detail.

If she could avoid having to acquire keys, since that would almost certainly involve Mr Gunnell, so much the better. There was a window facing outward to the grass and another that faced into the inner grounds of the school. It opened on hinges to the side and she judged that it should be possible to have it shut but unlocked so that it could be opened from the outside. The problem in this instance was that the tampering would need to be done close to the time it was needed. The longer it was left unlocked the more likely it was to be discovered. She made a decision and left it unlocked.

She left the church and checked the window from the outside. Placing a box under it would make it accessible and, while it would be easy to see someone climbing in, even at night, she could assume everyone's attention would be fixed on the dance. Satisfied, she headed back to her room.

Lunch came and went and then the long afternoon. There was no card playing on a Sunday, so even that possible distraction was taken from her.

Thankfully, her prayers were answered and Ena arrived with the meal that evening. The quality of the food had continued to improve as the staff were brought up to snuff by the chef. There was even the hope that the food for the dance would be exceptional.

"You spoke to Taliesin?"

"Yes, miss. And I did not like it one little bit. Made my blood run cold just listening to his voice. Like chalk on a blackboard."

"That's interesting but I'm more interested in what he sounded like."

"To be honest, miss, I was expecting him to be Irish like me."

"But he wasn't."

"No, miss, he was a German."

Maliha smiled, that at least confirmed that the man who called himself Taliesin was also the man who had bought the sweetshop.

"Good. What did he say?"

"He said he wanted to know about getting in to the school, just like you said he would," said Ena. "And then he wanted to know where all the sixth-form dormitories were."

Maliha frowned. "The dormitories?"

"Yes, ma'am."

"Did you tell him?"

"I said I couldn't help him very much because I don't go up there being stuck in the kitchens and the lower floors. But that was Friday."

"What do you mean?"

"He was there again today. And I saw his face."

"I know what he looks like." Maliha cursed herself, losing two days had completely confused her state of mind. Ena had been talking about what happened on Friday just as she had been asked but it was Sunday evening.

"Yes, ma'am." Ena was scowling.

Maliha cleared her throat. "I'm sorry for speaking so rudely. I was waiting outside the church on Friday hoping to catch a glimpse of him and he walked right by me."

"Did he not see you, miss?"

"I was in a tea shop, the one on the corner."

"I have been in there, it's quite nice."

"What happened today?"

"Well, I spent some time carrying a mop and bucket around the school yesterday afternoon. Nobody asks you what you're doing when you're a skivvy who looks like they have something to do."

That raised a smile on Maliha's face.

"You should do that more often, miss."

"What?"

"Smiling, it makes you look a lot more pleasant."

"And that's impertinent."

"Well, it seems to me, miss, we're at the same level on this matter. So I'm thinking a little impertinence is permitted, if you see what I mean, after all it wasn't as if I was saying something unpleasant."

"You said I don't look very nice unless I'm smiling."

"It's not that you don't look nice," she said. "More that the smile is an improvement. It's the difference of having an elegant grate that's empty, to a roaring warm fire."

Maliha changed the subject. "What did Taliesin say to you?"

"He wanted to know what I had found so I told him."

"And was he happy about it?"

"He did not seem like he was very happy, but not sad. No emotion, I think. Like you."

"I have emotions."

"Yes, miss."

"Why does he want to know about the dormitories?"

"I don't know."

Maliha shook her head and finished the meal in silence. She thanked Ena, who picked up the tray and left.

It was an absolutely certainty that she was wrong about the assassination attempt. Whatever Taliesin had in mind, it was not murder.

He was German for a start. Most of them, and a good proportion of the British upper classes with them, wanted closer ties to Britain since the Royal families were so closely related. It would make no sense to assassinate the princes.

Maliha was not convinced one way or the other. The only

thing she knew with certainty was that whatever action Taliesin intended to take, it would be next Saturday evening during the dance. At least she had notified the people who needed to know.

It was the murder of Ethel Jordan she should focus on. The conspiracy, whatever it was, was nothing more than a distraction. The fact they were connected was not important.

She stood and paced her room. "Ena was brought over from Ireland specifically to take up the position as kitchen maid. So that she could provide inside information." She said it out loud to try to make the thoughts form a coherent whole. "This was done before the dance had been moved. The dance has nothing to do with the conspiracy."

The dance has nothing to do with the conspiracy. If that's the case then the assassination of the princes *cannot* be the intention. And if the dance was not the target, then it must have everything to do with the school itself. Probably the girls.

Perhaps Taliesin wanted to kidnap one or more of the girls in order to extract a ransom. There were plenty of girls that would be suitable for that. Margaret was one of them, and plenty of others—in fact Ethel Jordan could have been a target since her father had a great deal of money.

But Taliesin had easy access to her. Patrick Hogan was Taliesin's man, and he was having plenty of private liaisons with Ethel. Did that mean it wasn't about money either?

She shook her head as she realised she had become side-tracked again.

"It's because I already know who killed Ethel Jordan," she said to the mirror. "The problem is that I don't really know why."

It was because she was pregnant, yes, and that if that had been revealed she would end up telling the truth about Patrick, and he led to Taliesin?

That was why she kept on coming back to the conspiracy, it was the reason why Ethel Jordan was now dead. It was the motive.

29

The scream and the crash of crockery from outside her room woke Maliha with a jolt. For a moment she had no idea where she was, expecting to see the dormitory. She returned to herself in a moment and jumped out of bed. The scream was followed by sobs and raised voices, Matron was one of them.

Maliha pulled on her dressing gown and put her feet into her slippers.

She unlocked and opened the door. Matron's voice got louder.

"Get Mr Gunnell up here to remove it."

Maliha looked down at the lump of fur at her feet. A lump of fur with a pale hairless tail.

A dead rat.

"Maliha! Get back in your room until Mr Gunnell has dealt with this."

She shut the door. The dead rat did not bother her. Neither did live rats. She knew what this was about, the same thing as being tripped in church. The jealousy was turning into a vendetta of practical jokes. She would have to be on her guard.

It complicated matters a little but it was something she had dealt with before. She could deal with it again. The other girls would be tied up in lessons most of the time.

The dead creature was removed and the stones outside the door scrubbed with carbolic. Breakfast arrived and Maliha was briefly questioned by Matron.

"Emily Solsbury is most likely the ring leader."

"Nasty piece of work," said Matron. "At least you knew where you stood with Ethel Jordan, mostly out of her way if you could because you knew what she might do. But Solsbury? She's the type that would hold out the hand of friendship while she poisoned your tea."

"I believe she is jealous that I currently have the ear of several of the aristocrats."

"Well, I'll make a note of it and pass it to Mrs Clemence."

Maliha made no comment, they both knew that nothing would come of it. While Mrs Ramsey might be concerned about trouble between the girls in the school, Mrs Clemence would simply sit on the information.

After breakfast Maliha dressed in her outdoor gear and went out of the school through the storeroom. The weather remained dry although the sky was cloudy.

The trip into Brighton proceeded as before, with the only difficult part being the stretch of grass from the back of the school to the trees and the gate. But since she was not dressed in uniform and had a scarf, she did not think she would be recognised even if someone was looking.

The coastguard men were up on the balcony of their station scanning the sea as usual. The younger one she had seen before waved. It would have been rude not to return his gesture so, despite her embarrassment, she waved back. Of course, if someone were to question him then he would comment that he had seen the same young woman walking backwards and forwards to the school. The position of his lookout was such that he could easily see across the valley to where she emerged from the trees.

Then she frowned. The coastguard possessed a fine tripod-mounted brass telescope that gleamed even in the light from the cloudy sky. It was designed to see for twenty miles to the horizon. It would be quite simple for them to train it on the school. And from here they would be able to see into at least one of the sixth-form dormitories quite easily.

She sighed and hoped that they did not do so, that propriety won out. But considering her experience of men up to now—Dr Jenkins, Mr Kennington in the bookshop, Patrick Hogan, and perhaps even her uncle back in India, it seemed that on balance at least half the men she encountered could not keep their lecherous thoughts inside their heads but had to express them in one way or another.

But she was soon past them. The train journey was uneventful and she walked up Old Steine to the Town Hall and turned left into North Street, catching a glimpse of the domes of the Royal Pavilion. She found the hardware shop she needed and, using some of the money she had left from Antonia, she bought a good-sized padlock, a hacksaw, some lubricating oil in a small can, and an alarm clock. She was not sure if she would need it but added some twine.

From there she went to Hanningtons, the big department store exclusive to Brighton, preparing to celebrate its first one hundred years. But by the time July came around Maliha expected to be back home in India.

The next task was to be somewhat awkward but it needed to be done. She made her way to the menswear department. She muttered under her breath trying to remember how to speak with an Indian accent. She conjured up the memory of her mother, very well spoken, but unmistakably Indian.

She chose the youngest-looking fellow on the sales floor and headed for him.

"Can I help you, miss?"

"Thank you, yes. My mistress has asked me to fetch some clothes. Please excuse me but she wishes, for a party, to dress as a gentleman. I must buy her clothes." It was not an outrageous suggestion, ever since the Prince Regent had made Brighton the playground of the aristocracy the parties were notorious. The idea that a woman might want to dress as a man for one such was not in the least unlikely. Nor would the reverse have been either.

"And, er, if you don't mind me asking, what are her measurements?"

"Similar to me, but taller. As tall as you."

"I see. And what sort of clothes?"

"Trousers. Jacket. Shirts, two of them. Tie and a cardigan? Does that seem enough?"

"A hat?"

"Yes, a hat of course. What a well-to-do gentleman might wear for an afternoon drive when the weather is not warm?"

"Of course, miss, if you'd like to come this way."

And so it went. Their mutual embarrassment allowed them to keep the conversation to a minimum but to get the job done. And Maliha walked away with a couple of bags containing hard-wearing cotton and tweed. Along with socks and a pair of shoes, they were the main problem as Maliha had never paid much attention to Jenny's feet. But Maliha's perfect memory filled in the details she needed.

Maliha took her purchases and returned to Old Steine, where she looked wistfully up the road to where the sweet shop stood. She had been shot at because she had been so foolish and open in that shop, not knowing the person behind the counter was in cahoots with Taliesin. The only reason she had remained safe, she imagined, was that he had other things to worry about and while she stayed in the school he could not easily get at her.

Unlike James Munroe, Taliesin did not have the option of watching her all the time.

She looked around to see if she could spot Munroe. She couldn't. He might not even be there.

This is not about assassination, it's something else.

The thought kept running through her mind. She knew what the problem was: she did not have enough information. All she could do was make assumptions and look where that had got her. Assumptions were the Devil's daydreams. Not that she believed in any kind of devil.

In all her readings her preference had always been in the direction of Buddhism. Unfortunately, managing to embroil herself in these events had disrupted any form of inner peace she might have been attaining. She was not an uncarved block, she was a lump of stone on a firing range.

Maliha shook herself back to present. She could not remain here standing outside the Town Hall, and by proxy, the police station. Someone would spot her eventually. Putting down one of her bags she hailed a steam cab, a Daimler Alexandra, and climbed in.

"The airfield, please." The words had jumped out of her mouth before she had even realised she was saying it. If Jordan carried such important customers, he would have a suitable air vehicle for the purpose, and she wanted to see it.

The cab was pointing in the right direction and they set off, crawling through the midday traffic. She should have gone back to school for lunch and would be missed but she was past caring about such things now.

As they escaped from the centre of town the traffic eased and they made good progress, arriving outside Jordan's Airline within twenty minutes. The doors to the main hangar were open sufficient to allow a person through but not a flyer. She had the driver pull up on the far side of the hangar away from the reception. He agreed to wait with her bags but left the meter running.

Maliha walked along the front of the huge concertina

door. Its panels were of wood and painted grey. Each one was set in a runner at the bottom and above; and was hinged with its neighbour. She concluded there must be a mechanism to operate it, since the weight would be far too much for one man, or even several.

She reached the opening and peered inside. It was dark and all she could see were lines of light seeping in through cracks and, in the case of the rectangular openings, doors. Slipping inside she waited just inside, and off to the side so her shape was not silhouetted against the light.

Her eyes adjusted.

Five flyers stood in silent shadowy ranks. Four were of the standard fixed-wing design, though one was much larger and mounted diesel-driven propellers on each wing. Its body was wide and long. That would be their long-distance machine, the one destined for South America next week. The fifth was a three-engined dynamically adjustable aero-thrust vehicle and, by the look of it, an A. V. Roe Stormy Petrel, one of the best models available—according to Aviator Weekly. The rotors were turned to the vertical, as if it was ready to launch upwards at any moment. It looked as if it might carry four or five passengers.

It was not a surprise that they had such a machine, any successful air transport company would possess one. It made it possible to pick up passengers from any point in a city, or country house, without the need for an airfield, which was the primary disadvantage of the fixed-wing flyers.

With her eyes fully adjusted she headed across the hangar. She tried to keep the sound of her shoes clicking on the hard surface to a minimum but it was so quiet the noise seemed loud enough to wake the dead.

The wall of the hangar that adjoined the reception building had a door on the lowest level and stairs going up what she judged to be two storeys. At the back of the space on this side was a set of rooms which she assumed would be for the mechanics and for storing machine parts.

A phone rang, echoing through the wide empty space. Maliha froze. She had been heading in a diagonal towards the biggest of the flyers but was still in the open. If someone came through it would be impossible for them not to see her.

The jangling bell repeated and repeated. She took a chance and ran on tiptoe. Light poured from the door that opened above her just as she made it under the nearest wing.

"Alfie! Pick up the bloody phone!" She did not recognise the voice as it thundered across the hangar, with just the slightest of echoes. "Alfie!"

The phone stopped mid-ring but continued jangling in her head. It had been so loud there must be an extra bell on the outside of the shed. In case the mechanic was working on a flyer.

The door above slammed and the light went out.

Maliha looked across the hangar at the sliver of light that was her exit. She was tempted to leave now; the place was not empty and she might be discovered at any moment. But there was no danger at present. She could hear a man, Alfie perhaps, talking intermittently.

She looked about again and her eyes came to rest on the three-rotor machine. That was where her interest truly lay. She hesitated no longer and headed along the fuselage of the big machine. The number of portholes suggested it might accommodate twenty passengers or more. A big dirigible could take a couple of hundred while the massive British-built dynamically adjustable aero-thrust skyliners carried five hundred or more, as well as the full complement of crew to fly it and look after the passengers. She was looking forward to the trip home on the *RMS Macedonia*.

The pilot's cabin had the expected two seats and a mass of controls. She had read a training manual that had explained the controls, so she knew what they were for—most of them— but that did not reduce the overwhelming impression of complexity.

She realised Alfie had stopped talking. If he came out of

the shed now she would be easy to spot but there was
something she wanted to check. Further along the body was
the passenger door. She turned the handle, it opened smoothly
and soundlessly. Oiled to perfection. The smell from inside
was beeswax. Maliha nodded to herself and climbed inside.
There was even less light here but what little light there was
reflected off polished brass and leather.

From the description she had read the seats, while large
and very comfortable, should be arranged in two ranks of two
with enough room for a small kitchen in the back. This was
different. The seats were ranged around the sides facing
inward, the floor was carpeted with a deep pile, and the walls
were panelled in wood, including the front bulkhead. Almost
like a very small drawing room, it screamed luxury.

Maliha jumped as music broke out and echoed through
the hangar. She did not recognise the tune, since music was
one form of art that could not be easily reproduced—and
certainly not in print—but the style suggested strongly that it
was from the music hall. Alfie must have a phonograph, and
one with the highest level of reverberation.

She peered through the opposite window and the volume of
the music redoubled as the door of the shed opened. A man in
overalls emerged, silhouetted against the electric light within, this
must be Alfie. As he moved from the direct light she saw he was
perhaps in his thirties, tall but walked with rounded shoulders.
Light glinted from his glasses. He was not heading towards her
but across the floor towards one of the other fixed-wing flyers.

Maliha dashed to the other side and pulled the door
closed. The snap of the lock seemed very loud to her but who
knew what could be heard through the din of a woman
singing about her lovely fruit.

Alfie came into view and was now heading away. She let
him walk a few more steps before opening the door once
more, jumping down and shutting it behind her. An act which
forced her to turn her back on Alfie but she was committed

now. She must move swiftly and with confidence but still on
tiptoe.

She did not head straight for the exit but to the nearer
wall, the one closest to the reception. The shadows here would
be the best way to hide herself. Forcing herself not to look at
the daylight through the open door, for fear of destroying her
night vision, she kept her eyes down and followed the line of
the wall.

She reached the front of the hangar and was pleased to
see that her assumption had been confirmed. There was a
small electric motor to drive the opening and closing of the
big doors.

The music stopped. Maliha froze again.

Then Alfie started singing the same song at the top of his
voice, which was a pleasant tenor. Maliha did not stop to
listen. If he was singing, all he would be able to hear would be
himself. She picked up her skirts and pelted for the gap in the
door. Even if he saw her he would never catch her.

Alfie did not stop singing about his lovely fruits as Maliha
zig-zagged through the opening. She did not slow down until
she was around the corner of the hangar. As she piled in and
slammed the door, she breathlessly ordered the cab to head
back to Blackrock.

She alighted just past the gasworks. From there she walked,
carrying her heavy bags, and nodding to the young coastguard
as she went.

It was about two o'clock when she arrived back and
secreted her purchases in the store room. Her food was cold
but still on the tray outside her room. She brought it inside
and ate the sausage and mash concoction. Somehow so much
better than Cook's. Even though it was stone cold. The
sausages were of far better quality, and the potatoes had been
mashed so thoroughly, perhaps with some oil, there was not a

single lump to be found. She could also taste garlic and there was an attractive sprinkling of herbs.

It was details like that that made all the difference. She hoped Cook would learn from this experience.

Then Matron knocked.

30

"Anyone would think I'm you're skivvy," she said entering without waiting to be invited. She had a package under her arm, which she dumped on the bed.

"Do you want me to clear a space for you in the store room?"

"I don't understand."

"Don't come the innocent with me, young lady." Matron crossed her arms. "You were out of the school again this morning and returned with several bundles—"

Maliha opened her mouth but was stopped by Matron's raised hand.

"No, don't deny it."

"I wasn't going to—"

But Matron continued as if Maliha had not spoken. "You need to be more discreet, Miss Anderson. You're getting careless. Coming and going in the hours of daylight. I sometimes wonder what this school is coming to."

"I wanted to say that it would be most helpful if I were allowed to store certain things in there," said Maliha.

"I see."

"With the dead rat this morning and being tripped in the church I can only see this vendetta increasing in intensity at least until the dance has come and gone. The perpetrators might well attempt to prevent me from attending by destroying my dress—when it arrives. If you were going to suggest having a secure location where they might be hidden, that would be ideal."

"Quite so," said Matron somewhat flustered as if the wind had been taken from her sails. "Good. You seem to have covered the same ground as me." She gestured at the parcel. "That's come from London by the mark on it. Kensington."

Maliha stared at the parcel and caught herself in what she could only describe as fear. Though she could not imagine why.

"Want me to open it?" said Matron.

Maliha glanced and saw a gentle smile on the woman's face.

"Sometimes it's hard to get nice things."

Matron pulled a pair of small scissors from a pocket in her skirt and snipped the string holding it all together. It wasn't the coarse string you could buy at any post office, it was smooth, dark blue and reflected the light. It was regulation brown paper that Matron removed from the inner box but even that was of a more expensive variety. The box inside was the usual card but coloured in deep blue with *Paquin* in cursive gold letters on the lid. A card slipped to the bed, Matron passed it to Maliha.

It was handwritten. "Miss Anderson, practice two hours each day but no longer than half an hour at a time. We expect elegance. Jeanne."

"What does it say?"

Maliha handed it back to Matron. "Oh, very nice, Jeanne Paquin's own hand I'll be bound. You're certainly circulating at the highest levels now. Shame she couldn't make something for me."

The fact that Jeanne Paquin made a point of pricing her

dresses reasonably and was happy to have anyone in her shop was probably not something Matron wanted to hear.

"Well open it," said Matron. "You might as well."

Maliha wasn't entirely sure what she had been expecting but wrapped in tissue paper to stop them from rubbing were a pair of white shoes. They were cut low to reveal to the top of the foot and a single strap and buckle went across the ankle.

"That must be three inches of heel," said Matron almost in horror. "And you never wear anything except flats. Well, she's right about practice. Assuming you don't break your ankle. You'll need a Faraday to keep you upright."

Maliha took one shoe out. She had been expecting quilted satin which was a popular style but they, she now realised, would not have the structural strength for such a high heel. The leather seemed warm to the touch and she ran her fingers across the sensual surface and then under the grip-less sole. The lining was soft and padded.

She sat down on the bed and unlaced her shoes. Then after a moment's hesitation took off her socks. The left shoe slipped on and she buckled it up. It fitted perfectly around the sides and back but her toes felt as if they were being crushed. Matron handed her the other shoe, which she had been examining, and Maliha put it on.

She had never owned anything like them before. Their luxury was almost overwhelming and she had to brush back a tear, and then remind herself that it was Lady Henrietta Creighton-Ward who had made this possible. They were a gift from someone for whom the expense meant nothing.

"Let me give you a hand up."

Maliha took the woman's hand and together they levered Maliha to her feet. It was like standing on a steep slope, that might collapse at any moment. She tried to relax and settle her feet into the shoe but it was unsettling to see everything from a new angle.

"One moment," said Matron, "there's another note."

Maliha was still holding Matron's hand and felt distinctly

unsafe when she stretched out to reach into the box. The new note was typewritten.

"Instructions," said Matron. "1. Place foot heel-toe when walking normally. 2. Take small steps. 3. Place foot flat when going downstairs. 4. Place toe-first when going upstairs. 5. Walk as if on a tightrope. 6. Allow hips to swing. 7. Practice."

"That seems straightforward enough," said Maliha, though the instructions sounded simple she expected the execution to be anything but. She took a deep breath, lifted her right foot and moved it. She allowed the heel to land first and then the sole. She realised she had not walked as if on a line and moved it to the side so it was in front of the other shoe.

Now she was unbalanced and gripped Matron's hand even tighter, but she lifted the left foot, swung it around and placed it in front of the right. Keeping the length of the stride short.

"My leg and hip muscles are already strained," she said as she took the next step, and the next. Matron moved with her but Maliha released her hand and headed for the opposite wall. It took a little longer to get there than she expected— short strides seemed inevitable—and there was a constant feeling that she might fall.

She bumped into the wall and placed the flat of her hands against it for support. Then placed her cheek on the cold surface.

"This is torture," she said.

"Do the shoes hurt?"

"No, but muscles I never knew I had are already complaining."

"Walk back."

Maliha pushed herself away from the wall but kept a hand on it as she turned around carefully. The heels were quite wide but she got the strong sense she might topple over at any moment.

There was another knock on the door.

"What?" Maliha almost shouted.

"Margaret! With shoes."

"Who?"

There was a momentary pause. "Sadie. With shoes."

"You better come in."

She barged in like a bull and stopped short just inside. "You got yours on." The she saw Matron. "Oh sorry, Matron."

"Don't you have a lesson this morning, Miss Creighton-Ward?"

"Free period, Matron."

"Very well. I should probably leave you girls to it. You'll no doubt have a lot more fun without me. But I will be annoyed if I have to deal with a sprained ankle and seriously displeased if it's a broken one."

She left.

"Go on then," said Margaret.

"What?"

"Walk to the bed or spend the rest of the day glued to the wall."

"Fine," muttered Maliha. She focused on the task and managed not to fall over as she moved across the room. Heel-toe, short strides, walking a line. She arrived at the bed but had nothing to hold on to so she stood there, nervously balanced trying not to stand on tip-toe.

"I'm so jealous, she's given you bigger heels than me."

"She's a sadist."

"A what?"

"Never mind. Aren't you going to put yours on then and we can teeter about the room together for half an hour."

Margaret did not need any prompting. She was like a puppy, thought Maliha, except when she was being sensible. It must be nice to be able to simply switch it off.

So, for the next half-hour, she tried to mimic her friend's *joie de vivre*. She was not sure whether she succeeded but she thought about the coming problems less than she had. Her aching legs finally demanded she stop and she simply lay down on the bed. Margaret crashed down beside her, laughing.

Mealtime came and went. Maliha took to her bed again with her aching hips. She had overdone the first practice session with her new shoes. They were very impractical but she had seen herself in the mirror and had to admit that the shoes demanded she maintain a good posture. Remembering how the dress had looked on her, she put the two images together and knew that she would make a striking figure. And would undoubtedly engender even more jealousy.

However, it was now imperative she attend the dance.

It was clear to her now that the relationship between Ethel and Pat had not been accidental—though the consequences would not have been part of the plan. Taliesin had placed Ena in the school and used Pat to get close to Ethel in order to gain leverage over her father and potentially gain access to the royals. If Mr Jordan was told his daughter would be hurt or killed if he didn't obey? Wouldn't that be enough?

Maliha realised she knew nothing of Ethel's mother. She sat up on the edge of the bed and pulled on the new shoes again. She needed to practice with them and she wasn't going far.

Going in straight lines was not too hard now as long as she launched herself in the right direction. She reached the door and got outside into the corridor. There were two half-flights of stairs between her and Matron's room. That would be good practice. She clung to the banister as she made her way down planting each foot flat as she went.

What she had not expected was the roughness of the floor, somehow wearing heels seemed to amplify the uneven surface and she had to be very careful where she planted her feet. She arrived at the door just as a couple of girls from the lower school were leaving. They stared up at her and she had the feeling she was towering over them.

Neither of them looked down at her feet, for which she was grateful., and she went inside before they got the chance to turn.

"Matron?"

"In here, dear," said the woman from her office. She looked up as Maliha came in and glanced down at her feet. "How's it going?"

"I think I'm getting the hang of it, it's just tiring."

"Good." Then, when Maliha said nothing and did not leave, she added. "Did you want something?"

"Can I sit down?"

"Help yourself."

Maliha sat with considerable relief. "I wanted to ask you something about Ethel Jordan."

"I'm sure you've discovered more about her than I know or want to know."

"Yes, but not about her mother."

"Her mother?"

"I don't know anything about her mother, is she alive, dead, estranged?"

"And why do you think I would know?"

"It might be in her records if it's important."

Matron shook her head in disapproval. "It would be quite improper of me to divulge any secrets of that nature. I believe we have covered this point previously?"

"You're right. I'm sorry." The aching in her leg muscles was distracting, would five days be enough to get her to the point where she could spend an evening wearing these shoes? Did she have any choice?

"You're still trying to discover her murderer?"

Maliha hesitated. "I am trying to find proof."

"You should tell the police."

"I have communicated with the one person I think will listen to me."

"I could speak to them."

"And when they ask you where you got your information?

It is fruitless to discuss this with the local constabulary, they have already made up their minds."

"I'm sorry, I can't help you."

"No," said Maliha and turned away wobbling a little. She had yet to gain the balance she needed for complex manoeuvres. "But I will be sending a letter, would you be able to find someone to send it?"

"Of course, my dear. Just one thing though. What was that nonsense earlier? Miss Creighton-Ward calling herself Sadie?"

"It's her name, one of her names."

"Yes, I looked up her file. I understand she goes by the name of Margaret among the girls."

"I call her Sadie."

"Why?"

"She wanted me to use something more personal."

"And you chose Sadie?"

"I don't like to be too predictable."

Back in her room, Maliha removed the torture devices from her feet and spent a moment enjoying the relief. Then she sat at the desk and grabbed her pen and a sheet of paper. If she was lucky she should catch the afternoon post, and if very lucky receive a reply late tomorrow, but certainly Thursday morning.

There was another possibility as well. Though it would mean leaving the safety of the school once more.

31

———

Margaret had visited in the evening again after dinner and they had practised walking in heels for half an hour. Her friend had tried to pry more information from her, but Maliha feigned ignorance. The latest news from London, via Lady Henrietta, was that the dresses would be delivered on Friday.

Maliha was not happy about that since it gave the ne'er-do-wells additional opportunities to cause damage. However, there was no way she could control that except hope they wouldn't be found, so there was no point worrying about it.

It was about eight-thirty when Margaret left and Maliha went to the card game with Matron, Mr Pimm and Mrs Clemence. The presence of the school secretary took Maliha aback but then everything was topsy-turvy now. Food preparations were probably almost round-the-clock now, so cook was lacking. And the school echoed to the sound of hammering and sawing throughout the day while the smell of drying paint permeated the air.

"It's a madhouse," said Mrs Clemence. "I have had to co-opt Mr Gunnell to ensure that everyone is doing the work they're supposed to. I hate having to rely on someone else but it really is far too much."

"You poor thing," said Matron. "If you need something to calm your nerves…" she let the sentence trail off.

"Mrs Ramsey's stash is enough for me."

Maliha did not draw attention to herself and Mrs Clemence ran on, incriminating herself as someone who frequently dipped into the headmistress's private reserve. The cards moved across the table, tricks were won and lost.

"I just worry about the girls," said Mrs Clemence starting up again. "I mean, all these men coming in and out, of course they have papers and orders, but it would be so easy for someone to get in."

"Never mind the girls," said Mr Pimm. "We could all be murdered in our beds." He gave Maliha a sly look and she allowed the beginnings of a smile to touch her lips.

"All of us, yes, Mr Pimm," said Mrs Clemence. "It's so dangerous opening up the school like this, we're just not safe."

"Don't listen to him," said Matron. "He's just trying to get a rise out of you."

Mrs Clemence played the next card so forcefully it flew off the table. Maliha retrieved it.

The game went on.

It was easier to stay awake when there was no requirement to pretend. Maliha read and watched the clock tick through to eleven-thirty. She dressed warmly and went down to the store room, where she collected the extra clothes, tools and padlock.

The side window of the chapel was open just as she had left it, and she climbed in. The sky was cloudy, which was unfortunate. With the hacksaw in hand she attacked the window latch. The noise seemed frightful in the cold quiet night, with only the sound of distant waves and the occasional owl or fox. But she kept at it until the part that actually held the window shut fell off.

Using adhesive, she glued the broken piece into the position where it would be if it was genuinely holding the window shut. The result was that with the window closed and lever in place it looked locked, yet a simple push (or pull from the other side) would open it.

A rag stuffed into the window frame, with an end hanging outside, jammed the window shut so even pressing on it quite hard would not open it. Yet simply pulling the rag on the outside would quickly and easily release the jam and the window would open. It would pass muster as long as no one pulled the rag before Saturday evening.

Maliha then headed down into the crypt.

Getting the hacksaw to cut through this padlock took considerably more work, and noise, than the window latch. But she kept at it, sometimes swapping hands, even though her left was considerably less effective. It was nearly two in the morning when she finally broke through and was able to remove the old lock. She replaced it with her new one. It wasn't as big but it would pass muster. Then she set about oiling the hinges and the bolts. She worked each one until she was sure it would move easily.

Then came the moment of truth. Maliha removed the padlock, undid all the bolts and pulled the door open. Stones scraped noisily as it swung inward, she closed it again and brushed the stone surface with her hands. At the second attempt the door opened silently. She moved it back and forth a little to ensure the oil was worked into the hinges. For the last time she closed it, set the bolts and put the padlock in place again.

In the crypt, she prepared the clothes and put the key to the padlock into the pocket of the trousers, attached to a length of twine which she also looped through a belt loop. She did not want it getting lost.

By half-past two the escape route was in place and ready to be used. Pleased with herself, she hid everything and headed back to her room with the intention of getting as much sleep as she could in the remaining hours.

She did not close her curtains but kept the lights off as well as she slowly removed her clothing. Through the window, the night was dark but highlighted in grey. The hedge and trees were thickest black while the field beyond curved up to the faintly blue horizon dotted with stars.

The fire had gone out in the grate but red embers still glowed there and the room had not lost all its warmth, though she got goose bumps as a cold draught played across her bare legs. There was something daring about standing naked by an open window, even though she knew there was no one out there, and even if there had been she would be invisible. Her skin helped to make her unnoticeable.

She stepped closer and pressed her palms against the cold metal of the window frames. Her eyes adjusted until she could make out the trees and bushes of the perimeter. An owl screeched. And a light flickered off to the right. It went dark again almost immediately, as if someone with an electric torch had been surprised by the sudden sound and then hidden it once more. It had been quite a way off to the right, though. She reimagined where she had seen it. The land rose gently in that direction and there was a patch of ground where the line of trees widened. That was where she had seen the light and that was a place a person might hide effectively, while the elevation would assist in seeing into the dormitories.

It wouldn't be the first time, every year there would be someone who thought it would be a good idea to see if they could spy on the dorms and see the girls in various states of undress. But to have one now seemed too much of a coincidence, it might just be a peeping tom, or it might be something more sinister.

Then she remembered she was in precisely the state of undress someone like that would want to see her. She backed away from the window and dressed herself for sleeping. If it had been under any other circumstances she would have simply reported it. The chance that it might be something related to the case meant she would have to investigate it herself first.

32

She yawned as she woke up to the knock on the door. There was sufficient light to illuminate the room but it was still early. She grabbed at her watch on the table by the bed and squinted at it. Eight o'clock. She glanced at the treacherous window, it must have become overcast during the night and what looked like early dawn wasn't.

The person on the other side of the door knocked again.

"Just leave the tray," she tried to say, but she just croaked. Instead of trying again, she threw back the covers and grabbed her dressing gown. The floor and air were very cold. She unlocked the door and pulled it open violently.

"Mornin', miss."

"Ena."

"Troubled night, miss?"

Maliha made an unladylike noise and went back into the room. The escapades of the previous night had left her considerably worse for wear and out of sorts. She sat in the chair by the desk and Ena put down the tray in front of her.

"Porridge and toast with a mug of tea."

"It all gets cold during the journey from there to here."

"You could eat with the other girls, miss."

"I've been all but banned." *Which suits me well enough.* She picked up her spoon and started on the porridge. It was as not as bad as she expected.

"Do you want the curtains pulled to, miss?

"Why?"

"You're in your nightie."

"I suppose."

Ena did it promptly, blocking out the already dim light and the teeming rain. It continued, however, to drum on the roof.

The maid turned and looked expectantly at Maliha. It was clear she had some news to impart but Maliha was in no mood to play games. She didn't ask but applied herself to her bowl.

"There's a commotion below stairs," said Ena finally.

"On top of everything else?"

"There's marines coming in tomorrow, they'll be deployed round the school for protection."

"You don't seem very happy about it."

"Taliesin won't be able to do anything, all we've done will be in vain."

"They will have expected it, it won't stop them."

"You think they're still about to blow up the princes?" she said. "What about everybody else?"

"I don't think that's their plan anymore because it makes no sense."

"Then what?"

"My best guess is kidnapping for ransom."

Ena looked doubtful. "Why would they do that on the day when the place will be alive with soldiers? Or in the school at all? If I wanted to kidnap one of the girls I'd do it on one of the days when they're allowed into the town."

Maliha stared at her as the realisation came over her. "Because this is the only day when the person they want to kidnap will be *least* guarded."

Maliah stared at the wall "Could they really want one of

the princes?" She said the words out loud just to hear how they sounded. "But there's no value in kidnapping the prince —whichever one."

"It would be a king's ransom, surely?"

"The government wouldn't pay it. And the entire British Empire would be after them." *Including a whole team of special agents who must usually be competent and trustworthy, unlike James Munroe.* "It would be suicidal. Which brings us back to assassination, except it can't be. The change in venue happened after they bought the sweetshop, and after they brought you into the school. It's something to do with the school as well as something to do with the princes."

"Perhaps they want to marry the boy off to one of the girls," said Ena and burst out laughing.

But Maliha did not laugh but just stared at her. Ena stopped laughing.

"I'm sorry, miss, I was just making a joke."

"No," said Maliha. "You're right. What if that is their plan?"

"I was joking, miss. Even I know the prince is barely more than a boy."

"He's not old enough to marry in the UK," said Maliha then thought for a moment. "Or anywhere in Europe."

"Betrothed?"

"If a child makes a promise it means nothing and to do so under duress, would be worse."

"Perhaps they would be abducted and held until they could be married."

"In which instance they would once again have the whole British Empire after them for a minimum of four years. And a coerced marriage could easily be annulled." *Henry VIII had done it enough times to make it an acceptable precedent for a king.*

Maliha sighed again. It just made no sense. Nothing about the situation made any sense, she must be missing critical information. And there were only four days left.

"Have you finished, miss?"

"What?"

"Your breakfast?"

Maliha looked down at the empty plates in front of her as if she was surprised to see them there. "Yes, thank you."

"I expect Taliesin will want information about those troops tomorrow. What should I tell him?"

Maliha stared at the window for a few moments. "Whatever you can that's the truth. Play along."

"I'd be happier slicing his neck with a knife."

"I know," Maliha said. "Ena, something I never asked, did your brother ever tell you how he met Ethel?"

"My brother was never one to keep his eyes to himself, he said he saw her playing in a hockey match, managed to speak to her."

"He was in the habit of walking up to any girl and speaking to them?"

Ena turned and faced back into the room. "He was not. He would look like all men and boys but lack the courage to speak to any one of them."

"And when it came to women she was formidable."

Ena nodded. "My brother had…"

"What?"

"A way with horses, miss."

Maliha gave a half-smile. "Well, Taliesin will have told him to do it."

"But he truly cared, miss."

"That must have come later."

She wondered how a girl like Ethel Jordan would have reacted to the attentions of a young Irish man. Shocked? Disbelieving? Or simply violent? Perhaps he had a way with women too. Perhaps she would change, the way Amelia had, perhaps with him she was as docile as a kitten. Though the claws of kittens were like needles.

The question of the light in the night now took her attention.

It may have been nothing. It might have been a farmer looking for livestock. There was even the faint possibility she had imagined it. And there was the chance, too, that it was important.

The weather continued inclement. She looked at the high-heeled shoes and decided to forgo their pleasure this morning. Instead she grabbed her umbrella, headed down to the storeroom and changed into her most weather-resistant clothes.

Under the circumstances she felt she was even less likely to be observed as she left by the window. Nobody would want to be out in this if they could help it. And the rain would help to hide her. She trudged through the pooling water on the path with the rain pattering on the umbrella. She did not relish the prospect of another bout of illness and pulled the scarf closer around her neck and up over her mouth and nose.

The umbrella caught on the branches as she passed through the perimeter trees, and water thumped down in huge drops from the disturbed boughs. Then she was through but instead of continuing towards Brighton, she turned back on her self and followed the path that led around the outside of the perimeter.

She went through the gate and found her feet sinking into clinging mud. She cursed the British weather and not for the first time. It must have taken her twice as long to walk the length of the back of the school than it should. She picked her way up the gentle rise, trying to find the less muddy parts and endeavouring to step only on tussocks of grass.

Her feet were sodden by the time she reached the place where the perimeter trees stopped at a wider area filled with bushes. The spring growth had not started but there was a lot of green here: rhododendrons. They were evergreens and their thick foliage would even keep off a deluge like this.

She could see where mud had been tracked form the path to the interior. She paused. This was dangerous, what if it was

Taliesin? Or a peeping tom with violent tendencies? She should have told Ena where she was going. Or Margaret.

Well, she had her umbrella and Ethel's knife in her pocket. That would have to be sufficient since she was not about to go back through the rain and mud to get support.

She followed the trail and closed her umbrella as she pushed through the tangles branches into the interior.

Her assessment was correct. It was reasonably dry beneath the canopy of leaves, though water still dripped through. She caught the scent of cigarettes and paused. There was no sound but the drumming of the rain.

"Who's here?" she called, she did not want to provoke a violent reaction of surprise by coming on someone unawares. But there was no reply. She pushed on coming to the more open area in the middle of the bush. There was a camp bed with blankets, though it looked decidedly damp. Some sort of stove with a small kettle. She put her hand against it, it was stone cold which suggested the occupant had not made a drink this morning.

He was certainly absent.

Further in, towards the school, was a black leather case lying flat. From the shine of both leather and brass beneath the splashes of mud it was clearly brand new. She crouched among the damp dead leaves and popped the locks. She had feared to find a telescope, what there was was infinitely worse. A very modern camera with a lens arrangement as big as her hand, clearly telescopic. She closed the lid and followed the trail of dirty leaves to a point that looked out on the school. From this vantage point the windows of several dormitories were in view, all of the lower school. There was even a convenient branch on which to rest the undoubtedly heavy camera, and it had been used.

She smelled fresh burning cigarette smoke before she heard him. She turned to face the threat and tied up her furled umbrella to make it more useful as a weapon, then put her hand on the knife in her pocket.

The man swore excessively as he pushed through the rhododendrons. She kept quite still and he did not seem to notice her.

He dropped a satchel to the floor and, without even a glance in her direction, set to attempting to light the burner, his lack of success and the increase in profanity suggested damp had got into his Vesta case.

"Must you swear quite so much?"

He turned his head slowly. He had a large nose and his hair was slick-flat. From the way the water droplets lay on it he must use some sort of hair grease.

"'Oo are you?"

"I am the person who's going to report you to the police."

He stood and she imagined he was trying to look threatening but she was at a higher point than him and he was not a tall man.

Then a nasty grin came over his face. "I know you—" He gave a short laugh. "You're that Alice Anderson girl."

"And you're a peeping tom."

At first he seemed genuinely surprised at her accusation and then he looked down at the ground.

"I ain't. I work for the Manchester Guardian."

Maliha squinted and the thousands of articles she had read flashed through her mind. "You're Ray Jennings." The surprise again. It was almost as if he couldn't keep his emotions off his face. "Yes, I know you. You write all the scurrilous items. The scandals and the break-ups, there's nothing that comes from your pen that is not hurtful."

"But you've heard of me."

"Only because I read everything."

"What about an interview then?"

"I beg your pardon?"

"Exclusive interview with the most important person in the case."

"Help you get on to the front page? I think not."

His face turned from its deceitful smile to an honest scowl. "Yeah, bet you'd do it for that Churchill cow, wouldn't ya?"

"I think you're missing the point, Mr Jennings, you have been taking photographs of the girls in their dormitories."

He glanced at the leather case. "What, that? That's not important."

The rain was letting up a bit but it made no difference beneath the dripping rhododendron. Maliha shivered, she needed to get back inside before she caught another cold.

"What do you mean?"

"Give me an interview and I'll sod off back to London."

She looked back at the camera case and frowned. Jenning's clothes were cheap and worn. The camera with that lens must have cost a year's wages, at least.

"Who's paying you?"

He froze like a rat in a suddenly illuminated room. "Nobody."

She took a step forward and brandished her umbrella. "You're lying."

"I ain't, I borrowed it."

She pressed the point of her umbrella on to the leather. "So, if something happened to it that would be a problem?"

"For gawd's sake, leave it!" In a sudden move he grabbed at the case and pulled it to his chest. "I borrowed it, right? I didn't want to bloody come 'ere. Camping out in March? I never been without a roof before. I hate this, alright? This is a load of crap."

"What pictures have you taken?"

"Nuffink."

She looked down and gathered her thoughts. "Mr Jennings, as you pointed out, I am a key witness in this case. I know the detective in charge very well."

Jennings flinched.

"I have no particular desire to turn you in, but can you imagine the kind of punishment they would mete out to a man taking photographs of young girls? Daughters of the aristocracy and the monied classes? Never mind the judicial punishment, what about the treatment you'd get from the police?"

"I don't want no police."

She smiled. "Neither do I. So far we are in agreement. What photographs have you got?"

"I got a few."

She seethed with hatred for the little man who seemed so unconcerned at his own disgusting behaviour, but she kept it in, made herself sound reasonable and calm.

"What sort?"

"Some of the younger girls, some of the older ones."

"Naked?"

"A few. Only the waist up though, the window ledges get in the way."

"I'm sure they do." Her voice was barely above a whisper. "And you were going to sell these?"

He shrugged. "There's trade in that."

"Especially if the victims don't know."

"I suppose."

Maliha closed her eyes, all she wanted to do was ram her umbrella through his heart—if she could find it.

"I could get rid if you gave me an interview."

Her eyes snapped open. "This is what's going to happen, Mr Jennings, you are going to destroy the films. Right now. And then you are going to return to London and go back to your nasty little job."

Now he looked scared. "I can't. I got to 'ave something."

"What do you mean?"

"I mean I got to have something." Then his demeanour changed from the fear back to the false levity. Hiding something. "Bloke's got to make a penny. Keep the wolf from the door."

There was something he wasn't telling her, something that put as much fear in him as the police. She didn't really care what trouble he was in but if giving him something

meant he destroyed the pictures, perhaps she should give
a bit.

"All right. But you burn the negatives right here and now.
And all the rest of your film. You get off back to London this
afternoon."

"Interview, yeah?"

"No," she said. "But it will be something you can use and
it'll be good enough to match up to one of Winifred
Churchill's pieces."

"What?"

"Film first."

"You think I'm stupid?"

Yes. "Or I could just get the police on you."

"Or I could just do you in right here and now."

"You may be slime, Mr Jennings, but I don't think you're a
murderer." She slipped the knife from her pocket. "Besides, I
did not come unarmed."

He peered at the small knife in her hand. "That does not
make me very afraid."

"Perhaps not, but I can still hurt you."

He held up his hand. "Alright. You gave a bit, I saw that. I
can do the same."

It took a while longer before he managed to get his stove
lit and the grey and brown films made a very bright bonfire.
He hadn't even finished the first reel.

"It's hard getting these candid pictures, boring 'n'all." He
liked to talk and didn't seem too concerned about he was
destroying the pictures he'd taken. However his lack of
empathy kept Maliha's anger bubbling. "I mean, you 'ave to
wait hours just 'oping one of the girls will take her top off and
jump around by a window. And top it all if you don't go quick
enough and snap it before she's gone or put her nightie on.
Didn't even get any really good ones."

Eventually it was done. Jennings pulled out a notebook
and pencil.

"What have you got then?"

"Amelia Johnson."

"The nutter what done the other one in."

"No."

"A different girl?"

"No."

"What then?"

"She didn't do it."

Jennings' eyes lit up. "Who did?"

Maliha shook her head. "You're missing the point."

"You ain't said nothing."

"Amelia is being accused of the crime and will be put away in an asylum without a trial so the police don't have to find the real culprit."

"So?"

"So, this is a bunch of toffs putting a poor girl away for nothing."

"But she's a nutter. I heard she likes to be hurt, you know, really hurt."

"That's true."

"So she's better locked up?"

"Considering the pain they're likely to inflict on her in that barbaric place, I expect she'll be very happy."

"Exactly."

Maliha sighed. "That was sarcasm. Mr Jennings, are you being deliberately obtuse? I find it hard to believe you have succeeded as well as you have by being stupid?"

"I just don't see any angle I can use?"

"Imprisoning a young girl without a trial for her entire life, when she should be in the bosom of her family? Letting the murderer go free to murder again? Are the toffs in on it?"

"You mean like a conspiracy?"

"Yes."

"Maybe the murderer was a toff and they're closing ranks."

"Yes."

"Maybe there's a whole trade in acquiring girls and letting toffs kill them."

"No."

"Could happen."

"You want to get published?"

"Fair point." Then his eyes lit up. "I could write a couple of different pieces, this ones got some legs."

Maliha suddenly felt very tired.

"Do what you like, but just do it in London."

"A decent bed is a good draw."

"I never want to see you again."

He stuck out his hand. "Deal."

She brushed past him and headed back into the muddy field. Her feet were cold and the shoes heavy with water.

Once back in her room she spent the remainder of the morning warming up, even to the point where she went back to bed and slept beneath the covers until lunch came knocking.

33

Wednesday morning arrived in the form of thundering noise. Two four-rotor flyers descended onto the back lawn outside Maliha's window. The building shook with the power of the machines—these were not diesel-powered but steam, which streamed from the inner workings of each rotor. Once she had ascertained the world was not ending, she was glued to the window watching them come down.

In a diesel machine there would be one engine for each rotor, but for a steam-driven flyer there was one furnace, one boiler from which the superheated steam was carried through pipes to the individual turbines that drove the rotors.

These were not the biggest machines but they were not small and once they had landed, well before the rotors stopped turning, forty marines discharged from each and formed ranks. Maliha imagined that Mrs Clemence would be very displeased since she had not mentioned the arrival of this military contingent on Monday evening.

Maliha dressed quickly and found her breakfast outside her door once again. It wasn't cold and she consumed it as quickly as she dared without getting indigestion. It was entirely possible the person delivering it had knocked while the flyers were landing; there was no way on earth that she could have heard anything.

She was a bit annoyed though, if the marines set up camp around the back it could put a distinct crimp in her plans for the two lovers—and it meant she would have wasted a lot of effort with the church. But there was no point in worrying yet, she would have to wait and see what their plans were. It would also prevent her making any further excursions during the day. She also suspected that the amount of work being performed was going to drop significantly as girls and teachers alike swooned over handsome men marching to and fro outside.

After breakfast, Maliha put on the high-heeled shoes and walked around the room for half an hour, contemplating the impossibility of the information she had to hand.

Taliesin had killed people to make his plan work and, as far as she knew, he had bludgeoned Ethel Jordan to death to prevent it being revealed. That he was up to no good was without question—and that was important because Maliha could have read the apparent evidence in a different way. If he hadn't killed so many innocents he might have been working for the crown—either crown.

He had arranged for Patrick Hogan to meet Ethel and somehow that led to her father, perhaps Taliesin threatened to kill Ethel if her father did not do as he was told. And Jordan Airways was used to transporting very special passengers in their luxurious flyer. Perhaps royalty, the fact that Jordan managed to keep his business out of the papers suggested he was keeping things quiet. That was why she had not known what he did—that, and the fact nobody talked about Ethel except to slander her.

But to what end?

Taliesin had purchased the sweet shop months ago, likewise arranged for Ena and her brother to be employed. This was before the dance had even been announced but it must have been in planning longer.

Maliha stopped in the middle of the room. She had found that holding her feet at an angle to one another provided greater stability when she was not walking. She was not, however, happy with the way her hips swayed when she was walking—the lascivious nature of the movement was not lost to her, and if she was wearing the clinging Paquin dress it would only emphasise the movement. She was sure Madame Paquin meant well, but she was not aware of the insults that the combination of Maliha's skin colour and such provocative behaviour would engender.

Maliha would become the subject of considerable male attention and that was not what she desired.

She changed out of her shoes and went in search of Matron.

"Do you know when the dance was arranged?"

Matron was in the room that adjoined her office that contained the various medicines, bandages, monthly supplies and other necessities for her job. Maliha leaned against the door frame as the woman opened a box marked as medical supplies. It contained tins of sanitary products.

"It was going to be at the Royal Pavilion."

"Yes, in a month or so," said Maliha, "but when was it first arranged?"

"Is it important, dear?"

"Yes."

Matron stopped and stood erect, her hand pressing against her hip as she levered herself to the vertical.

"How are the shoes?"

"Difficult, and I don't like the way they make my hips move."

Matron nodded and gave Maliha a long look before speaking again. "I don't know exactly."

"Even a rough estimate would be helpful."

"Remember Guy Fawkes night last year?"

"New moon, very dark, very clear, very cold. The fireworks were impressive."

"Of course, you remember," said Matron, "Mrs Clemence was agitated and told me about the plan. She was not at all happy about it, she does not think the girls should be gallivanting with young men. I think she must have said 'only trouble will come of it' at least six times in the one conversation."

Maliha sighed in relief. "Well, that's good."

"Is it, dear?"

"Whatever's being planned it has to do with the dance."

"I have no idea what you're talking about."

"I know."

"Is this still to do with poor Ethel's murder?"

"Yes. It's the motive for it."

"I thought the motive was her being in the family way."

"Only because the murderer thought she might reveal his plan when questioned about her condition."

Matron looked concerned. "Are the girls in danger?"

"With all these fine marines and Naval officers on hand?" Maliha crossed her fingers behind her back. "No danger at all."

Matron looked unconvinced. "What's going on?"

Maliha sighed. "I honestly don't know. I have collected a considerable quantity of facts but nothing seems to make much sense. If the dance had been a recent plan I would have absolutely no idea at all. You have at least been able to settle my mind on that."

There was another long moment of silence and then Matron made a humphing noise and came out of her side room. She went to the door of her office, shut it and turned the key in the lock. The rule was that if the door was shut, she was talking to someone privately and was not to be disturbed.

"Sit down, Maliha."

She did so as Matron sat opposite. "You wanted to know about Ethel Jordan's mother?"

"You don't have to tell me."

"Of course, I don't, dear, but there's no law that says I mustn't and, after all, the poor thing is dead and what you're asking is not something you couldn't find out another way eventually."

"I wrote to Somerset House," said Maliha.

"Ha! Not one to take no for an answer. I like that. This school was created to give girls real independence in a man's world. I don't understand the parents who send their children here and then simply marry them off into domestic slavery."

"Are *you* a suffragist, Matron?"

"Some women are happy belonging to their husbands, Miss Anderson, and if they are happy then I am happy for them. But for those who would not be, they should not be required to follow that path. You are one of the latter I should imagine."

"I cannot imagine myself married," said Maliha. "Though when I return to India my grandmother will make it her business to see me tied to a 'good husband'."

"Will you cooperate?"

"I will not."

Matron smiled and nodded. "You see that you do not."

She slid open the drawer of her desk and pulled out a manila folder.

"Ethel's father has been married three times. None of his wives is currently living."

"Foul play?"

Matron shook her head. "I don't have all the details, of course, but the first died in childbirth, the second of consumption, and the third in a traffic accident."

"Which one was Ethel's mother?"

"The second. Ethel had no siblings."

"I see. The family home is in Brighton."

"It is."

Maliha hesitated. "Does it give the death date of the third wife?"

Matron consulted the sheet. She might have been willing to give Maliha this information but she kept the details out of sight. It was a shame because just one glance would have been enough for Maliha to be able to peruse it at her leisure later.

"August, 1897."

"Thank you."

They sat silently.

"I should go," said Maliha. "I interrupted you."

"Leave the door open."

34

———————

Maliha checked the time. Everyone would be in class by now. She dressed for town, a glance outside indicated the sky was overcast but not raining. She put a scarf over her head, to disguise her colouration, and took her umbrella, just in case.

It was a risk but she needed to get into town. She came out of the main door of the infirmary and turned left into the courtyard. Usually it was quiet here but now the place was filled with marines, they seemed to be relaxing, but that process took the form of cleaning and checking weapons.

She forced herself not to look at the windows of the schoolrooms that surrounded her on three sides, though most were not on ground level. It took her only a few moments to get past the infirmary building and turn left again. One of the marines whistled and there was a sudden barrage of laughing and calls.

Naturally, she would be taken for being one of the staff and not a pupil. This was a satisfactory state of affairs though she closed her ears to the words they were saying. Some of them were quite crude.

As she had suspected the back gate was wide open. She walked out and turned left again heading for her usual exit. There was no guard mounted as yet and she escaped easily.

The walk to Volk's Electric Railway was becoming quite familiar, as was the coastguard station. She was not, however, expecting to get hailed.

"Miss!"

She could hardly ignore it so she stopped and looked up. It was the younger fellow—Margaret's one—he was standing up on the balcony but as soon as she turned he called down again.

"Wait!" and he disappeared into the building.

She considered moving on quickly but it would be rude and he would be able to catch up easily. A few moments later he cannoned out of the front door, almost stumbling as he took the steps at speed, rushed across the untidy grass and leapt the fence to come to a halt beside her, breathing heavily.

"Sorry 'bout that, miss."

She allowed him time to recover his breath, which did not take long, she could see from his general physique that he must be quite athletic. He did not even break a sweat, he probably indulged in something rather more robust than calisthenics.

"Can I help you?"

"Chief Boatman Alexander Goodiman."

"Hello."

"I hope you don't mind," he said with a smile that made Maliha feel as if she did, indeed, mind. "I seen thee and your friend pass by once or twice."

He didn't sound local but perhaps those in the coastguard service moved about like the other services.

"Yes?"

"There was a right business up at the school this morning."

"Royal Navy. Marines."

"Marines, is it?" He turned and looked at the school, the

flyers were grey shapes through the leafless trees. "That *is* a business. I know they having a right bash, but marines." He didn't seem to be talking to her any more.

"Is that all you wanted?" She looked at her watch. "I'm hoping to catch the train into town."

"Oh sorry, miss."

She gave a smile that sat on her face with no humour beneath. Turned and went away.

The train had not left by the time she reached it and the journey as far as the aquarium was uneventful, just as she preferred it.

She was working on the assumption that Frederick Jordan was a decent man and not any sort of habitual criminal. And if that was the case then he must be persuaded to be part of this conspiracy through some sort of blackmail. At first she had thought it might be threat against Ethel, after all she was completely besotted with Pat Hogan and that meant Taliesin could have disposed of her in a moment. Considering what he ended up doing, the threat was real. But with Ethel dead that wouldn't work.

After leaving the train, Maliha strode westward along the front and then turned up into one of the side streets until she reached the offices of the Brighton Gazette. She was directed to the morgue in the cellars and quickly located the August 1897 folder. She did not have to look far, the story had pride of place among the news stories of that day—and being August, they comprised mostly sightings of famous or aristocratic individuals and their entourages, along with warnings against thieves and pickpockets who flocked to the resort during the summer season.

Maliha read the article, flipping to page seven to continue. Amid the journalistic exaggerations were the commiserations for a father who had lost yet another wife, and the poor child who witnessed her mother's demise beneath the tread of a big steam-powered omnibus. Even with a Faraday device these machines were of considerable weight.

As was the custom, the newspaper gave the address of the Jordans and also mentioned a key witness, a railway worker by the name of Harold Gardiner, of 23 Boston Street.

From Maliha's recollection of the Brighton street plan, she placed Boston Street alongside the railway sidings of the London, Brighton and South Coast Railway company. All the railways in Britain had long-since been converted to Brunel's pneumatic design but there was still the need for storage of carriages.

There was no time like the present and it was less than a mile with most of that distance was along Queen's Road. Still, it was uphill and though it was not a steep incline it wore her out. She turned right at the station and then into the less reputable streets with their small terraced houses, almost all owned by the railway company to accommodate their staff.

Boston Street had a high brick wall on the left as Maliha entered it from the south. Smoke, steam and the rattling of trains and carriages rose from behind it. There were no less than three huge pumping stations that pushed the air into the tubes that carried the trains. The pub on the corner was unimaginatively called The Railwayman. Scruffy children played in the street as she made her way along to the house.

She stopped at the red wooden door covered in a layer of soot, like everything else here. You could see earlier attempts at cleaning the windows in the marks on the glass. She used the end of her umbrella to rap on the door as the dirt in the atmosphere she breathed threatened to clog her throat.

There was a long delay and finally an old man came to the door. He stared at her but whether it was the colour of her skin or the fact that some rich woman was standing at his door she could not guess.

"We don't give to charity," he said in a voice that had breathed too much of this air. He gulped down a cough that had threatened to explode at his words.

"I'm not collecting," she said before he had a chance to decide to close the door on her. "I'm looking for Mr Gardiner."

"I'm Gardiner."

"Harold Gardiner?"

The man stiffened. "What's your game? You a reporter?"

"I'm sorry? No, I'm not a reporter. I just wanted to ask him some questions."

"Hold a bloody seance then." He started to close the door.

"He's dead?"

"Yes, he's dead."

"When?"

"Last year, if you must know. Who are you and what do you want? The insurance money's all gone, so's all the rest and we got a couple a weeks to get out before they evict us." He glared at her. "You done?"

Maliha took a step back. "I'm sorry, I didn't know."

The glare softened. "What did you want to ask him?"

Maliha glanced around. The houses were a single room width and she could see a woman in the next house looking out at her. But there was no one in earshot as far as she could tell.

"It was about the woman who died under the bus."

The glare became sly. "Oh yes? What about it?"

"I just wanted to ask him about it. To tell me what he saw."

"He wouldn't've talked to the likes of you."

"Indian?"

"Yeah."

"But you are."

"Served over there in the Seventies. I liked it. I liked the women."

Maliha gave the humourless smile. "Did he tell you what he saw when the woman died?"

"What's it worth?"

"What do you want?"

"What I want I can't 'ave and prob'ly couldn't manage," he said. "So we won't talk about that, eh?"

"Let's not." She glanced around again and wondered how thin the walls were. She coughed without warning.

He laughed. "Live 'ere long enough and you get used to it. But it gets inside you and it'll kill you in the end. It's killed me."

"You're still moving."

"Not for long the doc says."

Maliha took a chance. "Your son saw the little girl push her mother under the bus, didn't he?"

The man's face took on a look of horror but he didn't deny it.

"But he didn't tell the police and blackmailed the husband. You can just nod."

He nodded. Maliha looked at her watch, it was coming up to midday.

"Thank you for your help." She turned to go back the way she had come.

"He died because of that, didn't he?"

Maliha glanced. "Yes."

"You going to tell the police?"

"Eventually," she said. "But I won't mention you."

"Don't you want to know who my boy told?"

"German, tall."

"You know."

"I know."

With that she headed back. She caught a taxi from the station and tried to clean off the sprinkling of soot as she walked past the coastguard and re-entered the school grounds. She was relieved there was nobody on the outer gate, and no one on the inner one. A number of marines were doing some sort of drill on the field beyond the school and there were no groups of them in the courtyard, however she ran into a group of five as soon as she entered the infirmary.

They stood aside as she went past.

"Excuse me, miss?"

She glanced at the badges on his arm. "Yes, Gunner?"

"Gunner Mitcham, miss."

"How can I help you, Gunner Mitcham?"

If he had been certain of her station and sure that she should not be in the infirmary he was no longer sure at all.

"We're familiarising ourselves with the layout and personnel of the school, miss, and I was wondering what you did here?"

"I am one of the pupils, Gunner."

"This is the infirmary."

"For complicated reasons that need not concern you I occupy a room here in the infirmary. The one upstairs that you probably found locked? Perhaps with a tray of food outside."

"There's a tray outside one of the rooms, yes."

"I'm a bit late for luncheon."

Some of the men pulled back and Gunner Mitcham looked at her nonplussed. "You live in the infirmary. Are you ill?"

"I can assure you I have nothing communicable. It suits me, and the school authorities, to spend the rest of my time until the end of the year here rather than one of the dormitories."

"I see, miss."

It was plain he did not see at all.

"Is that all?"

"That's all, miss."

Maliha headed to her room and lay down for a while. Until Margaret turned up.

"Royal Marines, aren't they handsome?"

They practised in the heels. Maliha felt she was becoming more comfortable with them and could walk without paying too much attention, although her muscles still ached.

Margaret was having far less difficulty, but then she was only on two inches.

They went outside to practice on the stairs and use the corridor for longer distances since the room alone had become too easy.

The windows of the half-flight of stairs gave out into the courtyard and Maliha stopped every time she reached it to look out. On one occasion Margaret came and stood beside her.

"I'm going to need your help on Saturday, Sadie," said Maliha as she watched cases of vegetables being unloaded from a steam truck.

"What do you need?"

"I will be keeping an eye out for whatever Taliesin is planning, I need you to make sure Jenny and Antonia get out of the school and to the taxi."

Margaret turned to her. "Really? That's so exciting."

"This is serious. If this goes wrong their lives will be ruined forever, and yours too."

"Oh pish. They can't touch me."

Maliha watched as a man on the back of the vehicle in the yard lifted a huge crate. He had plenty of muscles, and skin tanned by a life in the open, but even he should not have been able to raise that much. The truck must have a Faraday device that was still operating, bestowing him with the appearance of super-human strength. He passed the crate to three men beyond the edge of the vehicle and they were bowed beneath its weight.

"It would be more logical to have a Faraday grid laid out on the ground and then everyone could benefit," said Maliha to no one in particular.

"What?"

"Nothing." She brought to mind what Margaret had said even though she hadn't been listening. "Perhaps they can't touch you, but it could affect your marriage prospects."

"Nonsense, can't you imagine it, Lady Margaret

Creighton-Ward the woman who assisted two lovers in their elopement. I'll be the toast of society."

"It's not an elopement—" Maliha began and then broke off. It didn't matter, if Margaret was happy to do her part, in spite of the consequences, then so be it. "I have prepared the escape route. The window at the side of the church entrance has a piece of fabric sticking out. You pull that and the window will open. Once inside you make your way down to the crypt. There are men's clothes secreted there which should fit Jenny, a coat for Antonia and an umbrella. Just in case."

"Given Jenny's chest, I'm not sure that will work."

"I know but it will be dark and she has less to disguise than Antonia."

"True."

"She's also taller with short hair, so the assumption will be that she is the man. People can be very unobservant if you feed their preconceptions. The door from the church crypt to the grass at the back has been oiled and a new padlock put on. The key to the lock is in the men's trousers."

"What about the tickets for the flight?"

"I have them and will give them to you shortly before the time."

"Very well, so from there they sneak out to the taxi," said Margaret. "An excellent plan except for the matter of the Marines who have set up camp right in the path of the escape."

"Yes, that was unexpected and I have no doubt there will be a guard on the gate."

"How do you propose they get past armed soldiers?"

"I would suggest," said Maliha, "they do not attempt it at all. Instead cut straight across and go through the hedge and the trees onto the track and then pretend they've come from Overdean."

"It will make a mess of their clothes."

"There is a limit to what I can do," said Maliha, "but if

questioned they could mention they've come across the fields from Overdean and fell over."

Margaret nodded.

"And what will you be doing?"

"Exposing the murderer of Ethel Jordan."

35

Thursday morning. Maliha felt tied down. The marines were now organised and had patrols along the perimeter and guards posted at the gates. She could not get out and, even if she did, getting back in might be problematical. She could write letters but she had a feeling they might be opened and read.

Mid-morning she received a letter from Somerset House along with some packages from central London. The letter confirmed what she already knew: Frederick Jordan's third wife had died by falling under an omnibus. It was declared an accidental death and that was the end of it. She already knew far more than the coroner had determined, even if that knowledge was measured by dead bodies.

Maliha wished that Patrick Hogan was still alive, she was desperate to know the nature of his relationship with Ethel and how he had tamed the beast.

She turned her attention to the packages though she had a very good idea of what they contained. Silk underwear wrapped in tissue. Maliha sighed as she laid them out. It wasn't that she didn't like the strapless chemise, drawers,

stockings and garters—and all in the same shade of blue of
her dress so they would not be visible through it. Each item
exquisitely sewn and, she had no doubt, perfectly fitted for her.
It was simply that she would be so exposed. She reminded
herself that it was only one night and once it was over she had
no need to wear the dress or underwear ever again. These
were not clothes she would have any opportunity to put on
in India.

There were two sets of the entire ensemble. Maliha
repacked them and took them to Matron so they could be
placed out of the way securely. Even if she did not want to
wear them, she was also opposed to the idea of giving
satisfaction to the vicious practical jokers who might try to
damage them.

She spent an hour walking in her new shoes. Pacing the
corridor then descending and climbing the stairs. She had to
acknowledge it was becoming easier. Though her muscles
continued to ache, it was becoming less and she no longer had
to concentrate on maintaining her balance. She still found the
need to take small steps frustrating since she preferred to stride
ahead when she had a purpose.

Again and again she went over in her mind the facts that
she had at her disposal. Some things were now clear to her,
such as the role Frederick Jordan was to play. Other things
were a complete mystery since she still had no idea what
exactly Taliesin had planned.

Margaret turned up after luncheon with her shoes. Maliha
was happy enough to continue practising.

"Of the girls in the school, who would make the best
match for Prince Edward?"

"Me," said Margaret promptly and laughed. "I know, but I
am, after all I come from a solid aristocratic family. And we're
not poor like some."

"You're a bit old for him."

"That wouldn't matter and I'd be quite happy being
queen."

"Apart from you then."

"Antonia, she's a princess. And slightly closer to his age if you really think that's important."

"Not something she would want, obviously. Since she'd be required to produce an heir."

Margaret pulled a face. "Do you have to talk about that?"

"It's completely natural," said Maliha. "What about Katherine DeCourcy?"

"Too French."

"They came over with William the Conqueror. They beat your lineage by about five hundred years—and they go right back to Carolingians before that."

"That's the point. They're basically French and always have been, more importantly the family is Irish. They're not Church of England and that's why they never made it into royalty."

Maliha had to accept it. There was no way they would let a Catholic marry into the royal family.

"Who else then?"

Margaret stopped and stared into the nothing. "There's lot of new money, of course, but the royals like to keep it among the aristocrats. Honestly, there aren't a lot of other choices."

"You or Antonia?"

"Elektra Konstantin."

Maliha frowned. "Greek?"

Margaret grinned. "I know something you don't know. Ha!"

"Well?"

"Russian."

"But that name? Oh wait—" Maliha smiled. "—You're saying she's Nina Georgievna?"

It was Margaret's turn to scowl. "How do you do that?"

Maliha shrugged. "That won't work, she's another Catholic."

"The Grand Duchess would probably convert if it meant marrying into British royalty."

"Yes, but she's run away from her husband. That's far too much scandal."

"Well, you did ask for possibilities." Margaret walked away and tackled the stairs for perhaps the twentieth time that hour. While Maliha continued to ponder the possibilities.

The day wore on and Margaret went back to lessons. Maliha spent an hour writing down her thoughts in an exercise book she would probably never use for schoolwork again.

Something was planned and it involved a girl from the school and the princes. Probably the younger one. Ena's idea of some sort of arranged marriage did not hold water since the prince was too young—and the available girls were not extensive. It couldn't work.

Maliha did not think Lady Henrietta Creighton-Ward would allow her daughter to be forced into marriage since she was a Suffragette and had strong principles. And that left Antonia, but she would be out of the picture soon enough if their plan was successful.

But she knew now she would be able to expose Ethel's murderer and that would have to be enough. It would upset Taliesin's plans and that could only be a good thing.

Friday came and passed the same way as Thursday with much practising on the shoes. Even the stairs were now easy enough. As long as she steered clear of any uneven surface— like the cobbles in the courtyard—there should be no problem. She could avoid any need to dance, so that was satisfactory.

She was so bored she got the underclothes from Matron and tried them on. They clung to her skin and revealed every curve. The modern movement away from corsetry was good from one viewpoint but the revealing nature of the new style was quite embarrassing. She thought she would be happier hidden behind the walls of whalebone, even if it did restrict her movement.

But there was no option now.

She changed back into her school uniform. And spent the afternoon watching the marines as they trained on the grass at the rear. And counted off the minutes between the various patrols. She noted how often they changed the guards on the gate. School had seemed like a prison, now she understood what it really meant. Confined to her room by choice, but if she did choose to leave she could not go beyond the walls.

If she had a fanciful notion she might think of herself as a princess in a tower herself, but it was the other girls that were the princesses. Maliha was the beast and they would be glad to be rid of her. They did not mind allowing Irish, Greek or Russian girls into the school because their skin was white.

The threats were real. She suspected that Taliesin or his agents were now in the school but he would not make an attempt on her life now, since it would upset the plans for Saturday. The bullies who wished her harm—Emily Solsbury for one—would be planning something, probably for Saturday night. There had been no repeat of the rat incident but, in some ways that made Maliha even more concerned they were taking their time and hatching some plot.

There was little she could do to prepare for it except be aware it might happen. The book on the philosophy on Buddhism she had read suggested she should view all physical aspects as little more than lies. She wanted to be able to do that. She desperately wanted to be able to separate herself from worldly concerns, but she found it impossible.

The death of Ethel Jordan preyed on her—though in truth it was less the death of the girl and more the false accusation against Amelia Johnson. That the girl was not of sound mind made it worse. She could not defend herself and there was no one that would do it except Maliha.

It was truth that mattered. Truth was the only thing that mattered.

Without truth one could not make decisions, one could only make mistakes.

Lunch arrived carried by Ena. She looked tired and her hair was not as tidy as it usually was.

"Sit."

"I best not, miss, I've hardly slept the last two nights there is so much to be done and the chef is driving us like slaves. If I sit now I'll never wake up."

And then Margaret arrived, slightly surprised to see the scullery maid standing in the room.

"Ena, this is Sadie. Sadie, this is Ena."

The young Lady Margaret Creighton-Ward opened her mouth and then closed it again.

Ena gave a curtsy.

"Cat got your tongue, Sadie?"

"You just introduced me to a kitchen maid." Margaret looked over at Ena. "No offence."

"None taken, miss."

Maliha gazed at Margaret. "In our little adventure, Ena is your equal, Sadie."

"Stop calling me that!"

"You wanted a nickname, I gave you one."

"But the servants don't call me that." She looked towards Ena again. "No offence."

"None taken, miss."

"Ena is seeking to revenge herself on the man who killed her brother. The one who calls himself Taliesin. He is also the man who killed Ethel Jordan. Also, it seems, the man who killed the maid whose position Ena now occupies. The man who tried to shoot me, and injured you, Sadie." *And who killed a railwayman who happened to witness the death of Ethel's step-mother.* "So, as you can see, we are all in this together."

"Oh."

Maliha finished her food and Ena took it.

"I hope you manage to get more rest tonight," said Maliha. "I can't think that a tired staff is the best way to create a successful event."

"Chef says we have to work late tonight again but that we won't have to get up first thing. Except Mr Pimm and his staff for the bread making."

Ena left. Margaret still seemed in shock. "I thought you were my friend."

"Did I do something wrong?"

"You embarrassed me in front of a servant."

"The embarrassment was all yours, Sadie, you could simply choose not to be. You're no better than they are."

The war going on inside Margaret was almost visible. "I know I'm not better than them."

"You have what you have because of your parents."

"I know that."

"She has nothing because of her parents have nothing— and now one less child."

"I know."

"When women get the vote, Ena will have that vote too. Not just you. In that she will be your equal."

"I know."

"So, you can't go around treating servants like lesser creatures."

Margaret hesitated. "I don't. I treat them properly because that's the proper Christian thing to do but that doesn't mean we should be familiar. We shouldn't be on first name terms, we're different."

"Only by the rules of men, Sadie."

"I don't think I like you calling me that anymore," she said. "It sounds sleazy and common."

"All the more reason for you to hang on to it. Perhaps you should learn to be someone else."

"I don't think so, Maliha. I am not a bad person and I am happy being who I am."

"Well, there'll only be another day or so of this and then it will be over. You can go back to being Margaret Creighton-Ward and I'll go back to being the strange Indian girl that no one talks to."

Margaret frowned but it seemed she could find nothing to say. She left without a goodbye.

Maliha took a deep breath. "It's for the best, Sadie. Trust me."

36

Maliha found that she did not have any trouble sleeping that final night. She had spent the evening writing letters to her parents, to Matron, and to Mrs Ramsey. She apologised in all of them but expressed her love and appreciation to her parents. Matron she thanked for all her help, and to Mrs Ramsey she expressed gratitude for the education she had received.

The last letter was for form. It was not Mrs Ramsey she wanted to thank but the teachers that she really appreciated. She wanted them to understand they had given her a good start, even if she had outstripped them in most areas after that. Roedean was a good school for most of the girls, and she understood that. it simply wasn't for her.

She put the letters into her schoolbag, where they would be found if something bad happened to her. She went over her notes on the case but could find nothing more that she could have done, and no new insights.

If she had been her own agent and not been tied to the school she might have been able to do far more. There were leads she would have liked to have followed—like finding

Frederick Jordan and discussing his relationship with his daughter; or seeking out the asylum that held Amelia Johnson and perhaps giving her some hope. Searching the room that had been occupied by Patrick Hogan, tracking down the accommodation of Diederich Hößler and investigating the man in more detail. If only she had been able to understand his motives because then she would comprehend his intentions. What she knew was very vague.

But she was just a seventeen-year-old Indian girl in a girls' boarding school on the south coast of England, where it was always too cold and wet. There was a limit to what she could achieve.

So she slept well and woke promptly at seven-thirty.

Breakfast arrived an hour later with all the meats and bread that she could eat. The condemned was eating a hearty meal.

Maliha stayed in her room. Practised in the shoes for a while, she had become used to the way they made her hips sway, even though she was intensely aware of its sexually suggestive nature. She even attempted to run in them. It was extremely difficult and she resolved to avoid that if at all possible—besides, the short steps she was required to take meant that running was barely faster than a walk.

She stared out of the window. There was a light drizzle and the hills vanished into grey. She was tired of sitting around in her room and, she reasoned, perhaps spuriously, that she needed to recheck the school to see what changes the marines might have made in the name of security. She put on her coat and grabbed her umbrella.

Taking her time, she crossed the courtyard and entered the lower corridors. She went around the square, looking at the classrooms. It all seemed normal until she reached the dining room. The noise of people talking, shouting, hammering and working reached her before she got to the door.

Decorations were going up; the usual furniture was already gone and more was being brought in through the windows. The adjoining classrooms were receiving similar treatment. And a small classroom on the other side of the corridor was also being modified. If she was not mistaken that one would be used as a private area for the special guests. Somewhere a little more secure.

Those rooms had windows that gave onto an inner quad from which there were plenty of additional exits. However, that also meant there were other ways in. No doubt there would be marines posted in that area.

Maliha moved on. The school became normal again once she had left the dining room and all its bustle behind. The library door was locked and she decided it would be unwise to open it when anyone might come upon her. It also occurred to her that there would be men stationed in the tunnel, assuming they had not intentionally blocked it already.

On the floor above there was no sign of any changes. She did not go up to the dormitories but returned to the infirmary and fetched her new underwear from Matron.

Luncheon came and went, along with a printed invitation to the dance requesting her presence at half-past seven at the school office. She felt a wave of fear as she read it. Up to now she could have pretended it was all just imagination, now it was as real as the piece of card she held.

The call from Paquin came at about three o'clock in the form of a woman she did not recognise but from her stylish dress and make-up was clearly in Paquin's entourage. There were also two marines. Not in their red dress uniforms but in the modern khaki. That fact alone meant this exercise was being taken seriously.

"It is time," said the woman and she glanced nervously to her side where the men stood. "You have your undergarments and shoes?"

Maliha could not think of anything stranger than being escorted by armed soldiers to be outfitted in a dress that was so expensive it would feed a family in India for a year. Not that they were there for her safety, but only as a precaution against some kind of infiltration.

As was sometimes the case, a thought nagged at Maliha but just beyond her ability to see what it was. But it would come to her.

It was not only the visitors' suite that had been commandeered as dressing rooms, but three classrooms around it. More marines guarded the corridors and approaches but they did not come past the screens that had been set-up to obscure the inner corridors from view.

This part of the school had become a production line for beauty, though the number of girls involved was less than ten. Margaret and Antonia were already there; Emily Solsbury had yet to arrive. There was one other sixth-form girl and the rest that were present comprised three fifth-formers. Maliha did not bother digging for their names in her memory.

"This is it," said Margaret trying but failing to suppress her excitement.

"I hope we get something to eat before it starts," said Antonia.

"What colour is your dress?" Maliha asked her.

"Gold mostly, but it is lovely."

Of course, it was. It was a Paquin. Maliha doubted the woman was capable of creating anything that did not look wonderful on the person for whom it was designed. She gave Antonia an appraising look, were they about the same size? Possibly. Antonia was probably a little thinner in her torso though generously proportioned in front.

One by one each girl was called into one of the side rooms. Maliha's turn came, Margaret reached out and gave Maliha's hand a squeeze. Inside the room she was required to put on her new underwear and given a silk dressing gown. From there she was sent out into one of the classrooms where her hair was washed and cut. The girl ahead of Maliha, one of the younger ones, was having her hair done in a complex arrangement. Then it was Maliha's turn. She stared forwards while the stylist piled her hair in tight coils around her head.

The next stop was make-up. They had brought in comfortable chairs, which reminded Maliha of those found in a men's barber shop, and her back was supported all the way up to her neck.

It had not been that long since the wearing of make-up meant a woman had loose morals. Not that it stopped any woman from trying to look better. However, the person who came to work on Maliha's face stopped and stared.

It was apparent that no one had warned her that her subject did not have white skin. The conflict was obvious, she worked for Paquin, it was her role to put make-up on the woman wearing Paquin's dress. But Maliha was outside her experience.

In India it was common for women to try to whiten their skin, because the higher castes had progressively paler skin. And Maliha was Brahmin, and mixed race. Her skin was a lighter shade than most in her country. But as far as the British were concerned Maliha might as well have skin that was black as coal.

The woman got over her momentary surprise and stepped up beside Maliha's chair.

"You are Miss Anderson?"

Maliha smiled, the woman was Scottish, not Glaswegian like her father, but still it did remind her of him. "That's right."

"I'm Lettie, I'm supposed to do your make-up."

"Then this will be an adventure for both of us," said Maliha.

The woman smiled nervously and pressed her lips together. "Have you used make-up?"

"Never, it's not allowed in the school. And if you mean, do I know what works? No to that as well. A better question might be, do I need it?"

"I have my orders."

"Is that enough?"

"You haven't worked for Madame."

"No, that's true. Very well, let us see what can be done."

"Do you mind if I touch your face?"

Maliha shrugged and Lettie took that as a yes. She ran her fingers across Maliha's cheek and nodded to herself.

"Does it feel any different to a white girl?"

"No, not at all. But yours is quite dry and firm. There's no foundation I can use, none of it is the right shade, it would look ridiculous, I'd have to cover every exposed part of you."

Considering that would include Maliha's back, neck and chest, never mind the hands, she had to agree.

"Do you mind me saying you have lovely hair?"

Maliha smiled. "I don't mind."

The woman reached into her bag and pulled out a tray of plots in a range of reds. "If we can find the right one a good blusher will highlight your cheekbones. The overall structure of your face is very elegant we just need to emphasise it to complement the dress."

And there it was again. When it came to Paquin, everything was about the dress. Maliha's only purpose was to show the dress off to its best advantage, to make Paquin look like the best dressmaker in the world. The fact that it made Maliha appear to be someone who could *afford* a Paquin dress was its secondary function. It was beauty and materialism.

Lettie was staring at the colours, suddenly she jumped up. "Wait here." She disappeared with her make-up bag.

So Maliha waited. The other girls came and went. After a long while, Maliha heard the sound of a thundering steam-engine, accompanied by whooshing beat of rotors. It was not as noisy as the two military carriers but it still made the walls throb in response to its powerful motion. A shadow passed one of the windows though she could see nothing. If she was not mistaken it would be the two guests of honour arriving, in the luxurious flyer owned by Jordan Airways. And piloted by Frederick Jordan himself.

Finally, Lettie was back, after what seemed like an hour. She pulled out a new pot from her bag and was grinning. "Well, that put the cat among the pigeons."

"What happened?"

Lettie shook her head. "Trade secrets. But if Paquin wants something, there is no force on this earth to stand in her way. Not even a chef."

Maliha shook her head and sat back. It didn't matter.

Once she got properly started it did not take Lettie long. Despite what she had said previously, she did apply a foundation and then the rouge, which she worked carefully into Maliha's cheeks and then above her eyes. What surprised Maliha when she caught sight of it was the fact that it was a dark purple.

After half-an-hour Lettie stood back and smiled. "We'll be leaving the lips until just before you go down to the hall. Do you want to see?"

Maliha was not entirely sure she did but nodded anyway. Lettie pulled out a hand mirror and passed it over. Maliha held it up. She was expecting something grotesque but it was a different, perhaps beautiful, woman staring back at her. Her skin shade was unchanged but the colour on her cheeks and eyes glowed with a red-purple that Maliha would have sworn could not possibly enhance her features in an aesthetic way, and yet they did.

"Alright?" said Lettie.

"Yes," said Maliha almost wonder. "Yes, that is … surprising. Thank you."

"That's good. It's back to the main room now for you then."

She helped Maliha climb out of the chair, and with the robe wrapped around her she headed back.

"Oh goodness," said Margaret staring. "You're beautiful."

"Painted whore," growled Emily Solsbury, but somehow Maliha imagined her words came more from jealousy.

Margaret's make-up was subtle. The foundation perfectly blended and the rose in her cheeks looked like a natural blush, her eyelashes and eyebrows had been darkened too. Emily's was similar but somehow the fact that she frowned made her face look almost comedic.

Maliha did not respond but sat down beside Margaret. She checked her watch to find that three hours had gone by and it was shortly after six.

"*Mademoiselles* Anderson and Creighton-Ward. Please come through."

The voice of Paquin summoned them into the room where Maliha had got changed. She was there with half a dozen other women. The dresses were on hangers in the background.

Paquin strutted up to Margaret and gave her makeup and hair a long stare. "Good." Then she moved to Maliha. The examination took much longer than it had for Margaret but eventually Paquin nodded. "Very good."

Even though she had no real desire to be here, the fact that Madame approved of her was a considerable relief.

Paquin clicked her fingers. Margaret was guided to the other side of the room while Maliha was moved away from the wall. They were both required to stand on raised platforms, but they seemed solid. They were helped into their shoes as they stood there.

The dresses were brought forward. Maliha and Margaret locked eyes for a moment—sharing the fear and wonderment —before they were forced to pay attention as they were guided into their evening wear.

It did not take long for them to be buttoned in, although Maliha was not sure how she was going to get out of the dress, or whether going to the W.C. was even a possibility. Her creation clung to her from below her bust until it reached her thighs and then extended out in voluminous folds. The plain blue had been adorned with lace in tight patterns around the hem which seemed to climb her legs along the side and then explode across her bosom—it went some way to distracting from the décolletage, which was still embarrassing. The final touch was a gossamer blue wrap that would certainly not keep out the cold but added an indefinable air of otherworldliness to the ensemble.

Across from her, Margaret was pink and now Maliha could see how the make-up complemented the dress and vice versa. A dress with so many white flowers could have looked like a table arrangement but somehow it did not.

One of the women assisted Maliha in stepping down from the platform, the same for Margaret on the other side of the room.

"Walk for me," said Paquin.

So Maliha stood straight and walked across the room to Margaret with the unfamiliar movement of the silk around her legs and then together they returned. Once more Maliha caught a glimpse of herself in a long mirror. It was not her.

"Good enough." The *couturier* waved them aside and they stepped out into the waiting area. Emily Solsbury wasn't there but dressing was also being done in the other room as well. Antonia was now all in gold brocade. The fact that it looked almost like a wedding dress made Maliha smile. This dance was, in a way, the marriage between Antonia and Jenny. It was perhaps appropriate. The image was not lost on Antonia either, she was smiling so much it was as if she was going to break with happiness.

And that was the moment Maliha realised what it was that was bothering her.

She had sent a letter to Dr Underwood detailing her concerns, complete with the evidence she felt she had established. Yet, as far as she could tell, no action had been taken. Ena was still in contact with Taliesin, there had been no reports, and no gossip, that anyone had been arrested in regard to this evening's entertainment.

She might have expected even a non-committal acknowledgement thanking her for her information. She knew Dr Underwood respected her opinions. But there had been nothing.

To her mind that could mean only one thing: the letter had not reached its destination, and there was no one here that knew of the imminent attack—or whatever it was going to be—just her, Ena and Margaret.

She sat down and stared unseeing at the wall across the room.

37

———

There had been very little conversation in the room even when Emily Solsbury returned. She, too. looked completely different. Her ensemble had been inspired by Russian peasant dress and she was showing even more skin than Maliha, though she did not seem in the slightest embarrassed about it. For her, this was an opportunity to attract the attention of a suitable young man—assuming her existing plan did not work out.

Perhaps the other girls thought this way too, apart from the obvious exception.

For Maliha, she simply felt the weight of potential dangers on her shoulders. She must forestall whatever it was that Taliesin was planning. The only item to her advantage was that she knew what he looked like and would be able to recognise him. If she got the chance. And while she hoped for a cleaner resolution, at the very least she could cause a scene and prevent him from acting.

At seven o'clock, Paquin emerged from the side room with her entourage. One of them carried a large portrait camera on a tripod. They were arranged with Antonia in the middle and Maliha on one end. She hoped that her image would not appear on the film.

The group picture was taken and they proceeded to take individual images. Each of the girls smiled for the picture but Maliha could not bring herself to do it. Still the girls barely talked. The tension was simply too high.

At seven-twenty-five, they were called to line up in pairs, except for Antonia who was instructed to take the lead. Maliha and Margaret were to follow her. *As if we are her bridesmaids*, thought Maliha. It crossed her mind for one moment that Paquin knew what was happening, but that was ridiculous and she rejected it.

The door of the suite was opened and with Antonia in the lead they headed out, turning right to walk along the outer corridor. The screens had been removed and an escort of four marines, this time in dress uniform, led the way. A glance behind showed Maliha that there was half a dozen behind as well.

Someone was taking no risks, but why would they feel the need to protect the girls with so many men? Surely they were not *that* important?

Maliha's practice in her heels had been sufficient to allow her to concentrate on other matters as she walked. Now taller than most of the other girls because of the extra height she had been required to wear. Tall and slender, that had been Paquin's plan for her all along and she had emphasised it with the shoes. Maliha shook her head slightly, she was impressed by madame's skill both in design, but also in her ability to promote her wares.

But surely the girls were not that important? Unless one of them was, and that would fit with Taliesin's plans. He was interested in both the school and the princes. It was the two of them together that mattered, neither one singly.

And he had killed his way into a position where he could be present when someone from the school and someone from the Royal Family were in the same place.

The procession reached the next corner and turned inwards towards the stairwell. Maliha hoped the younger girls had practised stairs. They could not afford to have someone near the back bringing about an avalanche of debutantes. She had never imagined herself being a debutante and yet, by the definition of the word, that is precisely what she was.

Was she the first whose skin was not the purest white? It didn't matter, no one would report on her. Every other girl would be photographed and their names placed in the appropriate periodicals. But there was no such place for her, not even *The Times of India*.

Her concern about the stairs had been foreseen by others. First Antonia, Margaret and Maliha descended. The sound of many people filtered through the long corridors of the school and somewhere a chamber orchestra was playing a waltz. Maliha prayed that no one would ask her to dance, even though she had been given a dance card which now hung on a cord around her wrist.

They stood at the bottom while the next four descended. One of the fifth-formers wobbled on her heels but caught herself before anything catastrophic came to pass. And so it went until they were all on the ground floor and back in line.

They set off once more. Maliha wished that time would stop and that they would never reach the dining room. But the universe was cruel and did not hear her silent plea. The number of people in the corridors increased and no longer was it marines. Now there were just people. All staring at the group as it approached.

Three of their escort at the front stepped aside until it was just one who led the way. Behind them Maliha supposed the escort was also reduced. For one crazy hopeful moment she thought this might all be some cruel joke as their guide failed to turn left into the corridor on which the main doors to the dining room stood. But there was another entrance, a smaller one, further along.

Glancing up the passage they did not take, the number of

people loitering round the door scared her even more. She was acutely aware of how much of her skin was on show, and how the dress clung to her. And then the horror of the heels struck her. She had practised so much she had become used to how much her hips swayed as she walked and had forgotten. It was the eyes of the men who looked at her bust, then descended to her waist and remained glued to her hips as she walked past them. She might not be able to see but it was as if she could feel them staring at her rear.

She hated Madame Paquin.

But there was nothing she could do about it, if she did not move her hips, or failed to walk the tightrope with her feet, she would simply stumble and fall. The fashion into which she was shackled was a straitjacket. She swore never to wear anything like this ever again.

It was only a few hours. She had survived the school. She could do this. Besides, there was an enemy to be thwarted.

And then the moment came. The side door was opened and Antonia was gestured through. They were stopped for a moment, inside came an introduction for Antonia except it was "Princess Antonia Dumont of Hohenzollern" and there were appreciative noises from within. Then Maliha and Margaret followed. Unexpectedly there was a screen shielding them from the rest of the room and a man in uniform with a clipboard.

"Names."

"Lady Margaret Creighton-Ward."

"Maliha Anderson."

"Alice Anderson?"

"Yes."

"Go around the end of the screen, you will see Prince George and Prince Edward. You will curtsy and then proceed to stand beside Princess Antonia. Understand?"

They nodded. "Go."

Maliha let Margaret go first since she had senior rank, and it as always easier to follow. The two of them emerged into the dining room, now transformed and looking larger than it did when filled with dining tables and chairs. Margaret's name was announced and there was a pause, then Maliha was, too—using her Christian name. She did not react, though inside she allowed herself a moment of anger.

The princes were in full dress uniform; George had a great deal of regalia and Edward very little. Maliha and Margaret walked sedately across to a position in front of them and curtsied. Margaret pulled it off without a problem but it was something Maliha had not practised. And even if she had it would not have been in a long dress. She did the best she could and only wobbled a little, but it was probably going to be the least impressive curtsy they would see all evening.

They made their way across to Antonia, who was looking very pale. Maliha hoped she wasn't going to faint. Though she did not have a corset, she was fairly sure the other girls did. Though the skill of Paquin that meant they were well hidden.

Rather than do exactly as she was told, Maliha chose to stand on the other side of Antonia, half a step behind, just so she would be there in case anything happened.

In twos, the other girls emerged. Prince George continued to watch the process with alert eyes, but Maliha thought his son looked bored. And why wouldn't he be? He wasn't even fourteen and probably not interested in girls yet. Though that would most certainly change quite soon.

She studied his face, perhaps it wasn't boredom. Perhaps it was just indifference. As she stared at him the boy turned his head and looked at Antonia. Then he turned away. Antonia took a tiny step back and bumped Maliha. "Sorry."

But Maliha was not listening. The look on the boy prince's face had not been indifference, not at that moment. It had been a depth of contempt Maliha had only ever seen before when aimed at her. And that for the lovely and quite beautiful Antonia.

Antonia sniffed. Maliha stepped forward and saw a tear forming in her darkened eyelashes. It would ruin her make-up if allowed to escape. Maliha rummaged through the reticule she had been given, sure enough there was a hankie.

She gently pushed it into Antonia's hand and muttered. "Careful, don't smear the eye make-up."

Antonia gently dabbed at her eyes. Maliha was sure that no one else would realise that the emotion they might see here was anything more than being overcome by the event. But Maliha's mind whirled. Suddenly the truth of what was happening here came to her and she cursed herself for being such a fool. If she had known they could have changed how all of this happened.

Ena had half of the answer when she said that perhaps Taliesin wanted to forcibly marry the prince and princess. Except she had it the wrong way around. The prince and princess were already betrothed. It made sense, marry the English prince to a German princess and improve the relations between the two countries. The Germans had already tried to provoke war and failed, this was a diplomatic attempt to decrease the chance of conflict.

The French wouldn't like it but they were a minor player now.

But those who *wanted* war between Germany and Britain would want to prevent the marriage from happening. Even if it was a German renegade conspiracy it would not matter, there was no way the people of Britain would be able to separate an act of barbarism against their young prince, and the country from which the perpetrator came.

Taliesin had killed his way into a position where he could prevent that marriage, he *could* have simply killed Antonia— clearly he had no scruples about disposing of anyone who got in his way—but that would not have been public enough. It had to be done in such a way as to cause the most outrage in the hearts of the British people.

The idea was staggering and there would be no one here that would believe her.

The only question now was whether he intended only to

kill Antonia, or to go for the prince as well, and by what method he would do it.

And it was at that moment she almost cried herself, realising that she had prepared so badly. Made so many unwarranted assumptions and could not protect a girl who depended on her. A girl who simply wanted to run away with the person she loved.

The final three girls, including Emily Solsbury, came out and curtsied to the princes then came to take their places. This formal presentation was over and the dance proper would begin. The princes stood and moved off into the crowd, heading for the rooms that had been created for them, no doubt.

The band returned to their instruments and struck up with a sombre tune to cover the change in arrangements to the room. The crowds now moved forwards and filled the space. Madame Paquin's assistant came to them and told them they were now free to do as they wished but to remain close by because there might be more presentations later.

Maliha shook her head and turned to Antonia and Margaret wondering what she could tell them.

38

____

Maliha was braced for some action by Taliesin and yet nothing happened. The band played though nobody had yet begun to dance. That would come later.

A handkerchief was waved in her face. She took it and turned to Antonia.

"I know why you were crying," said Maliha. She checked around. Margaret was still with them but the other girls were talking in small groups. Like sprays of colourful flowers. The fact that Maliha could not see where Emily Solsbury had disappeared to, gave her some concern.

"No, you don't," said Antonia. "You can't."

Maliha glanced at Margaret. "Your parents promised you to the prince." Antonia looked as if she was about to cry again. "Don't cry. This is supposed to be a happy occasion."

Antonia sniffed. Maliha handed her kerchief back. "Blow your nose." _I sound like my father._

The girl turned away from the crowd and faced the wall behind as she dealt with her sniff.

Maliha continued while her eyes scanned the crowd, looking for Taliesin. "It doesn't matter what was promised.

You're leaving tonight as we planned. Margaret will guide you, she knows what needs to be done. Just get through the next two-and-a-half hours. That can't be hard."

"Chin up, Antonia," said Margaret. "We are British after all."

"Speak for yourself," said Maliha, which drew a laugh from Antonia despite the tears. She sniffed again. Maliha frowned, she hadn't been joking, she aimed a stern look at Margaret, who just grinned and winked.

Maliha hesitated and then decided she needed to say it. "There's something else. Something more important—"

"Girls, you look absolutely wonderful." Mrs Lancaster appeared. She had done well considering she did not have money to burn, the pale floral dress she wore was a modern style, in fact it looked like one of Paquin's low-cost designs for the masses.

Mrs Lancaster noticed Maliha's examination. "It's beautiful, isn't it?" She turned on the spot so the hem flared out. "My father said he couldn't possibly have his daughter attend a Royal bash in some old frock and splashed out for the one I wanted."

"You look lovely," said Margaret and the smile on her face was genuine—because this was Margaret Creighton-Ward, thought Maliha, who is always kind, honest and decent.

A gong rang to indicate that the food had been prepared.

"Oh no," said Antonia. "I have to go."

Maliha grabbed her arm before she could take more than a step. "Why? Where?"

"Antonia will eat with the princes and their entourage privately," said Mrs Lancaster. "She is, after all, a princess."

"It would have helped if you had told me these things, Antonia," said Maliha, "I would never have let things get this far."

"Miss Anderson?" said Mrs Lancaster. "What are you talking about?"

"I think," said Margaret. "I think it would be very

improper for Antonia to go to this private room without her attendants."

"You can't just barge in on a private meal," said Mrs Lancaster.

"It is perfectly acceptable etiquette for her to be accompanied. I imagine there won't be anyone else she knows there."

"My parents are travelling back from my father's holdings on Venus," said Antonia. "They didn't know the date had been changed. There's nobody close."

"And," said Margaret, "knowing these sort of arrangements, as I do, the vast majority of the Princes' retinue will be male. Would you send a princess into that, Mrs Lancaster?"

The teacher pursed her lips as if she wanted to disagree but was frustrated to find nothing to oppose. She gave a curt nod, as if agreeing out loud might somehow condemn her.

"Come along, your highness," said Margaret slipping her arm into Antonia's. "Let us face down the bastion of maleness with a brave face." They walked away from Mrs Lancaster with Maliha following a step behind and smiling at her friend's adept handling of the situation.

"By midnight you will be in the sky with your beloved," said Maliha in Antonia's ear. "But you will need to put a smile on that brave face. No one must suspect you will be disappearing later."

The crowd parted like the Red Sea as the three girls walked sedately toward the exit at the rear of the room. It was strange, Maliha thought, she had eaten in this room three times a day but now it was as if she had never seen the carved wood and plastered stone before.

There was a marine on each side of the door, and two more flanking the door opposite. There was still no chance of speaking to Antonia.

She had an idea. "Don't you need to check your make-up?" she said quickly and placed her hand on Antonia's shoulder. One of the marines moved as she did so.

"Pardon?" said Antonia pausing mid-step. Maliha let her arm drop.

"I think Madame Paquin would prefer it if you checked your make-up before going in. After what happened in the hall." Maliha looked at Margaret willing her to back Maliha up.

"That might be wise, your highness," said Margaret.

"Are you sure?" said Antonia. "Is there a problem?"

"Better safe than sorry."

"Library," said Maliha.

"Library?"

"It has electric light and a good mirror," said Maliha. "And it will be private."

"Very well," said Antonia.

Margaret turned her attention to the marines. "We need a couple of chaps to escort us to the library before we go in—" she nodded at the door opposite "—if you would be so kind?"

It took moments to organise and two minutes later Maliha unlocked the door to the library and they went inside. To allay any suspicions Maliha handed the key to the sergeant. "We'll be five minutes."

She pushed the door closed behind them. Antonia was staring at the place where she thought the body of Ethel must have lain. She missed it by several feet but Maliha didn't feel there would be any benefit in correcting her. What she did do was hurry to the bookshelf with the secret door and check it. It seemed solidly shut.

"What's this about, Maliha?" said Margaret. "It's not done to keep royalty waiting, even if she is a princess." Then she turned to Antonia. "Maliha's right, you should have told us. This changes everything."

"I wasn't supposed to tell anyone."

"You aren't supposed to be running away with Jenny," said Maliha, "but that's not the point." She took a deep breath.

"There is a man here tonight who's planning to…" she broke off.

"Planning to what?" said Antonia.

Margaret looked at Maliha and at her apparent inability to speak. "Are you sure, Maliha?"

Maliha nodded dumbly.

"Sure about what?"

"Politics," muttered Margaret with a venom that Maliha did not expect from her—it made Antonia stare as well.

"Sit down, Antonia, and take this handkerchief. Do not scream, we can't have the chaps outside forcing their way in and demanding to know what we've done to you."

Antonia sat and clutched Margaret's hankie. "Why? What are you going to do to me?"

Maliha put her hand on Margaret's arm. "It's alright, Sadie. Let me do it." She realised she was towering over Antonia and took a few steps back to reduce the angle. She would have crouched but she was not sure the dress could accommodate her.

"There is a man going by the name of Taliesin, who is planning to kill either you, or the young prince, or both. He wants to make sure that Germany and Britain form no closer alliance. He wants war between you, and it does not matter how many people he kills to ensure it happens." *And I'm sure he'll be very happy if he kills me as well.*

Under the make-up Antonia went very pale. "You're not serious."

"I wish I were not."

"How long have you known?"

"I have been very stupid, I should have realised before now but I did not. Only today. Even Ena almost got it right."

"Who's Ena?"

"Kitchen maid."

"Oh." Antonia stared straight ahead with unseeing eyes. She clutched the hankie but she did not cry. After a long moment she focused on Maliha. "You're saying he's doing this to push Britain and Germany further apart?"

"That's right."

There was another pause and then Antonia stood in one smooth motion. "Can you stop him?"

"I know what he looks like and I know his intentions. I do not know what method he will employ."

"That's why you wanted to stay with me."

"We're your bodyguard," said Margaret.

"But we need to proceed as if everything is normal," said Maliha. "Otherwise he will simply withdraw and try again another time."

They made their way back to the prince's private rooms and gained entry without too much difficulty: Antonia simply insisted. No one commented on them arriving late.

Prince George was the epitome of good manners and apologised to Antonia for the absence of his wife, who would have liked to have met her. And he went on with the platitudes. Antonia introduced Lady Margaret and then Maliha. She curtsied and managed not to wobble this time.

"Miss Anderson, this is a delight," he said. "Are you perhaps related to Iain Anderson the inventor of the Anderson valve? I believe he went out to India…?"

"My father, sir."

"Excellent. He's a credit to the nation. I know a good many engineers and I have to say that when his name comes up there is considerable jealousy—and admiration."

Much to her own surprise she found herself warming to the prince. The room seemed quite informal, the food was a buffet and there were plenty of chairs to go around, gathered in small groups for easy conversation—much as she imagined a gentleman's club might be. Along with the dense cloud of cigar smoke that was forming. But it was not too unpleasant though it did dull the senses.

She steered clear of the wine that was offered and found herself served with a plate of food. A quick glance showed that the prince was now seated with a number of men, including his son, which meant she and the others could also sit. They found a place in the corner. Maliha sat where she could watch the rest of the room.

Antonia said nothing but kept casting glances at the boy destined to be her husband. *But not if I can help it*, thought Maliha. The meal went on for about an hour, the noise and smoke increased as they drank and puffed.

"If they keep that up no assassin is going to be able to see anyone," said Margaret.

"That's not in very good taste," said Maliha.

"I thought the atmosphere could do with lightening."

Antonia giggled. She had drunk some of the wine. In fact, an entire glass. Margaret had just water.

But they need not have been concerned. Through the door they heard the musicians strike up another tune.

"Oh well," said the prince loudly. "Time to get out in public again." He stood and everyone followed suit. Someone whispered in his ear and he nodded.

"Lady Antonia, if you do not mind taking my arm. Edward, you'll have Lady Margaret—was that it, Margaret? Good. Good. The rest of you can fight over the lovely Miss Anderson." And he winked at her. She did not know where to look.

She ended up with a young man who looked slightly familiar. The cigar smoke must have addled her mind as she simply couldn't place him. Perhaps it was only a similarity.

"It will be a pleasure to escort you into the school," he said. "Rather than keep you out."

Recognition hit her like a train. "I—oh—"

"Say nothing, Miss Anderson, I'm sure you had an excellent reason for skipping lessons, I wish it were as easy for me."

The door ahead was opened and they walked out across the corridor and into the dining room.

"I had no idea you were a member of the aristocracy," she said.

"It pays to cultivate a middle-class accent," he said. "It makes it easier to make friends.

"I can imagine. What should I call you then?"

"Bertrand, you can call me Bertie if you like."

"Bertrand Harris?"

He nodded.

"The Earl of Malmesbury?"

"My father, yes. Could be worse."

"Worse?"

"My dad's a pretty decent sort. Same can't really be said for…" he didn't finish the sentence but nodded in the direction of the Prince George. "Not good with children apparently. And, if it's not treason to say so, his son doesn't get on well with others at the college. Though apparently, it's better than the last place he was in. Bit of a whiner, frankly."

In which case getting Antonia out of it would be doing her the greatest of favours, thought Maliha.

The band changed to a waltz and the prince set off across the clear floor with Antonia in his arms.

"Just give him a few seconds to get established and then we're off," said Bertrand.

"I'm not very good," said Maliha, "and I haven't practised in these shoes. I'd rather not."

"You're a funny one," he said. "But if you'd rather not, then that is how it will be."

Other people took to the dance floor and it steadily filled up. Margaret, however, did not dance with Edward. She was a foot taller than him and he was, after all, not quite fourteen.

Maliha gestured to Margaret who came over.

"Yours is a lot better than mine," she said, nodding at Bertrand.

"Should have come with the coastguard," said Maliha and smiled gently.

"Do you want something to drink?" he asked.

"I'll have a lemonade," said Maliha. "Margaret will have a wine."

Bertrand went off in search of lemonade.

"I don't want any wine," said Margaret.

"I wanted to get rid of him. The escape plan isn't going to work; even if the clothes haven't been found, the girls won't be able to sneak out. Antonia needs to change and she won't get the chance."

"What are we going to do?"

"We can fly out. Find Jenny and make sure we're ready to go at ten o'clock."

Bertrand returned far too swiftly with both drinks.

"Trust me, Sadie," said Maliha. Margaret frowned and then looked at Bertrand and her frown softened. She took the drink and walked away. Her hips swaying far more than they needed to. Bertrand watched her go.

"Thank you for the drink," said Maliha. "Lady Margaret Creighton-Ward would be an excellent dance partner."

"She does seem pleasant," he said. "But another time perhaps, I'll stick with you tonight."

But Maliha wasn't listening, her eyes were fixed on a man she didn't recognise who had approached the princes. She could see it wasn't Taliesin, but he might have accomplices.

"Who's he?" she said pointing.

"Viscount Wimborne, he's on the prince's personal staff. Fussy old coot but his heart's in the right place, or so I've heard."

Maliha knew he was making a joke but it wasn't a good one and she wasn't in the mood to pander to his vanity.

He must have noticed. "Are you alright, Miss Anderson? You seem quite on edge, if you don't mind me saying so."

She turned toward him, even with her additional inches he was taller. His arm, where she still had hers, was strong and she knew he knew how to handle a gun. But he didn't have one.

"Can I trust you?"

"It depends on what you want me to do."

"Good answer," she said. "I can't explain in detail right now but there is going to be an attempt on the lives of the young prince and Lady Antonia, tonight."

"That seems unlikely," he said.

"I know how unlikely it seems," she said through gritted teeth, "that's why it's hard to tell anyone about it, but I'm not wrong. You must know how precarious Britain's relationship with Germany is, well those two—Antonia and Edward—are betrothed in an attempt to bring the countries closer together. Some people oppose that, they want war." She took a deep breath. "I don't have time to go over everything now, but when I left the school I was investigating."

The angle of his mouth suggested he was sceptical but too polite to simply disagree.

"Why not just humour me? After all, if I'm wrong what harm has been done?"

"But if you're right?"

"People will die unless I can stop it. The man in charge calls himself Taliesin and he is not afraid of killing anyone who gets in his way."

"In that case, Miss Anderson, I will humour you. What would you like me to do?"

39
———

The evening wore on interminably. Maliha made a very pretty wallflower with Bertrand beside her. They had been allocated seats, which was a blessing. All the other girls, except Antonia, had at least a dozen men wanting to dance or talk to them. Maliha was not bothered by anyone. For her part she was not concerned, it allowed her to keep an eye on the proceedings.

Every now and then she would ask Bertrand who a particular person might be.

For his part, Bertrand did not say a great deal until, "I don't think that girl likes you."

"Which one? Most of them don't."

"The Russian-looking one. She keeps glancing over here and glowering at you. I think I got a glower, too."

"Emily Solsbury, no, she really doesn't. Probably thinks you shouldn't be sitting with me."

"None of her business."

"No."

They lapsed into silence again.

Madame Paquin made an appearance at about nine

o'clock dressed in her usual black and white—the only colours she had worn since the death of husband. But she left again shortly afterwards.

By ten o'clock Maliha was becoming concerned. Was he never going to turn up? Had she been completely wrong about the whole thing? Had she imagined it? She shook her head, no, she had not imagined Ethel's body and the other deaths were real enough.

The face of Amelia Johnson revealing her perverse pleasure was not something she could make up. It was true. It must be true.

"It is possible the man has not been able to gain entrance to the school," said Bertrand.

"He is not a man to be stopped by such a simple thing," she said. "He could pretend to be a member of the serving staff, or a guest."

"You said he's a German, why has he called himself Taliesin?"

"I don't know."

"Taliesin was a legendary Welsh bard."

Maliha stared around the room. "I know. Is that important?"

"Hoping to impress you."

"Why?" she said distractedly.

But before he could reply the band finished and the dancing stopped. There was a small commotion at the stage door and the band's conductor stood up to face the audience.

"Your Majesty, Your Highnesses, Lords, Ladies and gentlemen. It is with great pleasure that I introduce noted baritone Professor James Sauvage, recently arrived from the United States of America, where he now lives." He nodded in the direction of the rear entrance to the hall and began to delicately applaud with his baton tucked beneath his arm.

A portly man, who Maliha guessed to be in his sixties, stepped out and strode with firm steps across the floor. He looked completely at home with all eyes on him, and the generous applause. He shook hands with the conductor who then returned to his position in front of the band.

"Good evening, majesties—" he nodded to the royals, "—and everybody else." It could have been an insult but the wide smile on his face defused any ill-feeling. The man was the epitome of confidence and his voice was deep and sonorous. Maliha noted the American tones, but there was something else underneath it. "I know that I deserted this fair isle to live over there but you didn't move this occasion quite enough to get rid of me. I had to take an earlier flyer."

A murmur of appreciative laughter went through the room. Maliha grabbed Bertrand's hand hard.

"Ow," he said quietly.

"Get over there, get over to the princes and Antonia now," she hissed at him.

"To begin I would like to offer you a rendition of the beautiful song, *Calon Lân*, written by my friend Daniel James."

The Welshness of his voice became unmistakable in the title of the song he named. "Bertrand, he's the Taliesin, the Welsh bard. It's happening now. Do your duty, protect them."

She was grateful that he did not argue any more. She had been wracking her brains trying to think what form of attack Taliesin might use but the only thing that he could be sure about would be a gun at close quarters. Even a bomb big enough to bring down the building couldn't be sure to kill his targets. It was unlikely he considered his own life to be important.

Everyone was listening in rapt attention as the song filled the room with Sauvage's baritone. Maliha climbed to her feet and walked casually along the front of the audience. Bertrand was already in position trying to stand in the way without obviously blocking the view of the royals.

Maliha wanted to tell them to run but unless she drew Taliesin out he could try again in the future, perhaps without the complication of Ethel Jordan's death.

She could see the top of the door behind the screen. It

opened. Maliha reached the royal party and placed herself squarely in front of Antonia. Bertrand's gaze was fixed on her face, she nodded towards the door. He nodded back.

It was then that Taliesin stepped from behind the screen dressed as one of the waiting staff and carrying a tray. There were no glasses on it and it was tilted down in front of him. His right hand was behind it. Maliha wondered for a moment whether he would try to make a scene, no, he wouldn't. The more time he wasted the more chance he would fail. He would fire as soon as he had a clear shot.

Maliha snatched up her dress. He was less than twenty feet from her. In proper shoes she could have covered the distance in no time at all. She ran in the heels. Out of the corner of her eye she saw Bertrand moving, too.

The tray moved aside and she saw the gun being lifted. There was a moment's confusion in Taliesin's eye and then he recognised her. He pointed the gun at her heart. Bertrand raced past her and crashed into Taliesin. Maliha saw the flash as the gun went off. The sound blasted her ears and echoed through the hall. She did not know whether the band and singer had stopped, or she had simply been deafened.

She had just about reached them, Bertrand was trying to pin the German to the floor, when another shot rang out. Maliha jumped half expecting to feel pain but she seemed to be in one piece. Taliesin had stopped struggling and Bertrand stood up rapidly checking himself for injuries. There was blood on his shirt and Maliha was momentarily concerned.

She glanced round to see the princes being dragged away through the crowd. There were screams and barely restrained panic. The main doors were jammed with people, no doubt the soldiers outside were trying to get in. A woman was screaming. Margaret and Antonia had been forgotten it seemed. They stood there on a suddenly empty floor.

"Bertrand, do you know where the princes' flyer is? The one they came in on?"

He frowned. "Yes?"

"Get Antonia, Margaret and Jenny to it. They need to get out of here." He looked uncertain. "Please."

He nodded and gestured for the two girls to follow him. Margaret moved but Antonia seemed frozen to the spot, staring at the dying man on the floor.

"You need to go now," said Maliha. Margaret grabbed Antonia by the hand and pulled her towards the rear entrance, which was not blocked.

Maliha turned her attention back to the bleeding form of Taliesin. Blood was soaking into his side where he had shot himself. His face was screwed up in agony.

"The pain is what you deserve for what you have done, Diederich Hößler," she said.

"God is the only one with the right to judge me," he gasped out the words.

"You'll burn in hell," said Margaret.

"At least, I'll be able to tell Ena her brother is justly avenged," said Maliha.

Hößler groaned. "Miss Anderson, you were always a thorn in my side." Then he laughed grimly.

"You shouldn't have killed Ethel."

The prone man coughed blood. He raised his free hand weakly and gestured for her to come closer. Avoiding the red stain, she went down on one knee close to his head.

"The biggest joke of all, Miss Anderson—" he coughed blood again and closed his eyes. "—I didn't kill her."

Maliha stared at him as his face turned a ghastly shade. "You're lying," she whispered.

His eyes opened and seemingly with great effort focused on her. "Why would—"

The tension went out of his body and his eyes stared unfocused in her direction, but she knew he was no longer seeing her. She picked up the gun.

The crowd at the back of the hall finally succeeded in getting out. Two people lay prone near to it. Maliha hoped

they had not been killed in the crush, there did not need to be
more deaths laid at the feet of Taliesin.

She looked up at the band and the singer huddled in a
confused knot in the corner. Marines forced their way into the
room, guns raised.

"He's dead," she said. "He tried to assassinate the princes.
But he's dead."

She thought of Antonia and was galvanised into action.
She slipped off the shoes—there was no need for them
anymore—hitched up her dress and ran for the exit.

"Stop, miss!"

"I have to do something, I'll be back."

She pelted down the corridor. She knew the three-rotor
luxury flyer was in the quad at the front of the building. It
would have been cordoned off but the three aristocrats would
have been able to bluff their way through, especially after the
gunshots.

The stone flags were cold beneath her feet but it became
even colder when she got outside and ran across the grass.
The steam engine in the flyer was already thumping hard and
the rotors starting to turn.

A marine held up his hand to stop her.

"The princess is on the flyer, she can't go without me!"
Maliha shouted, carefully implying that she was a servant
without actually lying. He took the hint and let her go.

She reached it and banged on the door. Moments later it
swung open and a pair of male hands pulled her inside.

She sat down with a gentle bump as the Faraday was
engaged. She checked each face to make sure everyone was
here. They were. She wished she could see who was piloting
the vessel but she knew it had to be Frederick Jordan. They
would have trusted no one else.

The vehicle lifted.

"Does he know where he's going?" said Maliha.

"The airfield, yes."

"Why are we going to the airfield, Miss Anderson?" said

Bertrand. "I feel as if I have been co-opted into something that could be damaging to my family's reputation."

"No, it's fine," said Margaret. "Lovers escaping the strictures of their families and running away together. It's romantic."

"What lovers?" he looked around and saw Jenny and Antonia holding hands. "Oh."

He went bright red.

Maliha glanced at the couple as well. Antonia appeared particularly strained. Seeing someone shot dead would likely cause that.

"Except I am a Royal Navy cadet, Miss Creighton-Ward, the situation is rather different for me. I can see them giving me a medal for saving the life of the prince, but posthumously after they hang me for treason." The flyer was already coming in to land. The trip from one end of Brighton to the airfield was no distance at all.

They touched down smoothly and the Faraday was disengaged.

"I can't," said Antonia quietly. She lifted Jenny's hand and held it to her own wet cheeks.

"What are you saying?"

"I can't go. We can't do this."

"Of course, you can," said Margaret. "You must, it's the only way to be happy."

Antonia shook her head and tears flowed from her eyes. Maliha glanced at Bertrand but he was clearly a sensible male. He knew when not to talk. She knew what was coming.

"That man wanted to stop me from marrying the prince because he wanted war."

"But he's dead and gone," said Margaret.

"And if I don't marry the prince he's succeeded," said Antonia. "That's the end of everything, there'll be a war and more people will die. How many?" She turned to face Jenny. "What price should I be willing to pay? Is our love worth ten thousand lives? A thousand? A hundred? Ten?" She shook her head. "It's not even worth one. I can't be selfish. All I want to do is be with you, my love, but if someone dies because of that, how could I live with myself?"

Maliha stood up and opened the door. The steps descended and, with the aid of Bertrand's hand she descended to the concrete. It was cold and damp against the soles of her feet. Stones dug into her. Bertrand followed her down and helped Margaret to the ground. He shut the door behind them.

"Best let them be, I suppose," he said.

"You are a good man," said Margaret. "Why have we never met before?"

Maliha heard the sound of two booted feet hitting the ground on the other side of the flyer. "No time for that, here Bertrand take this." She reached into her reticule and pulled out Taliesin's gun.

He took it from her and it was too dark to see the expression on his face.

"Come on," she said and moved quickly round the end of the vehicle. A man was stomping away.

"Stop, Mr Jordan, my associate has a gun and will use it if necessary."

The man stopped and against the lights in the main building she saw him raise his hands.

"Why?" said Bertrand in her ear.

"Because this man killed his own daughter."

Frederick Jordan just stood there with his back to them. His lack of denial was telling enough.

"Why?" said Margaret coming up beside them.

"Because Ethel killed her step-mother by pushing her under a bus. And Taliesin was meticulous in his planning. He arranged for Patrick Hogan to meet Ethel in order to blackmail her father by threatening her death. But in her strange and twisted way Ethel loved Patrick and told him what she had done, probably to impress him. He told Taliesin. Did he try to blackmail you with that?"

Jordan still stood there but now he spoke. "He tried but he didn't know someone already was."

"So you agreed to work for him if he dealt with the blackmailer."

Jordan's silence was agreement.

It started to drizzle and the wind off the sea was cold.

"But there was still the fact that your daughter had killed your wife. And then you found out she was pregnant. You forced Patrick to tell you where they met."

"I didn't kill Patrick, that was Taliesin," said Jordan quickly.

"So, you went to the meeting in the beach hut instead of Patrick and you beat her to death."

"I didn't mean to. Yes, I hated her, but I wasn't going there to kill her. But she had this way of getting inside you and making you angrier and angrier. She laughed when I told her I knew what she'd done."

There was a long silence with just the wind and the rain. It was probably ruining Madame's dress, she'd never be able to wear it again. There was some good in this.

"Fly us back to the school, Mr Jordan."

"Can you trust him?" said Bertrand.

"You know how to fly, don't you?"

"Yes."

"And you have a gun."

"Very well."

Maliha and Margaret knocked on the door before opening it. Jenny and Antonia had both been crying copiously. Margaret fixed a brandy for both of them.

Ten minutes later they were landing back in the school grounds.

40

I t had been a long night with a great many questions. Maliha woke late. The resolution had not come out the way she had expected but the weight was gone from her shoulders.

She dressed slowly in her school uniform.

Through the window she could see activity in the courtyard as various carts were brought in and loaded. Both Royal Navy carriers were in the back, so the military had yet to leave though the royals had left as soon as the flyer had returned. Though not with Frederick Jordan at the helm. The police had been called and he was taken away.

She noticed a slip of paper under the door. "You ruined it for everyone, we're going to ruin you."

She scrunched it up and threw it in the grate. Petty, small-minded bullies without an ounce of knowledge as to what was going on around them. Not that Maliha was expecting any praise. Bertrand might get a medal, she doubted she would get even the slightest acknowledgement.

Her stomach informed her that it was quite hungry and she set out in search of a meal.

When she reached the ground floor the bustle outside seemed to have increased. She did not like crowds but she could brave it long enough to get to the kitchen. It was below stairs and she was forbidden to go there but she no longer cared.

Maliha waited until she was sure no cart was on the move —whether steam, diesel, electric or horse driven—and set off across the cobbles. She had spent so long in heels the previous day that flat shoes felt odd.

Then she saw a man directly opposite. James Munroe. She stopped stock-still. A horse whinnied in pain and the thunder of hooves and iron-shod wheels came from the right as a pair pulling a cart bore down on her. She tried to move but her shoe slipped on the wet stone and instead she fell where she stood directly in their path.

The next thing she knew Munroe blocked out the sky. Grabbing her by the shoulders, he yanked her across the ground. Pain ripped into her as a hoof came down on one of her legs, then something hit her thigh. For a fraction of a second the pain made Maliha scream and then she knew no more.

I'm still hungry was her first thought. Then her legs told her they were hurting.

She opened her eyes with a groan. She was lying in a room she recognised. Not the infirmary but one of the guest suite bedrooms. Empty of any evidence it had been used for dressing debutantes.

The sun was shining through the window. She found that both of her legs were in casts. The one on her right was just the lower leg but on the left it was from hip to foot. The dull pain that she had felt gave way to an intense itching.

She could not move but there was a small bell on the table by the bed. Stretching hurt but she reached it and rang hard.

The door opened and Ena poked her head in. "You're awake."

"Obviously."

"And still the pleasant girl you always were. But at least you're alive and still have both your legs."

"Was there a possibility I wouldn't?"

"A couple of the doctors were all for taking them off, or at least one of them."

"I'm hungry."

It took eight weeks before they agreed to remove the plaster on Maliha's right leg since it had not been too bad. But her left thigh had been broken and much of the tissue torn away.

The scarring was extensive. Just as well she wasn't on the hunt for a husband.

The police had interviewed her though they had the story anyway. Then James Munroe made an appearance.

"I suppose I owe you an apology," he said.

"You probably saved my life, I won't be reporting you to Dr Underwood."

"That's what I wanted to apologise for."

She frowned and her thigh ached.

He waited as if he expected her to say something. When she didn't he continued, though it was strange seeing a fully grown man acting like a naughty child. "I intercepted your letter to Dr Underwood. It never got to Scotland Yard."

"But I didn't report you."

"I know—I mean, I know *now*. I didn't even look at it, I just assumed that's what it was."

She nodded. "I suppose that explains why the authorities were so unprepared. Never mind." She was too tired for retribution. "I'm glad you were there."

"You blackmailed me into protecting you."

"I didn't think it was going to be from a runaway cart."

He stared at her. "You don't know?"

"Know what?"

"It was deliberate, one of the girls used an air-gun."

"Emily Solsbury."

"That's the one. Some of the teachers were all for having criminal charges brought."

"Mrs Ramsey wouldn't like that."

"No, but the girl got kicked out."

Which will do nothing to improve her attitude, thought Maliha. But that's not my problem. She closed her eyes and Munroe left without another word.

The end of term approached with interminable slowness, until it was suddenly only a week away but the doctors declared she was not well enough to travel. She must wait couple of weeks at least.

"You must come and stay with me," declared Margaret. "I'm having other friends over too. We'll be a jolly bunch, we can have adventures."

"You mean Jenny and Antonia?"

"I thought they could share the Green Suite."

"And they'll mope around the rest of the time."

"Oh, I imagine we won't see them much," said Margaret slyly. "Mater and Pater are off in the South of France all summer so we'll have the run of the place."

"Won't the servants talk?"

"Oh, I expect so, can't keep secrets from them, can we? But it's not as if it's against the law."

"It is for men. Your uncle."

"Nobody minds if you're discreet."

"Or rich."

Margaret changed the subject. "So you'll come?"

"On one condition."

"Anything."

"Arrange for Ena to work at your parents' estate."

"That scullery maid?"

"I think you meant to say 'that *Irish* scullery maid'."

"I did not."

"She's very bright and knows when to keep her mouth shut, she would make an excellent lady's maid," said Maliha. "With the right training, of course."

"You are joking, aren't you?"

Maliha offered a face that said categorically that *no*, she was not joking.

"But I have no control over that."

"Says the girl who offered to have the Home Secretary have a word with the local police."

Margaret acquiesced.

Maliha was looking forward to a return to Foxley Heath, to be in the middle of nowhere with no adults to bother her. Time to be alone, regardless of what Margaret wanted. Time to walk and strengthen her leg. It was, perhaps, just what the doctor ordered.

And Margaret was as good as her word. The three of them—Margaret, Jenny and Maliha—climbed into the rear of the limousine that Saturday after endless goodbyes from teachers and staff that included awkward hugs from Mrs Lancaster, and even a begrudging wave from Mr Gunnell standing at the door. And into the front of the vehicle, beside the driver, slid Ena. Margaret may have kept her word but she was not entirely happy since the only way she could get the girl onto the staff was as her own maid. Maliha found the situation quietly amusing.

This time Maliha had her own room. Margaret was officially removed to a small suite so that her new maid could sleep in an adjoining room so as to be on call at all times. While Jenny was given the Green Suite, in expectation of the arrival of her lover some time in the following week.

Summer in Britain was warm and damp but Maliha took every opportunity to walk. Though her leg ached at the end of every day, she forced herself to exercise. On the third day she was approached by Lassiter.

"Forgive my forwardness, Miss Anderson?" He was holding a walking stick. "The late duchess, my lord's mother, was afflicted by arthritis towards the end of her days, she found this stick to be of great assistance. You are her height, perhaps it might suit you too?"

Maliha took it, the bark along it's narrow length had been polished while the handle end was bulbous where the pale interior wood had been exposed and carved into an egg shape.

"Hazel?"

"Quite so, Miss. She called it her witching stick."

"Thank you," said Maliha. "That was very thoughtful."

Latimer gave a slight bow and withdrew. The stick was suited her very well.

A week passed and Antonia arrived. She managed the bare minimum of the social niceties before disappearing upstairs with Jenny.

By now Maliha was managing, with the assistance of the stick, to walk the entire circuit of the lake, which she judged to be about two miles, every day and, by the end of the week, she did not need to sit down for an hour or two to recover.

The ticket for her return to India was arranged but the day before she left she had a visitor in the form of Dr Underwood. She met him in the library, with Margaret sitting in the corner reading a book. The library seemed somehow appropriate, though Margaret assure her it had no secret passages, at least none that she knew of.

"Miss Anderson, a pleasure." Dr Underwood bowed then they sat in the large wing-backed chairs.

"Thank you, Dr Underwood, I am glad to see you before I

go back to India. I did try to warn you about the situation but my message did not reach you."

"Munroe admitted his part in the affair."

"He did not behave very honourably."

"He has been disciplined, but you need not be concerned about that I am here on a much more pleasant matter." He reached inside his jacket and pulled out an envelope. Before she had a chance to stand in order to reach for it he was on his feet and passing it over. "From a grateful gentleman."

Maliha recognised the Royal seal instantly, but this was not from the prince. Almost unwillingly she cracked the wax and pulled the letter from the envelope. It was handwritten.

Dear Miss Anderson,

I have been made aware of your efforts in preventing the assassination of two generations of royal princes. I am advised by my government that it would be politically problematic, because of some of your prior associations, for you to be publicly honoured over this matter.

However, please let me assure you that you have the personal gratitude of my wife and I. Your actions have not gone unnoticed by those to whom it matters the most.

I remain, in your debt,

Edward Saxe-Coburg

Maliha stared at it for a long time not sure whether to be happy or angry. Her *prior associations*, Princess Sophia and the Suffragettes, of course. She decided that she would be happy now, for the sake of Dr Underwood, and that she would be very angry once he had left.

She looked up and smiled. "Thank you, it is pleasing to receive some acknowledgement."

"There is, of course, the other matter." He gave Margaret a side-long glance.

"Other matter?"

"The one Mr Munroe spoke to you about?"

"I was under the impression he was acting without authority."

"He was, of course, however his judgement was not in error."

"So you, too, are offering me employment?" She saw Margaret jump slightly, she might be pretending to read but she had not turned a single page of the book.

"I am."

"I'm afraid my answer is the same, Dr Underwood, I have no desire for adventure and putting myself in physical danger has not turned out well for me. I know you mean well, and please understand that I appreciate the offer, but I must decline."

"Oh."

And that was that.

Margaret, Jenny and Antonia all offered to come to London with her to see her off but she insisted they did not. Though she did have to put up with them coming to the station at Royal Tunbridge Wells. Ena came as well, ostensibly as companion to her mistress but she too wanted to say goodbye.

They waited on the platform beside the massive tube of steel and glass through which the Faraday train ran—pushed forwards by air-pressure from the pumping station churning out plumes of smoke. None of them spoke, it was as if they had run out of things to say, or perhaps that it was not worth starting a new conversation that would be interrupted.

Antonia was crying but there was nothing new in that. Jenny comforted her.

Finally the tube vibrated and the train came thundering in —seen through the glass windows of the tube. It came to rest so that the train doors matched the ones in the tube and they opened together.

They all came on board to get her settled in her first-class compartment. Hugs, kisses and tears. Maliha tried to act the part but she already felt separated from them. She never intended to see them again.

And then she was alone in the compartment and they were standing on the platform. Two thicknesses of glass between them. They waved excitedly and she could see their lips saying *bon voyage* and *good luck*. She placed a smile on her lips and waved as the Faraday device switched on. And the people she had once known slipped into memory.

~end~

END NOTE

Thank you for reading *The Taliesin Affair*. If you enjoyed it perhaps you'll consider writing a review on your favourite website, and you can review on Amazon even if you did not buy it there.

If this is your first Maliha Anderson book you can continue reading with the Maliha Anderson Omnibus which contains the next three stories chronologically. Use this link:

https://bit.ly/maliha-anderson-omnibus

If you have read them all, please join the mailing list and read the free Maliha Anderson story:

https://bit.ly/join-maliha

If you're already on the mailing list as well – thank you!